D.C. Noir 2

Critical Praise for the Original *D.C. Noir*

"From the Chevy Chase housewife who commits a shocking act in Laura Lippman's 'A.R.M. and the Woman,' to the watchful bum protecting Georgetown street vendors in Robert Andrew's 'Solomon's Alley,' the tome offers a startling glimpse into the cityscape's darkest corners . . . Fans of the genre will find solid writing, palpable tension and surprise endings."
—*Washington Post*

"In George Pelecanos's Washington, every bar is smoky, every dame a looker, and 'mug' refers to a guy with a .38, not a latte at Starbucks. Pick up a copy of the book . . . and prepare to be transported to a different D.C. than tourists see."
—*Washingtonian*

"Mr. Pelecanos, as a champion of the city's grit, has done something noble and necessary. In a city lacking much homegrown literary talent, he has assembled a compelling mix of ex-convicts, retired police officers, former crime beat reporters and a few writing pros willing to turn their storytelling eye, whether jaundiced or tender, inward toward the neighborhood. Chocolate City certainly gets its due."
—*Washington Times*

"Those looking for redemption in humanity would do well to look elsewhere, but this set of gritty urban tales, written with all the requisite touches of shadow and fog of the noir masters, is a rare cut for crime aficionados and should pique the interest of anyone who calls the Dark City home."
—*Washington Examiner*

"[Pelecanos] delivers a wholly satisfying volume . . . [He] shows us how both trash-strewn alleys and oak-paneled offices can trap their occupants with dreams, compromise, and heartbreak."
—*Booklist*

"*D.C. Noir* is superior. In addition to his own first-rate story, there are the usual professional jobs you'd expect from Laura Lippman and James Grady, and good stories by two writers I'd not heard of before, Richard Currey and Jennifer Howard."

"While only a few of the contributors, such as editor Pelecanos, will be familiar to most readers, every story in this all-original noir anthology set in the nation's capital is well written."

"With an intimate knowledge of the city's nooks and crannies, Pelecanos is a street-level chronicler of changing neighborhoods and shifting trends."

"If you want political intrigue, go elsewhere. This anthology is a gritty glimpse of beyond the rotating political arena and into the shadows of D.C.'s most dangerous elements. The voices of the characters are distinctive and honest, reflecting the diversity of the locals."

D.C. NOIR 2

THE CLASSICS

EDITED BY GEORGE PELECANOS

AKASHIC BOOKS
NEW YORK

Published by Akashic Books | ©2008 Akashic Books
Series concept by Tim McLoughlin and Johnny Temple
D.C. map by Sohrab Habibion

ISBN-13: 978-1-933354-58-3
Library of Congress Control Number: 2008925937
All rights reserved | First printing

Akashic Books | PO Box 1456 | New York, NY 10009
info@akashicbooks.com | www.akashicbooks.com

Grateful acknowledgment is made for permission to reprint the stories and poem in this anthology. "A Council of State" by Paul Laurence Dunbar was originally published in *The Strength of Gideon and Other Stories* (New York: Dodd, Mead & Company, 1900); "Avey" by Jean Toomer was originally published in *Cane*, © 1923 by Boni & Liveright, renewed 1951 by Jean Toomer, used by permission of Liveright Publishing Corporation; "Trouble with the Angels" by Langston Hughes was originally published in *New Theatre* (July 1935), licensed here from *Short Stories* by Langston Hughes, © 1996 by Ramona Bass and Arnold Rampersad, reprinted by permission of Hill and Wang, a division of Farrar, Straus & Giroux, LLC; "The Man Who Killed a Shadow" by Richard Wright was originally published in French as "L'Homme qui tua une ombre" in *Les Lettres Française* (October 4, 1946) before its English publication in *Zero* (Spring 1949), licensed here from *Eight Men* by Richard Wright, © 1946, 1961 by Richard Wright, renewed © 1989 by Ellen Wright, reprinted by permission of HarperCollins Publishers; "The Last Days of Duncan Street" by Julian Mayfield was originally published in *Lunes de Revolución* (July 4, 1960), © 1960 by Julian Mayfield, reprinted by permission of Joan Cambridge; "Washington" by Julian Mazor was originally published in the *New Yorker* (January 19, 1963), © 1963 by Julian Mazor; *Cast a Yellow Shadow* (excerpt) by Ross Thomas was originally published by William Morrow & Co., Inc., in 1967, © 1967 by Ross Thomas; "Reflecting" by Rhozier "Roach" Brown is reprinted by permission of Rhozier T. Brown; "Nora" by Ward Just was originally published in the *Atlantic* (May 1973), © 1973 by Ward Just; "Our Bright Tomorrows" by Larry Neal is reprinted by permission of Evelyn Neal; "Kiss the Sky" by James Grady was originally published in *Unusual Suspects* (New York: Vintage, 1996), © 1996 by James Grady; "The Dead Their Eyes Implore Us" by George Pelecanos was originally published in *Measures of Poison* (Tucson, Arizona: Dennis McMillan Publications, 2002), © 2002 by George Pelecanos; "A Rich Man" by Edward P. Jones was originally published in the *New Yorker* (August 4, 2003), © 2003 by Edward P. Jones; "Wonderwall" by Elizabeth Hand was originally published in *Flights: Extreme Visions of Fantasy* (New York: Roc, 2004), © 2004 by Elizabeth Hand; "Christmas in Dodge City" by Benjamin M. Schutz was originally published in *Unusual Suspects* (New York: Vintage, 1996), © 1996 by Benjamin M. Schutz; *After* (excerpt) by Marita Golden was originally published by Doubleday, in 2006, © 2006 by Marita Golden.

ALSO IN THE AKASHIC NOIR SERIES:

FORTHCOMING:

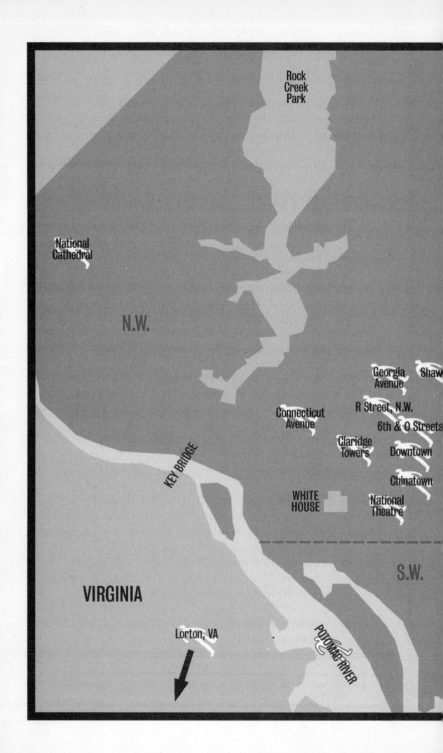

MARYLAND

Hyattsville, MD

Woodmore, MD

WASHINGTON, D.C.

N.E.

Kingman
Park

ED STATES
APITOL

S.E.

TABLE OF CONTENTS

PART III: IN THE SHADOWS OF FEDERAL CITY

INTRODUCTION
TOP-SHELF NOIR

When Johnny Temple, the publisher of Akashic Books, approached me with the idea of editing a sequel of sorts to *D.C. Noir*, our best-selling 2005 anthology of original Washington crime fiction, I told him I'd need to think on it. After all, I felt as if we'd covered the waterfront with that collection, and wasn't particularly interested in being involved with a second-tier batch of stories meant to cash in on the original. Johnny assured me that this would not be the case. What he was shooting for was the top-shelf of Washington short fiction, previously published stories of a noirish bent by some of the best writers who have come out of or written about this town. Now I was interested.

What I found, once I was in the hunt, was that it was not as easy as I imagined it would be to find stories that would fit the bill. I first spent several days at the Washingtoniana Room of the Martin Luther King Jr. Memorial Library, searching and reading, and found only a couple of stories that I liked. A young man who worked there put me in contact with a Margaret Goodbody, formerly of the MLK, now with the Bethesda Library in Montgomery County, Maryland. Ms. Goodbody suggested stories by Julian Mazor, Richard Wright, and Jean Toomer, which I eventually used, and helpfully pointed me in the direction of several databases and private collections. It's fair to say she got me going, and I'm very grateful for her assistance. In addition, Ibrahim Ahmad of Akashic Books was particularly diligent in researching, coordinating, and reviewing material that he felt would make a good fit for our project.

What Johnny Temple and I began to envision, as we got deeper into it, was a century-long overview of D.C. fiction that would focus on issues of race, ethnicity, politics, class, and the attendant struggles and changes that occurred in various eras of our history. In the finished product, the stories are arranged chronologically, in the order in which they were originally published, and geographically, by neighborhood or locale, to give you, in effect, a timeline and map of our literary city.

I have to say, I am very pleased with what we have compiled. The stories are high quality, the list of authors reads like lit royalty, and the package is handsome. Allow me also to give a nod to my friend, the accomplished photographer Jim Saah, whose evocative work once again appears on our cover. *D.C. Noir 2: The Classics* is a keeper.

Now, to the contributors.

The first name on my wish list was Edward P. Jones. I consider him to be the finest fiction writer to ever come out of Washington, D.C., and in the bargain he is a homegrown talent and graduate of Cardozo High School. From the collection *All Aunt Hagar's Children,* we chose "A Rich Man," which is not only a stunning piece of craftsmanship, but is full noir in its depiction of a man trapped inside a cage of his own making.

I next sought a contribution from Marita Golden, one of our most celebrated, popular, and talented local authors, and reached her in her office at the University of the District of Columbia, where she is currently serving as Writer-in-Residence. Ms. Golden's selection comes from *After,* her critically acclaimed novel on a police shooting and its psychological aftermath.

Our earliest-set tale was written by Paul Laurence Dunbar. (This is a fitting time to address our definition of "noir," which, with respect to this collection, is rather broad, particularly for the older stories. I tend to define noir by its psychological elements, rather than its crime elements or "visuals," which come from our natural association with film noir. Remember, it was the French who told us what noir "was" to begin with, a half-century after the publication of some of our early stories. As usual, I have digressed.) "A Council of State" is a telling and troubling story of the reality of racial politics in the Federal City at the turn of the last century. Dunbar, the son of escaped slaves, was the first eminent African American poet, as well as an accomplished short story writer, playwright, essayist, and novelist. Raised in Dayton, Ohio, he lived for a time in the LeDroit Park neighborhood of D.C., attended Howard University, and worked for about year at the Library of Congress, where the dusty environs were said to have worsened the tuberculosis that would end his life at the age of thirty-three. Dunbar Senior High School, D.C.'s first one exclusively for black teenagers—and for decades a model of academic achievement—was named in his honor, as were similar high schools in Baltimore and Fort Worth, Texas. It is fitting that his work be included here.

Julian Mayfield grew up in D.C. and was a notable actor, playwright, director, and novelist, as well as a Writer-in-Residence at Howard University and a political activist. He also cowrote, with Ruby Dee and Jules Dassin, the screenplay for the film *Up Tight!* Mr. Mayfield's story, "The Last Days of Duncan Street," is an affecting time-capsule snapshot of boys and a neighborhood.

Larry Neal was a writer, poet, and, with Amiri Baraka, one of the most significant members of the Black Arts Movement during the 1960s. For several years he was Executive Director of the District of Columbia Commission on the Arts and Humanities. His story, "Our Bright Tomorrows," is a meditation on loss, revolution, and the passage of time.

Jean Toomer, a leading light of the Harlem Renaissance, lived for many years, off and on, in Washington, D.C. The lyrical "Avey," taken from the landmark collection *Cane*, is set alternately on V Street and on the green of the Soldiers' Home along North Capitol Street, where "the ground is high" and the narrator, a dreamer unable to act on his love for the woman of the title, sees "the dawn steal over Washington. The Capitol dome looked like a gray ghost ship drifting in from sea."

Julian Mazor, a graduate of Woodrow Wilson Senior High School in the District (as is publisher Johnny Temple), made a splash in the literary world with his outstanding collection *Washington and Baltimore*, brought out by Knopf in 1968. Several of its stories were printed in the *New Yorker*, including our tale, "Washington," about a traveling young white man who gets off a bus in a black D.C. neighborhood and his ensuing afternoon adventure.

Elizabeth Hand moved to Washington in 1975 to attend Catholic University, where she studied playwriting and cultural anthropology. She worked in those years and beyond at the Smithsonian and was an active participant in the city's storied punk movement. Her novels and short fiction carry shades of autobiography and cross genre lines gracefully, with a reoccurring interest in outsider artists. "Wonderwall," harrowing and nakedly honest, is one of my very favorite D.C. short stories.

The *Washington Post* once called James Grady, fittingly, a "local legend." His early career as an investigative journalist and an innate curiosity for what lies beneath resulted in a deep understanding of the workings of this town that is evidenced in his auspicious body of work, which includes fourteen novels to date and numerous screenplays and short stories. "Kiss the Sky," set in the now-closed Lorton Correctional Complex, is a good example of Grady's ear for dialogue, rhythmic pacing, and cinematic eye.

Busboys and Poets, located at 14th and V streets in Northwest, is one of the most interesting, progressive bookstores to open in D.C. in the past decade. Its name was inspired by poet Langston Hughes, who lived in Washington in the 1920s and worked as a busboy at the Wardman Park Hotel to pay his bills. According to lore and the bookstore's press materials, Hughes, while on duty at the Wardman Park one night, slid several of his poems beside the dinner plate of poet Nicholas Vachel Lindsay. In the newspaper the following day, Lindsay spoke of his encounter with a "Negro busboy poet." We are honored to publish Mr. Hughes's story, "Trouble with the Angels," in this collection.

Ward Just is one of the finest authors to ever write about political Washington and, by extension, America. Many have traced his literary lineage to Henry James and Ernest Hemingway. I would add Graham Greene to the mix, in that Mr. Just is as concerned with the cost of a life devoted to politics and the spy game as he is the mechanics. "Nora," from the original edition of his story collection *The Congressman Who Loved Flaubert*, is a haunting example of his singular talent.

Benjamin M. Schutz was the author of seven Washington-based mystery novels and numerous short stories, for which he won both the Edgar Award and three Shamus Awards. He was a noted forensic and clinical psychologist whose knowledge of the human condition was strongly present in his fiction writing. Here we have "Christmas in Dodge City," which depicts a night in the life of a Cold Case squad detective. Mr. Schutz, who passed away early in 2008, will be missed.

It is an understatement to say that we are pleased to have a story from Richard Wright—one of the most important writers of the twentieth century—in this anthology. "The Man Who Killed a Shadow" is set largely in the National Cathedral, and it is an uncompromising, shocking, and thought-provoking work. There's a reason we subtitled this collection *The Classics*.

Ross Thomas's witty, urbane political thrillers, several of which take place in our town, are some of the finest Washington novels, regardless of genre, ever written. He wrote knowingly of the backroom deals made in the Federal City, of dinner parties in Georgetown, and of trysts in the Mayflower Hotel and three-martini lunches at Paul Young's Restaurant, but he could also riff accurately on any neighborhood of the four quadrants. Our selection comes from the novel *Cast a Yellow Shadow*, published in 1967, one year before the riots, six years after our streetcars had ceased operation. If there was a D.C. Literary Hall of Fame, Mr. Thomas would surely be in it.

Rhozier "Roach" Brown grew up in one of D.C.'s infamous alley dwellings. By his own admission, he came from a third-generation family of hustlers. In 1965, Roach Brown was sentenced to life in prison for his role in a robbery-murder, and alternated his serving time between St. Elizabeth's Hospital and Lorton Reformatory. While at Lorton, he wrote poetry and conceived of Inner Voices, a prisoner-led theatrical troupe that performed plays written by Brown, one of which was broadcast on National Public Television. In 1975, President Gerald Ford commuted Brown's sentence to time served. Brown has since been a local television producer, documentary filmmaker, has been appointed to congressional committees, and headed a media production and public relations firm. He was incarcerated again for a parole violation, and is now back out and writing, working with kids, and giving motivational speeches. We present his poem, "Reflecting," written in solitary at Lorton Reformatory.

I'll leave you to enjoy these outstanding stories. With pride, and once again with hope and anticipation, here is *D.C. Noir 2: The Classics*.

George Pelecanos
Washington, D.C.
June 2008

PART I

THE OLD SCHOOL

A COUNCIL OF STATE

BY PAUL LAURENCE DUNBAR

R Street, N.W.

(Originally published in 1900)

PART I

Luther Hamilton was a great political power. He was neither representative in Congress, senator nor cabinet minister. When asked why he aspired to none of these places of honor and emolument he invariably shrugged his shoulders and smiled inscrutably. In fact, he found it both more pleasant and more profitable simply to boss his party. It gave him power, position and patronage, and yet put him under obligations to no narrow constituency.

As he sat in his private office this particular morning there was a smile upon his face, and his little eyes looked out beneath the heavy grey eyebrows and the massive cheeks with gleams of pleasure. His whole appearance betokened the fact that he was feeling especially good. Even his mail lay neglected before him, and his eyes gazed straight at the wall. What wonder that he should smile and dream. Had he not just the day before utterly crushed a troublesome opponent? Had he not ruined the career of a young man who dared to oppose him, driven him out of public life and forced his business to the wall? If this were not food for self-congratulation pray what is?

Mr. Hamilton's reverie was broken in upon by a tap at the door, and his secretary entered.

"Well, Frank, what is it now? I haven't gone through my mail yet."

"Miss Kirkman is in the outer office, sir, and would like to see you this morning."

"Oh, Miss Kirkman, heh; well, show her in at once."

The secretary disappeared and returned ushering in a young woman, whom the "boss" greeted cordially.

"Ah, Miss Kirkman, good-morning! Good-morning! Always prompt and busy, I see. Have a chair."

Miss Kirkman returned his greeting and dropped into a chair. She began at once fumbling in a bag she carried.

"We'll get right to business," she said. "I know you're busy, and so am I, and I want to get through. I've got to go and hunt a servant for Mrs. Senator Dutton when I leave here."

She spoke in a loud voice, and her words rushed one upon the other as if she were in the habit of saying much in a short space of time. This is a trick of speech frequently acquired by those who visit public men. Miss Kirkman's whole manner indicated bustle and hurry. Even her attire showed it. She was a plump woman, aged, one would say about thirty. Her hair was brown and her eyes a steely grey—not a bad face, but one too shrewd and aggressive perhaps for a woman. One might have looked at her for a long time and never suspected the truth, that she was allied to the colored race. Neither features, hair nor complexion showed it, but then "colored" is such an elastic word, and Miss Kirkman in reality was colored "for revenue only." She found it more profitable to ally herself to the less important race because she could assume a position among them as a representative woman, which she could never have hoped to gain among the whites. So she was colored, and, without having any sympathy with the people whom she represented, spoke for them and uttered what was supposed by the powers to be the thoughts that were in their breasts.

"Well, from the way you're tossing the papers in that bag I know you've got some news for me."

"Yes, I have, but I don't know how important you'll think it is. Here we are!" She drew forth a paper and glanced at it. "It's just a memorandum, a list of names of a few men who need watching. The Afro-American convention is to meet on the 22d; that's Thursday of next week. Bishop Carter is to preside. The thing has resolved itself into a fight between those who are office-holders and those who want to be."

"Yes, well what's the convention going to do?"

"They're going to denounce the administration."

"Hem, well in your judgment, what will that amount to, Miss Kirkman?"

"They are the representative talking men from all sections of the country, and they have their following, and so there's no use disputing that they can do some harm."

"Hum, what are they going to denounce the administration for?"

"Oh, there's a spirit of general discontent, and they've got to denounce something, so it had as well be the administration as anything else."

There was a new gleam in Mr. Hamilton's eye that was not one of pleasure as he asked, "Who are the leaders in this movement?"

"That's just what I brought this list for. There's Courtney, editor of the *New York Beacon*, who is rabid; there's Jones of Georgia, Gray of Ohio—"

"Whew," whistled the boss, "Gray of Ohio, why he's on the inside."

"Yes, and I can't see what's the matter with him, he's got his position, and he ought to keep his mouth shut."

"Oh, there are ways of applying the screw. Go on."

"Then, too, there's Shackelford of Mississippi, Duncan of South Carolina, Stowell of Kentucky, and a lot of smaller fry who are not worth mentioning."

"Are they organized?"

"Yes, Courtney has seen to that, the forces are compact."

"We must split them. How is the bishop?"

"Neutral."

"Any influence?"

"Lots of it."

"How's your young man, the one for whom you've been soliciting a place—what's his name?"

Miss Kirkman did her womanhood the credit of blushing, "Joseph Aldrich, you mean. You can trust to me to see that he's on the right side."

"Happy is the man who has the right woman to boss him, and who has sense enough to be bossed by her; his path shall be a path of roses, and his bed a flowery bed of ease. Now to business. They must not denounce the administration. What are the conditions of membership in this convention?"

"Any one may be present, but it costs a fee of five dollars for the privilege of the floor."

Mr. Hamilton turned to the desk and made out a check. He handed it to Miss Kirkman, saying, "Cash this, and pack that convention for the administration. I look to you and the people you may have behind you to check any rash resolutions they may attempt to pass. I want you to be there every day and take notes of the speeches made, and their character and tenor. I shall have Mr. Richardson there also to help you. The record of each man's speech will be sent to his central committee, and we shall know how to treat him in the future. You know, Miss Kirkman, it is our method to help our friends and to crush our enemies. I shall depend upon you to let me know which is which. Good-morning."

"Good-morning, Mr. Hamilton."

"And, oh, Miss Kirkman, just a moment. Frank," the secretary came in, "bring me that jewel case out of the safe. Here, Miss Kirkman, Mrs. Hamilton told me if you came in to ask if you would mind running past the safety deposit vaults and putting these in for her?"

"Certainly not," said Miss Kirkman.

This was one of the ways in which Miss Kirkman was made to remember her race. And the relation to that race, which nothing in her face showed, came out strongly in her willingness thus to serve. The confidence itself flattered her, and she was never tired of telling her acquaintances how she had put such and such a senator's wife's jewels away, or got a servant for a cabinet minister.

When her other duties were done she went directly to a small dingy office building and entered a room, over which was the sign, "Joseph Aldrich, Counselor and Attorney at Law."

"How do, Joe."

"Why, Miss Kirkman, I'm glad to see you," said Mr. Aldrich, coming forward to meet her and setting a chair. He was a slender young man, of a complexion which among the varying shades bestowed among colored people is termed a light brown skin. A mustache and a short Vandyke beard partially covered a mouth inclined to weakness. Looking at them, an observer would have said that Miss Kirkman was the stronger man of the two.

"What brings you out this way to-day?" questioned Aldrich.

"I'll tell you. You've asked me to marry you, haven't you?"

"Yes."

"Well, I'm going to do it."

"Annie, you make me too happy."

"That's enough," said Miss Kirkman, waving him away. "We haven't any time for romance now. I mean business. You're going to the convention next week."

"Yes."

"And you're going to speak?"

"Of course."

"That's right. Let me see your speech."

He drew a typewritten manuscript from the drawer and handed it to her. She ran her eyes over the pages, murmuring to herself. "Uh, huh, 'wavering, weak, vaciliating adminstration, have not given us the protection our rights as citizens demanded—while our brothers were murdered in the South. Nero fiddled while Rome burned, while this modern'—uh, huh, oh, yes, just as I thought," and with a sudden twist Miss Kirkman tore the papers across and pitched them into the grate.

"Miss Kirkman—Annie, what do you mean?"

"I mean that if you're going to marry me, I'm not going to let you go to the convention and kill yourself."

"But my convictions—"

"Look here, don't talk to me about convictions. The colored man is the under dog, and the under dog has no right to have convictions. Listen, you're going to the convention next week and you're going to make a speech, but it won't be that speech. I have just come from Mr. Hamilton's. That convention is to be watched closely. He is to have his people there and they are to take down the words of every man who talks, and these words will be sent to his central committee. The man who goes there with an imprudent tongue goes down. You'd better get to work and see if you can't think of something good the administration has done and dwell on that."

"Whew!"

"Well, I'm off."

"But Annie, about the wedding?"

"Good-morning, we'll talk about the wedding after the convention."

The door closed on her last words, and Joseph Aldrich sat there wondering and dazed at her manner. Then he began to think about the administration. There must be some good things to say for it, and he would find them. Yes, Annie was right—and wasn't she a hustler though?

PART II

It was on the morning of the 22d and near nine o'clock, the hour at which the convention was to be called to order. But Mr. Gray of Ohio had not yet gone in. He stood at the door of the convention hall in deep converse with another man. His companion was a young looking sort of person. His forehead was high and his eyes were keen and alert. The face was mobile and the mouth nervous. It was the face of an enthusiast, a man with deep and intense beliefs, and the boldness or, perhaps, rashness to uphold them.

"I tell you, Gray," he was saying, "it's an outrage, nothing less. Life, liberty, and the pursuit of happiness. Bah! It's all twaddle. Why, we can't even be secure in the first two, how can we hope for the last?"

"You're right, Elkins," said Gray, soberly, "and though I hold a position under the administration, when it comes to a consideration of the wrongs of my race, I cannot remain silent."

"I cannot and will not. I hold nothing from them, and I owe them nothing. I am only a bookkeeper in a commercial house, where their spite cannot reach me, so you may rest assured that I shall not bite my tongue."

"Nor shall I. We shall all be colored men here together, and talk, I hope, freely one to the other. Shall you introduce your resolution today?"

"I won't have a chance unless things move more rapidly than I expect them to. It will have to come up under new business, I should think."

"Hardly. Get yourself appointed on the committee on resolutions."

"Good, but how can I?"

"I'll see to that; I know the bishop pretty well. Ah, good-morning, Miss Kirkman. How do you do, Aldrich?" Gray pursued, turning to the newcomers, who returned his greeting, and passed into the hall.

"That's Miss Kirkman. You've heard of her. She fetches and carries for Luther Hamilton and his colleagues, and has been suspected of doing some spying, also."

"Who was that with her?"

"Oh, that's her man Friday; otherwise Joseph Aldrich by name, a fellow she's trying to make something of before she marries him. She's got the pull to do it, too."

"Why don't you turn them down?"

"Ah, my boy, you're young, you're young; you show it. Don't you know that a wind strong enough to uproot an oak only ripples the leaves of a creeper against the wall? Outside of the race that woman is really considered one of the leaders, and she trades upon the fact."

"But why do you allow this base deception to go?"

"Because, Elkins, my child," Gray put his hand on the other's shoulder with mock tenderness, "because these seemingly sagacious whites among whom we live are really a very credulous people, and the first one who goes to them with a good front and says 'Look here, I am the leader of the colored people; I am their oracle and prophet,' they immediately exalt and say 'That's so.' Now do you see why Miss Kirkman has a pull?"

"I see, but come on, let's go in; there goes the gavel."

The convention hall was already crowded, and the air was full of the bustle of settling down. When the time came for the payment of their fees, by those who wanted the privilege of the floor, there was a perfect rush for the secretary's desk. Bank notes fluttered everywhere. Miss Kirkman had on a suspiciously new dress and bonnet, but she had done her work well, nevertheless. She looked up into the gallery in a corner that overlooked the stage and caught the eye of a young man who sat there notebook in hand. He smiled, and she smiled. Then she looked over at Mr. Aldrich, who was not sitting with her, and they both smiled complacently. There's nothing like being on the inside.

After the appointment of committees, the genial bishop began his opening address, and a very careful, pretty address it was, too—well worded, well balanced, dealing in broad generalities and studiously saying nothing that would indicate that he had any intention of directing the policy of the meetings. Of course it brought forth all the applause that a bishop's address deserves, and the ladies in the back seats fluttered their fans, and said: "The dear man, how eloquent he is."

Gray had succeeded in getting Elkins placed on the committee on resolutions, but when they came to report, the fiery resolution denouncing the administration for its policy toward the negro was laid on the table. The young man had succeeded in engineering it through the committee, but the chairman decided that its proper place was under the head of new business, where it might be taken up in the discussion of the administration's attitude toward the negro.

"We are here, gentlemen," pursued the bland presiding officer, "to make public sentiment, but we must not try to make it too fast; so if our young friend from Ohio will only hold his resolution a little longer, it will be acted upon at the proper time. We must be moderate and conservative."

Gray sprang to his feet and got the chairman's eye. His face was flushed and he almost shouted: "Conservatism be hanged! We have rolled that word under our tongues when we were being trampled upon; we have preached it in our churches when we were being shot down; we have taught it in our schools when the right to use our learning was denied us, until the very word has come to be a reproach upon a black man's tongue!"

There were cries of "Order! Order!" and "Sit down!" and the gavel was rattling on the chairman's desk. Then some one rose to a point of order, so dear to the heart of the negro debater. The point was sustained and the Ohioan yielded the floor, but not until he had gazed straight into the eyes of Miss Kirkman as they rose from her notebook. She turned red. He curled his lip and sat down, but the blood burned in his face, and it was not the heat of shame, but of anger and contempt that flushed his cheeks.

This outbreak was but the precursor of other storms to follow. Every one had come with an idea to exploit or some proposition to advance. Each one had his panacea for all the aches and pains of his race. Each man who had paid his five dollars wanted his full five dollars' worth of talk. The chairman allowed them five minutes apiece, and they thought time dear at a dollar a minute. But there were speeches to be made for buncombe, and they made the best of the seconds. They howled, they raged, they stormed. They waxed eloquent or pathetic. Jones of Georgia was swearing softly and feelingly into Shackelford's ear. Shackelford was sympathetic and nervous as he fingered a large bundle of manuscript in his back pocket. He got up several times and called "Mr. Chairman," but his voice had been drowned in the tumult. Amid it all, calm and impassive, sat the man, who of all others was expected to be in the heat of the fray.

It had been rumored that Courtney of the *New York Beacon* had come to Washington with blood in his eyes. But there he sat, silent and unmoved, his swarthy, eagle-like face, with its frame of iron-grey hair as unchanging as if he had never had a passionate thought.

"I don't like Jim Courtney's silence," whispered Stowell to a colleague. "There's never so much devil in him as when he keeps still. You look out for him when he does open up."

But all the details of the convention do not belong to this narrative. It is hardly relevant, even, to tell how Stowell's prediction came true, and at the second day's meeting Courtney's calm gave way, and he delivered one of the bitterest speeches of his life. It was in the morning, and he was down for a set speech on "The Negro in the Higher Walks of Life." He started calmly, but as he progressed, the memory of all the wrongs, personal and racial, that he had suffered; the knowledge of the disabilities that he and his brethren had to suffer, and the vision of toil unrequited, love rejected, and loyalty ignored, swept him off his feet. He forgot his subject, forgot everything but that he was a crushed man in a crushed race.

The auditors held their breath, and the reporters wrote much.

Turning to them he said, "And to the press of Washington, to whom I have before paid my respects, let me say that I am not afraid to have them take any word that I may say. I came here to meet them on their own ground. I will meet them with pen. I will meet them with pistol," and then raising his tall, spare form, he shouted, "Yes, even though there is but one hundred and thirty-five pounds of me, I will meet them with my fists!"

This was all very rash of Courtney. His paper did not circulate largely, so his real speech, which he printed, was not widely read, while through the columns of the local press, a garbled and distorted version of it went to every corner of the country. Purposely distorted? Who shall say? He had insulted the press; and then Mr. Hamilton was a very wealthy man.

When the time for the consideration of Elkins' resolution came, Courtney, Jones and Shackelford threw themselves body and soul into the fight with Gray and its author. There was a formidable array against them. All the men in office, and all of those who had received even a crumb of promise, were for buttering over their wrongs, and making their address to the public a prophecy of better things.

Jones suggested that they send an apology to lynchers for having negroes where they could be lynched. This called for reproof from the other side, and the discussion grew hot and acrimonious. Gray again got the floor, and surprised his colleagues by the plainness of his utterances. Elkins followed him with a biting speech that brought Aldrich to his feet.

Mr. Aldrich had chosen well his time, and had carefully prepared his speech. He recited all the good things that the administration had done, hoped to do, tried to do, or wanted to do, and showed what a very respectable array it was. He counseled moderation and conservatism, and his peroration was a flowery panegyric of the "noble man whose hand is on the helm, guiding the grand old ship of state into safe harbor."

The office-holders went wild with enthusiasm. No self-interest there. The opposition could not argue that this speech was made to keep a job, because the speaker had none. Then Jim Courtney got up and spoiled it all by saying that it may be that the speaker had no job but wanted one.

Aldrich was not moved. He saw a fat salary and Annie Kirkman for him in the near future.

The young lady had done her work well, and when the resolution came to a vote it was lost by a good majority. Aldrich was again on his feet and offering another. The forces of the opposition were discouraged and disorganized, and they made no effort to stop it when the rules were suspended, and it went through on the first reading. Then the convention shouted, that is, part of it did, and Miss Kirkman closed her notebook and glanced up at the gallery again. The young man had closed his book also. Their work was done. The administration had not been denounced, and they had their black-list for Mr. Hamilton's knife.

There were some more speeches made, just so that the talkers should get their money's worth; but for the masses, the convention had lost its interest, and after a few feeble attempts to stir it into life again, a motion to adjourn was entertained. But, before a second appeared, Elkins arose and asked leave to make a statement. It was granted.

"Gentlemen," he said, "we have all heard the resolution which goes to the public as the opinion of the negroes of the country. There are some of us who do not believe that this expresses the feelings of our race, and to us who believe this, Mr. Courtney has given the use of his press in New York, and we shall print our resolution and scatter it broadcast as the minority report of this convention, but the majority report of the race."

Miss Kirkman opened her book again for a few minutes, and then the convention adjourned.

* * *

"I wish you'd find out, Miss Kirkman," said Hamilton a couple of days later, "just what firm that young Elkins works for."

"I have already done that. I thought you'd want to know," and she handed him a card.

"Ah, yes," he said. "I have some business relations with that firm. I know them very well. Miss Anderson," he called to his stenographer, "will you kindly take a letter for me. By the way, Miss Kirkman, I have placed Mr. Aldrich. He will have his appointment in a few days."

"Oh, thank you, Mr. Hamilton; is there anything more I can do for you?"

"Nothing. Good-morning."

"Good-morning."

A week later in his Ohio home William Elkins was surprised to be notified by his employers that they were cutting down forces, and would need his services no longer. He wrote at once to his friend Gray to know if there was any chance for him in Washington, and received the answer that Gray could hardly hold his own, as great pressure was being put upon him to force him to resign.

"I think," wrote Gray, "that the same hand is at the bottom of all our misfortunes. This is Hamilton's method."

Miss Kirkman and Mr. Aldrich were married two weeks from the day the convention adjourned. Mr. Gray was removed from his position on account of inefficiency. He is still trying to get back, but the very men to whom his case must go are in the hands of Mr. Hamilton.

AVEY

BY JEAN TOOMER

Potomac River

(Originally published in 1923)

For a long while she was nothing more to me than one of those skirted beings whom boys at a certain age disdain to play with. Just how I came to love her, timidly, and with secret blushes, I do not know. But that I did was brought home to me one night, the first night that Ned wore his long pants. Us fellers were seated on the curb before an apartment house where she had gone in. The young trees had not outgrown their boxes then. V Street was lined with them. When our legs grew cramped and stiff from the cold of the stone, we'd stand around a box and whittle it. I like to think now that there was a hidden purpose in the way we hacked them with our knives. I like to feel that something deep in me responded to the trees, the young trees that whinnied like colts impatient to be let free . . . On the particular night I have in mind, we were waiting for the top-floor light to go out. We wanted to see Avey leave the flat. This night she stayed longer than usual and gave us a chance to complete the plans of how we were going to stone and beat that feller on the top floor out of town. Ned especially had it in for him. He was about to throw a brick up at the window when at last the room went dark. Some minutes passed. Then Avey, as unconcerned as if she had been paying an old-maid aunt a visit, came out. I dont remember what she had on, and all that sort of thing. But I do know that I turned hot as bare pavements in the summertime at Ned's boast: "Hell, bet I could get her too if you little niggers weren't always spying and crabbing everything." I didnt say a word to him. It wasnt my way then. I just stood there like the others, and something like a fuse burned up inside of me. She never noticed us, but swung along lazy and easy as anything. We sauntered to the corner and watched her till her door banged to. Ned repeated what he'd said. I didnt seem to care. Sitting around old Mush-Head's bread box, the discussion began. "Hang if I can see how she gets away with it," Doc started. Ned knew, of course. There was nothing he didnt know when it came to women. He dilated on the emotional needs of girls. Said they werent much different from men in that respect. And concluded with the solemn avowal: "It does em good." None of us liked Ned much. We all talked dirt; but it was the way he said it. And then too, a couple of the fellers had sisters and had caught Ned playing with them. But there was no disputing the superiority of his smutty wisdom. Bubs Sanborn, whose mother was friendly with Avey's, had overheard the old ladies talking. "Avey's mother's ont her," he said. We thought that only natural and began to guess at what would happen. Some one said she'd marry that feller on the top floor. Ned called that a lie because Avey was going to marry nobody but him. We had our doubts about that, but we did agree that she'd soon leave school and marry some one. The gang broke up, and I went home, picturing myself as married.

Nothing I did seemed able to change Avey's indifference to me. I played basket-ball, and when I'd make a long clean shot she'd clap with the others, louder than they, I thought. I'd meet her on the street, and there'd be no difference in the way she said hello. She never took the trouble to call me by my name. On the days for drill, I'd let my voice down a tone and call for a complicated maneuver when I saw her coming. She'd smile appreciation, but it was an impersonal smile, never for me. It was on a summer excursion down to Riverview that she first seemed to take me into account. The day had been spent riding merry-go-rounds, scenic-railways, and shoot-the-chutes. We had been in swimming and we had danced. I was a crack swimmer then. She didnt know how. I held her up and showed her how to kick her legs and draw her arms. Of course she didnt learn in one day, but she thanked me for bothering with her. I was also somewhat of a dancer. And I had already noticed that love can start on a dance floor. We danced. But though I held her tightly in my arms, she was way away. That college feller who lived on the top floor was somewhere making money for the next year. I imagined that she was thinking, wishing for him. Ned was along. He treated her until his money gave out. She went with another feller. Ned got sore. One by one the boys' money gave out. She left them. And they got sore. Every one of them but me got sore. This is the reason, I guess, why I had her to myself on the top deck of the *Jane Mosely* that night as we puffed up the Potomac, coming home. The moon was brilliant. The air was sweet like clover. And every now and then, a salt tang, a stale drift of sea-weed. It was not my mind's fault if it went romancing. I should have taken her in my arms the minute we were stowed in that old lifeboat. I dallied, dreaming. She took me in hers. And I could feel by the touch of it that it wasnt a man-to-woman love. It made me restless. I felt chagrined. I didnt know what it was, but I did know that I couldnt handle it. She ran her fingers through my hair and kissed my forehead. I itched to break through her tenderness to passion. I wanted her to take me in her arms as I knew she had that college feller. I wanted her to love me passionately as she did him. I gave her one burning kiss. Then she laid me in her lap as if I were a child. Helpless. I got sore when she started to hum a lullaby. She wouldnt let me go. I talked. I knew damned well that I could beat her at that. Her eyes were soft and misty, the curves of her lips were wistful, and her smile seemed indulgent of the irrelevance of my remarks. I gave up at last and let her love me, silently, in her own way. The moon was brilliant. The air was sweet like clover, and every now and then, a salt tang, a stale drift of sea-weed . . .

The next time I came close to her was the following summer at Harpers Ferry. We were sitting on a flat projecting rock they give the name of Lover's Leap. Some one is supposed to have jumped off it. The river is about six hundred feet beneath. A railroad track runs up the valley and curves out of sight where part of the mountain rock had to be blasted away to make room for it. The engines of this valley have a whistle, the echoes of which sound like iterated gasps and sobs. I always think of them as crude music from the soul of Avey. We sat there holding hands. Our palms were soft and warm against each other. Our fingers were not tight. She would not let them be. She would not let me twist them. I wanted to talk. To explain what I meant to her. Avey was as silent as those great trees whose tops we looked down upon. She has always been like that. At least, to me. I had the notion that if I really wanted to, I could do with her just what I pleased. Like one can strip a tree. I did kiss her. I even let my hands cup her breasts. When I was through, she'd seek my hand and hold it till my pulse cooled down. Evening after evening we sat there. I tried to get her to talk about that college feller. She never would. There was no set time to go home. None of my family had come down. And as for hers, she didnt give a hang about them. The general gossips could hardly say more than they had. The boarding-house porch was always deserted when we returned. No one saw us enter, so the time was set conveniently for scandal. This worried me a little, for I thought it might keep Avey from getting an appointment in the schools. She didnt care. She had finished normal school. They could give her a job if they wanted to. As time went on, her indifference to things began to pique me; I was ambitious. I left the Ferry earlier than she did. I was going off to college. The more I thought of it, the more I resented, yes, hell, thats what it was, her downright laziness. Sloppy indolence. There was no excuse for a healthy girl taking life so easy. Hell! she was no better than a cow. I was certain that she was a cow when I felt an udder in a Wisconsin stock-judging class. Among those energetic Swedes, or whatever they are, I decided to forget her. For two years I thought I did. When I'd come home for the summer she'd be away. And before she returned, I'd be gone. We never wrote; she was too damned lazy for that. But what a bluff I put up about forgetting her. The girls up that way, at least the ones I knew, havent got the stuff: they dont know how to love. Giving themselves completely was tame beside just the holding of Avey's hand. One day I received a note from her. The writing, I decided, was slovenly. She wrote on a torn bit of note-book paper. The envelope had a faint perfume that I remembered. A single line told me she had lost her school and was going away. I comforted myself with the reflection that shame held no pain for one so indolent as she. Nevertheless, I left Wisconsin that year for good. Washington had seemingly forgotten her. I hunted Ned. Between curses, I caught his opinion of her. She was no better than a whore. I saw her mother on the street. The same old pinch-beck, jerky-gaited creature that I'd always known.

Perhaps five years passed. The business of hunting a job or something or other had bruised my vanity so that I could recognize it. I felt old. Avey and my real relation to her, I thought I came to know. I wanted to see her. I had been told that she was in New York. As I had no money, I hiked and bummed my way there. I got work in a ship-yard and walked the streets at night, hoping to meet her. Failing in this, I saved enough to pay my fare back home. One evening in early June, just at the time when dusk is most lovely on the eastern horizon, I saw Avey, indolent as ever, leaning on the arm of a man, strolling under the recently lit arc-lights of U Street. She had almost passed before she recognized me. She showed no surprise. The puff over her eyes had grown heavier. The eyes themselves were still sleepy-large, and beautiful. I had almost concluded—indifferent. "You look older," was what she said. I wanted to convince her that I was, so I asked her to walk with me. The man whom she was with, and whom she never took the trouble to introduce, at a nod from her, hailed a taxi, and drove away. That gave me a notion of what she had been used to. Her dress was of some fine, costly stuff. I suggested the park, and then added that the grass might stain her skirt. Let it get stained, she said, for where it came from there are others.

I have a spot in Soldier's Home to which I always go when I want the simple beauty of another's soul. Robins spring about the lawn all day. They leave their footprints in the grass. I imagine that the grass at night smells sweet and fresh because of them. The ground is high. Washington lies below. Its light spreads like a blush against the darkened sky. Against the soft dusk sky of Washington. And when the wind is from the South, soil of my homeland falls like a fertile shower upon the lean streets of the city. Upon my hill in Soldier's Home. I know the policeman who watches the place of nights. When I go there alone, I talk to him. I tell him I come there to find the truth that people bury in their hearts. I tell him that I do not come there with a girl to do the thing he's paid to watch out for. I look deep in his eyes when I say these things, and he believes me. He comes over to see who it is on the grass. I say hello to him. He greets me in the same way and goes off searching for other black splotches upon the lawn. Avey and I went there. A band in one of the buildings a fair distance off was playing a march. I wished they would stop. Their playing was like a tin spoon in one's mouth. I wanted the Howard Glee Club to sing "Deep River," from the road. To sing "Deep River, Deep River," from the road . . . Other than the first comments, Avey had been silent. I started to hum a folk-tune. She slipped her hand in mine. Pillowed her head as best she could upon my arm. Kissed the hand that she was holding and listened, or so I thought, to what I had to say. I traced my development from the early days up to the present time, the phase in which I could understand her. I described her own nature and temperament. Told how they needed a larger life for their expression. How incapable Washington was of understanding that need. How it could not meet it. I pointed out that in lieu of proper channels, her emotions had overflowed into paths that dissipated them. I talked, beautifully I thought, about an art that would be born, an art that would open the way for women the likes of her. I asked her to hope, and build up an inner life against the coming of that day. I recited some of my own things to her. I sang, with a strange quiver in my voice, a promise-song. And then I began to wonder why her hand had not once returned a single pressure. My old-time feeling about her laziness came back. I spoke sharply. My policeman friend passed by. I said hello to him. As he went away, I began to visualize certain possibilities. An immediate and urgent passion swept over me. Then I looked at Avey. Her heavy eyes were closed. Her breathing was as faint and regular as a child's in slumber. My passion died. I was afraid to move lest I disturb her. Hours and hours, I guess it was, she lay there. My body grew numb. I shivered. I coughed. I wanted to get up and whittle at the boxes of young trees. I withdrew my hand. I raised her head to waken her. She did not stir. I got up and walked around. I found my policeman friend and talked to him. We both came up, and bent over her. He said it would be all right for her to stay there just so long as she got away before the workmen came at dawn. A blanket was borrowed from a neighbor house. I sat beside her through the night. I saw the dawn steal over Washington. The Capitol dome looked like a gray ghost ship drifting in from sea. Avey's face was pale, and her eyes were heavy. She did not have the gray crimson-splashed beauty of the dawn. I hated to wake her. Orphan-woman . . .

TROUBLE WITH THE ANGELS

BY LANGSTON HUGHES

National Theatre

(Originally published in 1935)

At every performance lots of white people wept. And almost every Sunday while they were on tour some white minister invited the Negro actor who played God to address his congregation and thus help improve race relations—because almost everywhere they needed improving. Although the play had been the hit of the decade in New York, its Negro actors and singers were paid much less than white actors and singers would have been paid for performing it. And, although the white producer and his backers made more than half a million dollars, the colored troupers on tour lived in cheap hotels and often slept in beds that were full of bugs. Only the actor who played God would sometimes, by the hardest, achieve accommodations in a white hotel, or be put up by some nice white family, or be invited to the home of the best Negroes in town. Thus God probably thought that everything was lovely in the world. As an actor he really got very good write-ups in the papers.

Then they were booked to play Washington, and that's where the trouble began. Washington, the capital of the United States, is, as every Negro knows, a town where no black man was allowed inside a downtown theater, not even in the gallery, until very recently. The legitimate playhouses had no accommodations for colored people. Incredible as it may seem, until Ingrid Bergman made her stand, Washington was worse than the Deep South in that respect.

But God wasn't at all worried about playing Washington. He thought surely his coming would improve race relations. He thought it would be fine for the good white people of the Capital to see him—a colored God—even if Negroes couldn't. Not even those Negroes who worked for the government. Not even the black congressman.

But several weeks before the Washington appearance of the famous "Negro" play about charming darkies who drank eggnog at a fish fry in heaven, storm clouds began to rise. It seemed that the Negroes of Washington strangely enough had decided that they, too, wanted to see this play. But when they approached the theater management on the question, they got a cold shoulder. The management said they didn't have any seats to sell Negroes. They couldn't even allot a corner in the upper gallery—there was such a heavy ticket demand from white folks.

Now this made the Negroes of Washington mad, especially those who worked for the government and constituted the best society. The teachers at Howard got mad, too, and the ministers of the colored churches who wanted to see what a black heaven looked like on the stage.

But nothing doing! The theater management was adamant. They really couldn't sell seats to Negroes. Although they had no scruples about making a large profit on the week's work of Negro actors, they couldn't permit Negroes to occupy seats in the theater.

So the Washington Negroes wrote directly to God, this colored God who had been such a hit on Broadway. They thought surely he would help them. Several organizations, including the Negro Ministerial Alliance, got in touch with him when he was playing Philadelphia. What a shame, they said by letter, that the white folks will not allow us to come to see you perform in Washington. We are getting up a protest. We want you to help us. Will you?

Now God knew that for many years white folks had not allowed Negroes in Washington to see any shows—not even in the churches, let alone in theaters! So how come they suddenly thought they ought to be allowed to see God in a white playhouse?

Besides, God was getting paid pretty well, and was pretty well known. So he answered their letters and said that although his ink was made of tears, and his heart bled, he couldn't afford to get into trouble with Equity. Also, it wasn't his place to go around the country spreading dissension and hate, but rather love and beauty. And it would surely do the white folks of the District of Columbia a lot of good to see Him, and it would soften their hearts to hear the beautiful Negro spirituals and witness the lovely black angels in his play.

The black drama lovers of Washington couldn't get any real satisfaction out of God by mail—their colored God. So when the company played Baltimore, a delegation of the Washington Negroes went over to the neighboring city to interview him. In Baltimore, Negroes, at least, were allowed to sit in the galleries of the theaters.

After the play, God received the delegation in his dressing room and wept about his inability to do anything concerning the situation. He had, of course, spoken to his management about it and they thought it might be possible to arrange a special Sunday night performance for Negroes. God said it hurt him to his soul to think how his people were mistreated, but the play must go on.

The delegation left in a huff—but not before they had

spread their indignation to other members of the cast of the show. Then among the angels there arose a great discussion as to what they might do about the Washington situation. Although God was the star, the angels, too, were a part of the play.

Now, among the angels there was a young Negro named Johnny Logan who never really liked being an angel, but who, because of his baritone voice and Negro features, had gotten the job during the first rehearsals in New York. Now, since the play had been running three years, he was an old hand at being an angel.

Logan was from the South—but he hadn't stayed there long after he grew up. The white folks wouldn't let him. He was the kind of young Negro most Southern white people hate. He believed in fighting prejudice, in bucking against the traces of discrimination and Jim Crow, and in trying to knock down any white man who insulted him. So he was only about eighteen when the whites ran him out of Augusta, Georgia.

He came to New York, married a waitress, got a job as a redcap, and would have settled down forever in a little flat in Harlem, had not some of his friends discovered that he could sing. They persuaded him to join a Red Cap Quartette. Out of that had come this work as a black angel in what turned out to be a Broadway success in the midst of the depression.

Just before the show went on the road, his wife had their first kid, so he needed to hold his job as a singing angel, even if it meant going on tour. But the more he thought about their forthcoming appearance in a Washington theater that wasn't even Jim Crow—but barred Negroes altogether—the madder Logan got. Finally he got so mad that he caused the rest of the cast to organize a strike!

At that distance from Washington, black angels—from

tenors to basses, sopranos to blues singers—were up in arms. Everybody in the cast, except God, agreed to strike.

"The idea of a town where colored folks can't even sit in the gallery to see an all-colored show. I ain't gonna work there myself."

"We'll show them white folks we've got spunk for once. We'll pull off the biggest actors' strike you ever seen."

"We sure will."

That was in Philadelphia. In Baltimore their ardor had cooled down a bit and it was all Logan could do to hold his temper as he felt his fellow angels weakening.

"Man, I got a wife to take care of. I can't lose no week's work!"

"I got a wife, too," said Logan, "and a kid besides, but I'm game."

"You ain't a trouper," said another, as he sat in the dressing room putting on his makeup.

"Naw, if you was you'd be used to playing all-white houses. In the old days . . ." said the man who played Methuselah, powdering his gray wig.

"I know all about the old days," said Logan, "when black minstrels blacked up even blacker and made fun of themselves for the benefit of white folks. But who wants to go back to the old days?"

"Anyhow, let's let well enough alone," said Methuselah.

"You guys have got no guts—that's all I can say," said Logan.

"You's just one of them radicals, son, that's what you are," put in the old tenor who played Saul. "We know when we want to strike or don't."

"Listen, then," said Logan to the angels who were putting on their wings by now, as it was near curtain time, "if we can't make it a real strike, then let's make it a general walk-out on the opening night. Strike for one performance anyhow. At least show folks that we won't take it lying down. Show those Washington Negroes we back them up—theoretically, anyhow."

"One day ain't so bad," said a skinny black angel. "I'm with you on a one-day strike."

"Me, too," several others agreed as they crowded into the corridor at curtain time. The actor who played God was standing in the wings in his frock coat.

"Shss-ss!" he said.

Monday in Washington. The opening of that famous white play about black life in a scenic heaven. Original New York cast. Songs as only Negroes can sing them. Uncle Tom come back as God.

Negro Washington wanted to picket the theater, but the police had an injunction against them. Cops were posted for blocks around the playhouse to prevent a riot. Nobody could see God. He was safely housed in the quiet home of a conservative Negro professor, guarded by two detectives. The papers said black radicals had threatened to kidnap him. To kidnap God!

Logan spent the whole day rallying the flagging spirits of his fellow actors, talking to them in their hotel rooms. They were solid for the one-day strike when he was around, and weak when he wasn't. No telling what Washington cops might do to them if they struck. They locked Negroes up for less than that in Washington. Besides, they might get canned, they might lose their pay, they might never get no more jobs on the stage. It was all right to talk about being a man and standing up for your race, and all that—but hell, even an actor has to eat. Besides, God was right. It was a great play, a famous play! They ought to hold up its reputation. It did white folks good to see Negroes in such a play. Logan must be crazy!

"Listen here, you might as well get wise. Ain't nobody gonna strike tonight," one of the men told him about six o'clock in the lobby of the colored Whitelaw Hotel. "You'd just as well give up. You're right. We ain't got no guts."

"I won't give up," said Logan.

When the actors reached the theater, they found it surrounded by cops and the stage was full of detectives. In the lobby there was a long line of people—white, of course—waiting to buy standing room. God arrived with motorcycle cops in front of his car. He had come a little early to address the cast. With him was the white stage manager and a representative of the New York producing office.

They called everybody together on the stage. The Lord wept as he spoke of all his race had borne to get where Negroes are today. Of how they had struggled. Of how they sang. Of how they must keep on struggling and singing—until white folks see the light. A strike would do no good. A strike would only hurt their cause. With sorrow in his heart—but more noble because of it—he would go on with the play. He was sure his actors—his angels—his children—would continue, too.

The white men accompanying God were very solemn, as though hurt to their souls to think what their Negro employees were suffering, but far more hurt to think that Negroes had wanted to jeopardize a week's box-office receipts by a strike! That would really harm everybody!

Behind God and the white managers stood two big detectives.

Needless to say, the Negroes finally went downstairs to put on their wings and makeup. All but Logan. He went downstairs to drag the cast out by force, to make men of darkies, to carry through the strike. But he couldn't. Not alone. Nobody really wanted to strike. Nobody wanted to sacrifice anything for race pride, decency, or elementary human rights. The actors only wanted to keep on appearing in a naïve dialect play about a quaint, funny heaven full of niggers at which white people laughed and wept.

The management sent two detectives downstairs to get Logan. They were taking no chances. Just as the curtain rose they carted him off to jail—for disturbing the peace. The colored angels were all massed in the wings for the opening spiritual when the police took the black boy out, a line of tears running down his cheeks.

Most of the actors *wanted* to think Logan was crying because he was being arrested—but in their souls they knew that was not why he wept.

THE MAN WHO KILLED A SHADOW

BY RICHARD WRIGHT

National Cathedral

(Originally published in 1946)

I t all began long ago when he was a tiny boy who was already used, in a fearful sort of way, to living with shadows. But what were the shadows that made him afraid? Surely they were not those beautiful silhouettes of objects cast upon the earth by the sun. Shadows of that kind are innocent and he loved trying to catch them as he ran along sunlit paths in summer. But there were subtler shadows which he saw and which others could not see: the shadows of his fears. And this boy had such shadows and he lived to kill one of them.

Saul Saunders was born black in a little Southern town, not many miles from Washington, the nation's capital, which means that he came into a world that was split in two, a white world and a black one, the white one being separated from the black by a million psychological miles. So, from the very beginning, Saul looking timidly out from his black world, saw the shadowy outlines of a white world that was unreal to him and not his own.

It so happened that even Saul's mother was but a vague, shadowy thing to him, for she died long before his memory could form an image of her. And the same thing happened to Saul's father, who died before the boy could retain a clear picture of him in his mind.

People really never became personalities to Saul, for hardly had he ever got to know them before they vanished. So people became for Saul symbols of uneasiness, of a deprivation that evoked in him a sense of the transitory quality of life, which always made him feel that some invisible, unexplainable event was about to descend upon him.

He had five brothers and two sisters who remained strangers to him. There was, of course, no adult in his family with enough money to support them all, and the children were rationed out to various cousins, uncles, aunts, and grandparents.

It fell to Saul to live with his grandmother who moved constantly from one small Southern town to another, and even physical landscapes grew to have but little emotional meaning for the boy. Towns were places you lived in for a while, and then you moved on. When he had reached the age of twelve, all reality seemed to him to be akin to his mother and father, like the white world that surrounded the black island of his life, like the parade of dirty little towns that passed forever before his eyes, things that had names but not substance, things that happened and then retreated into an incomprehensible nothingness.

Saul was not dumb or lazy, but it took him seven years to reach the third grade in school. None of the people who came and went in Saul's life had ever prized learning and Saul did likewise. It was quite normal in his environment to reach the age of fourteen and still be in the third grade, and Saul liked being normal, liked being like other people.

Then the one person—his grandmother—who Saul had thought would endure forever, passed suddenly from his life, and from that moment on Saul did not ever quite know what to do. He went to work for the white people of the South and the shadowlike quality of his world became terribly manifest, continuously present. He understood nothing of this white world into which he had been thrown; it was just there, a faint and fearful shadow cast by some object that stood between him and a hidden and powerful sun.

He quickly learned that the strange white people for whom he worked considered him inferior; he did not feel inferior and he did not think that he was. But when he looked about him he saw other black people accepting this definition of themselves, and who was he to challenge it? Outwardly he grew to accept it as part of that vast shadow-world that came and went, pulled by forces which he nor nobody he knew understood.

Soon all of Saul's anxieties, fears, and irritations became focused upon this white shadow-world which gave him his daily bread in exchange for his labor. Feeling unhappy and not knowing why, he projected his misery out from himself and upon the one thing that made him most constantly anxious. If this had not happened, if Saul had not found a way of putting his burden upon others, he would have early thought of suicide. He finally did, in the end, think of killing himself, but then it was too late . . .

At the age of fifteen Saul knew that the life he was then living was to be his lot, that there was no way to rid himself of his plaguing sense of unreality, no way to relax and forget. He was most self-forgetful when he was with black people, and that made things a little easier for him. But as he grew older, he became more afraid, yet none of his friends noticed it. Indeed, many of Saul's friends liked him very much. Saul was always kind, attentive; but no one suspected that his kindness, his quiet, waiting loyalty came from his being afraid.

Then Saul changed. Maybe it was luck or misfortune; it is hard to tell. When he took a drink of whisky, he found that it helped to banish the shadows, lessened his tensions, made the world more reasonably three-dimensional, and he grew to like drinking. When he was paid off on a Saturday night, he would drink with his friends and he would feel better. He felt that whisky made life complete, that it stimulated him. But, of course, it did not. Whisky really depressed him, numbed him somewhat, reduced the force and number of the shadows that made him tight inside.

When Saul was sober, he almost never laughed in the presence of the white shadow-world, but when he had a drink or two he found that he could. Even when he was told about the hard lives that all Negroes lived, it did not worry him, for he would take a drink and not feel too badly. It did not even bother him when he heard that if you were alone with a white woman and she screamed, it was as good as hearing your death sentence, for, though you had done nothing, you would be killed. Saul got used to hearing the siren of the police car screaming in the Black Belt, got used to seeing white cops dragging Negroes off to jail. Once he grew wildly angry about it, felt that the shadows would some day claim him as he had seen them claim others, but his friends warned him that it was dangerous to feel that way, that always the black man lost, and the best thing to do was to take a drink. He did, and in a little while they were all laughing.

One night when he was mildly drunk—he was thirty years old and living in Washington at the time—he got married. The girl was good for Saul, for she too liked to drink and she was pretty and they got along together. Saul now felt that things were not so bad; as long as he could stifle the feeling of being hemmed in, as long as he could conquer the anxiety about the unexpected happening, life was bearable.

Saul's jobs had been many and simple. First he had worked on a farm. When he was fourteen he had gone to Washington, after his grandmother had died, where he did all kinds of odd jobs. Finally he was hired by an old white army colonel as chauffeur and butler and he averaged about twenty dollars every two weeks. He lived in and got his meals and uniform and he remained with the colonel for five years. The colonel too liked to drink, and sometimes they would both get drunk. But Saul never forgot that the colonel, though drunk and feeling fine, was still a shadow, unreal, and might suddenly change toward him.

One day, when whisky was making him feel good, Saul asked the colonel for a raise in salary, told him that he did not have enough to live on, and that prices were rising. But the colonel was sober and hard that day and said no. Saul was so stunned that he quit the job that instant. While under the spell of whisky he had for a quick moment felt that the world of shadows was over, but when he had asked for more money and had been refused, he knew that he had been wrong. He should not have asked for money; he should have known that the colonel was a no-good guy, a shadow.

Saul was next hired as an exterminator by a big chemical company and he found that there was something in his nature that made him like going from house to house and putting down poison for rats and mice and roaches. He liked seeing concrete evidence of his work and the dead bodies of rats were no shadows. They were real. He never felt better in his life than when he was killing with the sanction of society. And his boss even increased his salary when he asked for it. And he drank as much as he liked and no one cared.

But one morning, after a hard night of drinking which had made him irritable and high-strung, his boss said something that he did not like and he spoke up, defending himself against what he thought was a slighting remark. There was an argument and Saul left.

Two weeks of job hunting got him the position of janitor in the National Cathedral, a church and religious institution. It was the solitary kind of work he liked; he reported for duty each morning at seven o'clock and at eleven he was through. He first cleaned the Christmas card shop, next he cleaned the library; and his final chore was to clean the choir room.

But cleaning the library, with its rows and rows of books, was what caught Saul's attention, for there was a strange little shadow woman there who stared at him all the time in a most peculiar way. The library was housed in a separate building and, whenever he came to clean it, he and the white woman would be there alone. She was tiny, blonde, blue-eyed, weighing about 110 pounds, and standing about five feet three inches. Saul's boss had warned him never to quarrel with the lady in charge of the library. "She's a crackpot," he had told Saul. And naturally Saul never wanted any trouble; in fact, he did not even know the woman's name. Many times, however, he would pause in his work, feeling that his eyes were being drawn to her and he would turn around and find her staring at him. Then she would look away quickly, as though ashamed. "What in hell does she want from me?" he wondered uneasily. The woman never spoke to him except to say good morning and she even said that as though she did not want to say it. Saul thought that maybe she was afraid of him; but how could that be? He could not recall when anybody had ever been afraid of him, and he had never been in any trouble in his life.

One morning while sweeping the floor he felt his eyes being drawn toward her and he paused and turned and saw her staring at him. He did not move, neither did she. They stared at each other for about ten seconds, then she went out of the room, walking with quick steps, as though angry or afraid. He was frightened, but forgot it quickly. "What the hell's wrong with that woman?" he asked himself.

Next morning Saul's boss called him and told him, in a nice, quiet tone—but it made him scared and mad just the same—that the woman in the library had complained about him, had said that he never cleaned under her desk.

"Under her desk?" Saul asked, amazed.

"Yes," his boss said, amused at Saul's astonishment.

"But I clean under her desk every morning," Saul said.

"Well, Saul, remember, I told you she was a crackpot," his boss said soothingly. "Don't argue with her. Just do your work."

"Yes, sir," Saul said.

He wanted to tell his boss how the woman always stared at him, but he could not find courage enough to do so. If he had been talking with his black friends, he would have done so quite naturally. But why talk to one shadow about another queer shadow?

That day being payday, he got his weekly wages and that night he had a hell of a good time. He drank until he was drunk, until he blotted out almost everything from his consciousness. He was getting regularly drunk now whenever he had the money. He liked it and he bothered nobody and he was happy while doing it. But dawn found him broke, exhausted, and terribly depressed, full of shadows and uneasiness, a way he never liked it. The thought of going to his job made him angry. He longed for deep, heavy sleep. But, no, he had a good job and he had to keep it. Yes, he would go.

After cleaning the Christmas card shop—he was weak and he sweated a lot—he went to the library. No one was there. He swept the floor and was about to dust the books when he heard the footsteps of the woman coming into the room. He was tired, nervous, half asleep; his hands trembled and his reflexes were overquick. "So you're the bitch who snitched on me, hunh?" he said irritably to himself. He continued dusting and all at once he had the queer feeling that she was staring at him. He fought against the impulse to look at her, but he could not resist it. He turned slowly and saw that she was sitting in her chair at her desk, staring at him with unblinking eyes. He had the impression that she was about to speak. He could not help staring back at her, waiting.

"Why don't you clean under my desk?" she asked him in a tense but controlled voice.

"Why, ma'am," he said slowly, "I just did."

"Come here and look," she said, pointing downward.

He replaced the book on the shelf. She had never spoken so many words to him before. He went and stood before her and his mind protested against what his eyes saw, and then his senses leaped in wonder. She was sitting with her knees sprawled apart and her dress was drawn halfway up her legs. He looked from her round blue eyes to her white legs whose thighs thickened as they went to a V clothed in tight, sheer, pink panties; then he looked quickly again into her eyes. Her face was a beet red, but she sat very still, rigid, as though she was being impelled into an act which she did not want to perform but was being driven to perform. Saul was so startled that he could not move.

"I just cleaned under your desk this morning," he mumbled, sensing that he was not talking about what she meant.

"There's dust there now," she said sternly, her legs still so wide apart that he felt that she was naked.

He did not know what to do; he was so baffled, humiliated, and frightened that he grew angry. But he was afraid to express his anger openly.

"Look, ma'am," he said in a tone of suppressed rage and hate, "you're making trouble for me!"

"Why don't you do your work?" she blazed at him. "That's what you're being paid to do, you black nigger!" Her legs were still spread wide and she was sitting as though about to spring upon him and throw her naked thighs about his body.

For a moment he was still and silent. Never before in his life had he been called a "black nigger." He had heard that white people used that phrase as their supreme humiliation of black people, but he had never been treated so. As the insult sank in, as he stared at her gaping thighs, he felt overwhelmed by a sense of wild danger.

"I don't like that," he said and before he knew it he had slapped her flat across her face.

She sucked in her breath, sprang up, and stepped away from him. Then she screamed sharply, and her voice was like a lash cutting into his chest. She screamed again and he backed away from her. He felt helpless, strange; he knew what he had done, knew its meaning for him; but he knew that he could not have helped it. It seemed that some part of him was there in that room watching him do things that he should not do. He drew in his breath and for a moment he felt that he could not stand upon his legs. His world was now full of all the shadows he had ever feared. He was in the worst trouble that a black man could imagine.

The woman was screaming continuously now and he was running toward the stairs. Just as he put his foot on the bottom step, he paused and looked over his shoulder. She was backing away from him, toward an open window at the far end of the room, still screaming. Oh God! In her scream he heard the sirens of the police cars that hunted down black men in the Black Belts and he heard the shrill whistles of white cops running after black men and he felt again in one rush of emotion all the wild and bitter tales he had heard of how whites always got the black who did a crime and this woman was screaming as though he had raped her.

He ran on up the steps, but her screams were coming so loud that when he neared the top of the steps he slowed. Those screams would not let him run any more, they weakened him, tugged and pulled him. His chest felt as though it would burst. He reached the top landing and looked round aimlessly. He saw a fireplace and before it was a neat pile of wood and while he was looking at that pile of wood the screams tore at him, unnerved him. With a shaking hand he reached down and seized in his left hand—for he was left-handed—a heavy piece of oaken firewood that had jagged, sharp edges where it had been cut with an ax. He turned and ran back down the steps to where the woman stood screaming. He lifted the stick of wood as he confronted her, then paused. He wanted her to stop screaming. If she had stopped, he would have fled, but while she screamed all he could feel was a hotness bubbling in him and urging him to do something. She would fill her lungs quickly and deeply and her breath would come out at full blast. He swung down his left arm and hit her a swinging blow on the side of her head, not to hurt her, not to kill her, but to stop that awful noise, to stop that shadow from screaming a scream that meant death . . . He felt her skull crack and give as she sank to the floor, but she still screamed. He trembled from head to feet. Goddamn that woman . . . Why didn't she stop that yelling? He lifted his arm and gave her another blow, feeling the oaken stick driving its way into her skull. But still she screamed. He was about to hit her again when he became aware that the stick he held was light. He looked at it and found that half of it had broken off, was lying on the floor. But she screamed on, with blood running down her dress, her legs sprawled nakedly out from under her. He dropped the remainder of the stick and grabbed her throat and choked her to stop her screams. That seemed to quiet her; she looked as though she had fainted. He choked her for a long time, not trying to kill her, but just to make sure that she would not scream again and make him wild and hot inside. He was not reacting to the woman, but to the feelings that her screams evoked in him.

The woman was limp and silent now and slowly he took his hands from her throat. She was quiet. He waited. He was not certain. Yes, take her downstairs into the bathroom and if she screamed again no one would hear her . . . He took her hands in his and started dragging her away from the window. His hands were wet with sweat and her hands were so tiny and soft that time and again her little fingers slipped out of his palms. He tried holding her hands tighter and only succeeded in scratching her. Her ring slid off into his hand while he was dragging her and he stood still for a moment, staring in a daze at the thin band of shimmering gold, then mechanically he put it into his pocket. Finally he dragged her down the steps to the bathroom door.

He was about to take her in when he saw that the floor was spotted with drippings of blood. That was bad . . . He had been trained to keep floors clean, just as he had been trained to fear shadows. He propped her clumsily against a wall and went into the bathroom and took wads of toilet paper and mopped up the red splashes. He even went back upstairs where he had first struck her and found blood spots and wiped them up carefully. He stiffened; she was hollering again. He ran downstairs and this time he recalled that he had a knife in his pocket. He took it out, opened it, and plunged it deep into her throat; he was frantic to stop her from hollering . . . He pulled the knife from her throat and she was quiet.

He stood, his eyes roving. He noticed a door leading down to a recess in a wall through which steam pipes ran. Yes, it would be better to put her there; then if she started yelling no one would hear her. He was not trying to hide her; he merely wanted to make sure that she would not be heard. He dragged her again and her dress came up over her knees to her chest and again he saw her pink panties. It was too hard dragging her and he lifted her in his arms and while carrying her down the short flight of steps he thought that the pink panties, if he would wet them, would make a good mop to clean up the blood. Once more he sat her against the wall, stripped her of her pink panties—and not once did he so much as glance at her groin—wetted them and swabbed up the spots, then pushed her into the recess under the pipes. She was in full view, easily seen. He tossed the wet ball of panties in after her.

He sighed and looked around. The floor seemed clean. He went back upstairs. That stick of broken wood . . . He picked up the two shattered ends of wood and several splinters; he carefully joined the ends together and then fitted the splinters into place. He laid the mended stick back upon the pile before the fireplace. He stood listening, wondering if she would yell again, but there was no sound. It never occurred to him that he could help her, that she might be in pain; he never wondered even if she were dead. He got his coat and hat and went home.

He was nervously tired. It seemed that he had just finished doing an old and familiar job of dodging the shadows that were forever around him, shadows that he could not understand. He undressed, but paid no attention to the blood on his trousers and shirt; he was alone in the room; his wife was at work. When he pulled out his billfold, he saw the ring. He put it in the drawer of his night table, more to keep his wife from seeing it than to hide it. He climbed wearily into bed and at once fell into a deep, sound sleep from which he did not awaken until late afternoon. He lay blinking blood-shot eyes and he could not remember what he had done. Then the vague, shadowlike picture of it came before his eyes. He was puzzled, and for a moment he wondered if it had happened or had someone told him a story of it. He could not be sure. There was no fear or regret in him.

When at last the conviction of what he had done was real in him, it came only in terms of flat memory, devoid of all emotion, as though he were looking when very tired and sleepy at a scene being flashed upon the screen of a movie house. Not knowing what to do, he remained in bed. He had drifted off to sleep again when his wife came home late that night from her cooking job.

Next morning he ate the breakfast his wife prepared, rose from the table and kissed her, and started off toward the Cathedral as though nothing had happened. It was not until he actually got to the Cathedral steps that he became shaky and nervous. He stood before the door for two or three minutes, and then he realized that he could not go back in there this morning. Yet it was not danger that made him feel this way, but a queer kind of repugnance. Whether the woman was alive or not did not enter his mind. He still did not know what to do. Then he remembered that his wife, before she had left for her job, had asked him to buy some groceries. Yes, he would do that. He wanted to do that because he did not know what else on earth to do.

* * *

He bought the groceries and took them home, then spent the rest of the day wandering from bar to bar. Not once did he think of fleeing. He would go home, sit, turn on the radio, then go out into the streets and walk. Finally he would end up at a bar, drinking. On one of his many trips into the house, he changed his clothes, rolled up his bloody shirt and trousers, put the blood-stained knife inside the bundle, and pushed it into a far corner of a closet. He got his gun and put it into his pocket, for he was nervously depressed.

But he still did not know what to do. Suddenly he recalled that some months ago he had bought a cheap car which was now in a garage for repairs. He went to the garage and persuaded the owner to take it back for twenty-five dollars; the thought that he could use the car for escape never came to his mind. During that afternoon and early evening he sat in bars and drank. What he felt now was no different from what he had felt all his life.

Toward eight o'clock that night he met two friends of his and invited them for a drink. He was quite drunk now. Before him on the table was a sandwich and a small glass of whisky. He leaned forward, listening sleepily to one of his friends tell a story about a girl, and then he heard:

"Aren't you Saul Saunders?"

He looked up into the faces of two white shadows.

"Yes," he admitted readily. "What do you want?"

"You'd better come along with us. We want to ask you some questions," one of the shadows said.

"What's this all about?" Saul asked.

They grabbed his shoulders and he stood up. Then he reached down and picked up the glass of whisky and drank it. He walked steadily out of the bar to a waiting auto, a policeman to each side of him, his mind a benign blank. It was not until they were about to put him into the car that something happened and whipped his numbed senses to an apprehension of danger. The policeman patted his waist for arms; they found nothing because his gun was strapped to his chest. Yes, he ought to kill himself . . . The thought leaped into his mind with such gladness that he shivered. It was the answer to everything. Why had he not thought of it before?

Slowly he took off his hat and held it over his chest to hide the movement of his left hand, then he reached inside of his shirt and pulled out the gun. One of the policemen pounced on him and snatched the gun.

"So, you're trying to kill us too, hunh?" one asked.

"Naw. I was trying to kill myself," he answered simply.

"Like hell you were!"

A fist came onto his jaw and he sank back limp.

Two hours later, at the police station, he told them everything, speaking in a low, listless voice without a trace of emotion, vividly describing every detail, yet feeling that it was utterly hopeless for him to try to make them understand how horrible it was for him to hear that woman screaming. His narrative sounded so brutal that the policemen's faces were chalky.

Weeks later a voice droned in a court room and he sat staring dully.

". . . The Grand Jurors of the United States of America, in and for the District of Columbia aforesaid, upon their oath, do present:

"That one Saul Saunders, on, to wit, the first day of March, 19—, and at and within the District of Columbia aforesaid, contriving and intending to kill one Maybelle Eva Houseman . . ."

"So *that's* her name," he said to himself in amazement.

". . . Feloniously, wilfully, purposely, and of his deliberate and premeditated malice did strike, beat, and wound the said Maybelle Eva Houseman, in and upon the front of the head and in and upon the right side of the head of her, the said Maybelle Eva Houseman, two certain mortal wounds and fractures; and did fix and fasten about the neck and throat of her, the said Maybelle Eva Houseman, his hand or hands—but whether it was one of his hands or both of his hands is to the Grand Jury aforesaid unknown—and that he, the said Saul Saunders, with his hand or hands as aforesaid fixed and fastened about the throat of her, did choke and strangle the said Maybelle Eva Houseman, of which said choking and strangling the said Maybelle Eva Houseman, on, to wit, the said first day of March, 19—, and at and within the said District of Columbia, did die."

He longed for a drink, but that was impossible now. Then he took a deep breath and surrendered to the world of shadows about him, the world he had feared so long; and at once the tension went from him and he felt better than he had felt in a long time. He was amazed at how relaxed and peaceful it was when he stopped fighting the world of shadows.

". . . By force and violence and against resistance and by putting in fear, did steal, take, and carry away, from and off the person and from the immediate, actual possession of one Maybelle Eva Houseman, then and there being, a certain finger ring, of the value of, to wit, ten dollars."

He listened now with more attention but no anxiety:

"And in and while perpetrating robbery aforesaid did kill and murder the said Maybelle Eva Houseman; against the form of the statute in such case made and provided, and against the peace and government of the said United States of America."

P.S. Thereupon Dr. Herman Stein was called as a witness and being first duly sworn testified as follows:

". . . On examination of the genital organs there was no evidence of contusion, abrasion, or trauma, and the decedent's hymen ring was intact. This decedent had not been criminally assaulted or attempted to be entered. It has been ascertained that the decedent's age was 40."

PART II

BURNING DOWN THE HOUSE

THE LAST DAYS OF DUNCAN STREET

BY JULIAN MAYFIELD

Kingman Park

(Originally published in 1960)

It was one of those bright days when that Washington sun wasn't taking any stuff off of anybody. There wasn't a cloud in the sky, and the wind wasn't a big wind at all, just a little itty-bitty breeze to take the edge off the sun's heat. It was a good day, man, because there wasn't any school, the grown folks were at work, and we could do anything that crossed our natural minds. It was a crazy day, man, because that night Joe Louis was going to knock the living stew out of a big German named Max Schmeling.

We could have gone swimming. There was the colored pool on the other side of town and the muddy Eastern Branch of the Potomac was only a few blocks away. We could have swiped pop bottles from old man Farbenstein's store yard and sold them back to him. Then we would have had enough money to ride across town to the picture show. A Bob Steele movie was playing at the Gem and a Tom Mix one was at the Alamo.

But this wasn't the kind of day when you went swimming or sat in a movie. You could do stuff like that anytime. But how often did Joe Louis have a chance to get into the same ring with that blabber-mouth Schmeling. That German had been doing a lot of talking about how badly he was going to beat

Joe. Naturally he thought he was better than Joe because he was white, but the newspapers were hinting that he thought he was better than everybody because he was a German. Well, you know Joe, he hadn't said much, but all of us knew what was bound to happen. Joe was nobody's talker, but he could dispose of a man before you could call his name. Yes, this was going to be a great night and we were prepared to celebrate it.

The bricks had come out of an empty lot in the middle of the block. They were red bricks that we had broken into halves, good bricks that were just right for throwing, bricks that you could aim at a white boy's head. The baseball bats would come in handy for any close fighting. A white boy wouldn't even know what had hit him if he got beaned with one of those Babe Ruth specials. We had a couple of knives and lots of milk bottles. It was going to be quite a night.

By mid-afternoon all our weapons were stored in Austin's basement. We lounged and talked on the grass near the basement door. Austin had a real grudge against the white boys. They had caught him near the Peoples Drug store the week before and knocked out two of his front teeth. He was a skinny little high-yellow kid with bow legs and curly hair. We thought his people were well-off because they lived in an entire house instead of a flat like the rest of us.

"Wait'll I catch one of them," Austin said, spitting through the space where his front teeth had been. "I'll knock his gut string out." He stood up, reached out with his left hand, and clutched the air. "I'll take that paddy boy like this, see, and I'll hold him up like this, see . . ." With one hand Austin lifted the imaginary white boy from the ground. "And I'll say, 'You're one of those paddy rats that jumped me last week.' And he'll say,

'No sir, Mister Austin, that must've been some other paddy rat, not me.' And I'll say, 'Well, that's too damned bad because you're gonna get it anyway.' He'll say, 'That ain't fair, Mister Austin.' And I'll say, 'Yes it is, because all you paddy boys look alike to me!'"

We laughed as Austin brought his right fist over and *wham!* the invisible white boy went sailing through the air.

Teeny Mae said, "Boy, I hear that Joe is in really good shape. Wonder how long it will take him to catch up with that German guy."

I said, "Three or four rounds." I wanted to give our man enough leeway. Sometimes Joe needed time to figure out a man's style.

Robert Jackson yelled, "Gowan! Joe'll stop that jerk in one round. Wanna bet?" I didn't want to bet. Robert had set himself up as leader of our gang and so far, because he was a year older than the rest (and presumably tougher), no one had challenged him.

"I'll show you." Robert stood up and took the Joe Louis stance, which was the only one any of us ever used. "This guy's got a hard right, see, but Joe will keep him off with that left jab. Now when this guy comes over with that right, see, Joe's gonna bring that left hard to the jaw like this. Then he'll whip it right in, and, man, that'll be the end of that German." Robert sprawled face downward on the grass like one of Joe's victims.

Fat Sammy said, "And that's when I'm going out and get myself a paddy boy."

We all agreed that, yeah, there was no better time to beat the paddy boys. Then we got into a loud argument about who had beaten up more white boys during the raid we had pulled after the last Joe Louis fight.

To understand this passion for scrapping with the white boys you have to feel what Joe Louis meant to the Duncan Street gang. We loved him. He was our *man*. He was right out there in front going for us. Some people called us hoodlums but in our minds there was no doubt Joe would have approved of the raids we went on after his ring victories. We justified them very simply. The white boys had a swimming pool nearby and we didn't. They could see movies right there in the neighborhood and we had to ride all the way up to the colored business district on U Street. And it was shame on you if, like Austin, you were caught alone by the white gang at 15th and H streets. I think sometimes we could not help wondering if there really was something wrong with us that made white folks treat us so badly. But Joe dispelled our doubts. He made us believe that each one of us was as good as anybody. He was our personal representative.

So it was give and take, man. You gave as much as you could and you took what you had to. Life was a crazy kind of thing full of school and the gang and fighting white boys. It was exciting because something was jumping every minute. Of course, the fever pitch ran highest whenever Joe fought. Those were the craziest nights of all. Talk about kicks, that was it.

When the sun got low it hung on a while, kissing everything in sight goodbye. It dropped away slowly as if it too wanted to stay on and hear the fight. Then the night eased down smoothly like warm milk and a gentle breeze cooled Duncan Street. I felt so good being a part of it all that I wanted to yell out loud.

Sammy's old man, Mister Speed, came home with a whole case of beer because he had invited friends over to hear the fight. We all had a good laugh on Teeny Mac when we saw his father, who was supposed to be a very strict Baptist, sneak a fifth bottle into the house. My pop sat down in the big easy chair, lit a White Owl cigar, and said he wasn't going to move until the fight was over.

By ten o'clock the sidewalks were deserted. Every radio in the block was tuned in to New York. Every mind pictured the Brown Bomber, always calm and deliberate, as he stepped through the ropes and raised his hand. We saw him standing before the German, softly pawing the canvas with his toe as the referee droned out the rules. Finally we saw him take off his robe and walk like a bronze god toward the center of the ring to begin his master work.

Well, I don't have to tell you what happened. That night Joe didn't have it, and this big German square did just what he said he was going to do to our ace man. He whipped the living daylights out of Joe. I just couldn't believe it. My eyes got hot and then the tears began to roll. My old man stopped puffing on his White Owl and didn't say a mumbling word. My kid sister was too young to understand, but she felt it and kept quiet. Mama sighed and said, "Well, you gotta lose sometimes, I guess," real sad like, and went into the kitchen. I felt just like nothing inside.

Of course, there was no rushing out of doors to snatch up our weapons and fight the white boys. One by one the members of the Duncan Street gang dragged tail out to the sidewalk under the lamplight where we usually gathered at night. We sat on the curbstone making figures in the sand. Robert Jackson kept spitting because that was what he did when he was mad or down in the blues. We must have sat there ten or fifteen minutes in complete, mournful silence. The beautiful day with the crazy sun had turned into a miserable night.

Finally, Teeny Mae said, "Boy, you know one thing? That didn't fight like no Joe Louis."

"You're goddamned right it didn't," said Austin, and we all agreed, yeah, they were right, that didn't fight like Joe Louis at all.

Then, as if someone had kicked him, Sammy yelled, "Something was wrong!" That's right, we chorused, something was damn wrong.

"Do you suppose they doped Joe?"

We turned and stared at Robert Jackson. He was serious. Our mouths opened in astonishment as the thought gripped us. It was such a simple explanation. We knew that Joe could beat Max Schmeling or anybody else any day in the week.

Sammy said, "You know they don't want no colored guy to be champ, man. My pop says they never did like Jack Johnson."

Now we were all furious. Imagine doing a nasty thing like that to Joe Louis! Robert Jackson said we ought to go beat some white heads just to make up for what they had done to poor Joe. He reminded us of the bricks and bats we had stored in Austin's basement. Robert Jackson said that 15th and H streets ought to be our first target because we could probably catch the whole white gang there. We jumped to our feet agreeing loudly that Robert had a damned good idea and we would show those sons of—*Crrraaaaaash!* A terrible shattering above our heads and pitch blackness. I stopped breathing. Not a soul moved. We were numb with fear as the fragments of the streetlamp showered us. For a moment there was a long, awful silence.

Then, small and hard, the white boy's voice from the alley. "Oh, you black bastards! We got you now!"

Man, I'm standing there like a dump on a log, and nothing in my hands. Then the bricks and bottles started falling, and the white boys came down on us like white on rice. The first brick hit me and I fell against Teeny Mae. Then we both started running and bumped into one another again. Teeny said, "Man, don't be holding me up," and I yelled, "Man, you get out of my way!" We both took flying leaps for a secret hiding place under Sammy's porch. Once there I huddled close to Teeny. My shoulder was throbbing where the brick had hit me.

Teeny said, "Man, ain't this something. Those guys done caught us off guard."

Obviously the 15th and H boys had felt so good about the German beating Joe that they had decided to pay us a surprise visit, something they had never dared before. They were dancing and yelling like Indians in the middle of Duncan Street, and throwing bricks and milk bottles at everything that moved. Then our parents started opening windows to see what all the noise was about, and the light from the houses poured down into the street. The victorious invaders hauled tail for their own territory, disappearing as suddenly as they had come.

We crawled out of our shelters and gathered under the shattered lamplight. You can imagine how we felt. It wasn't so much my shoulder or Robert Jackson's bleeding (his hand had been cut) or Austin's crying (he had lost another tooth). The hurt was deeper than that.

"Ira! Ira!" It was Teeny Mae's father calling him. "You out there, boy?"

Teeny looked up. "Yes sir, I'm here."

"What are you boys doing out there? What happened to that lamplight?"

Teeny didn't know what to say, and the rest of us could not help him. We just stood there with our heads bowed.

"Well, speak up, boys. What happened?"

We didn't know, not really. After that night we had our victories, especially after Joe became champ and gave Schmeling a good licking. But the spirit was never quite the same on Duncan Street. We were never so sure again.

WASHINGTON

BY JULIAN MAZOR

Shaw

(Originally published in 1963)

When I ran through Pennsylvania Station on a cloudy November afternoon, I was wearing a clean blue shirt with a soft unbuttoned collar, a brown knit tie, a brown herringbone suit, well-polished brown Spanish shoes, and an English overcoat—a gray herringbone—that I had worn for three years. I had some old letters stuffed into the inside pocket of my jacket, and after I had taken out my wallet to buy my train ticket I had trouble putting it back. I was afraid I would miss my train, so I slipped the wallet into the inside pocket of my overcoat, thinking I would sort things out when I was aboard. I had a hundred and forty-seven dollars in the wallet, a sum left over from my last pay check, and I was on my way to Washington, D.C., to see my family—my mother and father and an older sister who had recently got married. I had just left my job as a salesman-demonstrator-instructor in the tennis department of a famous New York department store, where I, John Lionel, was known as "Wright & Ditson." One day, for some reason, while demonstrating the proper service technique to a twelve-year-old boy and his mother, I tossed a tennis ball up in the air and hit a powerful cannonball service; the ball whizzed by the floor manager's—Mr. Palmerston's—ear, and smashed a glass case. Palmerston said it was nice knowing me and told me to pick up my check.

So long, Wright & Ditson. It was my third job since coming back from Europe, where I had served a tour in the Army, and although in a way I was a little concerned because I didn't seem to be going anywhere and didn't know where I wanted to go, I thought, Well, I'm only twenty-three and I've got time.

Somewhere near North Philadelphia, I ate a tuna-fish sandwich that I bought from a vender on the train, and about twenty minutes south of the Thirtieth Street Station I began to feel warm and a little strange. I thought I'd get some air, so I left my seat and went out to the platform between the cars. I leaned against the steel wall and smoked and looked out at the countryside. The cool air made me feel a lot better. I stayed out between the cars until the train was about a half hour past Wilmington, and then I returned to my seat in the coach.

I thought I'd get a book out of my suitcase and read for a while. When I looked up at the baggage rack, I saw that my overcoat was gone. I had forgotten to take the wallet out of it. I had placed the coat neatly folded over my suitcase, and there was no doubt that it was gone. I walked up and down the coach, looking at all the overcoats in the baggage racks, and then I returned to my seat and tried to be calm and think things out. Then I went up and down the car again. When I returned to my seat for the second time, feeling demoralized and enraged, a man sitting across the aisle asked me what was the matter, and I told him that my overcoat was gone. The man folded his newspaper and looked out the window for a while, and then he asked me to describe the coat. I told him that it was a gray herringbone, and that it had been on the rack above my seat. He took a deep breath and let it out slowly, and then, seeming embarrassed, he told me that he had seen a man pull my coat from the rack as the train got into Wilmington, and that he had, even then, found it a little strange, because this man was already wearing a camel's-hair coat.

I slumped down in my seat, feeling sick. I always do when somebody steals from me. For a while, I sat there thinking about my overcoat and how it had been part of the friendly continuity of my life. Then I got to my feet and went through my pockets and came up with fifty cents. I had lost my money, my Social Security card, and even my passport. I began to feel cold and hot alternately, and around Aberdeen I began to feel cramps and nausea. I figured it was the tuna-fish sandwich. Just outside of Baltimore, I became desperately sick and went to the men's room and threw up. I was sick again between Baltimore and Washington, and when the train finally pulled into Union Station and I stepped out into the cold, rainy afternoon, I felt like hell.

I didn't have enough money for a cab, and it was no use calling home. My family was out of town, visiting my sister's husband's family in Maryland. They would be coming back to Washington in the morning. So I got on a bus, and about twenty minutes later got off, in the rain, and transferred to another bus. While I was on the bus, the nausea and cramps came back and I decided I'd have to get off. I began to look for a bar or restaurant or hotel along the way, and when I saw a gasoline station in a very old, shabby neighborhood—a Negro neighborhood—I pulled the cord and picked up my suitcase and got off.

In the men's room of the gasoline station, I bathed my face in cold water, and went outside again. I was feeling much better, but weak. The rain was cold, and the wind had grown stronger, and I was shivering. I was about to cross the street and wait by a little yellow bus-stop sign, when I saw that I was in front of a small grocery store with a green awning slanting down over a dimly lighted display window. I decided to stand under the awning and watch for the bus from there.

Inside the grocery store, three Negroes were leaning against a long, white refrigerated case, or counter, talking and laughing. Another Negro, in a white apron, was behind the counter, leaning on it and reading a newspaper and eating a sandwich. I thought of going into the store and getting warm, but I had no excuse for going in, really—no money to buy anything with. So I stayed under the awning, which was flapping wildly in the wind. My teeth were chattering, and I felt a sore throat coming on, when I saw a Negro man and woman walking down the street in the rain, arguing. They'd walk without speaking, then stop and argue, then walk some more. Actually, it was more of a dramatic exercise than an argument. The woman would make wordless faces at the man, which unsettled him. He would get ready to say something, and then she would laugh at him. Then he would look surprised and cautious, as though he was searching for a little balance and leverage, and she would scream at him. Then she would tell him to shut up, and he would look surprised, and finally he would begin to scream at her, and then she would begin to laugh at him, which made him more unsteady. The man was squat and round, with a black moonface crowned by a porkpie hat. He was wearing a frayed and very wet fatigue jacket. His companion was mocha brown, and tall and wide. She was large-boned and hefty, but not fat, and although she was obviously strong, she was unmistakably feminine. She wore a man's raincoat and a pair of bedroom slippers without backs. She didn't wear stockings, and she didn't wear a hat. She had a wide nose and a wide mouth, and large, beautiful eyes. She walked ahead of the man into the grocery store, slamming the door after her, and he followed her in, looking worried and confused.

I leaned my back against the window and watched the rain water pour off the awning and splash over my shoes. I was standing in a puddle about an inch deep, but it hardly mattered any more. I was beginning to feel sick again. There was no sign of the bus. To take my mind off myself, I turned and faced the window, and I saw the woman dancing around the store with her arms outstretched and her eyes half closed. The men standing near the refrigerated case kept up a rhythmic clapping. She went on dancing around, having a marvelous time, while the man in the porkpie hat looked sullenly at the floor.

After a while, I turned around and faced the street again. I felt like a shipwreck hanging on a reef, or a piece of driftwood. I think I had a touch of delirium. I was thinking about what to do next, when the woman and the man in the porkpie hat came out of the grocery store.

"You deny that? You deny that?" he yelled at her. He was standing next to me under the awning.

"Go on, man. Go on. Go on," she said, walking away from him and moving indifferently into the rain.

"Now, you deny that?" he said. "Now where you going? You come on back here."

"You don't own me, baby," she said, walking on.

He gave a few preliminary grunts of frustration, and then he began to scream at her to come back, but she paid no attention to him. "You hear me? I'm talking to you! You come on back here," he said.

Halfway down the block, she stopped and turned around, put her hands on her hips, yelled something obscene at him, and then stretched out her arms and began to laugh.

"Honey, you getting wet. Now, you come on back here," he called imploringly.

She yelled something at him again.

"Now, honey, why you talk that way to me?" he yelled.

"Man, leave me alone. You make me sick," she said, moving on.

"Come on, honey, you know I don't feel good," he cried at her in a sad whine.

The woman crossed the street quickly, and the man watched her, moving his mouth without saying anything. He seemed too tired to go after her. For a while, he stood with his arms folded and shook his head. He didn't seem to know that I was there, even though only about a foot separated us. I was slightly behind him, still leaning against the window, when he turned around and looked surprised; then he closed his mouth and narrowed his eyes and looked angry.

"How are you?" I said.

"What you say?" he asked, putting a hand over his eyes.

"I said, 'How are you?'"

He held his hand over his eyes, considering the question. "That ain't what you said," he told me finally, still covering his eyes.

"O.K., that's not what I said."

I looked down at my feet, at the puddle I was standing in, trying to ignore him. I noticed that he was wearing a ripped pair of black, misshapen shoes and no socks, and that his pants legs were rolled up a little above his ankles. Suddenly he jumped into the puddle I was standing in and splashed me. I couldn't believe it.

"Now, what did you say?" he asked, folding his arms.

I didn't answer.

"You trying to make a fool out of me?" he asked.

"I'm not trying to make a fool out of you," I said. I looked down the street, feeling sick and desperate, but the street was empty and it was raining harder than ever.

"You mean you ain't trying but I am a fool anyhow. Right?" he said.

"I didn't say that."

"But that what you mean," he said. "You a wise guy. Right?"

"I'm just waiting for a bus. If I insulted you, it was unintentional," I said.

"Don't give me unintentional. I unintentional *you*."

He kicked the puddle, splashing my pants with water, and said he was going to knock me down. Then he stepped back, dropping his hands to the level of his belt, and measured me. I picked up my suitcase and moved it a few feet, setting it on a narrow ledge just below the window.

"Man, I'm gonna wipe you out," he said, opening and closing his hands several times.

I took a deep breath and let it out slowly. He looked very strong, and I am of medium height and rather frail. "Well," I said, "you're going to have the worst fight of your life."

"You gonna give it to me?" he asked, smiling.

I told him that I was going to beat the hell out of him, and then I brought my hands up.

"Man, will you look at that!" he said. "This is gonna be some fun."

He touched the brim of his hat, dropped his hands into position again, and, five feet away from me, began to bob and weave. "You come on in," he said. "I'm a counterpuncher."

I didn't move, but watched him closely, keeping my hands high. I told him I was a counterpuncher, too. He began to circle me, and I turned with him. He kept on going through this little shadowboxing routine, paying only nominal attention to me. He looked very good, very agile.

After a few minutes of circling and jabbing and hooking at the air, he stopped and looked at me. "You looks terrible," he said. We had maneuvered ourselves out into the rain, and the water was streaming over our faces. "You off balance," he said.

I told him not to worry about it, that I had fast hands and a good punch.

"The only thing you doing right is standing up," he said, shaking his head. He held up his hands in a truce gesture and walked over to me. He said he wanted to give me some basic instruction. He adjusted my hands slightly and pushed my head down so that it was protected by my left shoulder, and then he kicked my feet to a different position, saying I was standing flat-footed. "Now you looking good," he said.

"Well, it feels unnatural," I said, resuming my old position.

Then, to prove that my style was poor, he asked me to try to hit him. He said he wouldn't try to hit me but would just give me a little demonstration that would do more for me than all the talk in the world.

"I don't want to hit you," I said.

"Don't worry, you ain't going to," he said.

"Look, I'll take your word for it," I said.

"Come on, now," he said. "You got to see what I mean to really believe it."

So he began to bob and weave with his hands low, presenting his head as a slowly moving target. I watched his head bob for about thirty seconds, and tried to measure him. He kept talking the whole time. "You can't get set, see. Now you see it, now you don't. You all tied up."

I pulled my right hand back a few inches, and he broke into a wide grin, and then, while he was grinning, I feinted with my right hand and came hard with a left hook, catching him squarely on the side of the jaw. He whirled around and pitched forward on the pavement, landing hard on his chest and then rolling over on his side. He wasn't hurt. He grabbed his hat and jumped quickly to his feet, looking annoyed and embarrassed. "I'll be goddam," he said, one hand on top of his hat.

"I'm very sorry," I said. "Are you all right?"

"Some rain got in my eye," he said. "I ain't seen your left."

He said he wanted to give me a few more demonstrations, but I told him I'd had enough. I suddenly felt sick again, with the hot-and-cold business returning—the nausea and cramps and the rest. My legs became weak. Feeling I was going to faint, I walked over to the window and leaned against it. I decided to forget about the bus, for the time being, and go back to the men's room in the gasoline station. I took up my suitcase and started to walk away, when the man trotted over and grabbed me by the arm. "Where you going?" he asked.

"I'm not feeling well," I said, jerking my arm away. "Leave me alone."

"Man, what's wrong with you?" he asked, smiling. "You knock me down and *you* is mad."

Then he began to throw a flurry of punches at the air in front of me, bobbing and weaving, going into a series of strange forward and lateral hops and skips, dancing, and finally winding it up by running in place. I think he felt he was cheering me up, for he kept up the running for about two minutes, making faces, and then he stopped and said, "*Now* how you feeling?"

I told him to get out of my way, but he continued to block me, and I was too weak to try to run around him.

He jumped up in the air and closed his eyes and flapped his arms. "*Now* how you feeling?" he asked, after a few jumps.

I told him I was feeling worse than ever, and that if he really wanted to help me he would go away and leave me alone.

He said that I was just a little down and out, and there was nothing to worry about if I listened to him. He told me about his Opposite Theory. "If you feel like lying down, then stand up," he said. "If you feel like crying, then laugh."

I tried to get by him, but he grabbed me by the shoulder of my coat. "Maybe if you lie down you never get up. You thought of that?"

I broke away and started to run, but he caught up with me easily and clapped a huge hand on my shoulder and pressed down. I whirled around, dropped my suitcase, and threw a wild right hand at him, but he ducked under it neatly and countered, though intentionally missing, with a classic one-two. "Sickness all in the mind," he said.

I told him my sickness was in the stomach and that he should get the hell away from me, but he shook his head, half closing his eyes. "I ain't gonna let you give in to it," he said. "I gonna help you fight it."

He said he knew all about the body, because he was an ex-fighter, and most ex-fighters knew more about the human body than any doctor, and that every man has a secret place in him which fights sickness and pain, and the trick was to have faith in that secret place. He said you had to turn on that little secret power by doing just the opposite of what your body asked you to do.

While he was talking, I developed a headache, and I was about to ask him what this headache was telling me to do, so I could do the opposite, when I began to see objects in pairs and threes, and I knew I was going to fall. The nausea was so bad that I couldn't keep my mouth closed, and the ground seemed to tilt. I dropped down on one knee, pushing at the ground with both hands. "Get up," I heard him say, his voice far off. "Is you gonna lay down? Is you gonna quit?"

As I pushed at the ground, fighting it and the nausea, a bus went by, and the next thing I knew the man was grabbing me under the arms and pulling me to my feet. "We gonna make it," he said.

I tried to push him away. I succeeded in breaking free of one hand, but he had me by the collar with the other. "You doing fine," he said. "You got to keep moving around. It good for the circulation." The word "circulation" seemed to give him an idea, for he began to slap my face with his free hand.

I called him a stupid son of a bitch, hit him hard on the mouth, lurched and spun away from him, hearing my coat and shirt rip, and fell onto the pavement, where I crawled to the gutter and threw up. He stood near me. He kept saying, "You doing fine. You doing fine. You gonna be a new man now. We gonna clear you out."

As he was talking, the street lamps came on. I looked over at him and watched the rain bounce off his shoes. One of his pants legs had come unrolled in the scuffle, and the cuff was ripped.

"How you doing?" he asked, smiling, getting down on one knee and putting his hand on my forehead. His lip was bleeding. I knocked his hand away, and looked down at the fast-moving water in the gutter.

"Man, I is wounded," he said. He leaned over the gutter and brought some water up for his bloodied lip. "Look, I'm gonna tell you a joke," he went on. I got up and started to walk back to the awning, and he followed me, taking my suitcase from my hand and carrying it for me. "This man, he in a restaurant, and he say, 'Waiter, there is a fly in the soup,' and this waiter, he say, 'Don't worry, he can swim.'"

He began to laugh. We stood under the awning, and he continued to laugh at his joke while I looked down the street for the bus. He calmed down and then began to regard me seriously, putting a hand over his mouth.

"Say, you know who I am?" he asked.

I shook my head.

"I guess you heard of Ringo Brown," he said, "who fight in Griffith Stadium in 1939, '40, '41, and '46."

"If you're Ringo Brown, I never heard of you," I said.

"Aw, come on, man," he said, smiling. "I fight twenty-three preliminaries and one main event. I lose the main event. You remember Red Hickey, from Delaware?"

"No."

"I lose to him in a split decision. He was a good boy, but he never did nothing. I was a middleweight."

"You lost only one fight?" I said.

"Now, I ain't said that, but I never knocked out."

I pulled out a pack of cigarettes and a lighter. The pack was wet, but I managed to find two dry cigarettes, and I gave Ringo one.

We smoked for a while without saying anything, and then Ringo said, "Say, kid, what's your name?"

"John," I said. "John Lionel."

I saw a bus coming, and I picked up my suitcase and began to move away.

"Where you going?" Ringo asked.

"So long, Ringo," I said.

As I started to cross the street, he came and grabbed me by the arm. "John, I carry your bag," he said. "You tired."

"I'm all right. It's not heavy," I said.

"No, I carry it."

Ringo began to fight me for the suitcase, right there in the middle of the street. He pushed me with one hand and grabbed the suitcase away with the other. I ran over to the bus stop and called back to Ringo to bring the suitcase. The bus had stopped and was letting off passengers. Ringo just smiled at me from the other side of the street. I asked the driver to wait a second, but he took one look at me and closed the door and drove off. I walked over to Ringo and took the suitcase from him. "You're crazy," I said.

"They be another bus, John," he said, smiling. "One as good as another."

I walked back to the bus stop and decided to wait there, even though the rain was coming down harder than ever. Ringo followed me. "I try to do you a good turn and you don't let me. Don't you know that hurt?" he said.

"Get away from me!"

"Won't even let me carry his suitcase across the street," Ringo said, shaking his head.

He remained standing by me, his arms folded across his chest. I was beginning to feel faint again—not sick, only weak and tired and a little dizzy—and I put my hand over my face.

"Let's go to Billy's and have a sandwich," he said, slapping me on the shoulder. He pointed to the grocery store across the street.

"No, thanks," I said.

He said that a sandwich would build up my strength, and that he was hungry.

"I've only got a quarter," I said, "and that's for the bus."

"You can clean up at Billy's. He got a bathroom," Ringo

said. "You can watch for the bus inside the store and keep warm. You can dry off some."

I didn't say anything.

"Come on, John," he said. And then he grabbed my suitcase again and ran off across the street with it and into Billy's. I was so damned mad I slammed my hand against the bus-stop post, and then I followed Ringo across the street and into the grocery store.

"Here I am, Billy," Ringo was saying when I went in.

"Yeah, I see you," a slight, light-brown Negro said. He was the one in the white apron. The three Negroes leaning against the refrigerated case were smiling. Billy looked at Ringo, then at me, then back at Ringo.

"Now what you getting mad at? You mad at me, Billy?" Ringo said.

"What you doing with that suitcase?" Billy asked. "You going to catch a train?"

"Ain't this Union Station?" Ringo said, smiling at everyone.

"You ain't funny, Ringo. You just ain't funny," Billy said. "Give this man his suitcase."

"You got to be serious about everything. Nobody can take a joke," Ringo said, handing me the suitcase without looking at me.

"We seen the whole thing," Billy said. "We seen this man drop you, Ringo." Billy looked at me. "He deserved it," he said.

"You got that same tricky style, Ringo," one of the other Negroes said.

"He sure know how to fall," Billy said. "He an expert at that."

"Aw, man," Ringo said. "We wasn't in no fight. I teaching him some things."

"Yeah, you a real teacher, all right," Billy said. "You teach any man alive how to fall. But fighting something else."

Billy smiled at the other men, and then he looked at me. "You been sick, right?" he said.

I said yes, that I had an upset stomach. Billy said there was a bathroom in the back of the store, and that I could use it if I wanted to. I thanked him and said that I would like to clean up.

"I give you something for your stomach when you come back," Billy said. He took my suitcase and put it behind the counter, and then he led me back to the bathroom and switched on the light for me.

When I got back from the bathroom, Ringo was shadow-boxing in the middle of the room.

"Go. Go. Go. Hey!" one of the men said.

I walked over to Billy and stood beside him, watching the performance. Ringo was putting together some combinations to the head and body. "He won't go down. This sucker's tough," he said.

"They *all* tough, Ringo, for you," Billy said, and then he turned to me. "I lost more damn money on him," he said.

I asked Billy if Ringo had fought in Griffith Stadium.

"Yeah, I guess so," he said. "That was a long time ago. He look pretty good when there ain't nobody in his way. Say, how you feeling?" Billy looked seriously at me. I told him I was feeling a little tired.

"Well, I got something for you," he said, walking over to a shelf and taking down a large bottle of Coca-Cola syrup. He poured a little into a paper cup and handed it to me. "Drink that down and you be all right," he said.

I drank the syrup slowly and watched Ringo jump rope without a rope. His footwork was very good.

"See how his eyes is half closed," Billy said. "He really happy and stupid."

The three Negroes who had been leaning against the case stood up, nodded and smiled at Billy, and went out into the rain. Ringo continued to jump rope, but when he noticed that they had gone he seemed to lose interest. Looking distracted, as though he were trying to figure out what he could do next, he came over to Billy and me and broke out into a wide smile. "Hey, Billy, how about making me and John a sandwich," he said, tilting his head a little in a mock coyness that I hadn't seen before.

Billy turned to me, and I told him I didn't want a sandwich. Billy looked at Ringo and slowly shook his head. "Of course, you got the money. Right?" he said.

"John here, he carry the money," Ringo said.

I told Billy that all I had was a quarter.

"Even if you have the money, I ain't gonna let you buy him no sandwich," Billy said.

Ringo looked down at the floor and tapped his right foot nervously and scratched his leg. Then he put both hands over his eyes. Nothing happened. When Ringo finally took his hands away from his eyes, he said, "Billy, but I hungry."

"Hell, you always hungry, Ringo," Billy said. "But that don't mean you starving. It obvious you ain't no middleweight no more."

"That ain't nice," Ringo said, looking pained. "Why the world full of bad feeling?" He put his hands over his hat, crossing his fingers, and closed his eyes and began to twist and contort his mouth. He began to shake his whole body, without moving his feet or changing his position, and then, with his eyes still closed, he smiled. I looked over at Billy to see how he was taking it. He was leaning on the counter, reading the

Washington Post. I went behind the counter and picked up my suitcase.

Billy looked up from his paper. "Well," he said, "you *looking* better. How you *feeling?*"

"Much better," I said. "Thanks a lot, Billy." We shook hands.

"Look at that fool!" Billy said.

Ringo was still vibrating and smiling, but his eyes were open now. "What you doing with that suitcase?" he asked.

I didn't say anything, but moved toward the door to watch for another bus.

Ringo came up to me and put an arm around my shoulder. "So you going home," he said.

"That's right," I said.

"What you in a big hurry for?" he asked.

"So long, Ringo."

"I don't see no bus coming," he said.

I made sure I had a firm hold on my suitcase; then I tried to walk away, but he had a strong grip on my shoulder. "There ain't no bus coming," he said, smiling.

"Get lost, Ringo," I said.

"Go on, Ringo. Go on, now," Billy said. He came out from behind the counter.

"Look, there your bus, John," Ringo said.

I turned and looked out the window, but the street was clear. While I was looking down the street, Ringo slipped his forearm under my chin and pressed it against my throat. With his free hand he pressed the back of my head forward. "Now what you gonna do?"

I couldn't talk, because he was pressing too hard on my throat. I swung my suitcase, trying to hit him with it, but could only manage a light, slapping blow to the back of his legs.

Ringo began to laugh. "You can't do nothing, see? You can't do nothing."

Then he suddenly yelled and let me go.

I turned around, rubbing my throat, and saw Billy just back of Ringo, holding a large soda bottle. Ringo was grabbing at his ankle and hopping on one foot.

"Goddam, Billy," he said. "You nearly break my leg."

"Next time I break your head."

Ringo hopped over to the refrigerated case and sat on the front edge of it, holding his ankle. He looked from me to Billy, then back to me again. His eyes were half closed; his mouth was turned down exaggeratedly, like a clown's. "I just tired to death," Ringo said. "Man, you coulda hurt me, Billy."

"Yeah, sure," Billy said. "Now, why don't you shut up."

"I mess around," Ringo said. "But I don't hurt nobody."

"That's what you say," Billy said, putting the soda bottle back on the shelf.

I stood by the door, and finally I saw a bus turn the corner three blocks down. I pulled the quarter out of my pocket, grabbed my suitcase, and turned around for a final goodbye. "So long, Billy. Thanks," I said.

Billy waved and smiled at me. "So long, now."

As I backed through the door, I waved, knocking my hand against the doorframe. I dropped the quarter and it rolled under the refrigerated case, and I missed the bus again.

"Now, ain't that a damn shame!" Ringo said. He was all lit up, and had recovered his vitality.

Billy came over with a wooden yardstick to see if he could get the quarter out; it had become lodged between the case and the wall. He worked the yardstick in the crack until he had moved the quarter out onto the open floor. He picked it up, dusted it off on his apron, and handed it to me. "You having a bad day," he said. "Next time you keep it in your pocket." He slapped me on the back and told me I was going to make it.

Ringo looked at me with a wide and happy grin. "Well, Charlie, you having some rough luck," he said.

"My name's not Charlie," I said.

"Ain't you Charlie White Man?" Ringo said, smiling.

"Go on, Ringo. Go on," Billy said, looking at me apologetically.

"I got to admit that you is some fool, John," Ringo said, coming over to me. "You all set to go and then you drop the quarter." He laughed, closing his eyes, and put his hand on my shoulder.

I asked him if he wanted to rip the sleeve off this time.

"It look like you got a flower growing out of your shoulder," Ringo said, putting a finger on the ripped white lining that was puffing out. "Man, you look like hell. You know that?"

I took out my pack of cigarettes and lit one. Ringo watched me. I gave him the pack and told him to keep it and go away.

"You scares me," he said, taking my cigarette to light his. "I just can't figure you out."

Suddenly I got a terrible headache, and the room began to spin. Down the street another bus had appeared, but I decided it was no use even trying this time. I turned and looked at Billy, and he knew immediately that I was in some kind of trouble. "Don't you worry, now," he said. He pointed to the door that led to the bathroom. "See you soon," he said.

I walked unsteadily toward the door. There must have been a disturbance in my middle ear, because the ceiling seemed to rush at me and then rush away. I fell down, and began to crawl on all fours toward the door.

"He think he a horse," I heard Ringo say.

Billy helped me to my feet, steadied me, and walked me a few steps toward the bathroom. I told him I was all right and could make it the rest of the way. In the bathroom, I wasn't sick, but I was so dizzy that I couldn't stand up. I sat down on the floor and leaned against the wall for a few minutes, waiting for the dizziness to stop. Then I lay down and went to sleep.

Some time later, I felt someone nudging me lightly on the shoulder, and I woke up and saw Billy in his white apron, kneeling on one knee.

"You been in here about twenty minutes," he said. "I got to worry about you."

I stood up and walked over to the sink, feeling all right. The vertigo was gone. Billy switched on the light and stayed in the room while I washed up. "John, I think your luck is turning," he said.

When Billy and I went back into the big room, Ringo was talking to the woman I had seen him with earlier, outside the store. There was also another man—a large, dark-brown, sleepy-eyed Negro whom the woman called Tracy. "All right, Tracy, go on, knock him down," she said, pointing at Ringo.

Billy set a chair for me in the corner of the room farthest from Ringo and his friends. He saw that I was shivering, and he got his topcoat and told me to put it on. He also gave me another cup of Coca-Cola syrup, and said he was boiling some water for tea, and that I should just relax and take it easy.

"Knock him on his butt, Tracy," the woman said, looking fierce.

"Aw, honey, now," Tracy said, and then he smiled shyly at Ringo and folded his arms.

Ringo kicked some imaginary object, and turned on the

woman. "Ruby, why you always want to make trouble?" he said. "Now, Tracy's my friend."

"I want to see you fight," Ruby said. "You supposed to be a fighter. Well, I want to see you fight."

Billy came over with a glass jar of tea and half a lemon. He put the tea and lemon on top of a milk crate near my chair. Then he went behind the counter and came back with a sack of granulated sugar and a spoon. "This gonna give you some strength," he said, putting the sugar and spoon on the crate.

I thanked him, and, feeling comfortable and warm, sat back and watched the action. While Billy was bringing me the tea, Ruby had hit Ringo on the side of the head with her pocketbook, and now Ringo, looking pained, ignored her, folded his arms, and stared at the ceiling.

"Come on, Tracy, knock him down," Ruby bellowed, but Tracy, who was about six feet four and two hundred and fifty pounds, just looked down at the floor and smiled. "Now, Tracy, here, done spar with Joe Louis. Now, Tracy was a fighter!" she went on. "A heavyweight!" She looked at Ringo with scorn.

There was a long pause, during which Ringo took a deep breath and closed his eyes. "It don't matter what class a man fight in," Ringo said finally. "It only matter if he any good or not." He opened his eyes and looked at Ruby. "Now, I was a good middleweight."

"Uh-uh. You only fair, baby. At the most, you only fair," she said.

Ringo suddenly began to jump rope and put together some combinations, moving around the room with a wide smile and his eyes half closed. As he passed me the first time around, he winked and said, "How you doing, John?"

Billy was talking in a hoarse whisper to Tracy and Ruby. I couldn't hear what he said to them, but they were smiling. Ruby clapped her hands and threw her head back and shrieked, "Aw, come on, man, you killing me!"

Tracy covered his mouth with one of his enormous hands, trying to stifle the laughter, but some of it got through. He seemed a little embarrassed and shook his head. During Billy's whispering, Ruby looked at me from time to time and smiled and waved. Tracy looked at me once, too, and nodded shyly. Then Billy brought them over, and when I stood up, Ruby told me to sit down and save my strength.

"John, this here is Ruby Longstreet and Tracy James," Billy said.

We shook hands.

"Well, John, we sure glad to know you," Ruby said, shaking hands again.

I told her the pleasure was all mine.

"I seen you outside earlier, John," she said.

"I was waiting for a bus."

"I hear that fool Ringo done give you a fight lesson," she said. She looked at Ringo, who closed his eyes. "Come on, Ringo, open your eyes!" she said.

But he shut them tighter, and closed his mouth tight, too.

Billy laughed. "John knock him flat," he said.

"What you hit him with?" Tracy asked me.

"A left," I said.

"He still blind to a left hand," Tracy said.

I said that some rain had got in his eye.

"Some rain always getting in his eye," Ruby said. "If it ain't for the rain, he been champion."

Billy laughed, and Tracy covered his face with his hands and shook. Ringo turned his back on us and began to take very deep, noisy breaths.

"Aw, shut up, Ringo, you fat fool!" Ruby said.

I was trying to drink the tea, but I began to laugh so hard that I had to put the jar down, and then the laughter increased all around, and Ringo's breathing became noisier and his shoulders began to shake. I thought he was laughing, but he turned around and he was crying; tears were streaming down his face. "You all finish?" he asked.

"Will you look at that?" Ruby said.

I felt terribly sorry for him. "Come on, Ringo," I said. "What's the matter with you?"

"He just acting," Billy said.

Ringo pulled out a handkerchief and blew his nose and wiped his eyes, and then pulled up a crate and sat down next to me. "John, I feel lousy," he said. "How are you feeling?"

I told him I was feeling all right.

He patted me on the shoulder. "Well, I glad *you* feeling better," he said. He offered me a cigarette from the pack I had given him, and struck a match and gave me a light. "John, you my friend," he said. "They is some people don't know what friendship is." He looked around at everyone.

"Man, if you a friend," Billy said, "then there ain't no point having no enemy."

Ruby began to laugh, and she came over to Ringo and kissed him on top of the head. "Baby, why you so stupid?" she said, smiling widely at him. "Maybe you is the dumbest man in the whole world."

This revived Ringo, and he grabbed Ruby's arm and asked her to sit down next to him and be nice. Billy brought three more milk crates over, and Tracy and Ruby sat on two of them, and then Billy brought a pack of six cans of beer and an opener. "Ringo, because you such a good friend, we gonna have a little party," Billy said.

He went to the front door and locked it. He said there

wasn't any point staying open in all this rain anyhow. I drank my tea while the others drank beer, and then, feeling much better, I drank some beer, too. Ruby, holding her can of beer, announced she was going to sing a song. "I ain't Mahalia Jackson, but I can sing," she said.

She could, too. She sang a song, mostly humming it, while Ringo accompanied her with a little dance. He closed his eyes and put his hand in the pockets of his jacket and moved his feet very slowly back and forth.

"Where you coming from, John?" Ruby asked, when she had finished singing.

"New York," I said. "I came down on the train to see my family."

"Man, you have been travelling some," Tracy said, "and you still ain't home."

"When you with friends, you home. Ain't that right, John?" Ringo said.

Ruby said she liked to take train trips. "There ain't nowhere I want to go, but I *do* like the ride," she said.

She asked me if I had a good ride down, and I told them the story of my ride, how my overcoat and wallet had been stolen on the train, and how, after that, I had got sick.

"People get you sick every time," Ruby said thoughtfully.

"Sure," Billy said. "And then Ringo get you sick in Washington."

"I ain't get John sick," Ringo said. "I been helping John."

"You been *helping* John?" Ruby said. "Who else you *help* lately?"

"John ain't the only white man I ever help," Ringo said, smiling.

"Honey," Ruby said, leaning forward. "What other white man you nearly kill?"

"Few years ago I was working for this man name of Reddy," Ringo said, biting the corner of his lip. "In this junk yard out northeast."

"Yeah," Bill said. "I remember you and that *junk*."

"Well, one day," Ringo said, "Mr. Reddy is standing on the street watching these colored boys working on a trash truck. They up there singing and laughing, and Mr. Reddy, he say, 'Boys, you happy. You sure is happy. You have all the fun,' and one of them colored boys, he say, 'That's right, boss. We having some fun,' and they up there tossing them trash cans around and laughing, and Mr. Reddy, he watch them and smile, and then he walk over to me and he say, 'Ringo, you colored boys sure is happy,' and I say, 'Mr. Reddy, I ain't happy. Them niggers up on that truck may be happy, but I ain't,' and he get real angry, and he say, 'Don't give me no lip, Ringo,' and I laugh. 'Well, I sure ain't happy,' I say, 'with the wages you paying.' He fire me."

Billy guffawed and Tracy put his hands over his face and began to shake.

"How you *help* him, baby?" Ruby said, looking around at everybody.

Ringo spread his arms and turned his palms upward, and then he broke into a wide smile. "Well, I straighten him *out!*" he said.

Ruby laughed and slapped her thigh. Tracy, still shaking, kept his hands over his face, while Billy just looked at the floor and smiled.

Ringo started jumping rope with his eyes closed. Tracy leaned forward and touched Ruby's knee. "Ruby, you ain't gonna give that old moral?" he said, looking disgusted.

"I got to, baby," Ruby said. "O.K., Billy, you ask me."

Billy looked serious and folded his arms across his apron. "What's the moral of that story?"

"The moral of that story—" Ruby began, looking very serious.

"Aw, Ruby," Tracy said, shaking his head and looking at his feet. Ringo, with his arms straight out and his eyes closed, was standing completely still.

"The moral of that story," Ruby went on, holding up a hand for quiet, "is that, Ringo, honey, you sure is one dumb nigger."

They all began to laugh, moaning and groaning with laughter, leaning on one another, and, except for Ruby, Ringo laughed loudest and hardest. The laughter continued for about five minutes, gradually diminishing, then rising again. Ruby had her arms around Tracy's head, and Ringo sat on the floor. Billy had walked over to the counter and, leaning on it, his hands palms down on the top, laughed in gasps. I was laughing myself.

"Now, what you laughing at?" Ringo said to me from the floor. "That ain't nice."

Ruby looked over at me and said, "Honey, don't pay us no mind."

After a while, the laughter fell into silence. There were just the sounds of the wind, and Billy's shoes on the floor, as he walked around taking cans out of cartons and putting them on shelves. Only Ruby was still smiling. Tracy and Ringo seemed sad. They were looking down at their hands. Ringo, who had a very gentle expression, was biting his lip. Billy moved around looking preoccupied and tired. Ruby looked at me and winked, and I smiled at her. She was one of the most beautiful women I have ever seen. She nodded in the direction of Tracy and Ringo, and said to me, "They looking kind of blue," and Tracy looked up from his hands and smiled shyly, but Ringo continued to bite his lip and look down.

"Will you look at him?" Ruby said. "Ain't he cute?"

"Come on, Ruby. I ain't in the mood," Ringo said, looking up. His face was still very gentle.

"Is you sad, baby?" she said, going over and putting her hand on his cheek.

"I all right," Ringo said.

"I just don't know what I'm gonna do with you," Ruby said.

Tracy stood up and stretched and yawned, and then sat down again. He was smiling sleepily. "Boy, that laughing take a lot out of me," he said.

Billy said he guessed it was time he went home, and we all got up and walked slowly toward the door, with Ruby leading the way. Outside, it was foggy and still raining, though it had let up some. Billy came out and locked the door from the outside, and then we all walked up the street. I said I'd go with them a while and get the bus at the stop farther on.

"Well, we certainly glad you is gonna stay with us a while longer," Ruby said, smiling. She took my arm and Ringo's arm.

Tracy walked on ahead with Billy. Billy was wearing a neatly fitting raincoat, and as he walked, very erect and relaxed, he seemed much younger than he did in the grocery store. Tracy walked slouching forward. He was slightly pigeon-toed. "Look at Billy," Ruby said. "He look like a little boy with a big bear."

"Maybe we is them bears," Ringo said to me, looking across Ruby, "and, John, you is Goldilocks." Then he began to laugh very hard by himself.

"Aw, you ain't funny, Ringo," Ruby said, squeezing my arm. "You just ain't funny."

As we approached my bus stop, Ruby told me to take care of myself. "I hope you remember us," she said.

She called to Tracy and Billy to come back and say good-bye to me. They turned around and looked surprised, and then they walked back.

"Look, if you ever sick again," Ringo said, "you come on back and see us."

"Aw, shut up, Ringo," Ruby said. "He don't have to be sick to come back and see us. Right?" She put her arm around my shoulder as I shook hands with Ringo. "He talk like we is some hospital or something," she said.

"Aw, Ruby, you take everything I say and twist it," Ringo said. "Look, John, don't mind nothing I done."

I told Ringo he hadn't done anything.

"You lucky he ain't had more time," Billy said. "He can do some things."

I shook hands with Billy and thanked him for everything. Then Tracy stuck out his big hand. "So long, John," he said. "It been nice knowing you."

The bus was coming down the street rather slowly, because of the fog. When it pulled in, I picked up my suitcase and said goodbye again.

"Goodbye, honey!" Ruby yelled. "Take it easy."

Billy gave a serious little wave, and as I stepped into the bus, Ringo yelled, "I hope the bus break down!" and Ruby hit him on the head with her pocketbook. I heard Ringo say that he had said it for luck, and Ruby told him that she had also hit him for luck. I went to the back of the bus and waved to them from the rear window, and the fog closed in and covered them, and I couldn't see them any more.

CAST A YELLOW SHADOW (EXCERPT)

BY ROSS THOMAS

Downtown

(Originally published in 1967)

The call came while I was trying to persuade a lame-duck Congressman to settle his tab before he burned his American Express card. The tab was $18.35 and the Congressman was drunk and had already made a pyre of the cards he held from Carte Blanche, Standard Oil, and the Diner's Club. He had used a lot of matches as he sat there at the bar drinking Scotch and burning the cards in an ashtray. "Two votes a precinct," he said for the dozenth time. "Just two lousy votes a precinct."

"When they make you an ambassador, you'll need all the credit you can get," I said as Karl handed me the phone. The Congressman thought about that for a moment, frowned and shook his head, said something more about two votes a precinct, and set fire to the American Express card. I said hello into the phone.

"McCorkle?" It was a man's voice.

"Yes."

"This is Hardman." It was a soft bass voice with a lot of bulldog gravy and grits in it. Hardman, the way he said it, was two distinct words, an adjective and a noun, and both got equal billing.

"What can I do for you?"

"Make me a reservation for lunch tomorrow? Bout one-fifteen?"

"You don't need a reservation."

"Just socializin a little."

"I'm off the ponies," I said. "I haven't made a bet in two days."

"That's what they been tellin me. Man, you trying to quit winner?"

"Just trying to quit. What's on your mind?"

"Well, I got me a little business over in Baltimore." He paused. I waited. I prepared for a long wait. Hardman was from Alabama or Mississippi or Georgia or one of those states where they all talk alike and where it takes a long weekend to get to the point.

"You've got business in Baltimore and you want a reservation for one-fifteen tomorrow and you want to know why I haven't made book with you in two days. What else?"

"Well, we was supposed to pick somethin up off a boat over there in Baltimore and there was a little trouble and this white boy got hurt. So Mush—you know Mush?"

I told him I knew Mush.

"So Mush was bout to get hisself hurt by a couple of mothers when this white boy steps in and sort of helps Mush out—know what I mean?"

"Perfectly."

"Say wha?"

"Go on."

"Well, one of these cats had a blade and he cuts the white boy a little, but not fore he'd stepped in and helped out for Mush—know what I mean?"

"Why call me?"

"Well, Mush brings the white boy back to Washington

cause he's hit his head and bleedin and passed out and all."

"And you need some blood tonight?"

Hardman chuckled and it seemed to rumble over the phone. "Shit, baby, you somethin!"

"Why me?"

"Well, this boy got nothin on him. No money—"

"Mush checked that out, I'd say."

"No gold, no ID, no billfold, nothin. Just a little old scrap of paper with your address on it."

"Has he got a description, or do all white folks look alike?"

"Bout five-eleven," Hardman said, "maybe even six feet. Maybe. Short hair, little grey in it. Dark for an ofay. Looks like he been out in the sun a whole lot. Bout your age, only skinnier, but then, hell, who ain't?"

I tried to make nothing out of my voice; no tone, no interest. "Where do you have him?"

"Where I'm at, pad over on Fairmont." He gave me the address. "Figure you know him? He's out cold."

"I might," I said. "I'll be over. You get a doctor?"

"Done come and gone."

"I'll be there as soon as I can catch a cab."

"You won't forget about that reservation?"

"It's taken care of." I hung up.

Karl, the bartender I had imported from Germany, was deep in conversation with the Congressman. I signaled him to come down to the other end of the bar.

"Take care of the Right Honorable," I said. "Call him a cab—the company that specializes in drunks. If he doesn't have any money, have him sign a tab and we'll send him a bill."

"He's got a committee hearing tomorrow at nine in the

Rayburn Building," Karl said. "It's on reforestation. It's about the redwoods. I was planning on going anyhow so I'll pick him up in the morning and make sure he gets there."

Some people hang around police stations. Karl hung around Congress. He had been in the States for less than a year but he could recite the names of the one hundred Senators and the four hundred and thirty-five Representatives in alphabetical order. He knew how they voted on every roll call. He knew when and where committees met and whether their sessions were open or closed. He could tell you the status of any major piece of legislation in either the Senate or the House and make you a ninety to ninety-five per cent accurate prediction on its chance for passage. He read the Congressional Record faithfully and snickered while he did it. He had worked for me before in a saloon I had once owned in Bonn, but the Bundestag had never amused him. He found Congress one long laugh.

"Just so he gets home," I said, "although he looks as if he'll fade before closing." The Congressman was drooping a bit over his glass.

Karl gave him a judicious glance. "He's good for two more and then I'll get him some coffee. He'll make it."

I told him to close up, nodded good night to a handful of regular customers and a couple of waiters, walked east to Connecticut Avenue and turned right towards the Mayflower Hotel. There was one cab at the hotel stand and I climbed into its back seat and gave the driver the address. He turned to look at me.

"I don't ever go over there after midnight," he said.

"Don't tell me. Tell the hack inspector."

"My life's worth more'n eighty cents."

"We'll make it an even dollar."

I got a lecture on why George Wallace should be President on the way to the Fairmont Street address. It was an apartment building, fairly new, flanked by forty- or fifty-year-old row houses. I paid the driver and told him he needn't wait. He snorted, quickly locked all the doors, and sped off. Inside I found the apartment number and rang the bell. I could hear chimes inside. Hardman answered the door.

"Come in this house," he said.

I went in. A voice from somewhere, a woman's voice, yelled: "You tell him to take off his shoes, hear?"

I looked down. I was standing on a deep pile carpet that was pure white.

"She don't want her white rug messed up," Hardman said and indicated his own shoeless feet. I knelt down and took off my shoes. When I rose Hardman handed me a drink.

"Scotch-and-water O.K.?"

"Fine." I looked around the livingroom. It was L-shaped and had an orange couch and some teak and leather chairs, a dining table, also of teak, and a lot of brightly colored pillows that were carefully scattered here and there to make it all look casual. There were some loud prints on the wall. A lot of thought seemed to have gone into the room, and the total effect came off fairly well and just escaped being flashy.

A tall brown girl in red slacks swayed into the room shaking down a thermometer. "You know Betty?" Hardman asked.

I said no. "Hello, Betty."

"You're McCorkle." I nodded "That man's sick," she said, "and there ain't no use trying to talk to him now. He's out for another hour. That's what Doctor Lambert say. And he also say he can be moved all right when he wakes up. So if he's a friend of yours, would you kindly move him when he does wake up? He's got my bed and I don't plan sleeping on no couch. That's where Hard's going to sleep."

"Now, honey—"

"Don't honey me, you no good son-of-a-bitch." She didn't raise her voice when she said it. She didn't have to. "You bring in some cut-up drunk and dump him into my bed. Whyn't you take him to the hospital? Or to your house, 'cept that fancy wife of yours wouldn't have stood for it." Betty turned to me, and waved a hand at Hardman. "Look at him. Six-feet, four-inches tall, dresses just so fine, goes around pronouncing his name 'Hard-Man,' and then lets some little five-foot-tall tight twat lead him around by the nose. Get me a drink." Betty collapsed on the couch and Hardman hastily mixed her a drink.

"How about the man in your bed, Betty?" I said. "May I see him?"

She shrugged and waved her hand at a door. "Right through there. He's still out cold."

I nodded and set the glass down on a table that had a coaster on it. I went through the door and looked at the man in the bed. It was a big, fancy bed, oval in shape, and it made the man look smaller than he was. I hadn't seen him in more than a year and there were some new lines in his face and more grey in his hair than I remembered. His name was Michael Padillo and he spoke six or seven languages without accent, was handy with either a gun or a knife, and could make what has been called the best whiskey sour in Europe.

His other chief distinction was that a lot of people thought he was dead. A lot more hoped that he was.

The last time I had seen Michael Padillo he had been falling off a barge into the Rhine. There had been a fight with guns and fists and a broken bottle. Padillo and a Chinese called

Jimmy Ku had gone over the side. Somebody had been aiming a shotgun at me at the time and the shotgun had gone off, so I was never sure whether Padillo had drowned or not until I received a postcard from him. It had been mailed from Dahomey in West Africa, contained a one-word message—"Well"—and had been signed with a "P." He had never been much of one to write.

On dull days after the postcard came I sometimes sat around and drank too much and speculated about how Padillo had made it from the Rhine to the West Coast of Africa and whether he liked the climate. He was good at getting from one place to another. When he was not helping to run the saloon that we owned in Bonn he had been on call to one of those spooky government agencies that kept sending him to such places as Lodz and Leipzig and Tollin. I never asked what he did; he never told me.

When his agency decided to trade him for a couple of defectors to the East, Padillo tried to buy up his contract. He succeeded that spring night when he fell off the barge into the Rhine about a half-mile up river from the American Embassy. His agency wrote him off and no one from the Embassy ever came around to inquire about what happened to the nice man who used to own half of Mac's Place in Bad Godesberg.

Padillo's attempt to retire from the secret-agent dodge had involved both of us in a trip to East Berlin and back. During our absence somebody had blown up the saloon in revenge for some real or imagined slight so I collected the insurance money, got married, and opened Mac's Place in Washington a few blocks up from K Street, west of Connecticut Avenue. It's dark and it's quiet and the prices discourage the annual pilgrimages of high school graduating classes.

I stood there in the bedroom and looked at Padillo for

a while. I couldn't see where he had been cut. The covers were up to his neck. He lay perfectly still in the bed, breathing through his nose. I turned and went back into the livingroom with the white carpet.

"How bad is he hurt?" I asked Hardman.

"Got him in the ribs and he bled some. Mush say that boy damn near got both those cats. Moved nice and easy and quick, just like he'd been doin it all his life."

"He's no virgin," I said.

"Friend of yours?"

"My partner."

"What you gonna do with him?" Betty said.

"He's got a small suite in the Mayflower; I'll move him there when he wakes up and get somebody to stay with him."

"Mush'll stay," Hardman said. "Mush owes him a little."

"Doctor Lambert say he wasn't hurt bad, but that he's all tired out—exhaustion," Betty said. She looked at her watch. It had a lot of diamonds on it. "He'll be waking up in bout half an hour."

"I take it Doctor Lambert didn't call the cops," I said.

Hardman sniffed. "Now what kind of fool question is that?"

I should have known. "May I use your phone?"

Betty pointed it out. I dialed a number and it rang for a long time. Nobody answered. The phone was the push-button kind so I tried again on the chance that I had misdialed or mispunched. I was calling my wife and I was having a husband's normal reactions when his wife fails to answer the telephone at one-forty-five in the morning. I let it ring nine times and then hung up.

My wife was a correspondent for a Frankfurt paper, the one with the thoughtful editorials. It was her second assignment in the States. I had met her in Bonn and she knew about Padillo and the odd jobs he had once done for the quietly inefficient rival of the CIA. My wife's name was Fredl and before she married me it was Fraulein Doktor Fredl Arndt. The Doktor had been earned in Political Science at the University of Bonn and some of her tony friends addressed me as Herr Doktor McCorkle, which I bore well enough. After a little more than a year of marriage I found myself very much in love with my wife. I even liked her.

I called the saloon and got Karl. "Has my wife called?"

"Not tonight."

"The Congressman still there?"

"He's closing up the place with coffee and brandy. The tab is now $24.85 and he's still looking for two votes a precinct. If he had had them, he could have made the runoff."

"Maybe you can help him look. If my wife calls, tell her I'll be home shortly."

"Where're you at?"

"Right before the at," I said. Karl had no German accent, but he had learned his English from the endless procession of Pfc's who came out of the huge Frankfurt PX during the postwar years. As a seven-year-old orphan, he had bought their cigarettes to sell on the black market.

"Never end a sentence with a preposition," he recited.

"Not never; just seldom. I'm at a friend's. I have to run an errand so if Fredl calls, tell her I'll be home shortly."

"See you tomorrow."

"Right."

Hardman raised his six feet, four inches of large bone and hard muscle from a chair, skirted around Betty as if she would bite, and walked over to mix another drink. He was as close to a racketeer as Washington had to offer. I suppose. He was far up in the Negro numbers hierarchy, ran a thriving bookie operation, and had a crew of boosters out lifting whatever they fancied from the city's better department stores and specialty shops. He wore three- or four-hundred-dollar suits and eighty-five-dollar shoes and drove around town in a bronze Cadillac convertible talking to friends and acquaintances over his radio-telephone. He was a folk hero to the Negro youth in Washington and the police let him alone most of the time because he wasn't too greedy and paid his dues where it counted.

Oddly enough I had met him through Fredl, who had once done a feature on Negro society in Washington. Hardman ranked high in one clique of that mysteriously stratified social realm. After the story appeared in the Frankfurt paper, Fredl sent him a copy. The story was in German, but Hardman had had it translated and then dropped around the saloon carrying a couple of dozen long-stemmed roses for my wife. He had been a regular customer since and I patronized his bookie operation. Hardman liked to show the translation of the feature to friends and point out that he should be regarded as a celebrity of international note.

Holding three drinks in one giant hand, he moved over to Betty and served her and then handed one to me.

"Did my partner come off a ship?" I asked.

"Uh-huh."

"Which one?"

"Flyin a Liberian flag and believe it or not was out of Monrovia. She's called the *Frances Jane* and was carryin cocoa mostly."

"Mush wasn't picking up a pound of cocoa."

"Well, it was a little more'n a pound."

"How'd it happen?"

"Mush was waitin to meet somebody off that boat and was just hangin around waitin for him when the two of them jumped him. Next thing he knows he's lyin down and this friend of yours has done stepped in and was mixin with both of them. He doin fine till they start with the knives. One of them gets your friend in the ribs and by then Mush is back up and saps one of them and then they both take off. Your friend's down and out so Mush goes through his pockets and comes up with your address and calls me. I tell him to hang around to see if he can make his meet and if he don't connect in ten minutes, to come back to Washington and bring the white boy with him. He bled some on Mush's car."

"Tell him to send me a bill."

"Shit, man, I didn't mean it like that."

"I didn't think you did."

"Mush'll be back in a little while. He'll take you and your buddy down to the hotel."

"Fine."

I got up and walked back into the bedroom. Padillo was still lying quietly in the bed. I stood there looking at him, holding my drink and smoking a cigarette. He stirred and opened his eyes. He saw me, nodded carefully, and then moved his eyes around the room.

"Nice bed," he said.

"Have a good nap?"

"Pleasant. How bad am I?"

"You'll be O.K. Where've you been?"

He smiled slightly, licked his lips, and sighed. "Out of town," he said.

Hardman and I helped Padillo to dress. He had a white shirt that had been washed but not ironed, a pair of Khaki pants in the same condition, a Navy pea jacket, and black shoes with white cotton socks.

"Who's your new tailor?" I asked.

Padillo glanced down at his clothes. "Little informal, huh?"

"Betty washed em out in her machine," Hardman said. "Blood hadn't dried too much, so it came out easy. Didn't get a chance to iron em."

"Who's Betty?"

"You've been sleeping in her bed," I said.

"Thank her for me."

"She's in the next room. You can thank her yourself."

"Can you walk?" Hardman said.

"Is there a drink in the next room along with Betty?"

"Sure."

"I can walk."

He could, although he moved slowly. I carried the forbidden shoes. Padillo paused at the door and put one hand on the jamb to brace himself. Then he walked on into the livingroom. "Thanks for the use of your bed, Betty," he said to the tall brown girl.

"You're welcome. How you feel?"

"A little rocky, but I think it's mostly dope. Who bandaged me?"

"Doctor."

"He give me a shot?"

"Uh-huh. Should be bout worn off."

"Just about is."

"Man wants a drink," Hardman said. "What you like?"

"Scotch, if you have it," Padillo said.

Hardman poured a generous drink and handed it to Padillo. "How's yours, Mac?"

"It's okay."

"Mush'll be here any minute," Hardman said. "He'll take you down to the hotel."

"Where am I staying?" Padillo asked.

"At your suite in the Mayflower."

"My suite?"

"I booked it in your name and it's paid for monthly out of your share of the profits. It's small—but quietly elegant. You can take it off your income tax if you ever get around to filing it."

"How's Fredl?"

"We got married."

"You're lucky."

Hardman looked at his watch. "Mush'll be here any minute," he said again.

"Thanks for all your help—yours and Betty's," Padillo said.

Hardman waved a big hand. "You saved us having a big razzoo in Baltimore. What you mess in that for?"

Padillo shook his head slowly. "I didn't see your friend. I just turned a corner and there they were. I thought they were after me. Whichever one had the knife knew how to use it."

"You off that boat?" Hardman said.

"Which one?"

"The *Frances Jane.*"

"I was a passenger."

"Didn't run across a little old Englishman, name of Landeed, about fifty or fifty-five, with crossed eyes?"

"I remember him."

"He get off the boat?"

"Not in Baltimore," Padillo said. "His appendix burst four

days out of Monrovia. They stored him away in the ship's freezer."

Hardman frowned and swore. He put heart into it. The chimes rang and Betty went to open the door and admitted a tall Negro dressed in a crow-black suit, white shirt, and dark maroon tie. He wore sunglasses at two-thirty in the morning.

"Hello, Mush," I said.

He nodded at me and the nod took in Betty and Hardman. He crossed over to Padillo. "How you feeling?" His voice was precise and soft.

"Fine," Padillo said.

"This is Mustapha Ali," Hardman told Padillo. "He's the cat that brought you down from Baltimore. He's a Black Muslim, but you can call him Mush. Everybody else does."

Padillo looked at Mush. "Are you really a Muslim?"

"I am," the man said gravely.

Padillo said something in Arabic. Mush looked surprised, but responded quickly in the same language. He seemed pleased.

"What are you talkin, Mush?" Hardman asked.

"Arabic."

"Where you learn Arabic?"

"Records, man, records. I'll need it when I get to Mecca."

"You the goddamndest cat I ever seen," Hardman said.

"Where'd you learn Arabic?" Mush asked Padillo.

"From a friend."

"You speak it real good."

"I've had some practice lately."

"We'd better get you to the hotel," I told Padillo. He nodded and stood up slowly.

"Thanks very much for all your help," he said to Betty. She said it was nothing and Hardman said he would see me tomorrow at lunch. I nodded, thanked Betty, and followed Padillo out to Mush's car. It was a new Buick, a big one, and had a telephone in the front and a five-inch Sony television in the back.

"I want to stop by my place on the way to the hotel," I said to Mush. "It won't take long."

He nodded and we drove in silence. Padillo stared out the window. "Washington's changed," he said once. "What happened to the streetcars?"

"Took em off in 'sixty-one," Mush said.

Fredl and I lived in one of those new brick and glass apartments that have blossomed just south of Dupont Circle in a neighborhood that once was made up of three- and four-story rooming houses that catered to students, waiters, car washers, pensioners, and professional tire changers. Speculators tore down the rooming houses, covered the ground with asphalt, and called them parking lots for a while. When enough parking lots were put together, the speculators would apply for a government-insured loan, build an apartment house, and call it The Melanie or The Daphne after a wife or a girl friend. The rents for a two-bedroom apartment in those places were based on the supposition that both husband and wife were not only richly employed, but lucky in the stockmarket.

Nobody ever seemed to care what had happened to the students, waiters, car washers, pensioners and the professional tire changers.

Mush parked the car in the circular driveway where it said no parking and we rode the elevator up to the eighth floor.

"Fredl will be glad to see you," I told Padillo. "She might even invite you to dinner." I opened the door. The light from one large lamp burned in the livingroom, but the lamp had been knocked to the floor and the shade was lying a foot or so away. I went over and picked up the lamp, put it on the table, and replaced the shade. I looked in the bedrooms, but that seemed a foolish thing to do. She wasn't there. I walked back into the livingroom and Padillo was standing near the record player, holding a piece of paper in his right hand. Mush stood by the door.

"A note," I said.

"A note," he agreed.

"But not from Fredl."

"No. It's from whoever took her away."

"A ransom note," I said. I didn't want to read it.

"Sort of."

"How much do they want?"

Padillo saw that I didn't want to read the note. He put it down on the coffee table.

"Not much," he said. "Just me."

REFLECTING

BY RHOZIER "ROACH" BROWN
Lorton, VA
(Written in 1969)

Two hands resting on bars of steel
Wondering was all this really real
Living from day to day using dope
Death was waiting with a steel rope.

Living a life I thought was pretty cool
Moving in a hurry and breaking all the rules
Stepping on anyone who got in my way
Never expecting any dues to pay.

I was hooked quite early, and dying quick
Staying high and fly, and pretty slick
The world passed by and I was in a deep nod
To awake a young old man and find no God.

Wine and reefers were a part of my song
Getting my kicks and doing wrong
It's a miracle, how I managed to survive
Riding a pale white horse, bent on suicide.

Her eyes are moist, bursting from within
Alone and crushed, her man in the pen

Patiently she tried and done all she could
It didn't work, it just wasn't any good.

I killed all the love that stood in my path
Love was for suckers, and I was in a Hip Bag
If only I had listened, or even cared
My youth and dreams, wouldn't die in here.

I knew all the angles, and how to score
But all it's brought me was time and a steel door.

A few days of fun and years of pain
Is the price I pay for doing my thing.
Now I hurt in a way I've never known
For the rest of my life, I'll be alone.

Here in the House of Time, grown men cry
I, too, am one of them and I know why
My brand of cigarettes tells of a hip young fool
Who destroyed his life and family being real KOOL.

NORA

BY WARD JUST

Connecticut Avenue

(Originally published in 1971)

N ora believed that my stories were old-fashioned. She said once, "Friend, why don't you write something up-to-date, immediate. The romantics are dead. Friend, they're *gone*." She was really very serious about it, and I had to tell her that hers was a liverish idea whose time had not yet come. Not that it made any difference, because in 1965 nobody would buy the stories except an obscure review in the Midwest, whose payment was in prestige. In the first six months of 1965 I had two payments of prestige with a third on the way. For eats, as Nora liked to call them, I worked as a researcher for *Congressional Weekly Digest*, an expensive private newsletter which purported to give its subscribers advance information on legislation pending before the House and Senate. I was paid a hundred dollars a week for reading the *Congressional Record* and reporting my findings to the editor, who would rearrange them into breathless verbless sentences.

But that had little to do with Nora Bryant. She was English and had come to Washington as correspondent for one of the popular London dailies. She had good looks, and good brains to go with the good looks, but she was admired for her idiosyncrasies. Nora believed that America was alive and Britain was dead; interesting, amusing in its way, but dead nonetheless. She thought that this country was open to possibilities and in perpetual motion in a way that Britain was not. She had a wide circle of American friends, and spent as little time at the British embassy as she could manage; the ambassador there was an aging peer whom she called the kandy-kolored tangerine-flake stream-lined baron. In a bewitching West Riding accent she spoke American slang, and the effect was hilarious: Somerset Maugham imitating Allen Ginsberg. Her specialty was southern politicians and she told me it was a high point of her life here when she spent an evening with the then-occupant of the White House and came away with enough vocabulary to last her a month or more. She came to my apartment after dinner at the White House, still laughing over all the wonderful words and phrases she'd learned. I tried to pump her about the man himself, what he was like. How much did he drink? What was on his mind? Was his mood hot or cold?

"I didn't have a thermometer up his bum, friend," she said.

"Come on, Nora! Give! What did he say about the war? Anything about—"

She laughed and shook her head.

"Nora . . ."

"That dog won't hunt," she said, and that was that.

We'd met at a party on Capitol Hill, and I was quickly taken with her because she asked me about my stories. Under any normal circumstance a writer doesn't like to be asked what he's working on, except in Washington no one cared at all. No one ever asked me about my fiction, so my identity was frozen at "researcher for *Congressional Weekly Digest*," a job I despised and was defensive about. Nora understood right away. She was persistent in asking about the stories and it was clear to me as I answered her that I hadn't thought them out clearly. She saw this, too, but did not press it. She told me to keep working, and everything would be fine.

"You'll be jake," she said. "You're a writer, I can see that."

"Oh? Just how?"

"You don't know what you think."

Nora is barely five feet tall, and I come in at just under six feet four. In a brief moment of anger I saw her as a little girl who worked for a second-string London newspaper, looking up at me and figuratively patting me on my head; the patronage was unmistakable and outrageous, but I was charmed. At our first meeting, listening to her voice and watching her glide around the room, I fell half in love with her. She seemed wonderfully cheerful and inquisitive, intelligent and sure of herself, and I liked the attention. It was a large, jumbled party and she left it early, and two days later called me at my apartment.

"I've got a pretty good tip," she said. "Will that do you any good at that thing you work for? That newsletter?" She sounded brisk and impatient.

"Sure," I said. Gottschault, the editor, paid me a ten-dollar bonus for any authentic inside story, anything that had not been printed elsewhere. I had never taken advantage of this, because I seldom read the newspapers and therefore did not know what was news and what wasn't.

"All right," she said. "The Senate Finance Committee will take up the oil section of the tax bill on Thursday. They will report it on Friday. There will be one day of discussion, in private. No more."

"Thursday, huh?"

"Yes, Thursday. Now does that suggest anything to you?"

"No," I said.

"Well, today is Wednesday. That might suggest to you that the oil section *has already been written*."

"Stop the presses," I said.

"Would you like to have that? For your very own?"

"Are you under the Official Secrets Act?"

"I'll send it over by messenger."

"Are you serious?" I suspected a joke.

"Yes," she said, and rang off.

The document arrived that afternoon, and when I gave it to Gottschault he whooped with pleasure and literally did stop the presses to get it in the newsletter. Then he gave me a twenty-dollar bonus, but when I asked Nora to dinner to celebrate, she declined.

I don't remember when she started calling me "friend." It was probably the period when she began dropping in at my apartment unannounced. This was a two-room apartment in a brownstone off Connecticut Avenue. I'd know she was there when I heard the phonograph; Brahms if she was in a good mood, Bunk Johnson if she was not. She'd taken to American jazz along with everything else and loved to listen to the blues when she was low. I worked in my bedroom and would finish whatever passage I was writing and join her and we'd sit and talk, sometimes all night. Washington politicians fascinated her, she thought they had nothing in common with the ones she knew in Britain. She came to modify that opinion, but in the first months in Washington she was as intrigued as a biologist investigating a new species. Nora developed categories for the politicians that she met.

It was clear from the first month that there would be no romance. I was never exactly sure why. She seemed to want a friend, someone off the Washington political circuit, who was compatible and what she called "talkable." I was pleased and flattered—romance or no—because I was being very reclusive and difficult at that time of my life, and Nora was one of the ornaments of Washington. She had her own center of gravity, a distinct and (I thought) hard-won personal style. Late at night we tried to analyze the town, what made it work, why some men were successful and others were not, why women seemed to fail, and what each had to do with the other.

A couple of times a month she'd give me a document or memcon—she'd picked up government slang, a "memcon" is a memorandum of conversation—and as a result of that I was a boon to Gottschault. Now he was paying me a hundred and twenty-five dollars a week, plus a thirty-dollar bonus for really important items. Items that were exclusive. Because of Nora's tips, Gottschault had become very popular at the National Press Club bar. It was clear to everyone that he had inside information, "inside skinny," as Nora called it. I enjoyed the extra money, but more than that I enjoyed Nora. I'd wait for her unannounced visits, when we'd sit and drink coffee or beer and talk. The longer she stayed in Washington, the more doubts she had about America; but she never regretted leaving London. Of course she was by then one of the best-known foreign correspondents in town. Her copy was nothing much to read because of the form in which she was obliged to write. The editor of her paper had a theory that no paragraph should be longer than two sentences, no sentence longer than ten words, and no word longer than three syllables. Once she wrote a two-hundred-word political story entirely in haiku, but her foreign desk mixed up the paragraphing so it came out wrong. But it was a noble effort, and (as a matter of fact) excellent haiku.

It was partly Nora's encouragement that gained me my

first real sale, a story to the *Saturday Evening Post* for eight hundred dollars. I'd received word in the morning and immediately rang her up at her office. But she'd gone. I was agitated the rest of the day, because I wanted to share this news with her. I'd been working on fiction for two years and this was the first evidence I had that I could sell my stories for money. I felt wonderful and spent most of the day congratulating myself that I hadn't "cheated" or "lowered my standards" or pandered to "the popular taste." I had eight hundred dollars and virtue, too. At four in the afternoon, I heard the phonograph. Bunk Johnson.

I opened the bedroom door right away and saw Nora sitting on the couch. It had taken me four months to write the story, Nora had followed it from the beginning. I trusted her absolutely, and now I looked at her and grinned and told her I'd sold the story and mentioned the amount. She knew everything about it, including how difficult the writing had been. I was certain that with this story behind me, I'd fly. "Nora, it's really going to move now. The bastards can't ignore me any longer," I said, and scooped her up in my arms. She was so tiny and light it was like lifting a doll. She put her arms around my neck and kissed me on the cheek. She was crying, and I began to laugh.

"Oh, come on. No tears. Think of this, a real sale. Money. I've the letter right here. They really like it. They're thinking of putting my name on the cover of the magazine. Do you know how many copies they sell a week? Five or six million copies." I held her tightly and laughed. "Every dentist in America reads the *Saturday Evening Post*."

When I put her down she was still crying. I started to say something funny, but understood then that the tears had nothing to do with me or the magazine. There was something frightening to me about Nora in tears, Nora hurt with no visible wounds. She cried without covering her eyes.

She stopped crying after a minute, and I went into the kitchen and made tea. She was sitting quietly in the middle of the sofa, a bleak look on her face, her hands in her lap, listening to Bunk Johnson. We had become very close over the six months, and I had a strong protective instinct toward her; it was partly fatherly, and strongly sexual. She had been the one encouraging me, and now I wanted to help her. I thought she was too strong to be hurt that badly by anyone.

"Do you want to talk?"

She shook her head.

"Drink your tea," I said.

She held the cup in both hands, sipping the tea.

"Trouble," she said.

"A man?"

She nodded, yes.

She was involved with someone, and I knew it was serious. She was the only woman in Washington who took sex seriously enough to be private about it. She had her own standards, which were uninhibited and seemed to me healthy; she said she loved the pleasure that sex gave her and never confused that with anything else. Beyond that, she was discreet. From time to time she stayed at my apartment, although we never slept together; different stars, wrong chemistry, she said. Those nights she was usually in flight from a bore or a sponge. She was cheerful about it, acknowledging that sometimes she picked the wrong man, and vice versa. But Nora's life was not an open book.

"Well, I'm a mess today."

I wanted desperately to say the right thing. She had always

encouraged me when I needed encouragement, and I felt very much in her debt. I knew right away that this had something to do with her current liaison, the details of which I knew practically nothing.

"You tell me what you want to tell me," I said, as gently as I could.

"I have to write a story this afternoon."

"Well, I'll write the story. You tell me what it's about, and I'll write it. Then you can rest for a bit and tell me what you want to tell me later."

She smiled at that: "Friend, you can't write a story for my paper. You don't know how, your sentences are too long. Won't work."

"I'll cable London and tell them that you've got the flu."

"Would you do that?"

"Of course."

"No need to cable, just call Judson." Judson was the bureau chief, the man she worked for.

I telephoned, Judson was out, so I left word with the answering service. Then I went to Nora, who was stretched out full-length on the couch. It took an hour to get the essentials out of her, but I still didn't have the man's name. It didn't matter to me who he was, except from one or two things she said I gathered he was someone important. She told me the usual things, what he was like, what they talked about, how they'd met, what he meant to her, and how it was ended. It was "permanent," she said, but ended. He wanted to get a divorce from his wife, and that was the last—definitely the last—thing she wanted. It would ruin his career, and he would be no good at anything else. She would become an ego doctor, and she wanted no part of that; she saw it as martyrdom and it seemed to her wrong. If you're an architect or a lawyer and you get into trouble, you can resign and go practice some-where else. If you're a politician and get into trouble, that's the end of it.

"I can't see him as anything else, and I don't want to see him as anything else. I don't care a hoot in hell," she said. "Getting married doesn't mean anything to me. It never did. I don't care about it. He gets his . . . juice from politics. Politics and me. If politics goes, there's only me. You know what happens then." She shook her head. "It's a disaster."

"Does he know the way you feel?"

"Yes, and he says it doesn't matter what I feel."

"Doesn't *matter?*"

"Yes, he says it matters to him. 'The only way,' he says. 'The only decent way.' Besides, he hates his wife."

"Oh."

"He says he doesn't want to go on sleeping with me in motel rooms." She smiled wanly. "Well, that's rather sweet, really."

"I guess it is."

"The thing is, he's really an awfully good politician. I mean . . . he's really *good*. Damned good. You know?"

"Look, Nora. Who is he?"

"You don't know?" She was incredulous.

"How would I know?"

"I thought everybody knew."

"Maybe everybody does. I don't."

When she told me, I shook my head. I'd had no idea.

He was a midwestern senator, about forty, one of those who is always named on the lists of Most Effective Legislators, and for the last two elections as one of the many vice-presidential possibilities. As senators go in Washington, he had what the

press calls high visibility. He was not a member of the lead-
ership, but he had an independent base of his own, particularly among academics. He had been a university president at
twenty-eight and resigned to run for the Senate. That was a
highly implausible sequence except that this particular university president's father had been governor, and his brother
now published the state's largest newspaper. That was all I
knew about him, except that he was a Washington politician
who was clean. He was intelligent, he was not a thief, and he
seemed to know his own mind.

Nora stayed with me three days, she barely moved from
the sofa. Her spirits improved, her confidence returned. In the
mornings we drank coffee, in the afternoons tea, and in the
evenings beer. She told me the story of the romance, how he
had enchanted her . . .

"I mean literally enchanted," she said. Then she went on
to list the things they did together, her tone of voice changing.
She became wistful, a most un-Nora tone of voice. She talked
of the future, too, how he'd plotted his political career, the
plans he had for the next national convention; this was before
he decided to divorce his wife. But she thought he had a self-
destructive part of him, and that was not always unappealing,
surrounded as he was by success.

And not once in the first weeks did they ever speak of politics. They spent a weekend together in Nova Scotia, "and this
was in December. Gosh, friend, did you ever spend a weekend
in December in Nova Scotia? I was touched, he used my name
to register at the hotel. Mr. and Mrs. N. Bryant. The way he
did it, he was . . . oh, I don't know what he was doing. I took it
to mean he regarded us as equals. We spent that time in Nova
Scotia, and other weekends in other wonderful places. Have
you ever been to Chincoteague Island? And all the time he

was legislating in the Senate, and passing me the documents, the bad ones, to get them out in the open." She laughed. "He used to call me his publisher. He loved to see them all in print, then listen to the bitching and moaning inside the committee. The FBI was called in to investigate the leak. I thought it was all obvious, too obvious, so I passed some of the stuff on to you. Didn't you ever wonder where it came from?"

"Well, I thought you just picked it up . . ."

"Friend, you don't just 'pick up' the sort of stuff I was passing on to you. It was all golden." She smiled proudly. "He loved it, really loved doing it, watching the reaction . . ."

"The romance, Nora. It sounds to me a little heavy, it isn't the sort of thing you pursue in motel rooms."

"But it is! Why not? It was just fine, it was going along just fine. Nothing wrong, he'd have to go home from time to time. But his wife didn't really care. I mean he was under no pressure. Not from her. Not from me. Now it's ended."

"Say again why."

"He'd be ruined without his political life. I *know that*. What do we do now? Does he open a law office, become a lobbyist? How about a beachcomber?"

"My God, you can get a divorce and still run for office. A hell of a lot of guys do that. You can divorce, remarry, and run for office. There's no law . . ."

"You don't understand. He's a Catholic. He wants to marry me. You don't recover from that. Not in his state. No, he'd have to give up politics altogether. Go do something else."

"You've talked it all out?"

"Until I'm out of breath! He won't listen. He wants to wait a year or two, then marry. He says he's through with motels and through with his wife. But he doesn't know what I know.

Which is that without politics he's a different man, and not as good a man. It's the self-destructive part."

"Nora, someone isn't defined entirely by what they do. People have other sides to them, sides that have nothing to do with . . . plumbing or writing or politics."

"Not him," she said.

"So you've refused absolutely to marry him."

She nodded slowly.

"What did he say?"

"He said he was going to get the divorce anyway."

"And then?"

"And then I'll change my mind, he said."

The next day Nora left, sad but in control. She was talking now about going back to England or cajoling her editor into a long assignment abroad, Africa or the Far East. She told me that she would never, never marry the man; it would destroy both their spirits, they'd be hypnotized for the rest of their lives by what he'd thrown away. She knew in her heart it was irretrievable. She said she understood the political mind too well not to understand that. If a man gives up power against his will it haunts him. And there was no need, she said. No need at all. Just before she left my apartment she made the only anti-American remark I'd ever heard from her. She generally regarded this country with great affection and enthusiasm, and it amused her to write pro-American articles for her Yankee-baiting London newspaper.

"Goddamned American innocence," she said. "Destructive virtue."

"Thank you, Graham Greene," I replied. The remark irritated me, it was unjustified; it was true of course, but unjustified. "Can't you see your man is in a bind, too?"

"Well, we're all in a bind. But he's the one who's forcing it, *and there's no need.*"

I couldn't quarrel with that.

A week later, she called me for a favor. She said she would ask me the favor if I would cook her dinner. We ate a memorable meal, and she was full of praise for the *Saturday Evening Post* story and one other story I was working on. All the time she was talking, I was looking at her and wishing the stars and chemistry had been right. She was in good form, looking as beautiful as I'd ever seen her. She'd had another of her dinners at the White House and was full of new stories and phrases. She was pouring coffee when she said she needed the favor right away.

"He's coming over here tonight," she said.

"Great," I said.

"Just for an hour or two. It's better to talk here, was what I thought. Not that there's very much to talk about. Can you make yourself scarce?"

I smiled at the Americanism. "Sure."

"He's due in about ten minutes."

"I'll go now."

"You can come back in an hour."

"I'll make it an hour and a half."

"I appreciate it. Friend."

"Just keep the door closed, and I'll know you're still here if I get back too early."

So I left, half-angry, half-sad. There was a bar down the street that had a color television set. I hadn't been in the bar in six weeks, but it was empty as usual and I took a seat at the far end, backed up against the wall, and drank draft beer for two hours. I thought I had better give them all the time they needed. While I sat and drank beer I thought about Nora and how she would handle it. It occurred to me that there were a hundred jobs in Washington that the senator could get, all of them close to the—what did they call it?—"the center of events." There were jobs in this town other than elective ones. Editing newsletters. Influence peddling. I began to think of him as an undersecretary of state or an assistant secretary of defense. Depending, of course, on how messy the divorce was. Whether or not the press picked it up. Well. No adulterers in the Pentagon. But as I sat and drank the beer, I understood that the speculations didn't matter. What mattered was Nora, and how she saw it. She'd staked out her territory and was a very determined woman. She loved him, so she understood him, and she understood Washington, too; that was the essence of it. It seemed to me that the way she had constructed her argument made retreat impossible.

The night baseball game ended, and I was alone in the bar. The barman and I were watching the late news. There was film from Saigon and a report on the West Coast dock strike. We were chatting quietly, and then the barman moved off to serve a late arrival who had taken a table in the rear. I was preparing to go, when I caught the last of a sentence from the television announcer: ". . . the senator and his wife had been married for fourteen years." There was no more, but I knew they were talking about Nora's man. I turned to go and saw him then, at the table in the rear of the room, near the color television set. He was staring into his drink, a stricken look on his face. He hadn't taken off his overcoat, its khaki collar concealed his cheeks and jaw. He was almost as big as I am, hunched over the table in the overcoat, his hat on the chair beside him. He stared at the drink and clicked the ice with his finger, apparently unconscious of the surroundings. I turned back to the bar and in a moment I left, leaving a five-dollar bill and walking straight out the door.

I ran up the street to the brownstone, let myself in, and sprinted up the stairs to the second floor. The door was partly ajar, and I could hear Bunk Johnson's blues inside. Nora was sitting on the couch, a drink in front of her, staring at the bookshelves.

"He's gone now," she said. She waited a moment, concentrating, then went on. "He made an announcement tonight; he and his wife are separating. He prepared an announcement, a press release. He and his staff. Is that what you do in Washington? If you decide to get a divorce, leave someone's bed, do you first prepare an announcement to give to the newspapers? Before you've packed, said good-bye?"

"If you're a senator, I guess you do."

"Television, too, I suppose."

"I guess so. I heard it on the news ten minutes ago."

"I suppose you'd want the largest possible distribution, no part of America ignorant of any personal fact. Do you suppose he'll have a briefing for the wire services? Off the record? Deep background, perhaps. Lindley Rule with a release date?" She'd begun to cry.

"Nora, Nora."

"No need," she said.

"Well, *he* thought there was."

"Yes, he did. He did he did he did."

"How was he when he left?"

"He didn't like it," she said.

"It isn't the worst thing I've ever heard a man do."

"No, not the worst. Unless you regard futility as an offense. Or ignoring other people's feelings. Or your own . . . your own sense of yourself. To destroy a part of yourself, what you are, what you have, in obedience . . . to some stupid . . ."

I wanted to say something to shock her. "How can you be so goddamned sure?"

It was then that she made the remark about romantics dead and dying, although as I look back on it now, that can be taken two ways. In any case, the senator was duly divorced, and Nora got her assignment abroad. I didn't see her again for six years, when I was in London on a holiday and rang her up and we had lunch at the Ritz. It was an elegant lunch, and we talked about everything but that. I was waiting for her to bring up the subject and I suppose she was waiting for me. But there was nothing to be said about it, at that late date. Nothing useful or illuminating or constructive. But I could never tell her, then or later, that I'd seen him that night in the bar, hunched over the table, staring at the glass, clicking the ice cubes with his fingernail. In light of everything since, she'd been right as rain.

OUR BRIGHT TOMORROWS

BY LARRY NEAL

Georgia Avenue

(Written circa 1973)

Martin Luther King was dead.
A gloom descended upon me; and it was as if my body was outside of me like some kind of haunting shadow.

One night during that semester I dreamed I saw my ghost drifting across the campus toward me like a puff of stream. My face drifted above the stream. And although I knew it was my ghost, my face was without definition.

I followed the ghostly twin to a crossroads.

"On one side of this road," I thought I heard her say, "there is a river of blood. On the other side there is a river of milk. Life could not exist without either. You will have to choose. But there is pain always . . ."

And now in the cool spring air, I made my way across the campus to the Arts and Humanities building. I liked this time of evening best. Now I would have access to the practice room where I could play what I wanted without the vulgar intrusions and comments of Dr. Reed, who was the chairman of the music department.

I would hang around the library and try to work on my paper on the history of the violin in the development of European music. Needless to say, I found all of that quite boring. Did you know that from 1600 to 1750 Cremona was the center for great violin making? And that Antonio Stradivari was Nicolò Amati's pupil? Yes, it was boring like Dr. Reed, who must have been teaching this course since the days when this university was five shacks by a dirt road which later came to be called Georgia Avenue. His note cards were frayed and dirty, and he affected a kind of gay British accent.

I was never good at writing papers, but I somehow managed to get by with good grades. In my senior year, I found it harder and harder to work. I was feeling disconnected, a little batty even. And now the death of Dr. King, my hero. It was, nonetheless, my last year. I would have to bear down.

I tried taking notes from Petherick's book on Antonio Stradivari, but after fifteen minutes into it, I found it hard to stay awake. I would doze off, and then suddenly jerk myself awake like one of these junkies down on U street. This can't go on.

I played my scales and exercises. Then I worked on the piece by Schumann. I worked hard until I had built up a sweat. But I stumbled through the Hindemith, and finally gave up on the Bartók.

Outside, there was a large crowd of students clustered around the big oak tree just opposite the library. A notoriously controversial student by the name of Jennie Forman was speaking through a white bullhorn. The campus police were there almost in full strength. She wore a high bushy Afro; and she had on an army jacket with red, black, and green epaulets. She must have been quite popular with the male students, because there were a lot of good-looking brothers guarding her.

She shouted through the bullhorn. The sound bounced off of the buildings surrounding the campus green: "You call this education?! Think about it. What are these bourgeois Toms preparing us for? I'll tell you . . . Have any of you heard of the Congo, or Vietnam . . . ?" She paused, waiting for an answer. "What about imperialism?"

"Tell it like it is, sister!" a male voice boomed out.

"Brainwash! Make you docile, afraid, and white-minded like them. We have to shake up this university. Find out which members of the board are investing in South Africa. We got to expose the running-dog lackeys in the political science department. The revolution must begin here because this is where we are."

The crowd cheered her wildly.

"This is nothing but a nigger factory. Look around you. The world is changing. The dark world of Africa, Asia, and Latin America is coming into its own. Students all over the world are making the revolution . . . And what are we doing? Joining fraternities and sororities . . ." She seemed to look directly at me. I looked around somewhat self-consciously; there was no one there from either a fraternity or sorority. I shuddered a little, and for some reason I thought of the dream with my ghostly twin at the crossroads. The brisk evening air made me shudder again.

The moon seemed to rise over Douglass Hall now, casting a cool blue light over the tall oak tree under which she stood; that oak tree which was the traditional place for radical speeches on the state of everything from the politics of Reconstruction to the quality of the food in the cafeteria.

She wasn't much bigger than me. Underneath the army jacket, her faded blue jeans were tight around her firm body. She was surely intelligent, but there was something of the tigeress about her. Even standing back on the edge of the crowd, I could feel her force. But I could never wear my hair like that. My mother would kill me. A disgrace to the race, she would say. And not proper by anyone's standard of beauty.

"Let's shut this mother down!" someone shouted. Then they started throwing bottles at the campus guards. Then two more campus patrol cars sped into the main gate. On one car there was a loud speaker: *"This is an illegal assembly. All students are requested to disperse. Those failing to move on will be reported to the dean's office."*

The guards began moving in on the students. But she continued to shout over the bullhorn as they dispersed. Who was she anyway? Her name came up all the time in our rap sessions. And I had seen her from a distance. She always looked determined, like she was mad in quest of something that was speeding ahead of her. One day I had seen her working in the reading room of the library. I watched her furiously taking notes as she went through several volumes of books piled high beside her on the long mahogany table. She was a top-notch student, but the men she went around with were always making trouble. They disrupted student council meetings with their crazy ideas. All that talk about blackness and black people. It was *black this* and *black that*. They should just be happy, I thought, happy to have the opportunity to get an education in this world. The crowd broke up. I went back to the practice room in the basement of Arts and Humanities.

It was dangerous to be out anyway. Maybe the District police would have to come on campus like they did last week when Stokely was here. They say that during the rioting and looting Stokely tried to get the crowd off the street. "Go home!" he said. "Go home! Get off the street . . . We're not ready to fight!"

Ready for what? I thought . . . Did people like him really believe that we would ever be ready to fight these white people? It all made me feel very sick and strange. But I had cried for

Dr. King. Yes, I had cried and that was that. There wasn't any need to do anything else. I had done all I could; and hadn't my roomie and I, with several other girls, wept for the man of peace, as we drank cognac and ginger ale the night I had my first puff of marijuana?

The Arts and Humanities building was semi-dark. But on the top floors light shined from the windows of the art studios. Several of the painters would linger working and talking long into the night. I wondered if painters were more gregarious than musicians. What about me? Was I just one of the herd around here? Was Jennie Forman right when she attacked the lifestyles of students like me and my sisters in the sorority? Who the hell does she think she is, and why does she believe that she has to be right?

Wide dust mops shoved the day's debris along the marbled corridors. Along the corridor walls were pictures of the founders of the university.

These old photographs showed some determined people. You could tell by looking at them intently and studying their faces, and then you would zero in on their eyes; their eyes looking straight ahead to the future at you! *At me!* I would shout in my head, and smile. But there they were beige faces, brown faces, yellow faces, black faces, red faces, and damn near white faces all looking forward at me, fine brown Linda Frazier who hasn't even given up any pussy yet. Linda Frazier who fears the dark crossroads. They were looking at me sternly but sincerely. I was standing in the way of one of the janitors, who pushed a mound of trash along the wall beneath the photographs. I stepped out of the way.

I wondered whether these janitors ever picked up any of the trash and read it. Like if, say, a religious lady was cleaning the office of a professor of theology; and suppose she found a pile of notes on say the Eschatogical Vision in the Book of Revelations; or one on the Hermeneutics of Divine Providence. I wondered what that poor woman would think. I wondered how the God she lived by and prayed to would compare with the analytical abstractions of the theologians . . .

I set up the music and began working on my various scales and exercises. I went through the exercises automatically, remembering the dream of my ghost in the fog hovering above the crossroads near the rivers of blood and milk. Graduation was one month away. What would I do then? Enter the conservatory in New York? Graduate work? Then maybe a job in an all-white symphony orchestra? Maybe no job, just frustration and anger. I could always teach. I went from the exercises to a piece by Hindemith. I worked the first eight bars of the piece and then stopped. How come I wasn't as dynamic as Jennie Forman? What made her so tough? I played the piece through. I liked the way it moved, especially the rhythm in the middle sections. It was beautiful, but as I played, it was as if I was drifting out of myself and hovering like a bird looking down on myself . . .

Next, I improvised on a blues song that my grandfather used to sing. I played the piece in A minor. I just played and played from my heart. I wept as I played and thought about my father and mother, both graduates from this university. I thought about how they were so unlike my granddaddy who died last winter, right before Christmas.

Granddaddy always made my mother mad singing and humming this old blues song. She used to say, "Daddy, you still singing those ole-time songs? Folks up north don't wanna hear that stuff . . . It reminds them of slavery . . ."

Grandfather: "I was never a slave for nobody. I worked for myself all of my life, took care of your mother, and sent you to college. I'll be singing this song until the day I die . . ." Then he would go back to humming. But neither Mommy or Daddy liked it. And Dr. Reed didn't like it either.

Dr. Reed: "The department would like to discourage our students from playing such music as jazz and blues in the practice rooms. The time allotted for these facilities should be used constructively. The classical forms require dedication and discipline. You may, however, play that kind of material on your own, preferably off campus . . ."

Having said this, Dr. Reed posted a notice on the bulletin board outside of the department office that read:

ATTENTION
ALL MUSIC MAJORS

It is strictly forbidden to use the practice rooms
for anything other than the study of music directly
related to the concerns of the department.

DR. ARNOLD REED
CHAIRMAN OF THE DEPT. OF MUSIC

Needless to say, we constantly disobeyed this directive. No one was ever caught. But it was said that Dr. Reed had spies who reported on the activities of the music majors. Someone tapped on the door. I stopped abruptly. A pair of light brown eyes peered through the little window in the door. I opened it slowly; it was the tall ascetic student from the rally. Up close, he was very handsome, much more than I had previously thought. He was inside of the little room now.

"Sorry to disturb you," he said, "I was passing this room when I heard your playing—beautiful."

"Thank you. I thought you were one of Reed's mysterious spies."

"Yes, Dr. Reed . . . He's one of our targets."

"Targets?"

"Yes, he is a running-dog lackey. And we want him out of this university."

"But why?"

"Because he's not black enough."

"Black?"

"Not physically, but spiritually . . . He's one of those super-brainwashed Negroes who believes that we can't be educated unless we become mentally and culturally whitened."

"I see," I said softly. There was a long pause. I glanced at my music stand.

"What is your name, Sister?"

I was taken back not so much by the word "sister," but there was something special about the way he said it. A warm blue wave passed quickly over me; and in a flash I felt our future closeness.

"Linda."

"My name is Eugene, but I'm thinking about changing it."

"Changing it?"

"It lacks power."

"Power? What does your name have to do with power?"

"I don't know . . . That's what I'm trying to find out . . . But—Linda what?"

"Frazier," I said.

"Well, Linda, we must claim this century in our name. Do you understand . . . ?"

And then he sat down at the piano and played a variation of my granddaddy's blues. I joined in, and we played together until the night watchman came to close the building.

Then I knew it was clear, I had to fall in love with him.

Later, we walked across town and surveyed the burned-out stores in the riot corridor. "The people have spoken," he said quietly, "but it is us and future generations that will make the revolution."

"How?" I said.

"We must each find a way . . . I'm going in law . . . Jennie's got her plan . . ."

"Any place for a violinist in the revolution?" I laughed.

We had crossed the street and were looking at the titles in the Drum and Spear bookstore: *The Wretched of the Earth, Muntu, Don't Cry, Scream, Black Fire, Toward the African Revolution, The Collected Works of Marcus Garvey, Song for Mumu, The Dead Lecturer, The Selected Military Writings of Mao Tse-Tung* . . .

"We're going to start by dealing with the administration."

"What's gonna happen?"

"Something that should have happened a long time ago."

I certainly don't want to be involved in any kind of mess, I thought, not now with only a month to go before I graduate . . . My mother would kill me.

"You should talk to Jennie."

"I don't know her, but she seems so hard." I tried not to show any jealousy.

"Not hard. Determined. The Sisters will have to make the revolution also. Jennie is a poet and a committed revolutionary."

From the tone of his voice, I could easily surmise that he really admired her. I had only known him for two hours, and already I was jealous of her.

"We're having a meeting tomorrow. You should stop by . . . Stokely and Marion will be there. Plus some people from Philly . . . a group called R.A.M."

"Ram?"

"The initials stand for the Revolutionary Action Movement."

"If I get a chance, I'll check it out." I was lying. This was going too far.

It was a clear night. We lingered for a moment in front of the large apartment building that the university had purchased and converted into a dormitory. Then he walked me to the security desk as the armed night guard eyed him suspiciously.

Looking around the foyer, he said: "This place is an armed camp since the rebellion." The guard wore what I later learned was a .38 caliber police special. Eugene grasped my hand and shook it gently. "Keep on pushin'," he said and walked out of the door.

My heart was jumping like crazy when I got in the elevator. He was nice, but he was a little strange. I tried picturing him sitting with us back home at dinner. I strained to imagine how my bank executive father would talk to him. Would they clash, and ruin dinner? Or maybe they would just talk about sports and money like most men did. But what would they think of me?

I entered my room. My roommate was sleeping, but the radio was still on. I turned it off, undressed, and then stood before the mirror stark naked. I checked out my hips and thighs. I turned around sideways to check out my behind. I touched myself all over. My hands were very hot and moist. I massaged my face with cold cream. Then I turned off the light and sat on the edge of the bed in the dark, thinking . . .

As I dozed off, my ghostly twin smiled in the fog at the crossroads . . . Granddaddy's blues echoed in the distance over the cool murmur of rivers . . .

* * *

We met for lunch the next day. That was nice. But then I didn't see him again for several days. With a great deal of effort, I suppressed the storm that raged inside of me. After all, wasn't I a senior—not just a senior, but a mature senior? I'm not a genius, but for the most part, with painful effort, I always manage, manage somehow, to pull through, sometimes with honors even. I guess I get my staying power from my father, who really wanted a son, but who, as my mother tells it, jumped with joy when I was born. I am not frivolous. I play to win.

It was mother's wish that I major in music. She had wanted to be a classical pianist and concertize all over the world. She was a child prodigy, and depending on your point of view, that was either a curse or a blessing. It had all come to nothing. After a meteor-like burst of fame, it had suddenly all come to nothing. The novelty wore off. And against Daddy's wishes she ended her professional career. And then they had me. And that was that.

The note I held in my hand was from Dr. Reed. I sat outside of his office that morning nervously chatting with the secretaries in the office. They were talking about the riots.

"Them folks sure showed their asses over in Northeast where I live. Grabbing junk out of Allen's and Woolworth's and next to that the liquor store. Girl, you should have seen that mess they were dragging out of the Lerner shops . . ."

Her intercom buzzed. She picked up the phone.

"You may go in now, Miss Frazier . . . And good luck, child."

What did she mean, *good luck?*

Dr. Reed's back was turned to me as he looked out of the window onto the campus green. He was a dark, pompous man who clearly thought highly of his long-standing success. He held what looked like a list of grades in his hands. I stood there uncomfortably for a moment. Still looking out of the window, he said: "Have a seat, Miss Frazier." Then he slowly spun around in that plush leather chair. The wall behind him was full of plaques and photographs. In each photograph, he was giving or receiving some kind of award. His PhD diploma was prominently displayed between two cheap reproductions of Renoir and Degas.

"Your grades are not bad, Miss Frazier. I want to congratulate you on having been a good student. But it is essential that you obey the rules this institution . . ."

He found out!

". . . It has come to my attention that you have violated my directive concerning proper use and conduct in the practice rooms."

He had me.

"Now that you're ready to graduate, you'll need excellent departmental recommendations. And, Miss Frazier, I sincerely believe that all of us here want you to succeed in your chosen endeavors. But you must obey my rules, Miss Frazier . . . What is happening to civilization? You can play that other music in one of those terrible clubs on U Street. But your applications and general deportment as a student at this university indicate that you have higher aspirations . . . Keep those aspirations, my child; it is so easy for us, as a people, to fall prey to the baser aspects of human existence."

Wow!

"Do you have anything to say for yourself, Miss Frazier?" He pressed his sleekly manicured fingers together to form a V, which seemed to point directly at my heart.

I got up slowly, barely able to speak. I bit down on my bottom lip to keep from breaking into tears. But I would not let him break me down. I mumbled some kind of something and excused myself as I groped my way out of there. A menacing, electronic curse whirred in the air. Somehow, I made it past Fannie and the other secretaries in the outer office. It was like an echo chamber in a Frankenstein movie . . . They said something about pink lingerie being dragged along the street as state troopers stood guard over the burning carcass of the city.

On the phone, she had a soft voice, with a lyrical sort of poignancy about it. It was clearly a different voice from the one she had at the rally; and now muted by the phone, it was a marvelous antidote to the whirring menace that continued to plague my memory of yesterday's encounter with Dr. Reed.

"We're having a party Friday night at our place on Ontario Road . . . Abdul said to call . . . So, how about it?"

"Thanks, but who's Abdul?"

"You know him as Eugene . . . He's changed his name."

Why did he have to do that now? All of the fantasies churning within my young heart had Eugene and I on location in some distant erotic country. For a moment, I was angry with him for not sharing his transformation with me.

"Are you still there, Sister?"

"Yes," I said, "I'm looking forward to meeting you in person . . . Eugene speaks very highly of you."

It was a fantastic party!!! Where had all these people been hiding? Most of them were from the university, but I had never seen them before. There were colorful and zany students from the theatre department. Painters from the art department. Mad musicians who I didn't even know existed. Two or three maverick professors from the English department—one, a woman with a red turban whose long brown arms danced in a circle of passionate wit. Where had all of these people been my four years at this university? There were revolutionary activists from Philadelphia, Cleveland, Detroit, and Harlem. There were different sets of people, all over the house:

In the living room, Jennie was engaged in a spirited debate on the need for a black revolutionary army. Jennie said that was suicidal because the masses had to be organized. The argument was fierce, but there was a great deal of laughter interspersed throughout.

Down in the basement, they were dancing to the music of Martha and the Vandellas, Mary Wells, the Supremes, and the mighty James Brown. In the corner of the basement, somebody passed me a joint, but I turned it down. I get silly and lose prospective when I smoke.

And in the kitchen, there were poets, at least ten of them. There was a thin dark string bean of a woman whose poetry reminded me of my granddaddy's voice. It was so full of the earth and the sound of life as it is actually lived. The way it made you feel was more like music than literature. It was not like the poetry we studied in Dr. Brawley's class. That poetry was "beautiful" (like most of my classical repertoire), but beautiful in a distant kind of way. The art of this poetry sprang from the urge to name things anew. As the old folks often said: This is the kind of food that sticks to the ribs. This poetry made you sing and laugh and weep and curse your enemies. Enemies? *Who are our enemies?* the poets asked.

Then Jennie's turn came to read, her voice sometimes blazing with images of moribund worlds crumbling. In her poems, women and men died the romantic death of righteous revolutionaries, uttering inspiring slogans as they fought desperately and then died under the awesome firepower of the enemy. There was always something a little corny and sentimental about her concept of change; but that night I loved her poems uncritically. Yet something about her frightened me. She was so much freer than me. Her poems about being a woman, for example, were disturbingly erotic and daring.

And so we partied on into the night, some of us down in the basement shimmying to the music of Smokey Robinson; and others, like me, Jennie, and Eugene, in the kitchen digging on Coltrane while on the stove simmered big pots of peas and rice and spicy creolized stewed chicken.

In a quiet corner, away from the din, I tried to get acquainted with Jennie. I talked on and on about my musical studies; about whether or not I should go to the conservatory, or just get married and have a lot of babies. I went on about how I longed to see places like Paris and Vienna.

Suddenly, she interrupted me: "Don't you have any commitment to anything other than yourself?" Her question stopped me dead. She was so smug with me then, and her voice was heavily weighted with a tone of moral and intellectual superiority. Yes, compared to her, I was confused about everything. Jennie seemed to have a firm grip on things.

Her family belonged to what she called the "responsible working class." Her father was a railroad man whose overalls smelled of oil and coal. Her mother worked in a food processing plant in the Frankford section of North Philadelphia. She was the oldest of three children: a brother and a sister. By "responsible" she meant that they were never wards of the state.

They all worked hard. They paid the rent, and later the mortgage, on time. They voted. Did jury duty. Paid taxes. Made sure that there was food on the table. Stood over them while they did their school work. Read them good books. Scraped together money to take them to shows at the Pearl Theatre. And finally, kept them alive and out of jail.

So against all of my best intentions, that night we became friends.

"We need to make a revolution," she said. "There's no reason for people to have to live like our people do in this society. This system must inevitably fall. And upon its ashes we must build a new society . . . That's what I'm about. What are you about, Sister?"

There was a sudden burst of laughter from the kitchen. I sat there kind of scramble-headed. But she was coolly and quietly arrogant as she waited for me to answer. What could I say that could even begin to compare with her grand apocalyptic visions?

Up until those weird dreams of which I have previously spoken, my life had seemed very ordinary and well made.

But I was not spoiled. No, I am not middle-class lace and frills. To be sure, by some abstract standard of accomplishment, we lived better than most Negroes. But my people have never made a big deal about it. You might call my people "conservative," but it really wouldn't mean anything to them. Because they hate oppression and degradation. They never put on airs, but they are certain that they can run this society better than most so-called white people. So life was no crystal stair for them. Like most black people, however superficially fortunate, they have had to claw and scratch for every crumb they could snatch from the white man's table. With all of this in mind, I found the words to answer her.

"Bitch," I said quietly, "please don't try that shit on me . . . I am a person and my name is Linda Frazier."

She looked at me stunned for a moment. Then she started laughing. I don't know whether she was laughing at me or with me; but we laughed together, long and hard . . .

* * *

It was a long weekend. Sometime between that Friday night and Monday morning, I made love to Eugene and plotted with them the takeover of the university. So, I let go. Not knowing where any of this would take me, I became a spring child running wild. My blood afire, my nipples moist with milk . . .

Monday morning we seized the president's office, which was located in the administration building. We took over the switchboard. About six hundred of us. All of the campus crazies and passionate ideologues. We chanted and sang slogans as we charged across the campus. We locked the president and his entire staff in the offices. Jennie was in charge of logistics. "Abdul" set up a communications network with other college campuses. I was part of the arts-attack team. We moved on the Arts and Humanities building. We cornered Dr. Reed and the music staff in a department meeting. Our banners demanded black music: Ellington, Parker, Coltrane . . . They trembled. Dr. Reed and his supercilious flock of incompetents trembled. Seeing them like this, we realized that we had power. In the swirl, I caught a glimpse of Dr. Reed giving me an imploring look. He knew I was with them. But still his mouth was twisted in a painful "Why?"

We pressed our demands on them. A few of the bolder teachers tried to defend the policies of the department, but we shouted them down. Then we played our stomps, rags, blues, and be-bop. We played everything "out," wailing plaintive, atonal black screeching sounds that made us scream with power. Dr. Reed tried to cover his ears, but the sound was so righteous and judgmental that, despite himself, he was compelled to listen. Yes, it was chaos, but it was good.

We ran the university for seven days. On the heels of our rebellion, more spread to other campuses around the country.

Eugene's press briefings were superb. We made the six o'clock news. Our voices went out on radios and tape recorders all around the world. Yes, it was dangerous. But in a snap I had somehow become reckless in my passion. And in my dreams now, the face of my spectral twin alternately changed her expression from stern acquiescence to wry, cryptic laughter. On the whole, though, she seemed to be thoroughly enjoying herself. Because now I was free to go on. Toward what and where?

No, it was not difficult to wash out my permanent and display this kinky hair like it was a bejeweled diadem. Of course, I briefly thought about my mother's shock. But I was grown now, and our tomorrows loomed bright before us.

Well, we won most of our demands. Seniors like myself, Eugene, and Jennie would be allowed to graduate. A joint committee of students and faculty members was set up to plan an Afro-American Studies program. The director of the cafeteria promised better food. It was a strange and exhilarating victory. Two nights before graduation day, Eugene and I were back at it furiously. We lay under the sheets together.

"I've been accepted to law school."

"Where?"

"Columbia."

I was impressed.

"What about you?"

"The conservatory."

"That's an odd combination."

"What's an odd combination?"

"A lawyer with a violinist for a wife."

"We'll have to tell Jennie . . ."

"Oh yes, Jennie," he said as he slide inside of me again . . .

* * *

The next day I met Jennie at the West Indian restaurant on Georgia Avenue. She was unusually buoyant. Maybe a little high even.

"Well, this is it, ole girl," she said, "we finally made it out of this plantation."

"What are you gonna do now?" That was the question everyone was asking each other.

But before she could answer, I said: "Go ye forth, Children, and tear down the walls of Jericho."

She laughed, flashing an exquisite set of teeth. She had recently washed her hair, and there was about her the scent of coconut oil. "Of course, Jericho must fall, my Sister. What will be your contribution?"

"Why must I make a contribution?"

"Because there is no such thing as personal anything as long as the Beast rules the planet."

"But why must I give my life to that? This is the only life I know. I want to make music and have babies. Is there really anything wrong with that?"

"No, but you can't collaborate with this system."

"Collaborate?"

"Yes, collaborate!" She was suddenly very angry. Then she paused and softly stroked my hand with her fingertips. "Why don't you come with me?"

"Where?"

"Chicago, to help organize a revolutionary party."

"Jennie, I wouldn't be good at that, and besides, Eugene and I are getting married." I felt her fingers pause.

"Oh, I see . . . So you two have really been at it. I wish somebody could have told me before now."

"We were planning to tell you tonight." I knew I was taking him away from her; I hadn't consciously planned it that way, but in the whirl of events my body seemed on fire. My womanhood came down on me, and Eugene got to be a habit I couldn't break.

"I love you, Linda." It hung in the air like smoke from a stick of marijuana.

"I love you too, Jennie."

She almost wept, but held back. "I have an appointment now. Good luck, my Sister." She kissed me on the cheek and walked out of the restaurant.

She must have left campus the next day, because she did not march down the aisle. She was a summa cum laude student, and they called her name. But she was not there. I met Eugene's entire family of doctors and lawyers. My family liked his family and his family liked mine. And there was nothing unusual about the rest.

So we married, but there is really nothing very special about us. We take it for granted that we love each other, and that we should succeed in whatever we do. Eugene is a tough lawyer, one of the best of a new breed of black constitutional attorneys specializing in the First Amendment. Me? I'm still trying to get into an orchestra. In the meantime, I fly back and forth to Europe for special concerts. The reviews are good, but nothing big has broken for me over here. I just go on working my stuff on Eugene, playing an occasional gig, and keeping this diary. I suspect that we will have children soon. And as Jennie would say, we will raise them in the proper knowledge of themselves. And what of Jennie now?

She's on the run, living in Paris or Algeria as a political exile. Expatriate—

Eugene was out of town. I was working on a new composition about seven years ago when the phone rang. I started not to answer it because it seemed to ring so harshly. It was Jennie. She was wanted for murdering a Chicago policeman. It was in all of the papers. Hadn't she considered that our phone might be tapped? After all, Eugene had successfully defended movement people. I wiped the instrument clean and put it in the case. I went to the bank and withdrew two thousand dollars in cash. Suppose they found out and Eugene lost his license to practice law? Suppose they have been followed? This was Jennie's vortex, no doubt out it.

It was a dingy Irish bar on the West Side. She was not alone. The man was a little younger than Jennie. He wore a suit and a raincoat. He did not take his hat off. We sat at the table facing the door. With his left hand he sipped his drink, but underneath the table, the right hand held a large-caliber weapon. Jennie introduced me to him, but I didn't really hear his name.

"Sister, you sure look good. How's Abdul?"

"He's fine. But he stopped calling himself Abdul several years ago." I don't know why I was compelled to tell her that. She could have just as well remembered him as Abdul.

"How's your musical career coming?"

I laughed nervously. "It just limps along."

How could she seem so calm in a situation like this? Suddenly, the real danger I was in confronted me. The man kept his eyes on the door. It seemed he got slightly agitated and alert every time a police car passed the bar . . .

An awkward pause. "Would anybody like anything to eat?" I asked. No. They had eaten already. The drinks were just fine.

"I'm sorry we don't have time, my Sister. Are you able to help?"

I clutched my bag with the money in it. I would be lying if I said that she looked good. She had lost weight and it showed in her face, which was now gaunt with strain.

Just as I was about to feel sorry for her, she said: "Life is funny, isn't it, girl? And we ain't even turned forty yet." Then she laughed a little, and with a gesture hinted that we should go to the ladies' room together.

In the john, she said: "I'm sorry we'll have to cut this visit short, my Sister."

"I understand," I said, fighting back the tears.

I took out the money, all the time thinking about Eugene and imagining if the FBI burst in there right then. But nothing happened. I gave it to her. She took it and grasped my hand tightly. Then she kissed me full in the mouth, and said: "For a better world."

"For a better world," I replied

"Thanks. Now, when we get back to the table, you will stay with us for about three minutes. We will leave first . . . You understand?" Yes, I said. "After a while, you can leave. Good luck with everything, Linda."

I did just as she said, but that was the longest five minutes of my life. The last time I saw her in person was in that awful West Side bar. But I read about her in the Paris papers and in *Freedomways* magazine. It is rumored that she operates a gun-running ring for African liberation movements from an office in Paris. Jennie has found her river.

About me, there isn't much here to say. Except, perhaps, that the children must come now. We're working on that. I look forward to playing for them. Our parents are quite proud of us. I do find myself a little nervous these days—some hovering tension lurking in the air. We're doing well, but the pressure to keep up is great. We have a house on a quiet treelined street in Westchester. I go to club meetings once a month. I work with the church choir; and once in a while, for kicks, I get my hair done at Henri Bendel's . . .

PART III

IN THE SHADOWS OF FEDERAL CITY

KISS THE SKY

BY JAMES GRADY

Lorton, VA

(Originally published in 1996)

F lat on his back at night when the TV and radio whispers and the coughs and sobs faded away, Lucus let his arm float up until his fingers pressed against a concrete sky and told him where he was.

What's going on, he thought, remembering a song from another Death City son who'd been big back when Lucus had been an outside man. Now . . .

Grounded, man: Got to maintain. All day. All night.

Night meant the admin killed the cells' overheads. Dudes with desk lamps had to snap them off. Unblinking walkway bulbs on the tiers cast a pale light into every cell.

Same as ever, cell lights snapped on at 7 a.m. that cold autumn morning.

From the bunk under his, Lucus heard H.L.S. whisper: "Think they's gonna go for it today?"

Lucus said nothing.

Jackster lay on the cot an arm's length from H.L.S.'s bunk, waiting to take his cue from the two gray men the admin had sardined him with, waiting before putting his feet on the floor and figuring on whether to take his meal card, make for breakfast.

"Maybe it's all cool," said Jackster. "Maybe it's chilled."

"They been rocking the cradle," said H.L.S. "Put a dude

to sleep with *its-forgots,* put steel in him when he's dreaming. They thinks they got a beef, they got a beef, and it don't blow away in the wind. Hard luck."

"I know what you're saying," said Jackster, not backing down like a punk but not pushing like a fool. "What you gonna do, Lucus?"

Silence answered those whispers in cell 47, tier 3, Administrative Building 3, Central Facility of the Lorton Correctional Complex, which drew its residents from the streets of Washington, Death City, a half hour drive north on a Virginia highway.

Then from down the tier came the buzz of a cell door as officers called a D-Dude out, the tinkle of chains as they strapped him in full restraints—hands linked to a chain belt in front, ankle hobbles, a lead line and chains to the next guy in line.

D-Designate residents were linked up to be marched to and from the mess hall, the first cons for breakfast and last for dinner. Lunch got carted to them in their cells, a universally unpopular feeding system negotiated between Eighth Amendment court rulings and the administration.

When the jerks moved the D-Dudes to the mess hall, other cons were supposed to stay in their cells. Their gates might be locked, but it was easier for the guards to yell the corridors clear and march the D-Dudes past open cells as fast as the shackled men could shuffle. D-Dudes shuffled fast: In full restraints, you were a soft mark to get tore up.

Two years into his stretch, Lucus became a D-Designate after he and Marcus jumped the hospital bus guards, stole the vehicle, and damn near made it to the freeway before troopers threw up a roadblock. Lucus shot a trooper in the leg with a bus guard's pistol. After a SWAT sharpshooter cracked Marcus's head open, Lucus was able to press the guard's revolver into Marcus's dead hand, then surrender unharmed. The trooper who got shot couldn't make a positive ID on which orange-jumpsuited convict had pulled his trigger, so dead Marcus ate that beef. Lucus only got tabbed for an escape.

That adventure added five to his forty, kept him in chains for the next seven years.

Chains tinkled past the cell. Lucus drilled his eyes into the concrete ceiling.

H.L.S. swung off his lower bunk, went to the seatless toilet, urinated.

"Man," he said, "hard luck, my plumbin's so creaky, can't go but half the night without hitting porcelain and I still gots to go first thing in the a.m.!"

"I hear that," said Lucus.

A rhythm worked its way down the tier, squeaky shoes followed by a loud clunk, moving closer: the fat Guard Rawlins unlocking the manuals on each cell door. Rawlins threw their bolt, squeaked down the line.

Jackster whispered: "What *are* you going to do, Lucus?"

Respectful. Wary. But pushing.

The warning Klaxon echoed through the five tiers of Building 3, then came the sledgehammer clang of all the cells unlocking electronically.

Lucus sat up.

Cell doors were slid open by their residents. Lucus didn't need to remind his two cellmates to leave their door shut that day. To sleep warm in the seasonally cold cell, he wore his orange jumpsuit over a white T-shirt—the seven-inch shank hidden along his heart-side forearm, inside the orange sleeve, held in place by a fuzzy red wristband like the iron-pumpers sported. Two winters before, a fish with a machine-shop job thought he could wolf out Lucus with the shiv he'd made right under the jerks' eyes. Lucus broke both the fish's arms and one of his knees, kept the blade, and left the fish to gimp around like a billboard.

At their cell sink, H.L.S. splashed water on his face.

"I'm hungry," said Lucus. He slid to the floor, slipped into his sneakers. Glanced to the man at the sink whose hair was white: "You hungry, Sam?"

H.L.S.—Hard Luck Sam.

"Hell yes," he answered. "If it's gonna keep running out, got to put more in."

"Want to stroll, Darnell?" said Lucus. *Darnell*, not *Jackster*: not using the dude's street name. Not dissing the younger man, but underlining who was who.

"Think I'll hang here for a while," answered Darnell.

Jackster, thought Lucus, *you keeping safe distance?*

"I ain't that hungry," added the young man.

Justifying, thought Lucus. *Making sure I bought what he sold.*

"What's hunger got to do with it?" Sam put on his shoes.

Could have just been H.L.S. running off at the mouth again.

But Lucus knew better.

And the flicker in Darnell's eyes said that he *wondered*.

Central Facility's dining hall could hold all 2,953 residents, but by the time Lucus and Sam made their way through the checkpoints out of their cellblock and the chain-link fence tunnel to the dining hall, half of the bolted-down picnic-style tables were empty.

Lucus recognized several crews of younger inmates clustered at their usual tables, a politicization of geography that mirrored neighborhoods from which those men drew their identity. Here and there sat old timers like Sam and him, neither apart from nor a part of any group. Tattoos from a biker gang filled the corner table; they were laughing. Spanish babbled from three tables. Two Aryan Brotherhood bloods kept themselves close to the main doors—close to the control station where two guards sat. Two more guards punched inmates' meal passes as they moved into the food line. Three guards strolled the aisles, their faces as flat as the steel tables.

The dining hall smelled of burnt coffee and grease. Breakfast was yellow and brown and sticky, though the cornbread from the prison bakery was fresh.

Sam carried his tray behind Lucus, sat with him at the table that emptied of other convicts as soon as Lucus arrived. The exodus might have been coincidental, Lucus couldn't be sure. He was grateful for Sam staying where he didn't have to be.

"You lookin good this morning," Lucus told him.

"Hard luck is, I look like myself."

Five tables away, Lucus spotted Twitch—6'3" of too-tight piano wire, a guy with kinky hair like the man who thought up the atomic bomb. Lucus had seen a picture of that guy in the prison library encyclopedia when he started the program and learned to read good. Twitch bunked four cells down from Lucus. Twitch lifted a spoonful of yellow toward his grim mouth—the spoon jerked, and yellow glopped down to the tray. Nobody laughed or dissed Twitch: He was a straight-arrow postal worker who'd bought his ticket here when he beat a man to death when the guy complained about slow mail service.

Twitch met Lucus's eyes.

Hope you're taking your medication, thought Lucus. Twitch's lawyers lost the insanity plea, so their client bused it to the prison population instead of a loony bin, but the courts let admin make sure Twitch took pills to keep him functional.

In the chessboard of tables, two men sat surrounded by an invisible bubble. One was thin and coughed; the other looked fine. The Word was they had the Ultimate Virus, and once that was the Word, those men were stuck where they were.

Someone snickered to the right.

Easy, casual, Lucus drifted his eyes to the laughter.

Two tables over, sitting by himself, bald head on 300 pounds of barbell muscle and sweet-tooth fat: Cooley, pig-blue eyes, thick lips. In the world, Cooley cruised for hitchhikers and lone walkers, made page one when Five-O tied him to three corpses.

Why ain't you a D-Designate? Lucus said to himself, knowing the answer, knowing that Cooley played the model prisoner, except for maybe once or twice a year when he found some unconnected sheep where the admin wasn't watching. Cooley left 'em alive, which kept the heat off, and always washed his hands.

Twitch heard Cooley snicker, jerked his head toward that mountain of flesh.

Don't do it, Twitch, thought Lucus. He made his mind a magnet for Twitch's eyes. *Don't be a fool today. Crazy as you are, Cooley'll eat you alive and love the memories in his lockdown. Ride your pills. Keep it cool.*

Magic worked: Twitch's eyes found Lucus, blinked. Bused his tray and left.

"Hard luck," muttered Sam. "Twitch losing a cushy government job like that."

Lucus smiled.

Sam lowered his voice and talked with tight lips: "Ears?"

Lucus shook his head.

Sam told him his back was empty, too, then said: "So what are you going to do?"

"I'm in the flow of events," said Lucus.

"Just you?"

"Gotta be who it's gotta be, and it's gotta be just me."

Sam said: "Believe I can—"

"You can't help me enough," said Lucus. "That'd just be one more body in the beef. That'd force it up to big-time, but it's not enough to back it down. I won't let you stand on that line and get slaughtered since it ain't gonna do no good no how . . . But bro," finished Lucus, "I hear you. And thanks."

"Hard luck." The older man sighed. Lucus wasn't sure if it was with sorrow or relief. "So you're in the flow."

"There it is."

"I be on the river banks." Sam shrugged. "Never know."

Then, for all the room to see, he held out his hand and slapped five with Lucus.

"What about Jackster?" Sam asked.

"Yeah," said Lucus. "What about our Darnell?"

Darnell had folded the cot, leaned it next to the toilet. His footlocker was jammed up against the wall. With the small desk, the sink, the rust-stained toilet, and built-in footlockers designed for only two prisoners in this Resident Containment Unit, enough space remained for him to pace eight steps along the front of the cell bars.

"You getting your exercise, Jackster?" asked Lucus when he and Sam got home.

H.L.S. stretched out on his bunk—feet facing the front of the cell. "Why didn't you take it to the rec? They got three new ping-pong balls and you loves to watch that talk-show lady strut her stuff."

"Figured I'd just hang here," said Darnell. "Wait for you."

"Wait for us to what?" Lucus kept his voice flat, easy. He perched on top of the desk, the open front of the cell and Darnell filling his eyes.

"Shit, man, I don't know!" said Darnell, pacing, staring out across the walkway, across the yawning fifty-foot canyon between their wall of tiered cells and the identical scene facing it. "We're partnered here, I figured—"

"Partnered?" said Lucus. "Don't recall signing on with anybody when they put me in here. You remember anything like that, Sam?"

"I disremember nothing and I don't remember that."

"Shit, man," said Darnell. Not turning around.

"Course, we do have to live together," said Lucus.

"Yeah," said Darnell. "That's what I'm talking 'bout."

"I mean," said Lucus, "we all gots the same cell number."

Darnell humphed.

"Numbers, man," chimed in Sam from the lower bunk, "they can be hard luck."

"What you mean?" snapped Darnell.

"Why, nothing, Jackster," said Sam, flat on his back, hard to see. "Just talking about numbers. Luck. Like when I went to that sporting house outside of Vegas. Man, they trot the women out in a line, I'm gassed, blow and booze and riding a hell of a score, squinting at them long legs, them firm—"

"Stop it, man!" hissed Darnell. "Don't kill me like that!"

"How do you want us to kill you?" said Lucus, sweet and low.

Jackster didn't reply.

"Just a story!" came the words from the lower bunk. "It ain't about women, it's about numbers. Them ladies all had these number tags on 'em, kind of like our designations, only you couldn't tell as much from reading theirs, just their number. Some of 'em were dog meat, but I spot number nine and she's so fine—"

"I heard this shit already," said Jackster.

"And I choose her, tells the man nine, pay him, go to the room and skin down—and who strolls in but the skaggiest bowser in the line who's so untogether, she's number six but her number's on upside down!"

"Hard luck," said Lucus, rolling out Sam's punch line.

"Yeah," spit out Jackster, "like when old H.L.S. here, him already a two-time fall man, cases his apartment rip so bad that the lady done showed up coming home—"

"She got sick at work." Sam's tone was flat. Hard. "She wasn't supposed to."

If Jackster knew what he was hearing, he didn't show it.

"Yeah," he said, "hard luck that lamp you whomped her upside the head with—"

"She wasn't supposed to be screaming, getting in the way of me getting gone."

"And hard luck when you dropped out her window and the alley dumpster lid caved in on you, and hard luck it was empty so's you hit steel bottom and busted your foot instead of bouncing off a pile of dirty Pampers, and—"

"You talking about *my* crime."

Even Darnell heard the sound of gravestone from the man on the bottom bunk.

Can't let this shit roll down today, thought Lucus; said: "Enough hard luck out there to fill our happy home." *Zero the score so H.L.S. won't need to.* "Kind of like when somebody sells three bags of rock to a roller wearing a beard over his badge, deal going down just in time to catch the new mandatory-sentencing guidelines."

Darnell's eyes risked flicking from the lower bunk to Lucus.

Lucus smiled: "Some guys just ain't cut out for the spy game."

"I don't play no games," said Darnell. But his edge was jagged, backing away.

The air inside the room eased out the open cell door, whirled into the cacophony of shouts and radios and sweat in the cellblock.

"The point of the story," said Sam, his words round and smooth again, "is numbers. Some people get their number wrong, and look what hard luck that brings."

"I got my number," mumbled Darnell, "don't worry about it."

"I won't," said H.L.S. "I be glad for you."

"What about you, Lucus?" said Darnell.

"What about me *what?*"

"You gotta be working on your number," said Darnell. He met Lucus eye for eye. "Like you said, we live together, no choice. That means your number's chained to mine."

"I know about chains," said Lucus.

"Me too," said Jackster. "And us being linked, it's righteous I should get to know what's what and figure my score around your play." He shrugged. "Ain't saying I'll throw with you, but I gots to do the stand-up thing by the guys I'm bunking with."

Chaos and chatter from the tier filled their cell.

"Time for me to hit the shower." Lucus snagged his towel, stepped past Darnell. "You boys play nice while I'm gone." Then Lucus was on the walkway, strolling down the tier, his towel looped in his left hand. Inside his sleeve rode the shiv.

Split the walkway toward the right, stay closer to the rail

than the cells. Not so close it's an easy bull-charge to push you over, but better than walking next to the bars where you're an easy pull into a cell for a pile-on of badasses and blades. Ripping it up on the walkway meant that the tussle might get seen by the tier monitor in the tower. He could punch the horn, maybe get nightsticks there while you still had some pieces left. In the cells, you'd fall into a setup so savage it'd be history before anyone got there, even if the monitor saw you snatched.

Usually when Lucus walked the tiers, dudes sang out to him, gave him a nod, or even strolled up to jazz. That morning, the guys hanging outside the open cells and doing their busies inside sent him no words. Guys in his path rolled away.

"Hey, sir," Lucus said to the guard behind the desk at the cage entrance to the shower rooms, "okay if I catch a shower so's I won't stink up the boss's office today?"

Security plans for the Central Facility called for two corrections officers to be on front desk duty at the cleansing unit's entrance, and for one officer to be stationed "in visual range" of the showers in each of the five locker rooms. The building's architect had taken the "custody and care" charge of incarceration laws seriously. Under the latest budget plan, however, there was only enough manpower for one front desk officer.

That pockmarked guard had seven years left to his pension. Whenever he found a dollar bill on a walkway, he failed to smell fermenting homebrew. The guard skimmed the clipboard of demerit denials and didn't find Lucus's name or designation. "Number two and four are busted out," he said.

"Believe I'll try three," replied Lucus, signing his name and number on the second line of the log book.

The guard frowned, spun the log book around, and double-checked the scrawl on the line above Lucus's name.

"I thought you could read, boy."

Keep it level—hell, slam it straight back at the fat son of a bitch: "Do my numbers too."

"You know who's in there?"

"I don't care."

Flat out, the power mantra.

The guard shook his head, scrawled his initials in the column. Said: "Never figured you for that scene, Lucus."

Like all its counterparts, Unit 3's locker room had no lockers. Wooden benches were bolted to the floor. A set of prison-orange clothes and a DayGlo undershirt were neatly stacked up in the empty dressing room when Lucus walked in. From inside the tiled shower area came the sound of rushing water and billowing steam.

Lucus stripped to his skin, stacked his clothes by the wall opposite the other pile. A scar snaked around his left ribs where he'd been too slow seven years before. He held the shiv along his forearm, his other hand fanned a path through the warm fog.

There, against the far wall, under the last of all twenty spraying shower spigots, shoulder-length permed tresses protected by a flowered shower cap, saying: "And *lo*, it is the man himself."

"Who you expecting, Barry?" Lucus walked through the lead-heavy rain.

Barry was six feet three inches of rippling muscles. Long, sinewy legs that let him fly across the stage of the city ballet or lightspeed kick the teeth out of dudes inside who were dumb enough to think his style equaled weakness. The shower steam made the mascara over Barry's right eye trickle down his cheek like a midnight tear.

"Expecting?" Barry turned his bare shoulder toward

Lucus, flashed his floodlight smile, and swung his arms out from his sides, up above his head, hands meeting in a point as he stretched to his tiptoes, eyes closed in ecstasy. He held position for a full count, then fluttered his arms down, cupped his hands shyly above his groin, and lowered his chin, eyes closed: a sleeping angel scarred by the midnight tear.

One heartbeat.

Barry's eyes popped open and he beat his lashes toward the man with the shiv.

"Why, I've been waiting for only you." Barry cocked poses with each beat as he sang: "Just *you*, indeed, it's *you*, only *you*, yes it's *true* . . ." Whirling around, dancing, singing: "No-body bu-ah-ut—" Cobra coiled, shrinking back on one cocked leg, both pointing fingers aimed right at Lucus's heart: "*Yooou!*"

"Good thing you came," said Lucus.

"What else is a girl supposed to do?" Barry leered. "My pleasure."

"No, man," said Lucus, "my payoff."

"Oh my, yes," replied Barry, washing. "Lucus to Mouser to Dancer—why, you'd think we're playing *baseball!*"

"We ain't playing shit."

"Certainly not, manchild." Barry smiled. "And right you were. The play's been called, the sign is on for a hit."

"When?"

"Well, that nervous Nellie was all *denial*, you see, as if he hadn't been cruising around the yard, too scared to make a move, afraid his bros would put him down. Those savages! As if *they've* never grabbed a punk in these very tiled walls and made the poor boy weep! But of course *my man* wasn't really doing it, you understand, just accepting my smitten appreciation of him being such a stud."

"When?"

"Let a girl tell her story or you'll never get anywhere with her!"

"We're where we are and where we're going. You been paid, you come across."

"Always." Barry savored the moment. "What did Mouser owe you that he swapped my debt to him for?"

"Enough," said Lucus. "Now give me what I bought: When?"

"Why, today, dear man."

Lucus showed nothing.

"Probably in the afternoon exercise."

Yard time, thought Lucus. *Starts at 3:30.* About five hours away.

Barry washed his armpits.

"My simple little use-to-be-a-virgin's crew has traded around and rigged the stage and done the diplomacy and even rehearsed wolf-packing. They have a huge enough chorus to smother any friends of their featured star who try to crimp the show and make it more than a solo death song."

Water beat down on the two men.

"What else?" said Lucus.

"Nothing you'd want. He cried. I think he actually feels guilty. That's the only charming thing about him—though he does have nice thighs. Not as nice as yours."

"Does he suspect that he was set up with you or that he ran his mouth too much?"

"He's all ego and asshole," said Barry. "He can't conceive that he's been bought and sold and suckered clean."

"How about his bros? By now, they might know about you two."

"Not from him. He's too scared of getting branded to confess, cagey enough to not let it slip out. If they do know, no worry:

Like you said, I used to middleman powder for upscale customers from a boy tied to their crew. That makes *moi* acceptable."

"We're square." Lucus stepped back, his eyes staying on Barry as he moved toward the door.

"How about a little something for the road?" Barry smiled. "It'll calm your nerves. For free. For you, from me."

"I got what I need for the road."

"Oh, if only that were true for all of us! If only we could all *believe* that!"

Lucus turned, disappeared in the steam. In the locker room, he dressed. *Don't run. Don't show one bead of sweat.*

"You get what you was after?" asked the guard as he signed Lucus out.

"Guess I did."

"Guess I did—*sir.*"

"Yeah." Lucus saw his reflection in the guard's eyes, saw how it shrank because of what that guard thought happened in there. *That's* his *problem,* thought Lucus. He went back to the cell.

Spent the morning on his cot, like he had nothing to do.

Jackster and H.L.S. puttered about, neither one leaving Lucus.

"Lunchtime," announced Lucus, swinging off his bunk. "Come on, Jackster. Today you eating with the men."

"I eat where I want," snapped Darnell.

"Why wouldn't you want to eat with us?" asked Lucus.

Darnell mumbled—then obeyed Lucus's gesture to lead the way.

A table emptied when Lucus and his cellmates sat down.

Lunch was brown and brown and gray, with coffee.

Jackster kept sneaking looks at other tables, locking eyes with bros from his old neighborhood.

H.L.S. ran down "Chumps I have known."

Like Dozer, a Valium freak who bypassed a pharmacy's alarm system, then overindulged in bounty and nodded off in the baby-food aisle. The cops woke him.

And Two-Times Shorty, a midget who tried to bully an indy whore into being his bottom lady. She chased him through horn-honking curbside shoppers and lost tourists looking for the White House, pinned him on the hood of a Dodge, and pounded about a hundred dents in him with her red high-heeled shoe. Tossed him buck naked into a dumpster. Climbing out, pizza parts stuck to his naked torso, Shorty grabbed the offered hand of a fine-looking woman. *What the hell,* he figured, *second time's the charm,* and he reeled off his *be-mine* pimp spiel. She slapped policewoman bracelets on him.

Then there was Paul the Spike, who tested heroin on street dogs. While he was slicing and dicing a batch of Mexican, Paul heard a knock on the door. Because of the 'sclusionary rule, he beat the narco charges but drew ninety days for cruelty to animals.

"Hard luck can bite anybody's ass," said Sam, "but it always eats up chumps."

"I ain't no chump," said Jackster.

Sergeant Wendell entered the mess hall, scanned the mostly empty rows of tables.

"Who said you were?" Lucus let his eyes leave the sergeant to study Darnell.

"No fool better!"

Sergeant Wendell started toward them.

"Trouble with young punks today," said Sam, "they got no *finesse.* Our day, needed to smoke a guy, you caught him in private, did your business, and everything's cool. These days, you young punks let fly on street corners and wing some poor girl coming home from kindergarten. No respect for nothing, no style or—"

"Style?" snapped Jackster. "You got no idea, man, no *idea* what style is!"

"Resident Ellicot!" yelled Sergeant Wendell.

"Yes, sir?" answered Lucus.

"What the hell are you doing?"

"I was just—"

"You know your damn schedule as well as I do! Your ass belongs in Administrator Higgins's office as of ten minutes ago!"

"On my way, sir!" Lucus stood.

H.L.S. pulled Lucus's tray so Lucus wouldn't need to bus it.

"Why'd you make me have to come fetch you?" Wendell asked as he marched Lucus along in front of a dozen sets of eyes.

"Just guess I ain't so smart," said Lucus.

"Don't give me that shit," said Wendell, who was no fool and a good jerk, though no con had ever been able to buy him. "Move!"

Assistant Administrator Higgins kept his office *almost* regulation. Sunlight streaming through the steel mesh grille over his lone window fell on a government low-bid desk positioned in line with the file cabinets and the official calendar on the wall next to facility authority and shift assignment charts. But Higgins had taken out the regulation steel visitors' chairs bolted to the floor in front of his desk and had risked replacing them with more inviting, freestanding wooden fold-up chairs that a strong man could use to batter you to death.

Higgins was a bantamweight in chain-store suits and plain

ties. He wore metal frame glasses that hooked around his ears. Glasses on or off, his dark eyes locked on who he was talking to. That afternoon, he slowly unhooked his glasses, set them on the typed report in the middle of his otherwise blank desk, and fixed those eyes on Lucus.

"So, do you understand this report?" asked Higgins.

"I can read now, so that ain't what I gots to talk to you about."

"That was on your meeting request." Higgins leaned back in his chair.

"The administration," started Lucus, "they got to like what I been doing. They been catching hell on the news, in the TV ads from those two citizens running for senator. I heard the warden—"

"Chief administrator," corrected Higgins.

"Oh yeah, I forgot. Change the name and everything's okay. Long as there's no trouble."

"What do you mean, *trouble?*"

"There's some that say the understaffing helps you guys, cause it'll inspire something to happen, and then you all can say, *See? We need more budget. Jobs.*"

"I don't see it that way."

"Maybe some of the guards do."

"The officers are paid to watch inmates, not make policy. I need to be told about any of them who act differently."

"I ain't the telling kind," said Lucus. "I just sensitive to your problems about image and keeping up the good show so the warden don't get bad press and take heat from his buddy the governor and every other politician looking to get elected."

"What's this got to do with anything?"

"I just glad to help out—with things like that charity program on your desk."

"You've done good work, Lucus."

"What will it get me?"

Higgins frowned. "You knew that isn't the way this works."

Lucus shrugged. "Things change."

"Don't go con on me now, resident."

"Sir, you was the one who showed me about attitude, about getting out from behind it and how nothing would change if I didn't. So I been workin on my attitude, what's behind it, what I do. But where's it getting me? Still right here."

"You're down for Murder One, five counts . . . plus. Where do you expect to be?"

"Oh, I'm a criminal," said Lucus. "No question about that. I can do the time for what I did, but man, let my crime justify my punishment."

"Five murders," said Higgins. "*Plus*."

"I already done my *plus* in chains." *Stay calm.* "But I never did no murders."

"The law—"

"Sir, I know the law. We were sticking up gamblers. The law made them crooks, which made them marks. The law did that—not me. Figure, heist a crook, he can't holler for cops. Rodney had the gun, had them fools lined up against that wall, told me to check out the basement. We agreed before we went in there: in and out with cash, nobody hurt, nobody can do shit about us. I'm in the basement looking for whatnot, I hears those *pop-pop-pops* . . . Man, Rodney done me just as much as he done them dudes!"

"Not quite," said Higgins.

"Yeah, well, what's done is done, but I didn't kill nobody. It's the law and Rodney that made me guilty."

"You chose to rob, you chose to run with a trigger-happy

partner, you chose your juvie record, your prior theft and assault rec—"

"Yes, sir," said Lucus, interrupting with polite formality. *Got to hurry this up.* "I admit I'm guilty, but fitting my crimes with two twenty-year stretches, back to back, no parole—no right man can do that kind of justifying."

"It's a done deal, Lucus. I didn't think you were fighting that anymore."

"I got a lot of time to mess with it. Nineteen more years."

"Might just be enough to make yourself a new life."

"Yeah. Starting when I'm sixty-two."

"Starting every time you breathe." Higgins blinked. "You want something."

"This new attitude you helped me get," said Lucus. "Working programs—with my program in my head. Not getting in any beefs since I got out of chains—"

"At least none that you got caught for," said Higgins.

"I been doing good time."

"The law isn't about doing good time. That's what you're supposed to do as a minimum. No matter what you do in here, every day is on the payback clock, and you gotta get to zero before you can claim you're owed."

"Maybe yes, maybe no. Maybe not always."

Higgins shrugged. "What do you want?"

"A transfer," said Lucus.

"What?"

"Out of here. Right now. Not a parole, you couldn't pull that off. But you could take a paper out of that desk, sign it, and there it is, a transfer out of the Wall to the Minimum-Security Farm. Effective soon as the ink is dry. Call the duty sergeant and—"

"You're down for hard time. You're a five-count killer with

one escape and one shot-up officer—don't tell me where that gun was found—plus a jacket full of incidents."

"All before I changed my attitude."

"Never happen. I never bullshitted you it would."

"The transfer ain't for me. It's for my son."

Higgins blinked.

Blinked again, and in the administrator's dark eyes, Lucus saw mental file cabinet drawers slide open.

"Kevin," said Higgins. "Kevin Ellicott, down for . . ."

"Last year, a nickel tour for what they could get him on instead of big dope. He's done angel time for thirteen months."

"Your boy runs with the Q Street Rockers," said Higgins. "They're no church choir."

"I didn't say he was a genius. What he is, sir, is a juicer. Just about to become a full-bore alcoholic, if he stays in here much longer. And what's that gonna solve? How's that gonna make life easier for the warden? What justice is—"

"Doesn't add up," said Higgins. "He can get pruno as easy at the Farm as here."

"Maybe if he gets into the Farm's twelve-step program—"

"It's *his* maybes, not yours. Why isn't he asking? Why are you doing this?"

"He's my son. I wasn't there to bring him up. Hell, if I had been around before I got my attitude program, probably wouldn't have done him much good. Maybe he could have learned better street smarts, but . . . he stays in here, he dies in here."

"Of alcoholism?" said Higgins.

"Dead is dead," said Lucus.

They watched each other for a dozen heartbeats.

"And you think a transfer to the Farm will keep him alive."

"It'll give him a chance."

"What aren't you telling me?" asked Higgins.

"I'm telling you everything I can," answered Lucus.

"That you *can*? You got to learn that we create most our own *cans* and *can'ts*."

"We do?" Lucus paused; said: "You always say that we pay for them too."

"That's right."

"Yeah," said Lucus. "That's right. So if somebody's already paid, then he deserves a *can*."

Softly, Higgins said, "Don't blow it, Lucus. Whatever's going down, don't blow everything you've accomplished."

"What's that, sir? Any way I cut it, I still got nineteen years to go. What could I blow?"

"The way you get to look at yourself in the mirror."

"I see a man there now. I'll see a man there tomorrow."

"If you won't help me," said Higgins, "I can't help you."

"I've been helping you—sir. Look at the report on your desk. Let the warden take credit for it, keep his image shiny. I ain't asking nothing for me. Who I am, what I've done, what I can do—one way or the other, all that should pay for something."

Higgins shook his head: "You can't bargain for your son."

"Then what the hell can I do?"

"Let him do his own life."

"You telling me, no transfer for him?"

"That's the way it has to be."

"Thought we defined our own possibilities." Lucus stood. "Are you through with me—sir?"

"We're through, resident."

Lucus walked to the door, turned back. "Answer me one question, sir?"

"Maybe."

"Why do what you do? Every day, come in here, locked up just like us, with us. Bucking the admin, the law, and the Word and the attitudes: Why you do it?"

"I got kids too."

Lucus nodded as he opened the door. "Too bad."

Clock on the wall facing the sergeant's desk: 1:52. Hour and a half to go.

Close that door behind you, thought Lucus, then said: "Hey, sergeant, got some book work to do. Can you cut me a library pass? It ain't my regular day till tomorrow."

Sergeant Wendell wrote the pass without bothering his boss behind the closed door. Wendell knew about Lucus and his Help the Homeless Project, all the grants and reports.

The library filled the second floor of the recreation complex. Lucus shivered as he hurried through the outside fenced tunnel from admin building to the rec. Couldn't help himself, he turned his face up to the cold sun as if to kiss the sky like he was a free man with a future. His exhaled clouds floated through the chain-link fence. The blade hugged his arm.

Inside the rec, Lucus glanced at the standing-room-only crowd of orange jumpsuits watching a soap on the prison's big-screen TV that the Feds had confiscated in a drug bust. Cons laughed and joked, but soaked up the story about a beautiful blonde in slinky dresses. Lucus couldn't spot *that face* in the crowd, but he knew it was there.

The guard at the library door blinked at Lucus's pass with eyes that coveted first-floor duty where he could watch TV too.

The A-Designate con working as librarian stood by the checkout desk, stacking books on a delivery cart to be rolled along the tiers. Another A-Designate replaced books on a shelf. Three residents sat at tables, surrounded by law books and yellow legal pads.

Over in the corner, reading at his Thursday table: James Clawson. The Man.

An orange tent loomed in front of Lucus: Manster, the only creature in the institution bigger than Cooley. Manster stayed out of chains because whatever he wanted from another con, the other con gave up. Outside, Manster had pistol-whipped a cop to death.

"I'm here to see the Man," Lucus told Manster.

"Maybe." Manster kept his eyes on Lucus, coughed to get the Man's attention.

The three other iron men between the Man's table and the world made a space for their ruler to check out the petitioner. He read to the end of the paragraph, glanced through the orange jumpsuits, and let Lucus fall into his eyes.

"How you doin', J.C.?" said Lucus.

"Lucus the lone wolf," replied J.C. "Join me."

J.C. picked up some chump's pink commissary pass, used it as a bookmark for the page he was reading, then closed the volume. He turned the book so Lucus could see the cover: a picture of a suit-and-tie dude with a cocked sword in one hand and a briefcase in the other. The book's title read: *Corporate Samurai—Classic Japanese Combat Principles for the 21st Century's Global Business Economy.*

"Are you still reading, Lucus?"

"When I got time."

"You know what the underlying fallacy of this book is?" asked J.C., who was working on his MBA, correspondence and good-faith-in-your-prison-jacket style.

"Ain't read it."

"You don't need to. Look at the cover."

The suit with a briefcase and a sword and a going-places face.

"Give a twelve-year-old a dime and a nine," said J.C., "and he'll punch a dozen red holes in Mr. Global Business Corporate Samurai before that sword even gets close."

A national gang once sent a crew from Angel Town to Death City to "negotiate" J.C.'s outfit into their fold. A freezer truck carted the five gangbangers back to L.A., dumped the meat in their hood.

"Business ain't my thing," said Lucus.

"It's the wave of the future," counseled J.C., who was down on a drug kingpin sentence running longer than any life.

"I've got something for you," said Lucus.

"Ah."

"But I need something too."

"Of course you do. Or you wouldn't be here. Respect and such, you've been smart about it. But it's always been Lone-Wolf Lucus."

"I've had bad luck at partnering."

"Perhaps prison has taught you something."

"Oh yeah," said Lucus. "Deal is, there's trouble coming down. You run most of what moves inside here."

J.C. shrugged.

"Trouble comes down," said Lucus, "all the politics buzzing outside, the admin will tighten the screws, and that'll crimp business, be bad for you."

"The innocent always suffer," said J.C. "What 'trouble' has made you its prophet?"

"There's a hit on, likely for this afternoon. The guarantee is it won't be quick and clean, and you don't need any out-of-hand mess tightening the screws on your machine."

"What's the 'guarantee'?"

"I am." *Risk it.* Maybe he knows, maybe not. Maybe he gave the nod, maybe he just heard the Word and let it melt in his eyes.

"The hit's on my boy—Kevin. He got drunk, got in a stupid beef over a basketball game in the yard. Trash flew, couple pushes before some guards walked by and chilled it down. Dude named Jerome's claimed the beef with my boy, and Jerome and his Orchard Terrace Projects crew gonna make it a pack hit."

"This is just a beef? Not turf or trade?"

"Nothing ever stays clean, J.C. You know that. The Orchard Terrace crew does my boy, it'll make them heavy—balance of power shifting don't do you no good."

"Unless the teeter-totter dips my way," said J.C.

"Far as I know, you ain't in this."

Gotta be that way! Or . . .

J.C. sent his eyes to one of his lieutenants.

"Lucus's punk runs with the Q Street Rockers," said the man whose job it was to know. "Wild boys. Orchard Terrace crew, they been proper, smart."

J.C. sat for a moment. Closed his eyes and enjoyed the sunshine streaming through the grilled window. "You're in a hard place," he told Lucus.

"Life story."

"What do you want from me?" asked J.C.

"Squash the hit—you could do it, no cost."

"Everything costs. What's in that play for me?"

"Your profits stay cool," said Lucus.

"Your concern for my profits is touching."

"We got the same problem here."

"No," sighed J.C., "we don't. If I squash the hit, then *I* tilt the teeter-totter. Why should I become the cause instead of just one of the bystanders? Your boy picked his crew—"

"It's a neighborhood thing, he didn't pick."

"He didn't grow up," said J.C. "Now, if he runs to me out of fear, wants to join up . . . I'd be signing on a weak link. I'd gain more if I fed him back to the Orchard Terrace boys— then they'd owe me. Better to be owed by lions than to own a rabbit."

"I figured that already."

"What else is in your column of calculations?"

Fast, everything's rushing so fast, too fast.

"You quash the hit," said Lucus, drawing the bottom line, "I'll owe you one."

"Well, well, well. What would you owe me?" asked the man with a wallet full of souls.

"Eye for an eye. One for one."

"Eye for an eye plus interest." J.C. smiled. His teeth were white and even. "You really aren't a businessman, Lucus."

"I am who I am."

"Yes. A gray legend when I walked in here. Lone wolf and wicked. You mind your step, never push but never walk away. Smart. Smarter than smart—schooled."

"I'm worth it."

"You ever kill anybody, Lucus?"

"I'm down for five murders—plus."

"My question is," said the man whose eyes punished lies, "have your hands ever drained blood?"

"Nobody ever quite died," confessed Lucus.

"*Quite* is a lot." J.C.'s smile was soft. "I know you're stand-up. You'd keep your word, wear my collar. But the fit would be too tight. And down the line, who knows what problems that would mean?"

Lucus felt his stomach fall away. His face never changed.

"So . . . I can't help you. Your boy's beef is none of my

business—either way, I promise you that. He makes it clean, I'm not in his shadow. But his future is his future."

Lucus nodded. Pushed his chair back from the table slowly and felt the meats close in by his sides, ready.

"Whatever happens," said Lucus, "remember I gave you heads-up, fair warning. Nothing coming your way from me. Or my boy."

"We'll see," J.C. shrugged. "If we're square on that, we're square."

On his way out the library door, Lucus checked the clock: 2:01. Less than ninety minutes until the turnout in the yard.

What was left was the hardest thing.

Lucus found them in the TV room, backs to the wall, street cool—running their mouths and eyeing beautiful people on the tube.

"Well, what's up here?" said one of them as Lucus neared.

Brush past that fool like December wind.

Look at yesterday's mirror—a young man against a wall, thick hair with no gray, taller and flatter muscles, no scar across the bridge of the nose, but *damn*: a mirror.

"We gotta talk," Lucus told the apparition.

"Say what?" said the young man. Lucus smelled pruno on the boy's breath. Fear in his sweat.

Fuck your fear! telepathed Lucus. *If you can't kill it, use it and ride it smart!* But he said: "Say, *now*."

"Old man," answered his son, "anything you got to say, you say it right here, right now, in front of my bros."

"I thought you grew up to be enough of a stallion you didn't need nobody to protect you from facing your old man."

Catcalls and laughs bounced off Lucus—bounced off him and hit his son. Lucus knew they were all measuring Kevin, seeing how he'd handle this. Wondering if maybe Lucus could wolf their bro down. And if the old man could do it . . .

Kevin knew all this too, sensed Lucus. *Damn yes: My son ain't all fool.*

"Well, shit!" said Kevin. "You been worrying 'bout talking to me for nineteen years, you might as well get it off your back now."

Kevin swaggered out of his crew, headed toward an empty corner by the moth-eaten pool table whose cues and balls hadn't been replaced after the last riot. Pressed his back against the wall, made Lucus turn his eyes from the distant crowd.

Good move! thought Lucus. "We haven't got much time."

"You never did have the time, did you?"

"I never had much choice. Your grandma didn't want to be bringing you down to no lockup, get you thinking that was just another part of family life, and your mother—"

"She'd have sold me for a nickel bag."

"She did what she could by you, got you to her mother. Gave up the only thing she ever loved all-out."

"I should drop by the cemetery, spray tag *Yo, thanks!* on her stone."

"Don't throw your shit on her grave."

The chill in Lucus's voice touched his son.

"Why'd you two go and have me anyway?"

"Wasn't what we were thinking of," answered the father.

"Yeah, I know. A little under-the-jackets action sitting in chairs in minimum security's visitor hall."

"Least you know who your father is."

"Hell of a family that gives me." Kevin shook his head. "I don't know who the hell you are. You're the big Never There."

"Nothing kept you from catching a bus out here when you turned eighteen, signing the visitor's log, calling me out."

Kevin shrugged: "I figured I'd make it here soon enough."

There it is, thought Lucus. *Got to tend to business!* But he said: "Outside . . . you got a woman?"

Kevin looked away, said: "They's all bitches and whores."

"Thinking and talking like that," said his father, "no wonder you're in prison. No woman who's worth it will stick around you when you got that attitude."

"Yeah, well . . . no ladies no how was beating down my crib door." Kevin looked at his father; looked away, said: "That woman Emma, works down at the dry cleaners for them Koreans. She calls herself your wife."

"We ain't got no law on it." Lucus shrugged, prayed for the clock not to tick. "Her old man died in a bust-out, I got to know her through that. Phone calls, letters. We understand each other."

"You don't even have minimum-security visiting privileges. The glass stays up when she visits you. What's she see in it?"

Lucus shrugged. "Safe sex."

Made him laugh!

"We got no time," said Lucus. "There's a hit on you today. Likely in the yard."

Kevin blinked: "Jerome said—"

"Words are weapons! Ain't you learned that?"

"You ain't been my teacher, so you can't give me grades."

"If I'd been learnin you, you wouldn't have got drunk, got in a chump beef over yard basketball! And if you *had* run up against it, you would have done it right."

"Yeah? Like how?"

"Like you'd have kept it personal! Man to man. Walked

into Jerome's crew and called him out—put him on the spot. Then you'd have had a chance."

"What chance did I ever have for anything?" hissed Kevin. "You think I'm chump enough to ask him—"

"You don't 'ask' for anything from anybody!"

"Force a throw-down, strap our arms together, toss the blade on the floor, and—"

"And you got an even chance! You let it buck up to you dissing him and his whole crew, you got a war, not a battle."

"I got my own crew!"

"Yeah. There's more of the other dudes, and the guys on your side would never sell anybody out. Or dodge getting cut up. They gonna *die* for you."

"That's the way it is."

"If that's the way it is, this wouldn't be Plea-Bargain City."

"So what do you want me to do, Mr. Smart-Time Con?"

"You got one chance. Go to the admin. Feed them a pruno still: Robinson, Building 2, Tier 2, in the bus the auto mechanics practice on. Trade that bust for a crash transfer to—"

"You want me to rat? You a fool? That's evil! And suicide!"

"No, that's smart. Robinson wants to kick the juice—like you need to. He knows lockdown cold turkey is his only way. I already cut a deal with him. You just gotta make your move—and right now."

"You're one treacherous mother," said Kevin.

"Believe it."

"But I go to the Farm, the Orchard Terrace guys—"

"They got no crew there."

"They will."

"That's tomorrow. You're scheduled to die today. With the time you done, keep your jacket clean and when the courts make the admin thin the herd, you're prime for early release. Could be outta here in a year. Besides, we'll fix tomorrow when—"

"The Farm boys would know I ratted."

"Not if Robinson puts out the Word how you two tricked the admin."

"My crew would cut me loose."

"No loss."

"They're all I got!"

"Not anymore."

Lucus heard the babble behind him; knew a hundred eyes were checking them out. Knew the clock was ticking.

"You just don't understand," said Kevin. "If I run from—"

"You're not running *from*, you're running *towards*. And don't tell me I don't understand."

"I just gotta do what I gotta do. If what's gonna happen's got to happen, that's just the way it's gotta be."

"Kevin?"

"Yeah?"

"Don't hand me bullshit street jive. That's all hollow words you stack up in front of your face to keep from seeing you're too lazy or too stupid or too scared to walk smart. *What's gotta be, gotta be*—shit: You sit there where the 'be' shit is, you ain't being stand-up strong, you're making yourself the most powerless chump in the world."

"You don't get it, do you, old man?"

"Yes, I do."

"Why are you doing this?"

"Just because I done a lot of wrongs don't mean I can't do one right."

"Why this? Why me?"

"You're what I got," whispered Lucus.

Kevin pushed off the wall. "See you."

"I can save your life!"

"No, you can't," said his son. Nineteen-year-old Kevin spread his arms out like Jesus. "Besides, what's it worth?"

And he walked away. Strutted toward his bros.

Nowhere to run, nowhere to hide, Lucus went back to his cell.

Jackster and H.L.S. were there, waiting out the last few minutes before yard time.

Nobody said anything.

Soon as Kevin got sent to the institution, Lucus put the few pictures the boy's grandmother had grudgingly sent him in a paperback book where, like now, he could flip through them without a ritualized search that might betray his heart. With those childhood snapshots were pictures that Emma had somehow scissored from high school yearbooks for both years Kevin had attended.

Lucus glanced at his cell walls. Pictures of wide outdoors. Pictures of Emma—she sent him a new one every three months. *Who says we can't grow old together?* she once told him through the phone and glass in the maximum designates' visitation room.

Couple minutes to go, Lucus leaned on the bars. Stared nowhere.

"What you doing?" asked Jackster.

"Nothing," mumbled Lucus.

"What you gonna do?" asked Jackster.

Lucus stood wordless until the Klaxon blared the *"All out"* for those residents with permission to choose the ninety-minute exterior exercise, general population period.

The blade rode up Lucas's sleeve when he slipped into his blue-denim prison jacket. As his cellmates grabbed their jackets, Lucus said: "Nice day out there."

The yard.

Inside the Wall, chop a couple football fields and box them in a square with three mammoth cellblocks, double chain-link fences topped with razor and barbed wire. Build guard towers for snipers. Lay down a running track that circles inside the fence a couple steps from the dead zone trip wire. Pave a dozen basketball half-courts in one corner, stick some rusted barbells and concrete benches beside them. Paint some white lines on a cellblock and call them handball courts. Smack in the center, throw up a water tower surrounded by a chain-link fence. Build chain-link fence funnels from the cellblocks and admin building.

Loose the animals down those funnels.

The D-Designates clink out there with their chains for thirty minutes after breakfast. General population gets ninety minutes in the afternoon. A-Designates have lunch to dinner access.

Institution procedures assign twelve pairs of corrections officers to roaming yard patrol during general population period. The budget that day sent five pairs of jerks out to the yard.

Several hundred inmates funneled through the tunnels.

Go to the core, thought Lucus. Go to the center of the yard, where you can watch and be ready to move any which way.

H.L.S. casually strolled a step behind Lucus's right side.

No matter how Jackster shuffled, the old dudes hung behind him a half-step and herded him where they wanted.

J.C. and a squad paraded toward the concrete chess tables in the best sun. J.C. showed his empty face to Lucus. Manster sent the lone wolf a sneer.

Lucus thought: *The hitters'll take their time, make sure the play is set.*

Kevin and a handful of his crew entered the yard laughing and looking drunk.

Count six, thought Lucus. *Q Street Rockers supposed to be a dozen strong.*

Barry strolled by with three attentive supplicants under his protection.

The orange-jumpsuited and blue-jacketed sea of inmates parted for Cooley. The hulk's beady eyes jumped around the yard, seeking a fish.

"Yo, Jackster!" An inmate Darnell's age popped out of the crowd twenty feet away, a worn brown basketball spinning in his hands. "We shooting hoops or what?"

"Ah . . ." Darnell looked to his cellmates. "I got a game."

"Better win," said Lucus. And he smiled.

Darnell got an empty stare from Hard Luck Sam.

Jackster followed the man with the ball to a half-court.

Twitch stood by the water-tower fence, alone, an invisible wind roaring around him. His gloves were gone, strips of an old blue shirt were wrapped around his hands. Twitch's eyes bore through Lucus.

Lucus used both hands to rub his temples, like to rub away the pain.

Jerome and a posse of his Orchard Terrace crew, a dozen dudes, strolled into the yard, headed for turf opposite Kevin and his bros. Like nothing was on.

Looking once at Jerome, the world couldn't tell him apart from Kevin.

There, in the crowd on Kevin's flank, positioning by the dead zone wire: one, two—no, three Orchard Terrace boys, the O.T.s fanning out and holding. Waiting.

Making the box, thought Lucus. No need to check the other flank, O.T.s would be there too.

The shiv burned along Lucus's forearm.

Across the yard, a b-ball game filled a court, the ball clinking through the chain hoop, bouncing off the backboard.

Jackster caught a pass, made a fast break to the hoop, and laid the ball up in the air. A teammate tipped it in. Dude on the other team slapped Jackster five and jogged down the court with him, mouths a-working. Time out and the five-slapper waved a sub in for himself. Time in. Standing on the sidelines, a spectator got the word on the game from the five-slapper. Dunk shot. Ball in play. Spectator got bored, strolled away from the courts, through the crowd, cut left, cut right, materialized alongside the O.T. posse. Whispered in the main man's ear. Got a nod. The main man put his arm around Jerome, leaned in to him.

Standing beside Lucus, H.L.S. said: "Catch that?"

"Oh yeah," said Lucus. Two tan uniformed jerks picked their way through the orange-jumpsuited crowd: Adkins and Tate, a too-lean and too-short combo who always got stuck with yard duty and always walked the same beat. They headed for their shake-the-water-tower-fence-gate check, after which they would angle toward the barbells.

Lucus saw the O.T. posse adjust their cluster, the flankers anticipating the patrol, not letting anybody use the guards to outmaneuver the game plan.

Adkins, the lean guard, swung the keys retracto-chained to his belt. Shorty Tate kept his eyes on the ground, like he was looking for something. Everybody knew his eyes were in the dust so the cons wouldn't see his fear. As if they needed to see it. Fear hung like smoke over the small man, who wished yard officers were armed and he didn't have to rely on the wall snipers.

Adkins swung his keys and complained about the union

and the World Series. Tate locked his eyes in the dust, thinking about how after checking the gate to the water tower, they'd only need to—

Twitch threw a punch smack between Tate's shoulder blades, and the small guard crashed into the dust.

Adkins dropped his keys and the retracto-chain snapped them back to his belt. But before he could whirl around, Twitch was on his back, sliding a thick strip of old shirt around the guard's neck. One end of the strap was tied to Twitch's wrist. He looped it around his hand, cinched it tight so the shiv in his fist was locked with the point digging into the guard's neck.

"Nobody move!" screamed Twitch. "Anybody moves, I cut his head off and let the mice run out! Nobody moves!"

The cons cared *zero* about Adkins, but Twitch's play stunned them into stillness.

On the ground, Tate gasped, but managed to push the button on his belt radio.

Twitch backed toward the water tower, hugging Adkins in front of him with the knife pinned at the base of his skull.

Guards ran through the jumpsuited crowd, yelled into their radios.

"Nobody come any closer! Nobody move!" Twitch yelled to the charging guards. "Don't you clear the yard! You clear the yard, I cut off his head and let the mice run out! Swear to Jesus, you clear the yard, you come at me, he's dead! Dead! Mice! Ain't gonna let you clear the yard! No Attica! No clean shots!"

The guard captain reached the inner ring of spectators near Lucus and called out: "Everybody hold your positions! Everybody! No prisoner moves! Officers stay back! . . . It's okay!" he shouted to Twitch as the inmate kept backing toward the water-tower fence. The captain's words flew over Tate, who stayed facedown in the dust and prayed that the snipers' aim was true. "You're okay!"

A react squad of guards charged out of the admin building. Shotguns, *man*, buckshot loads bouncing on SWAT belts. They formed a skirmish line facing the cons to be sure nobody tried to cop a point in this psycho drama.

On the wall, snipers ran to position. Lucus saw sunlight glint off a scope.

Twitch kept yelling, "Nobody move!" He made Adkins unlock the water-tower gate, stayed pressed against the guard. The Klaxon blared.

Higgins, radio in hand, moved next to the captain as Twitch maneuvered himself and his hostage up the spiral steel staircase along the outside of the water tower.

"What the hell is he doing?" asked Higgins.

"We can't get a clean shot," said the captain.

"Nobody move down there!" yelled Twitch. "Nobody move or we'll all die!"

Higgins radioed a report to the warden.

In his mind, Lucus saw the state police cars in the town a mile beyond the wall, cops choking down donuts and slurping coffee as they turned on their red-and-blue spinning party lights and roared toward the prison.

Somewhere, Lucus knew, a TV news camera crew was racing to their helicopter.

Standing on a metal ledge fifty feet above the yard, knife against the guard's spine, Twitch screamed down: "Don't move! Kill him if you do! Mice!"

Radios crackled.

The dudes started to buzz, whisper, but stood still cause the admin had turned out the shotguns and snipers.

Higgins's radio squawked; it was the warden: "What does he want?"

Cool and careful, Lucus stepped forward.

"Administrator Higgins!" yelled Lucus, going for the man in charge. "I can do it!"

"Freeze and stow it!" yelled the captain. A guard swung a shotgun toward Lucus.

"I can do it!" pleaded Lucus.

"Do what?" asked Higgins.

"Get your man down from there alive. Twitch, he thinks I'm, like, one of him. You know I'm the only guy in here who he believes."

Captain said: "What the—"

"He's crazy, sir," said Lucus. "But he ain't stupid."

"He's a dead man!" snapped the captain.

"Drop him, your guy falls too," said Lucus, adding: "Sir. Hell to pay for that. Hell to pay even if you just kill Twitch. TV cameras coming. Ask the warden what he wants on the 6 o'clock news."

"Resident," snapped the captain, "you're ass—"

"How will you do it?" said Higgins.

"Careful, sir. Real careful. I can do it, I promise you that. But," added Lucus, "I'm gonna need something from you."

"We don't—" started the captain.

"What?" interrupted Higgins, who knew the true priorities.

"I can't bargain Twitch down off of there with just *Be nice* bullshit," said Lucas.

"That man's crazy!" barked the captain.

"Dead on, sir. And there's nothing you can threaten him with that he don't already do to himself in his cell. But you let me tell him he can get transferred to a state hospital—"

"The courts put him in here as sane," said the captain.

"Wasn't that a smart move." Lucus jerked his thumb toward the men on the water tower. "You can administratively transfer him to the state hospital for a ninety-day evaluation. Hell, they get him in there. Unless you or his lawyer squawks, they'll keep him on an 'indefinite treatment term.' No doctor gonna risk his state job turning loose a man with a knife talking about mice."

"Why would that work?" asked Higgins.

"Cause I'll sell Twitch the truth. Hospital is co-ed. Nurses. Better drugs, better beds, more sun, people who treat him like he is. He might be crazy, but he ain't no fool . . . Course, there is one more problem."

"What?" chorused the captain and Higgins.

"Why risk my ass doing that? Long climb up that tower. Long fall down."

"You get my man back," ordered the captain, "or—"

"Or what—sir? My lockup order don't make me a hostage negotiator. I get punished for being a no-volunteer, some lawyer will make the admin eat it big-time."

"What do you want?" asked Higgins.

"Nothing much," said Lucus. "A righteous deal—admin breaks its word on this, it'll get brutal in here, then real soon admin will need credibility with us residents to save something or somebody else."

"What do you want?" repeated Higgins.

"That little matter we talked about earlier will do."

Captain said: "What?"

Higgins pushed his steel eyes against Lucus. Lucus didn't fold. Higgins bargained in the radio with the warden.

"That a TV news helicopter I hear chopping close?" said Lucus.

Higgins lowered his radio. Told Lucus: "Go."

Sam, Kevin, and Darnell, Cooley and J.C. and Manster, Jerome and the O.T. posse, Barry, Higgins, and the admin—everybody watched Lucus. Heard him yell to Twitch that he was coming up. Heard him talking about deals, making it cool. Watched Lucus climb that spiral staircase as his words faded in the October wind. Watched three men on a platform high above the yard. Watched them with cold eyes and sniper-scoped rifles—for maybe ten minutes: Nobody took their eyes off the three men to time it.

A helicopter chopped the air above the institution.

Movement on the ledge—a sliver of glistening steel tumbled down through the sky to the yard.

Guard Adkins scurried down the water-tower steps.

Higgins, into the radio: "No fire! Repeat, no fire!"

Half a dozen guards grabbed Twitch when he reached the bottom of the stairs, handcuffed him, and led him away. Everybody knew the guards would use rubber hoses on him inside, but even the meanest jerk knew the deal had to stand.

Lucus walked toward Higgins and H.L.S.

Higgins said something to the captain, who frowned, but nodded when the message was repeated as a command.

The captain and two of his shotgun boys marched through the crowd of prisoners. Marched up to Kevin.

"You!" yelled the captain. "Let's go!"

"Me?" said Kevin as the shotguns swung his way. "Hey! What's this shit? I didn't do anything! I didn't do anything!"

And as the guards hustled him away to pack his personal gear, the yard watched.

Higgins nodded to Lucus, went home to his family.

The Klaxon sounded *"Return to cells."* Shotguns on the yard watched everybody shuffling back inside.

J.C. was lost in the crowd.

For a heartbeat, Lucus glimpsed Jerome and the O.T. posse.

Roll up on that boy next yard time, thought Lucus. *Brace him, but let him back down. His posse won't be so hot to dance with me, and he'll know it. The Word will advise him to keep his cool: The chump he wanted ain't around no more, the beef is over, and a respected, evil dude like me . . . Word is, don't mess with Lucus.*

Walking beside Lucus, like he was reading the man's mind, H.L.S. said: "What about our spy boy Darnell?"

"Oh, I'll think of something for Jackster."

"Hard luck," said Sam.

As they strolled to the tunnel, other dudes kept a respectful distance from the two old cons.

Sam said: "I gots to know. Just exactly what did you tell Twitch to make him drop the blade and climb down from there?"

Lucus whispered: "Same thing I said to make him grab the guard in the first place."

THE DEAD THEIR EYES IMPLORE US

BY GEORGE PELECANOS

Chinatown

(Originally published in 2002)

S omeday I'm gonna write all this down. But I don't write so good in English yet, see? So I'm just gonna think it out loud.

Last night I had a dream.

In my dream, I was a kid, back in the village. My friends and family from the *chorio*, they were there, all of us standing around the square. My father, he had strung a lamb up on a pole. It was making a noise, like a scream, and its eyes were wild and afraid. My father handed me my Italian switch knife, the one he gave me before I came over. I cut into the lamb's throat and opened it up wide. The lamb's warm blood spilled onto my hands.

My mother told me once: Every time you dream something, it's got to be a reason.

I'm not no kid anymore. I'm twenty-eight years old. It's early in June, 1933. The temperature got up to one hundred degrees today. I read in the *Tribune*, some old people died from the heat.

Let me try to paint a picture, so you can see in your head the way it is for me right now. I got this little one-room place I rent from some old lady. A Murphy bed and a table, an icebox and a stove. I got a radio I bought for a dollar and ninety-nine. I wash my clothes in a tub, and afterwards I hang the *roocha* on a cord I stretched across the room. There's a bunch of clothes—*pantalonia* and one of my work shirts and my *vrakia* and socks—on there now. I'm sitting here at the table in my union suit. I'm smoking a Fatima and drinking a cold bottle of Abner-Drury beer. I'm looking at my hands. I got blood underneath my fingernails. I washed real good but it was hard to get it all.

It's 5, 5:30 in the morning. Let me go back some, to show how I got to where I am tonight.

What's it been, four years since I came over? The boat ride was a boat ride so I'll skip that part. I'll start in America.

When I got to Ellis Island I came straight down to Washington to stay with my cousin Toula and her husband Aris. Aris had a fruit cart down on Pennsylvania Avenue, around 17th. Toula's father owed my father some *lefta* from back in the village, so it was all set up. She offered me a room until I could get on my feet. Aris wasn't happy about it but I didn't give a good goddamn what he was happy about. Toula's father should have paid his debt.

Toula and Aris had a place in Chinatown. It wasn't just for Chinese. Italians, Irish, Polacks, and Greeks lived there too. Everyone was poor except the criminals. The Chinamen controlled the gambling, the whores, and the opium. All the business got done in the back of laundries and in the restaurants. The Chinks didn't bother no one if they didn't get bothered themselves.

Toula's apartment was in a house right on H Street. You had to walk up three floors to get to it. I didn't mind it. The milkman did it every day and the old Jew who collected the rent managed to do it too. I figured, so could I.

My room was small, so small you couldn't shut the door all the way when the bed was down. There was only one toilet in the place, and they had put a curtain by it, the kind you hang on a shower. You had to close it around you when you wanted to shit. Like I say, it wasn't a nice place or nothing like it, but it was okay. It was free.

But nothing's free, my father always said. Toula's husband Aris made me pay from the first day I moved in. Never had a good word to say to me, never mentioned me to no one for a job. He was a sonofabitch, that one. Dark, with a hook in his nose, looked like he had some Turkish blood in him. I wouldn't be surprised if the *gamoto* was a Turk. I didn't like the way he talked to my cousin either, 'specially when he drank. And this *malaka* drank every night. I'd sit in my room and listen to him raise his voice at her, and then later I could hear him fucking her on their bed. I couldn't stand it, I'm telling you, and me without a woman myself. I didn't have no job then so I couldn't even buy a whore. I thought I was gonna go nuts.

Then one day I was talking to this guy, Dimitri Karras, who lived in the 606 building on H. He told me about a janitor's job opened up at St. Mary's, the church where his son Panayoti and most of the neighborhood kids went to Catholic school. I put some Wildroot tonic in my hair, walked over to the church, and talked to the head nun. I don't know, she musta liked me or something, cause I got the job. I had to lie a little about being a handyman. I wasn't no engineer, but I figured, what the hell, the furnace goes out you light it again, goddamn.

My deal was simple. I got a room in the basement and a coupla meals a day. Pennies other than that, but I didn't mind, not then. Hell, it was better than living in some Hoover Hotel. And it got me away from that bastard Aris. Toula cried when I left, so I gave her a hug. I didn't say nothing to Aris.

I worked at St. Mary's about two years. The work was never hard. I knew the kids and most of their fathers: Karras, Angelos, Nicodemus, Recevo, Damiano, Carchedi. I watched the boys grow. I didn't look the nuns in the eyes when I talked to them so they wouldn't get the wrong idea. Once or twice I treated myself to one of the whores over at the Eastern House. Mostly, down in the basement, I played with my *pootso*. I put it out of my mind that I was jerking off in church.

Meanwhile, I tried to make myself better. I took English classes at St. Sophia, the Greek Orthodox church on 8th and L. I bought a blue serge suit at Harry Kaufman's on 7th Street, on sale for eleven dollars and seventy-five cents. The Jew tailor let me pay for it a little bit at a time. Now, when I went to St. Sophia for the Sunday service, I wouldn't be ashamed.

I liked to go to church. Not for religion, nothing like that. Sure, I wear a *stavro*, but everyone wears a cross. That's just superstition. I don't love God, but I'm afraid of him. So I went to church just in case, and also to look at the girls. I liked to see 'em all dressed up.

There was this one *koritsi*, not older than sixteen when I first saw her, who was special. I knew just where she was gonna be, with her mother, on the side of the church where the women sat separate from the men. I made sure I got a good view of her on Sundays. Her name was Irene, I asked around. I could tell she was clean. By that I mean she was a virgin. That's the kind of girl you're gonna marry. My plan was to wait till I got some money in my pocket before I talked to her, but not too long so she got snatched up. A girl like that is not gonna stay single forever.

Work and church was for the daytime. At night I went to the coffeehouses down by the Navy Yard in Southeast. One of them was owned by a hardworking guy from the neighborhood, Angelos, who lived at the 703 building on 6th. That's the *cafeneion* I went to most. You played cards and dice there if that's what you wanted to do, but mostly you could be yourself. It was all Greeks.

That's where I met Nick Stefanos one night, at the Angelos place. Meeting him is what put another change in my life. Stefanos was a Spartan with an easy way, had a scar on his cheek. You knew he was tough but he didn't have to prove it. I heard he got the scar running protection for a hooch truck in upstate New York. Heard a cheap *pistola* blew up in his face. It was his business, what happened, none of mine.

We got to talking that night. He was the head busman down at some fancy hotel on 15th and Penn, but he was leaving to open his own place. His friend Costa, another *Spartiati*, worked there and he was gonna leave with him. Stefanos asked me if I wanted to take Costa's place. He said he could set it up. The pay was only a little more than what I was making, a dollar-fifty a week with extras, but a little more was a lot. Hell, I wanted to make better like anyone else. I thanked Nick Stefanos and asked him when I could start.

I started the next week, soon as I got my room where I am now. You had to pay management for your bus uniform— black pants and a white shirt and short black vest—so I didn't make nothing for a while. Some of the waiters tipped the busmen heavy, and some tipped nothing at all. For the ones who tipped nothing you cleared their tables slower, and last. I caught on quick.

The hotel was pretty fancy and its dining room, up on the top floor, was fancy too. The china was real, the crystal sang when you flicked a finger at it, and the silver was heavy. It was hard times, but you'd never know it from the way the tables filled up at night. I figured I'd stay there a coupla years, learn the operation, and go out on my own like Stefanos. That was one smart guy.

The way they had it set up was, Americans had the waiter jobs, and the Greeks and Filipinos bused the tables. The coloreds, they stayed back in the kitchen. Everybody in the restaurant was in the same order that they were out on the street: the whites were up top and the Greeks were in the middle; the *mavri* were at the bottom. Except if someone was your own kind, you didn't make much small talk with the other guys unless it had something to do with work. I didn't have nothing against anyone, not even the coloreds. You didn't talk to them, that's all. That's just the way it was.

The waiters, they thought they were better than the rest of us. But there was this one American, a young guy named John Petersen, who was all right. Petersen had brown eyes and wavy brown hair that he wore kinda long. It was his eyes that you remembered. Smart and serious, but gentle at the same time.

Petersen was different than the other waiters, who wouldn't lift a finger to help you even when they weren't busy. John would pitch in and bus my tables for me when I got in a jam. He'd jump in with the dishes too, back in the kitchen, when the dining room was running low on silver, and like I say, those were coloreds back there. I even saw him talking with those guys sometimes like they were pals. It was like he came from someplace where that was okay. John was just one of those people who made friends easy, I guess. I can't think of no one who didn't like him. Well, there musta been one person, at least. I'm gonna come to that later on.

Me and John went out for a beer one night after work, to a saloon he knew. I wasn't comfortable because it was all Americans and I didn't see no one who looked like me. But John made me feel okay and after two beers I forgot. He talked to me about the job and the pennies me and the colored guys in the kitchen were making, and how it wasn't right. He talked about some changes that were coming to make it better for us, but he didn't say what they were.

"I'm happy," I said, as I drank off the beer in my mug. "I got a job, what the hell."

"You want to make more money, don't you?" he said. "You'd like to have a day off once in a while, wouldn't you?"

"Goddamn right. But I take off a day, I'm not gonna get paid."

"It doesn't have to be like that, friend."

"Yeah, okay."

"Do you know what 'strength in numbers' means?"

I looked around for the bartender cause I didn't know what the hell John was talking about and I didn't know what to say.

John put his hand around my arm. "I'm putting together a meeting. I'm hoping some of the busmen and the kitchen guys will make it. Do you think you can come?"

"What we gonna meet for, huh?"

"We're going to talk about those changes I been telling you about. Together, we're going to make a plan."

"I don't want to go to no meeting. I want a day off, I'm just gonna go ask for it, eh?"

"You don't understand." John put his face close to mine. "The workers are being exploited."

"I work and they pay me," I said with a shrug. "That's all I know. Other than that? I don't give a damn about nothing." I pulled my arm away but I smiled when I did it. I didn't want to join no group, but I wanted him to know we were still pals. "C'mon, John, let's drink."

I needed that job. But I felt bad, turning him down about that meeting. You could see it meant something to him, whatever the hell he was talking about, and I liked him. He was the only American in the restaurant who treated me like we were both the same. You know, man to man.

Well, he wasn't the only American who made me feel like a man. There was this woman, name of Laura, a hostess who also made change from the bills. She bought her dresses too small and had hair bleached white, like Jean Harlow. She was about two years and ten pounds away from the end of her looks. Laura wasn't pretty but her ass could bring tears to your eyes. Also, she had huge tits.

I caught her giving me the eye the first night I worked there. By the third night she said something to me about my broad chest as I was walking by her. I nodded and smiled, but I kept walking cause I was carrying a heavy tray. When I looked back she gave me a wink. She was a real whore, that one. I knew right then I was gonna fuck her. At the end of the night I asked her if she would go to the pictures with me sometime. "I'm free tomorrow," she says. I acted like it was an honor and a big surprise.

I worked every night, so we had to make it a matinee. We took the streetcar down to the Earle, on 13th Street, down below F. I wore my blue serge suit and high button shoes. I looked like I had a little bit of money, but we still got the fisheye, walking down the street. A blonde and a Greek with dark skin and a heavy black moustache. I couldn't hide that I wasn't too long off the boat.

The Earle had a stage show before the picture. A guy named William Demarest and some dancers who Laura said were like the Rockettes. What the hell did I know, I was just looking at their legs. After the coming attractions and the short subject the picture came on: *Gold Diggers of 1933*. The man dancers looked like cocksuckers to me. I liked Westerns better, but it was all right. Fifteen cents for each of us. It was cheaper than taking her to a saloon.

Afterwards, we went to her place, an apartment in a rowhouse off H in Northeast. I used the bathroom and saw a Barnards Shaving Cream and other man things in there, but I didn't ask her nothing about it when I came back out. I found her in the bedroom. She had poured us a couple of rye whiskies and drawn the curtains so it felt like the night. A radio played something she called "jug band"; it sounded like colored music to me. She asked me, did I want to dance. I shrugged and tossed back all the rye in my glass and pulled her to me rough. We moved slow, even though the music was fast.

"Bill?" she said, looking up at me. She had painted her eyes with something and there was a black mark next to one of them where the paint had come off.

"Uh," I said.

"What do they call you where you're from?"

"Vasili."

I kissed her warm lips. She bit mine and drew a little blood. I pushed myself against her to let her know what I had.

"Why, Va-silly," she said. "You are like a horse, aren't you?"

I just kinda nodded and smiled. She stepped back and got out of her dress and her slip, and then undid her brassiere. She did it slow.

"*Ella*," I said.

"What does that mean?"

"Hurry it up," I said, with a little motion of my hand. Laura laughed.

She pulled the bra off and her tits bounced. They were

everything I thought they would be. She came to me and un-buckled my belt, pulling at it clumsy, and her breath was hot on my face. By then, God, I was ready.

I sat her on the edge of the bed, put one of her legs up on my shoulder, and gave it to her. I heard a woman having a baby in the village once, and those were the same kinda sounds that Laura made. There was spit dripping out the side of her mouth as I slammed myself into her over and over again. I'm telling you, her bed took some plaster off the wall that day.

After I blew my load into her I climbed off. I didn't say nice things to her or nothing like that. She got what she wanted and so did I. Laura smoked a cigarette and watched me get dressed. The whole room smelled like pussy. She didn't look so good to me no more. I couldn't wait to get out of there and breathe fresh air.

We didn't see each other again outside of work. She only stayed at the restaurant a coupla more weeks, and then she disappeared. I guess the man who owned the shaving cream told her it was time to quit.

For a while there nothing happened and I just kept work-ing hard. John didn't mention no meetings again, though he was just as nice as before. I slept late and bused the tables at night. Life wasn't fun or bad. It was just ordinary. Then that bastard Wesley Schmidt came to work and everything changed.

Schmidt was a tall young guy with a thin moustache, big in the shoulders, big hands. He kept his hair slicked back. His eyes were real blue, like water under ice. He had a row of big straight teeth. He smiled all the time, but the smile, it didn't make you feel good.

Schmidt got hired as a waiter, but he wasn't any good at

it. He got tangled up fast when the place got busy. He served food to the wrong tables all the time, and he spilled plenty of drinks. It didn't seem like he'd ever done that kind of work before.

No one liked him, but he was one of those guys, he didn't know it, or maybe he knew and didn't care. He laughed and told jokes and slapped the busmen on the back like we were his friends. He treated the kitchen guys like dogs when he was tangled up, raising his voice at them when the food didn't come up as fast as he liked it. Then he tried to be nice to them later.

One time he really screamed at Raymond, the head cook on the line, called him a "lazy shine" on this night when the place was packed. When the dining room cleared up, Schmidt walked back into the kitchen and told Raymond in a soft voice that he didn't mean nothing by it, giving him that smile of his and patting his arm. Raymond just nodded real slow. Schmidt told me later, "That's all you got to do, is scold 'em and then talk real sweet to 'em later. That's how they learn. Cause they're like children. Right, Bill?" He meant coloreds, I guess. By the way he talked to me, real slow the way you would to a kid, I could tell he thought I was a colored guy too.

At the end of the night the waiters always sat in the dining room and ate a stew or something that the kitchen had prepared. The busmen, we served it to the waiters. I was running dinner out to one of them and forgot something back in the kitchen. When I went back to get it, I saw Raymond spitting into a plate of stew. The other colored guys in the kitchen were standing in a circle around Raymond, watching him do it. They all looked over at me when I walked in. It was real quiet and I guess they were waiting to see what I was gonna do.

"Who's that for?" I said. "Eh?"

"Schmidt," said Raymond.

I walked over to where they were. I brought up a bunch of stuff from deep down in my throat and spit real good into that plate. Raymond put a spoon in the stew and stirred it up.

"I better take it out to him," I said, "before it gets cold."

"Don't forget the garnish," said Raymond.

He put a flower of parsley on the plate, turning it a little so it looked nice. I took the stew out and served it to Schmidt. I watched him take the first bite and nod his head like it was good. None of the colored guys said nothing to me about it again.

I got drunk with John Petersen in a saloon a coupla nights after and told him what I'd done. I thought he'd get a good laugh out of it, but instead he got serious. He put his hand on my arm the way he did when he wanted me to listen.

"Stay out of Schmidt's way," said John.

"Ah," I said, with a wave of my hand. "He gives me any trouble, I'm gonna punch him in the kisser." The beer was making me brave.

"Just stay out of his way."

"I look afraid to you?"

"I'm telling you, Schmidt is no waiter."

"I know it. He's the worst goddamn waiter I ever seen. Maybe you ought to have one of those meetings of yours and see if you can get him thrown out."

"Don't ever mention those meetings again, to anyone," said John, and he squeezed my arm tight. I tried to pull it away from him but he held his grip. "Bill, do you know what a Pinkerton man is?"

"What the hell?"

"Never mind. You just keep to yourself, and don't talk about those meetings, hear?"

I had to look away from his eyes. "Sure, sure."

"Okay, friend." John let go of my arm. "Let's have another beer."

A week later John Petersen didn't show up for work. And a week after that the cops found him floating downriver in the Potomac. I read about it in the *Tribune*. It was just a short notice, and it didn't say nothing else.

A cop in a suit came to the restaurant and asked us some questions. A couple of the waiters said that John probably had some bad hooch and fell into the drink. I didn't know what to think. When it got around to the rest of the crew, everyone kinda got quiet, if you know what I mean. Even that bastard Wesley didn't make no jokes. I guess we were all thinking about John in our own way. Me, I wanted to throw up. I'm telling you, thinking about John in that river, it made me sick.

John didn't ever talk about no family and nobody knew nothing about a funeral. After a few days, it seemed like everybody in the restaurant forgot about him. But me, I couldn't forget.

One night I walked into Chinatown. It wasn't far from my new place. There was this kid from St. Mary's, Billy Nicodemus, whose father worked at the city morgue. Nicodemus wasn't no doctor or nothing, he washed off the slabs and cleaned the place, like that. He was known as a hard drinker, maybe because of what he saw every day, and maybe just because he liked the taste. I knew where he liked to drink.

I found him in a no-name restaurant on the Hip-Sing side of Chinatown. He was in a booth by himself, drinking something from a teacup. I crossed the room, walking through the cigarette smoke, passing the whores and the skinny Chink gangsters in their too-big suits and the cops who were taking money from the Chinks to look the other way. I stood over

Nicodemus and told him who I was. I told him I knew his kid, told him his kid was good. Nicodemus motioned for me to have a seat.

A waiter brought me an empty cup. I poured myself some gin from the teapot on the table. We tapped cups and drank. Nicodemus had straight black hair wetted down and a big mole with hair coming out of it on one of his cheeks. He talked better than I did. We said some things that were about nothing and then I asked him some questions about John. The gin had loosened his tongue.

"Yeah, I remember him," said Nicodemus, after thinking about it for a short while. He gave me the once-over and leaned forward. "This was your friend?"

"Yes."

"They found a bullet in the back of his head. A twenty-two."

I nodded and turned the teacup in small circles on the table. "The *Tribune* didn't say nothing about that."

"The papers don't always say. The police cover it up while they look for who did it. But that boy didn't drown. He was murdered first, then dropped in the drink."

"You saw him?" I said.

Nicodemus shrugged. "Sure."

"What'd he look like?"

"You really wanna know?"

"Yeah."

"He was all gray and blown up, like a balloon. The gas does that to 'em, when they been in the water."

"What about his eyes?"

"They were open. Pleading."

"Huh?"

"His eyes. It was like they were sayin' please."

I needed a drink. I had some more gin.

"You ever heard of a Pinkerton man?" I said.

"Sure," said Nicodemus. "A detective."

"Like the police?"

"No."

"*What*, then?"

"They go to work with other guys and pretend they're one of them. They find out who's stealing. Or they find out who's trying to make trouble for the boss. Like the ones who want to make a strike."

"You mean, like, if a guy wants to get the workers together and make things better?"

"Yeah. Have meetings and all that. The guys who want to start a union. Pinkertons look for those guys."

We drank the rest of the gin. We talked about his kid. We talked about Schmeling and Baer, and the wrestling match that was coming up between Londos and George Zaharias at Griffith Stadium. I got up from my seat, shook Nicodemus's hand, and thanked him for the conversation.

"*Efcharisto, patrioti.*"

"*Yasou, Vasili.*"

I walked back to my place and had a beer I didn't need. I was drunk and more confused than I had been before. I kept hearing John's voice, the way he called me "friend." I saw his eyes saying please. I kept thinking, I should have gone to his goddamn meeting, if that was gonna make him happy. I kept thinking I had let him down. While I was thinking, I sharpened the blade of my Italian switch knife on a stone.

The next night, last night, I was serving Wesley Schmidt his dinner after we closed. He was sitting by himself like he always did. I dropped the plate down in front of him.

"You got a minute to talk?" I asked.

"Go ahead and talk," he said, putting the spoon to his stew and stirring it around.

"I wanna be a Pinkerton man," I said.

Schmidt stopped stirring his stew and looked up my way. He smiled, showing me his white teeth. Still, his eyes were cold.

"That's nice. But why are you telling me this?"

"I wanna be a Pinkerton, just like you."

Schmidt pushed his stew plate away from him and looked around the dining room to make sure no one could hear us. He studied my face. I guess I was sweating. Hell, I *know* I was. I could feel it dripping on my back.

"You look upset," said Schmidt, his voice real soft, like music. "You look like you could use a friend."

"I just wanna talk."

"Okay. You feel like having a beer, something like that?"

"Sure, I could use a beer."

"I finish eating, I'll go down and get my car. I'll meet you in the alley out back. Don't tell anyone, hear, because then they might want to come along. And we wouldn't have the chance to talk."

"I'm not gonna tell no one. We just drive around, eh? I'm too dirty to go to a saloon."

"That's swell," said Schmidt. "We'll just drive around."

I went out to the alley where Schmidt was parked. Nobody saw me get into his car. It was a blue '31 Dodge coupe with wire wheels, a rumble seat, and a trunk rack. A five-hundred-dollar car if it was dime.

"Pretty," I said, as I got in beside him. There were hand-tailored slipcovers on the seats.

"I like nice things," said Schmidt.

He was wearing his suit jacket, and it had to be eighty

degrees. I could see a lump under the jacket. I figured, the bastard is carrying a gun.

We drove up to Colvin's, on 14th Street. Schmidt went in and returned with a bag of loose bottles of beer. There must have been a half-dozen Schlitz's in the bag. Him making waiter's pay, and the fancy car and the high-priced beer.

He opened a coupla beers and handed me one. The bottle was ice cold. Hot as the night was, the beer tasted good.

We drove around for a while. We went down to Hains Point. Schmidt parked the Dodge facing the Washington Channel. Across the channel, the lights from the fish vendors on Maine Avenue threw color on the water. We drank another beer. He gave me one of his tailor-mades and we had a couple smokes. He talked about the Senators and the Yankees, and how Baer had taken Schmeling out with a right in the tenth. Schmidt didn't want to talk about nothing serious yet. He was waiting for the beer to work on me, I knew.

"Goddamn heat," I said. "Let's drive around some, get some air moving."

Schmidt started the coupe. "Where to?"

"I'm gonna show you a whorehouse. Best secret in town."

Schmidt looked me over and laughed. The way you laugh at a clown.

I gave Schmidt some directions. We drove some, away from the park and the monuments to where people lived. We went through a little tunnel and crossed into Southwest. Most of the streetlamps were broke here. The row houses were shabby, and you could see shacks in the alleys and clothes hanging on lines outside of them. It was late, long time past midnight. There weren't many people out. The ones who were out were coloreds. We were in a place called Bloodfield.

"Pull over there," I said, pointing to a spot along the curb where there wasn't no light. "I wanna show you the place I'm talking about."

Schmidt stopped and cut the engine. Across the street were some houses. All except one of them was dark. From the lighted one came fast music, like the colored music Laura had played in her room.

"There it is right there," I said, meaning the house with the light. I was lying through my teeth. I didn't know who lived there and I sure didn't know if that house had whores. I had never been down here before.

Schmidt turned his head to look at the row house. I slipped my switch knife out of my right pocket and laid it flat against my right leg.

When he turned back to face me he wasn't smiling no more. He had heard about Bloodfield and he knew he was in it. I think he was scared.

"You bring me down to niggertown for *what*?" he said. "To show me a whorehouse?"

"I thought you're gonna like it."

"Do I look like a man who'd pay to fuck a nigger? *Do* I? You don't know anything about me."

He was showing his true self now. He was nervous as a cat. My nerves were bad too. I was sweating through my shirt. I could smell my own stink in the car.

"I know plenty," I said.

"Yeah? *What* do you know?"

"Pretty car, pretty suits . . . top-shelf beer. How you get all this, huh?"

"I earned it."

"As a Pinkerton, eh?"

Schmidt blinked real slow and shook his head. He looked out his window, looking at nothing, wasting time while he decided what he was gonna do. I found the raised button on the pearl handle of my knife. I pushed the button. The blade flicked open and barely made a sound. I held the knife against my leg and turned it so the blade was pointing back.

Sweat rolled down my neck as I looked around. There wasn't nobody out on the street.

Schmidt turned his head. He gripped the steering wheel with his right hand and straightened his arm.

"What do you want?" he said.

"I just wanna know what happened to John."

Schmidt smiled. All those white teeth. I could see him with his mouth open, his lips stretched, those teeth showing. The way an animal looks after you kill it. Him lying on his back on a slab.

"I heard he drowned," said Schmidt.

"You think so, eh?"

"Yeah. I guess he couldn't swim."

"Pretty hard to swim, you got a bullet in your head."

Schmidt's smile turned down. "Can *you* swim, Bill?"

I brought the knife across real fast and buried it into his armpit. I sunk the blade all the way to the handle. He lost his breath and made a short scream. I twisted the knife. His blood came out like someone was pouring it from a jug. It was warm and it splashed onto my hands. I pulled the knife out and while he was kicking at the floorboards I stabbed him a coupla more times in the chest. I musta hit his heart or something because all of a sudden there was plenty of blood all over the car. I'm telling you, the seats were slippery with it. He stopped moving. His eyes were open and they were dead.

I didn't get tangled up about it or nothing like that. I wasn't scared. I opened up his suit jacket and saw a steel revolver with wood grips holstered there. It was small caliber. I didn't touch the gun. I took his wallet out of his trousers, pulled the bills out of it, wiped it off with my shirttail, and threw the empty wallet on the ground. I put the money in my shoe. I fit the blade back into the handle of my switch knife and slipped the knife into my pocket. I put all the empty beer bottles together with the full ones in the paper bag and took it with me as I got out of the car. I closed the door soft and wiped off the handle and walked down the street.

I didn't see no one for a coupla blocks. I came to a sewer and I put the bag down the hole. The next block I came to another sewer and I took off my bloody shirt and threw it down the hole of that one. I was wearing an undershirt, didn't have no sleeves. My pants were black so you couldn't see the blood. I kept walking toward Northwest.

Someone laughed from deep in an alley and I kept on.

Another block or so I came up on a group of *mavri* standing around the steps of a house. They were smoking cigarettes and drinking from bottles of beer. I wasn't gonna run or nothing. I had to go by them to get home. They stopped talking and gave me hard eyes as I got near them. That's when I saw that one of them was the cook, Raymond, from the kitchen. Our eyes kind of came together but neither one of us said a word or smiled or even made a nod.

One of the coloreds started to come toward me and Raymond stopped him with the flat of his palm. I walked on.

I walked for a coupla hours, I guess. Somewhere in Northwest I dropped my switch knife down another sewer. When I heard it hit the sewer bottom I started to cry. I wasn't crying cause I had killed Schmidt. I didn't give a damn nothing about him. I was crying cause my father had given me that knife, and now it was gone. I guess I knew I was gonna be in

America forever, and I wasn't never going back to Greece. I'd never see my home or my parents again.

When I got back to my place I washed my hands real good. I opened up a bottle of Abner-Drury and put fire to a Fatima and had myself a seat at the table.

This is where I am right now.

Maybe I'm gonna get caught and maybe I'm not. They're gonna find Schmidt in that neighborhood and they're gonna figure a colored guy killed him for his money. The cops, they're gonna turn Bloodfield upside down. If Raymond tells them he saw me I'm gonna get the chair. If he doesn't, I'm gonna be free. Either way, what the hell, I can't do nothing about it now.

I'll work at the hotel, get some experience and some money, then open my own place, like Nick Stefanos. Maybe if I can find two nickels to rub together, I'm gonna go to church and talk to that girl, Irene, see if she wants to be my wife. I'm not gonna wait too long. She's clean as a whistle, that one.

I've had my eye on her for some time.

A RICH MAN

BY EDWARD P. JONES

Claridge Towers

(Originally published in 2003)

Horace and Loneese Perkins—one child, one grand-child—lived most unhappily together for more than twelve years in Apartment 230 at Claridge Towers, a building for senior citizens at 1221 M Street, N.W. They moved there in 1977, the year they celebrated forty years of marriage, the year they made love for the last time—Loneese kept a diary of sorts, and that fact was noted on one day of a week when she noted nothing else. "He touched me," she wrote, which had always been her diary euphemism for sex. That was also the year they retired, she as a pool secretary at the Commerce Department, where she had known one lover, and he as a civilian employee at the Pentagon, as the head of veteran records.

He had been an army sergeant for ten years before be-coming head of records; the secretary of defense gave him a plaque as big as his chest on the day he retired, and he and the secretary of defense and Loneese had their picture taken, a picture that hung for all those twelve years in the living room of Apartment 230, on the wall just to the right of the heating-and-air-conditioning unit.

A month before they moved in, they drove in their burgundy-and-gold Cadillac from their small house on Chesa-peake Street in Southeast to a Union Station restaurant and promised each other that Claridge Towers would be a new beginning for them. Over blackened catfish and a peach cobbler that they both agreed could have been better, they vowed to devote themselves to each other and become even better grandparents. Horace had long known about the Commerce Department lover. Loneese had told him about the man two months after she had ended the relationship, in 1969. "He worked in the mail room," she told her husband over a spaghetti supper she had cooked in the Chesapeake Street home. "He touched me in the motel room," she wrote in her diary, "and after it was over he begged me to go away to Florida with him. All I could think about was that Florida was for old people."

At that spaghetti supper, Horace did not mention the dozens of lovers he had had in his time as her husband. She knew there had been many, knew it because they were written on his face in the early years of their marriage, and because he had never bothered to hide what he was doing in the later years. "I be back in a while. I got some business to do," he would say. He did not even mention the lover he had slept with just the day before the spaghetti supper, the one he bid good-bye to with a "Be good and be sweet" after telling her he planned to become a new man and respect his marriage vows. The woman, a thin school-bus driver with clanking bracelets up to her elbows on both arms, snorted a laugh, which made Horace want to slap her, because he was used to people taking him seriously. "Forget you, then," Horace said on the way out the door. "I was just tryin to let you down easy."

Over another spaghetti supper two weeks before moving, they reiterated what had been said at the blackened-catfish supper and did the dishes together and went to bed as man and wife, and over the next days sold almost all the Chesapeake

Street furniture. What they kept belonged primarily to Horace, starting with a collection of six hundred and thirty-nine record albums, many of them his "sweet babies," the 78s. If a band worth anything had recorded between 1915 and 1950, he bragged, he had the record; after 1950, he said, the bands got sloppy and he had to back away. Horace also kept the Cadillac he had painted to honor a football team, paid to park the car in the underground garage. Claridge Towers had once been intended as a luxury place, but the builders, two friends of the city commissioners, ran out of money in the middle and the commissioners had the city government people buy it off them. The city government people completed Claridge, with its tiny rooms, and then, after one commissioner gave a speech in Southwest about looking out for old people, some city government people in Northeast came up with the idea that old people might like to live in Claridge, in Northwest.

Three weeks after Horace and Loneese moved in, Horace went down to the lobby one Saturday afternoon to get their mail and happened to see Clara Knightley getting her mail. She lived in Apartment 512. "You got this fixed up real nice," Horace said of Apartment 512 a little less than an hour after meeting her. "But I could see just in the way that you carry yourself that you got good taste. I could tell that about you right off." "You swellin my head with all that talk, Mr. Perkins," Clara said, offering him coffee, which he rejected, because such moments always called for something stronger. "Whas a woman's head for if a man can't swell it up from time to time. Huh? Answer me that, Clara. You just answer me that." Clara was fifty-five, a bit younger than most of the residents of Claridge, though she was much older than all Horace's other lovers. She did not fit the city government people's definition of a senior citizen, but she had a host of ailments, from high blood pressure to diabetes, and so the city people had let her in.

Despite the promises, the marriage, what little there had been of it, came to an end. "I will make myself happy," Loneese told the diary a month after he last touched her. Loneese and Horace had fixed up their apartment nicely, and neither of them wanted to give the place up to the other. She wanted to make a final stand with the man who had given her so much heartache, the man who had told her, six months after her confession, what a whore she had been to sleep with the Commerce Department mail-room man. Horace, at sixty, had never thought much of women over fifty, but Clara—and, after her, Willa, of Apartment 1001, and Miriam, of Apartment 109—had awakened something in him, and he began to think that women over fifty weren't such a bad deal after all. Claridge Towers had dozens of such women, many of them attractive widows, many of them eager for a kind word from a retired army sergeant who had so many medals and ribbons that his uniform could not carry them. As far as he could see, he was cock of the walk: many of the men in Claridge suffered from diseases that Horace had so far escaped, or they were not as good-looking or as thin, or they were encumbered by wives they loved. In Claridge he was a rich man. So why move and give that whore the satisfaction?

They lived separate lives in a space that was only a fourth as large as the Chesapeake Street house. The building came to know them as the man and wife in 230 who couldn't stand each other. People talked about the Perkinses more than they did about anyone else, which was particularly upsetting to Loneese, who had been raised to believe family business should stay in the family. "Oh, Lord, what them two been up to now?" "Fight like cats and dogs, they do." "Who he seein now?" They each bought their own food from the Richfood on 11th Street or from the little store on 13th Street, and they could be vile to each other if what one bought was disturbed or eaten by the other. Loneese stopped speaking to Horace for nine months in 1984 and 1985, when she saw that her pumpkin pie was a bit smaller than when she last cut a slice from it. "I ain't touch your damn pie, you crazy woman," he said when she accused him. "How long you been married to me? You know I've never been partial to pumpkin pie." "That's fine for you to say, Horace, but why is some missing? You might not be partial to it, but I know you. I know you'll eat anything in a pinch. That's just your dirty nature." "My nature ain't no more dirty than yours."

After that, she bought a small icebox for the bedroom where she slept, though she continued to keep the larger items in the kitchen refrigerator. He bought a separate telephone, because he complained that she wasn't giving him his messages from his "associates." "I have never been a secretary for whores," she said, watching him set up an answering machine next to the Hide-A-Bed couch where he slept. "Oh, don't get me started bout whores. I'd say you wrote the damn book." "It was dictated by you."

Their one child, Alonzo, lived with his wife and son in Baltimore. He had not been close to his parents for a long time, and he could not put the why of it into words for his wife. Their boy, Alonzo Jr., who was twelve when his grandparents moved into Claridge, loved to visit them. Horace would unplug and put away his telephone when the boy visited. And Loneese and Horace would sleep together in the bedroom. She'd put a pillow between them in the double bed to remind herself not to roll toward him.

Their grandson visited less and less as he moved into

his teenage years, and then, after he went away to college, in Ohio, he just called them every few weeks, on the phone they had had installed in the name of Horace and Loneese Perkins.

In 1987, Loneese's heart began the countdown to its last beat and she started spending more time at George Washington University Hospital than she did in the apartment. Horace never visited her. She died two years later. She woke up that last night in the hospital and went out into the hall and then to the nurses' station but could not find a nurse anywhere to tell her where she was or why she was there. "Why do the patients have to run this place alone?" she said to the walls. She returned to her room and it came to her why she was there. It was nearing three in the morning, but she called her own telephone first, then she dialed Horace's. He answered, but she never said a word. "Who's this playin on my phone?" Horace kept asking. "Who's this? I don't allow no playin on my phone." She hung up and lay down and said her prayers. After moving into Claridge, she had taken one more lover, a man at Vermont Avenue Baptist Church, where she went from time to time. He was retired, too. She wrote in her diary that he was not a big eater and that "down there, his vitals were missing."

Loneese Perkins was buried in a plot at Harmony Cemetery that she and Horace had bought when they were younger. There was a spot for Horace and there was one for their son, but Alonzo had long since made plans to be buried in a cemetery just outside Baltimore.

Horace kept the apartment more or less the way it was on the last day she was there. His son and daughter-in-law and grandson took some of her clothes to the Goodwill and the rest they gave to other women in the building. There were souvenirs from countries that Loneese and Horace had visited as man and wife—a Ghanaian carving of men surrounding a leopard they had killed, a brass menorah from Israel, a snow globe of Mount Fuji with some of the snow stuck forever to the top of the globe. They were things that did not mean very much to Alonzo, but he knew his child, and he knew that one day Alonzo Jr. would cherish them.

Horace tried sleeping in the bed, but he had been not unhappy in his twelve years on the Hide-A-Bed. He got rid of the bed and moved the couch into the bedroom and kept it open all the time.

He realized two things after Loneese's death: His own "vitals" had rejuvenated. He had never had the problems other men had, though he had failed a few times along the way, but that was to be expected. Now, as he moved closer to his seventy-third birthday, he felt himself becoming ever stronger, ever more potent. God is a strange one, he thought, sipping Chivas Regal one night before he went out: he takes a man's wife and gives him a new penis in her place.

The other thing he realized was that he was more and more attracted to younger women. When Loneese died, he had been keeping company with a woman of sixty-one, Sandy Carlin, in Apartment 907. One day in February, nine months after Loneese's death, one of Sandy's daughters, Jill, came to visit, along with one of Jill's friends, Elaine Cunningham. They were both twenty-five years old. From the moment they walked through Sandy's door, Horace began to compliment them—on their hair, the color of their fingernail polish, the sharp crease in Jill's pants ("You iron that yourself?"), even "that sophisticated way" Elaine crossed her legs. The young women giggled, which made him happy, pleased with himself, and Sandy sat in her place on the couch. As the ice in the Pepsi-Cola in her left hand melted, she realized all over again that God had never promised her a man until her dying day.

When the girls left, about three in the afternoon, Horace offered to accompany them downstairs, "to keep all them bad men away." In the lobby, as the security guard at her desk strained to hear, he made it known that he wouldn't mind if they came by to see him sometime. The women looked at each other and giggled some more. They had been planning to go to a club in Southwest that evening, but they were amused by the old man, by the way he had his rap together and put them on some sort of big pedestal and shit, as Jill would tell another friend weeks later. And when he saw how receptive they were he said why not come on up tonight, shucks, ain't no time like the present. Jill said he musta got that from a song, but he said no, he'd been sayin that since before they were born, and Elaine said thas the truth, and the women giggled again. He said I ain't gonna lie bout bein a seasoned man, and then he joined in the giggling. Jill looked at Elaine and said Want to? And Elaine said What about your mom? And Jill shrugged her shoulders and Elaine said Okay. She had just broken up with a man she had met at another club and needed something to make the pain go away until there was another man, maybe from a better club.

At about eleven-thirty, Jill wandered off into the night, her head liquored up, and Elaine stayed and got weepy—about the man from the not-so-good club, about the two abortions, about running away from home at seventeen after a fight with her father. "I just left him nappin on the couch," she said, stretched out on Horace's new living-room couch, her shoes off and one of Loneese's throws over her feet. Horace was in the chair across from her. "For all I know, he's still on that couch." Even before she got to her father, even before the abortions, he knew that he would sleep with her that night. He did not even need to fill her glass a third time. "He was a fat man," she said of her father. "And there ain't a whole lot more I remember."

"Listen," he said as she talked about her father, "everything's gonna work out right for you." He knew that, at such times in a seduction, the more positive a man was the better things went. It would not have done to tell her to forget her daddy, that she had done the right thing by running out on that fat so-and-so; it was best to focus on tomorrow and tell her that the world would be brighter in the morning. He came over to the couch, and before he sat down on the edge of the coffee table he hiked up his pants just a bit with his fingertips, and seeing him do that reminded her vaguely of something wonderful. The boys in the club sure didn't do it that way. He took her hand and kissed her palm. "Everything's gonna work out to the good," he said.

Elaine Cunningham woke in the morning with Horace sleeping quietly beside her. She did not rebuke herself and did not look over at him with horror at what she had done. She sighed and laid her head back on the pillow and thought how much she still loved the man from the club, but there was nothing more she could do: not even the five-hundred-dollar leather jacket she had purchased for the man had brought him around. Two years after running away, she had gone back to where she had lived with her parents, but they had moved and no one in the building knew where they had gone. But everyone remembered her. "You sure done growed up, Elaine," one old woman said. "I wouldna knowed if you hadn't told me who you was." "Fuck em," Elaine said to the friends who had given her a ride there. "Fuck em all to hell." Then, in the car, heading out to Capitol Heights, where she was staying, "Well, maybe not fuck my mother. She was good." "Just fuck your daddy then?" the girl in the backseat said. Elaine thought about it as they went down Rhode Island Avenue, and just before they turned onto New Jersey Avenue she said, "Yes, just fuck my daddy. The fat fuck."

She got out of Horace's bed and tried to wet the desert in her mouth as she looked in his closet for a bathrobe. She rejected the blue and the paisley ones for a dark green one that reminded her of something wonderful, just as Horace's hiking up his pants had. She smelled the sleeves once she had it on, but there was only the strong scent of detergent.

In the half room that passed for a kitchen, she stood and drank most of the orange juice in the gallon carton. "Now, that was stupid, girl," she said. "You know you shoulda drunk water. Better for the thirst." She returned the carton to the refrigerator and marveled at all the food. "Damn!" she said. With the refrigerator door still open, she stepped out into the living room and took note of all that Horace had, thinking, A girl could live large here if she did things right. She had been crashing at a friend's place in Northeast, and the friend's mother had begun to hint that it was time for her to move on. Even when she had a job, she rarely had a place of her own. "Hmm," she said, looking through the refrigerator for what she wanted to eat. "Boody for home and food. Food, home. Boody. You shoulda stayed in school, girl. They give courses on this. Food and Home the first semester. Boody Givin the second semester."

But, as she ate her eggs and bacon and Hungry Man biscuits, she knew that she did not want to sleep with Horace too many more times, even if he did have his little castle. He was too tall, and she had never been attracted to tall men, old or otherwise. "Damn! Why couldn't he be what I wanted and have a nice place, too?" Then, as she sopped up the last of the yolk with the last half of the last biscuit, she thought of her best friend, Catrina, the woman she was crashing with. Catrina Stockton was twenty-eight, and though she had once been a heroin addict, she was one year clean and had a face and a body that testified not to a woman who had lived a bad life on the streets but to a nice-looking Virginia woman who had married at seventeen, had had three children by a truck-driving husband, and had met a man in a Fredericksburg McDonald's who had said that women like her could be queens in D.C.

Yes, Elaine thought as she leaned over the couch and stared at the photograph of Horace and Loneese and the secretary of defense, Catrina was always saying how much she wanted love, how it didn't matter what a man looked like, as long as he was good to her and loved her morning, noon, and night. The secretary of defense was in the middle of the couple. She did not know who he was, just that she had seen him somewhere, maybe on the television. Horace was holding the plaque just to the left, away from the secretary. Elaine reached over and removed a spot of dust from the picture with her fingertip, and before she could flick it away, a woman said her name and she looked around, chilled.

She went into the bedroom to make sure that the voice had not been death telling her to check on Horace. She found him sitting up in the bed, yawning and stretching. "You sleep good, honey bunch?" he said. "I sure did, sweetie pie," she said and bounded across the room to hug him. A breakfast like the one she'd had would cost at least four dollars anywhere in D.C. or Maryland. "Oh, but Papa likes that," Horace said.

And even the cheapest motels out on New York Avenue, the ones catering to the junkies and prostitutes, charged at least twenty-five dollars a night. What's a hug compared with that? And, besides, she liked him more than she had thought, and the issue of Catrina and her moving in had to be done delicately. "Well, just let me give you a little bit mo, then."

Young stuff is young stuff, Horace thought the first time Elaine brought Catrina by and Catrina gave him a peck on the cheek and said, "I feel like I know you from all that Elaine told me." That was in early March.

In early April, Elaine met another man at a new club on F Street, N.W., and fell in love, and so did Horace with Catrina, though Catrina, after several years on the street, knew what she was feeling might be in the neighborhood of love but it was nowhere near the right house. She and Elaine told Horace the saddest of stories about the man Elaine had met in the club, and before the end of April he was sleeping on Horace's living-room floor. It helped that the man, Darnell Mudd, knew the way to anyone's heart, man or woman, and that he claimed to have a father who had been a hero in the Korean War. He even knew the name of the secretary of defense in the photograph and how long he had served in the Cabinet.

By the middle of May, there were as many as five other people, friends of the three young people, hanging out at any one time in Horace's place. He was giddy with Catrina, with the blunts, with the other women who snuck out with him to a room at the motel on 13th Street. By early June, more than a hundred of his old records had been stolen and pawned. "Leave his stuff alone," Elaine said to Darnell and his friends as they were going out the door with ten records apiece. "Don't

242 // D.C. Noir 2

take his stuff. He loves that stuff." It was eleven in the morning and everyone else in the apartment, including Horace, was asleep. "Shhh," Darnell said. "He got so many he won't notice." And that was true. Horace hadn't played records in many months. He had two swords that were originally on the wall opposite the heating-and-air-conditioning unit. Both had belonged to German officers killed in the Second World War. Horace, high on the blunts, liked to see the young men swordfight with them. But the next day, sober, he would hide them in the bottom of the closet, only to pull them out again when the partying started, at about four in the afternoon.

His neighbors, especially the neighbors who considered that Loneese had been the long-suffering one in the marriage, complained to the management about the noise, but the city government people read in his rental record that he had lost his wife not long ago and told the neighbors that he was probably doing some kind of grieving. The city government people never went above the first floor in Claridge. "He's a veteran who just lost his wife," they would say to those who came to the glass office on the first floor. "Why don't you cut him some slack?" But Horace tried to get a grip on things after a maintenance man told him to be careful. That was about the time one of the swords was broken and he could not for the life of him remember how it had happened. He just found it one afternoon in two pieces in the refrigerator's vegetable bin.

Things toned down a little, but the young women continued to come by and Horace went on being happy with them and with Catrina, who called him Papa and pretended to be upset when she saw him kissing another girl. "Papa, what am I gonna do with you and all your hussies?" "Papa, promise you'll only love me." "Papa, I need a new outfit. Help me out, willya please?"

Elaine had become pregnant not long after meeting Darnell, who told her to have the baby, that he had always wanted a son to carry on his name. "We can call him Junior," he said. "Or Little Darnell," she said. As she began showing, Horace and Catrina became increasingly concerned about her. Horace remembered how solicitous he had been when Loneese had been pregnant. He had not taken the first lover yet, had not even thought about anyone else as she grew and grew. He told Elaine no drugs or alcohol until the baby was born, and he tried to get her to go to bed at a decent hour, but that was often difficult with a small crowd in the living room.

Horace's grandson called in December, wanting to come by to see him, but Horace told him it would be best to meet someplace downtown, because his place was a mess. He didn't do much cleaning since Loneese died. "I don't care about that," Alonzo Jr. said. "Well, I do," Horace said. "You know how I can be bout these things."

In late December, Elaine gave birth to a boy, several weeks early. They gave him the middle name Horace. "See," Darnell said one day, holding the baby on the couch. "Thas your grandpa. You don't mind me callin you his granddad, Mr. Perkins? You don't mind, do you?" The city government people in the rental office, led by someone new, someone who took the rules seriously, took note that the old man in Apartment 230 had a baby and his mama and daddy in the place and not a single one of them was even related to him, though if one had been it still would have been against the rules as laid down in the rule book of apartment living.

By late February, an undercover policeman had bought two packets of crack from someone in the apartment. It was a woman, he told his superiors at first, and that's what he wrote in his report, but in a subsequent report he wrote that he had

bought the rocks from a man. "Start over," said one of his superiors, who supped monthly with the new mayor, who lived
for numbers, and in March the undercover man went back to
buy more.

It was late on a warm Saturday night in April when Elaine
woke to the crackle of walkie-talkies outside the door. She
had not seen Darnell in more than a month, and something
told her that she should get out of there because there might
not be any more good times. She thought of Horace and Catrina asleep in the bedroom. Two men and two women she
did not know very well were asleep in various places around
the living room, but she had dated the brother of one of the
women some three years ago. One of the men claimed to be
Darnell's cousin, and, to prove it to her, when he knocked
at the door that night he showed her a Polaroid of him and
Darnell at a club, their arms around each other and their eyes
red, because the camera had been cheap and the picture cost
only two dollars.

She got up from the couch and looked into the crib. In the
darkness she could make out that her son was awake, his little
legs kicking and no sound from him but a happy gurgle. The
sound of the walkie-talkie outside the door came and went.
She could see it all on the television news—"Drug-Dealing
Mama in Jail. Baby Put in Foster Care." She stepped over the
man who said he was Darnell's cousin and pushed the door
to the bedroom all the way open. Catrina was getting out of
bed. Horace was snoring. He had never snored before in his
life, but the drugs and alcohol together had done bad things
to his airway.

"You hear anything?" Elaine whispered as Catrina tiptoed
to her.

"I sure did," Catrina said. Sleeping on the streets required keeping one eye and both ears open. "I don't wanna go back to jail."

"Shit. Me neither," Elaine said. "What about the window?"

"Go out and down two floors? With a baby? Damn!"

"We can do it," Elaine said, looking over Catrina's shoulder to the dark lump that was Horace mumbling in his sleep. "What about him?"

Catrina turned her head. "He old. They ain't gonna do anything to him. I'm just worried bout makin it with that baby."

"Well, I sure as hell ain't gonna go without my child."

"I ain't said we was," Catrina hissed. "Down two floors just ain't gonna be easy, is all."

"We can do it," Elaine said.

"We can do it," Catrina said. She tiptoed to the chair at the foot of the bed and went through Horace's pants pockets. "Maybe fifty dollars here," she whispered after returning. "I already got about three hundred."

"You been stealin from him?" Elaine said. The lump in the bed turned over and moaned, then settled back to snoring.

"God helps them that helps themselves, Elaine. Les go." Catrina had her clothes in her hands and went on by Elaine, who watched as the lump in the bed turned again, snoring all the while. Bye, Horace. Bye. I be seein you.

The policeman in the unmarked car parked across 12th Street watched as Elaine stood on the edge of the balcony and jumped. She passed for a second in front of the feeble light over the entrance and landed on the sloping entrance of the underground parking garage. The policeman was five years from retirement and he did not move, because he could see quite well from where he sat. His partner, only three years on the job, was asleep in the passenger seat. The veteran thought the woman jumping might have hurt herself, because he did not see her rise from the ground for several minutes. I wouldn't do it, the man thought, not for all a rich man's money. The woman did rise, but before she did he saw another woman lean over the balcony dangling a bundle. Drugs? he thought. Nah. Clothes? Yeah, clothes more like it. The bundle was on a long rope or string—it was too far for the man to make out. The woman on the balcony leaned over very far and the woman on the ground reached up as far as she could, but still the bundle was a good two feet from her hands.

Just let them clothes drop, the policeman thought. Then Catrina released the bundle and Elaine caught it. Good catch. I wonder what she looks like in the light. Catrina jumped, and the policeman watched her pass momentarily in front of the light, and then he looked over at his partner. He himself didn't mind filling out the forms so much, but his partner did, so he let him sleep on. I'll be on a lake fishin my behind off and you'll still be doin this. When he looked back, the first woman was coming up the slope of the entrance with the bundle in her arms and the second one was limping after her. I wonder what that one looks like in a good light. Once on the sidewalk, both women looked left, then right, and headed down 12th Street. The policeman yawned and watched through his sideview mirror as the women crossed M Street. He yawned again. Even at three o'clock in the morning people still jaywalked.

The man who was a cousin of Darnell's was on his way back from the bathroom when the police broke through the door. He frightened easily, and though he had just emptied his bladder, he peed again as the door came open and the light of the hallway and the loud men came spilling in on him and his sleeping companions.

Horace began asking about Catrina and Elaine and the baby as soon as they put him in a cell. It took him that long to clear his head and understand what was happening to him. He pressed his face against the bars, trying to get his bearings and ignoring everything behind him in the cell. He stuck his mouth as far out of the bars as he could and shouted for someone to tell him whether they knew if the young women and the baby were all right. "They just women, yall," he kept saying for some five minutes. "They wouldn't hurt a flea. Officers, please. Please, Officers. What's done happened to them? And that baby . . . That baby is so innocent." It was a little after six in the morning, and men up and down the line started hollering for him to shut up or they would stick the biggest dick he ever saw in his mouth. Stunned, he did quiet down, because, while he was used to street language coming from the young men who came and went in his apartment, no bad words had ever been directed at him. They talked trash with the filthiest language he had ever heard but they always invited him to join in and "talk about how it really is," talk about his knowing the secretary of defense and the mayor. Usually, after the second blunt, he was floating along with them. Now someone had threatened to do to him what he and the young men said they would do to any woman that crossed them.

Then he turned from the bars and considered the three men he was sharing the two-man cell with. The city jail people liked to make as little work for themselves as possible, and filling cells beyond their capacity meant having to deal with fewer locks. One man was cocooned in blankets on the floor beside the tiered metal beds. The man sleeping on the top bunk had a leg over the side, and because he was a tall man the leg came down to within six inches of the face of the man lying on the bottom bunk. That man was awake and on his back and picking his nose and staring at Horace. His other hand was under his blanket, in the crotch of his pants. What the man got out of his nose he would flick up at the bottom of the bunk above him. Watching him, Horace remembered that a very long time ago, even before the Chesapeake Street house, Loneese would iron his handkerchiefs and fold them into four perfect squares.

"Daddy," the man said, "you got my smokes?"

"What?" Horace said. He recalled doing it to Catrina about two or three in the morning and then rolling over and going to sleep. He also remembered slapping flies away in his dreams, flies that were as big as the hands of policemen.

The man seemed to have an infinite supply of boogers, and the more he picked, the more Horace's stomach churned. He used to think it was such a shame to unfold the handkerchiefs, so wondrous were the squares. The man sighed at Horace's question and put something from his nose on the big toe of the sleeping man above him. "I said do you got my smokes?"

"I don't have my cigarettes with me," Horace said. He tried the best white man's English he knew, having been told by a friend who was serving with him in the army in Germany that it impressed not only white people but black people who weren't going anywhere in life. "I left my cigarettes at home." His legs were aching and he wanted to sit on the floor, but the only available space was in the general area of where he was standing and something adhered to his shoes every time he lifted his feet. "I wish I did have my cigarettes to give you."

"I didn't ask you bout *your* cigarettes. I don't wanna smoke them. I ask you bout *my* cigarettes. I wanna know if you brought *my* cigarettes."

Someone four cells down screamed and called out in his sleep: "Irene, why did you do this to me? Irene, ain't love worth a damn anymore?" Someone else told him to shut up or he would get a king-size dick in his mouth.

"I told you I do not have any cigarettes," Horace said.

"You know, you ain't worth shit," the man said. "You take the cake and mess it all up. You really do. Now, you know you was comin to jail, so why didn't you bring my goddam smokes? What kinda fuckin consideration is that?"

Horace decided to say nothing. He raised first one leg and then the other and shook them, hoping that would relieve the aches. Slowly, he turned around to face the bars. No one had told him what was going to happen to him. He knew a lawyer, but he did not know if he was still practicing. He had friends, but he did not want any of them to see him in jail. He hoped the man would go to sleep.

"Don't turn your fuckin back on me after all we meant to each other," the man said. "We have this long relationship and you do this to me. Whas wrong with you, Daddy?"

"Look," Horace said, turning back to the man. "I done told you I ain't got no smokes. I ain't got your smokes. I ain't got my smokes. I ain't got nobody's smokes. Why can't you understand that?" He was aware that he was veering away from the white man's English, but he knew that his friend from Germany was probably home asleep safely in his bed. "I can't give you what I don't have." Men were murdered in the D.C. Jail, or so the *Washington Post* told him. "Can't you understand what I'm sayin?" His back stayed as close to the bars as he could manage. Who was this Irene, he thought, and what had she done to steal into a man's dreams that way?

"So, Daddy, it's gonna be like that, huh?" the man said, raising his head and pushing the foot of the upper-bunk man out of the way so he could see Horace better. He took his hand out of his crotch and pointed at Horace. "You gon pull a Peter-and-Jesus thing on me and deny you ever knew me, huh? Thas your plan, Daddy?" He lowered his head back to the black-and-white-striped pillow. "I've seen some low-down dirty shit in my day, but you the lowest. After our long relationship and everything."

"I never met you in my life," Horace said, grabbing the bars behind him with both hands, hoping, again, for relief.

"I won't forget this, and you know how long my memory is. First, you don't bring me my smokes, like you know you should. Then you deny all that we had. Don't go to sleep in here, Daddy, thas all I gotta say."

He thought of Reilly Johnson, a man he had worked with in the Pentagon. Reilly considered himself something of a photographer. He had taken the picture of Horace with the secretary of defense. What would the bail be? Would Reilly be at home to receive his call on a Sunday morning? Would they give him bail? The policemen who pulled him from his bed had tsk-tsked in his face. "Sellin drugs and corruptin young people like that." "I didn't know nothin about that, Officer. Please." "Tsk-tsk. An old man like you."

"The world ain't big enough for you to hide from my righteous wrath, Daddy. And you know how righteous I can be when I get started. The world ain't big enough, so you know this jail ain't big enough."

Horace turned back to the bars. Was something in the back as painful as something in the stomach? He touched his face. Rarely, even in the lost months with Catrina, had he failed to shave each morning. A man's capable demeanor started with a shave each morning, his sergeant in boot camp had told him a thousand years ago.

The man down the way began calling for Irene again. Irene, Horace called in his mind. Irene, are you out there? No one told the man to be quiet. It was about seven and the whole building was waking up and the man calling Irene was not the loudest sound in the world anymore.

"Daddy, you got my smokes? Could use my smokes right about now."

Horace, unable to stand anymore, slowly sank to the floor. There he found some relief. The more he sat, the more he began to play over the arrest. He had had money in his pocket when he took off his pants the night before, but there was no money when they booked him. And where had Catrina and Elaine been when the police marched him out of the apartment and down to the paddy wagon, with the Claridge's female security guard standing behind her desk with an oh-yes-I-told-you-so look? Where had they been? He had not seen them. He stretched out his legs and they touched the feet of the sleeping man on the floor. The man roused. "Love don't mean shit anymore," the man on the lower bunk said. It was loud enough to wake the man on the floor all the way, and that man sat up and covered his chest with his blanket and looked at Horace, blinking and blinking and getting a clearer picture of Horace the more he blinked.

Reilly did not come for him until the middle of Monday afternoon. Somebody opened the cell door and at first Horace thought the policeman was coming to get one of his cellmates.

"Homer Parkins," the man with the keys said. The doors were supposed to open electronically, but that system had not worked in a long time.

"Thas me," Horace said and got to his feet. As he and the

man with the keys walked past the other cells, someone said to Horace, "Hey, Pops, you ain't too old to learn to suck dick." "Keep moving," the man with the keys said. "Pops, I'll give you a lesson when you come back."

As they poured his things out of a large manila envelope, the two guards behind the desk whispered and laughed. "Everything there?" one of them asked Horace. "Yes." "Well, good," the guard said. "I guess we'll be seein you on your next trip here." "Oh, leave that old man alone. He's somebody's grandfather." "When they start that old," the first man said, "it gets in their system and they can't stop. Ain't that right, Pops?"

He and Reilly did not say very much after Reilly said he had been surprised to hear from Horace and that he had wondered what had happened to him since Loneese died. Horace said he was eternally grateful to Reilly for bailing him out and that it was all a mistake as well as a long story that he would soon share with him. At Claridge, Reilly offered to take him out for a meal, but Horace said he would have to take a rain check. "Rain check?" Reilly said, smiling. "I didn't think they said that anymore."

The key to the apartment worked the way it always had, but something was blocking the door, and he had to force it open. Inside, he found destruction everywhere. On top of the clothes and the mementos of his life, strewn across the table and the couch and the floor were hundreds and hundreds of broken records. He took three steps into the room and began to cry. He turned around and around, hoping for something that would tell him it was not as bad as his eyes first reported. But there was little hope—the salt and pepper shakers had not been touched, the curtains covering the glass door were intact. There was not much beyond that for him to cling to.

He thought immediately of Catrina and Elaine. What had he done to deserve this? Had he not always shown them a good and kind heart? He covered his eyes, but that seemed only to produce more tears, and when he lowered his hands the room danced before him through the tears. To steady himself, he put both hands on the table, which was covered in instant coffee and sugar. He brushed broken glass off the chair nearest him and sat down. He had not got it all off, and he felt what was left through his pants and underwear.

He tried to look around but got no farther than the picture with the secretary of defense. It had two cracks in it, one running north to south and the other going northwest to southeast. The photograph was tilting, too, and something told him that if he could straighten the picture, it all might not be so bad. He reached out a hand, still crying, but he could not move from the chair.

He stayed as he was through the afternoon and late into the evening, not once moving from the chair, though the tears did stop around five o'clock. Night came, and he still did not move. My name is Horace Perkins, he thought just as the sun set. My name is Horace Perkins, and I worked many a year at the Pentagon. The apartment became dark, but he did not have it in him to turn on the lights.

The knocking had been going on for more than ten minutes when he finally heard it. He got up, stumbling over debris, and opened the door. Elaine stood there with Darnell Jr. in her arms.

"Horace, you okay? I been comin by. I been worried about you, Horace."

He said nothing but opened the door enough for her and the baby to enter.

"It's dark, Horace. What about some light?"

He righted the lamp on the table and turned it on.

"Jesus in heaven, Horace! What happened! My Lord Jesus! I can't believe this." The baby, startled by his mother's words, began to cry. "It's okay," she said to him, "it's okay," and gradually the baby calmed down. "Oh, Horace, I'm so sorry. I really am. This is the worst thing I've ever seen in my life." She touched his shoulder with her free hand, but he shrugged it off. "Oh, my dear God! Who could do this?"

She went to the couch and moved enough trash aside for the baby. She pulled a pacifier from her sweater pocket, put it momentarily in her mouth to remove the lint, then put it in the baby's mouth. He appeared satisfied and leaned back on the couch.

She went to Horace, and right away he grabbed her throat. "I'm gonna kill you tonight!" he shouted. "I just wish that bitch Catrina was here so I could kill her, too." Elaine struggled and sputtered out one "Please" before he gripped her tighter. She beat his arms, but that seemed to give him more strength. She began to cry. "I'm gonna kill you tonight, girl, if it's the last thing I do."

The baby began to cry, and she turned her head as much as she could to look at him. This made him slap her twice, and she started to fall, and he pulled her up and, as he did, went for a better grip, there was time enough for her to say, "Don't kill me in front of my son, Horace." He loosened his hands. "Don't kill me in front of my boy, Horace." Her tears ran down her face and over and into his hands. "He don't deserve to see me die. You know that, Horace."

"Where, then!"

"Anywhere but in front of him. He's innocent of everything."

He let her go and backed away.

"I did nothin, Horace," she whispered. "I give you my word, I did nothin." The baby screamed, and she went to him and took him in her arms.

Horace sat down in the same chair he had been in.

"I would not do this to you, Horace."

He looked at her and at the baby, who could not take his eyes off Horace, even through his tears.

One of the baby's cries seemed to get stuck in his throat, and to release it the baby raised a fist and punched the air, and finally the cry came free. How does a man start over with nothing? Horace thought. Elaine came near him, and the baby still watched him as his crying lessened. How does a man start from scratch?

He leaned down and picked up a few of the broken albums from the floor and read the labels. "I would not hurt you for anything in the world, Horace," Elaine said. Okeh Phonograph Corporation. Domino Record Co. RCA Victor. Darnell Jr.'s crying stopped, but he continued to look down at the top of Horace's head. Cameo Record Corporation, N.Y. "You been too good to me for me to hurt you like this, Horace." He dropped the records one at a time: "It Takes an Irishman to Make Love." "I'm Gonna Pin a Medal on the Girl I Left Behind." "Ragtime Soldier Man." "Whose Little Heart Are You Breaking Now." "The Syncopated Walk."

WONDERWALL

BY ELIZABETH HAND

Hyattsville, MD

(Originally published in 2004)

A long time ago, nearly thirty years now, I had a friend who was waiting to be discovered. His name was David Baldanders; we lived with two other friends in one of the most disgusting places I've ever seen, and certainly the worst that involved me signing a lease.

Our apartment was a two-bedroom third-floor walkup in Queenstown, a grim brick enclave just over the District line in Hyattsville, Maryland. Queenstown Apartments were inhabited mostly by drug dealers and bikers who met their two-hundred-dollars-a-month leases by processing speed and bad acid in their basement rooms; the upper floors were given over to wasted welfare mothers from P.G. County and students from the University of Maryland, Howard, and the University of the Archangels and St. John the Divine.

The Divine, as students called it, was where I'd come three years earlier to study acting. I wasn't actually expelled until the end of my junior year, but midway through that term my roommate Marcella and I were kicked out of our campus dormitory, precipitating the move to Queenstown. Even for the mid-1970s our behavior was excessive; I was only surprised the university officials waited so long before getting rid of us. Our parents were assessed for damages to our dorm room, which were extensive; among other things, I'd painted one wall floor-to-ceiling with the image from the cover of *Transformer*, above which I scrawled, *Je suis damné par l'arc-en-ciel*, in foot-high letters. Decades later, someone who'd lived in the room after I left told me that, year after year, Rimbaud's words would bleed through each successive layer of new paint. No one ever understood what they meant.

Our new apartment was at first an improvement on the dorm room, and Queenstown itself was an efficient example of a closed ecosystem. The bikers manufactured Black Beauties, which they sold to the students and welfare mothers upstairs, who would zigzag a few hundred feet across a wasteland of shattered glass and broken concrete to the Queenstown Restaurant, where I worked making pizzas that they would then cart back to their apartments. The pizza boxes piled up in the halls, drawing armies of roaches. My friend Oscar lived in the next building; whenever he visited our flat he'd push open the door, pause, then look over his shoulder dramatically.

"Listen—!" he'd whisper.

He'd stamp his foot, just once, and hold up his hand to command silence. Immediately we heard what sounded like surf washing over a gravel beach. In fact it was the susurrus of hundreds of cockroaches clittering across the warped parquet floors in retreat.

There were better places to await discovery.

David Baldanders was my age, nineteen. He wasn't much taller than me, with long, thick black hair and a soft-featured face: round cheeks, full red lips between a downy black beard and mustache, slightly crooked teeth much yellowed from nicotine, small well-shaped hands. He wore an earring and a bandana that he tied, pirate-style, over his head; filthy jeans, flannel shirts, filthy black Converse high-tops that flapped when he walked. His eyes were beautiful—indigo, black-lashed, soulful. When he laughed, people stopped in their tracks—he sounded like Herman Munster, that deep, goofy, foghorn voice at odds with his fey appearance.

We met in the Divine's drama department, and immediately recognized each other as kindred spirits. Neither attractive nor talented enough to be in the center of the golden circle of aspiring actors that included most of our friends, we made ourselves indispensable by virtue of being flamboyant, unapologetic fuck-ups. People laughed when they saw us coming. They laughed even louder when we left. But David and I always made a point of laughing loudest of all.

"Can you fucking believe that?" A morning, it could have been any morning: I stood in the hall and stared in disbelief at the department's sitting area. White walls, a few plastic chairs and tables overseen by the glass windows of the secretarial office. This was where the other students chain-smoked and waited, day after day, for news: casting announcements for department plays; cattle calls for commercials, trade shows, summer reps. Above all else, the department prided itself on graduating "working actors"—a really successful student might get called back for a walk-on on *Days of Our Lives*. My voice rose loud enough that heads turned. "It looks like a fucking dentist's office."

"Yeah, well, Roddy just got cast in a Trident commercial," David said, and we both fell against the wall, howling.

Rejection fed our disdain, but it was more than that. Within weeks of arriving at the the Divine, I felt betrayed. I wanted—hungered for, thirsted for, craved like drink or drugs—High Art. So did David. We'd come to the Divine expecting Paris in the 1920s, Swinging London, Summer of Love in the Haight.

We were misinformed.

What we got was elocution taught by the department head's wife; tryouts where tone-deaf students warbled numbers from *The Magic Show*; Advanced Speech classes where, week after week, the beefy department head would declaim Macduff's speech—*All my pretty ones? Did you say all?*—never failing to move himself to tears.

And there was that sitting area. Just looking at it made me want to take a sledgehammer to the walls: all those smug faces above issues of *Variety* and *Theater Arts*, all those sheets of white paper neatly taped to white cinder block with lists of names beneath: callbacks, cast lists, passing exam results. My name was never there. Nor was David's.

We never had a chance. We had no choice.

We took the sledgehammer to our heads.

Weekends my suitemate visited her parents, and while she was gone David and I would break into her dorm room. We drank her vodka and listened to her copy of *David Live*, playing "Diamond Dogs" over and over as we clung to each other, smoking, dancing cheek to cheek. After midnight we'd cadge a ride down to Southwest, where abandoned warehouses had been turned into gay discos—the Lost and Found, Grand Central Station, Washington Square, Half Street. A solitary neon pentacle glowed atop the old *Washington Star* printing plant; we heard gunshots, sirens, the faint bass throb from funk bands at the Washington Coliseum, the ceaseless boom and echo of trains uncoupling in the railyards that extended from Union Station.

I wasn't a looker. My scalp was covered with henna-stiffened orange stubble that had been cut over three successive nights by a dozen friends. Marcella had pierced my ear with a cork and a needle and a bottle of Gordon's gin. David usually favored one long drop earring, and sometimes I'd wear its mate.

Other times I'd shove a safety pin through my ear, then run a dog leash from it around my neck. I had two-inch-long black-varnished fingernails that caught fire when I lit my cigarettes. I kohled my eyes and lips, used Marcella's Chloe perfume, shoved myself into Marcella's expensive jeans even though they were too small for me.

But mostly I wore a white poet's blouse or frayed striped boatneck shirt, droopy black wool trousers, red sneakers, a red velvet beret my mother had given me for Christmas when I was seventeen. I chain-smoked Marlboros, three packs a day when I could afford them. For a while I smoked clay pipes and Borkum Riff tobacco. The pipes cost a dollar apiece at the tobacconist's in Georgetown. They broke easily, and club owners invariably hassled me, thinking I was getting high right under their noses. I was, but not from Borkum Riff. Occasionally I'd forgo makeup and wear army khakis and a boiled-wool navy shirt I'd fished from a dumpster. I used a mascara wand on my upper lip and wore my bashed-up old cowboy boots to make me look taller.

This fooled no one, but that didn't matter. In Southwest I was invisible, or nearly so. I was a girl, white, not pretty enough to be either desirable or threatening. The burly leather-clad guys who stood guard over the entrances to the L&F were always nice to me, though there was a scary dyke bouncer whom I had to bribe, sometimes with cash, sometimes with rough foreplay behind the door.

Once inside all that fell away. David and I stumbled to the bar and traded our drink tickets for vodka and orange juice. We drank fast, pushing upstairs through the crowd until we reached a vantage point above the dance floor. David would look around for someone he knew, someone he fancied, someone who might discover him. He'd give me a wet kiss, then stagger off; and I would stand, and drink, and watch.

The first time it happened David and I were tripping. We were at the L&F, or maybe Washington Square. He'd gone into the men's room. I sat slumped just outside the door, trying to bore a hole through my hand with my eyes. A few people stepped on me; no one apologized, but no one swore at me, either. After a while I stumbled to my feet, lurched a few steps down the hallway, and turned.

The door to the men's room was painted gold. A shining film covered it, glistening with smeared rainbows, like oil-scummed tarmac. The door opened with difficulty because of the number of people crammed inside. I had to keep moving so they could pass in and out. I leaned against the wall and stared at the floor for a few more minutes, then looked up again.

Across from me, the wall was gone. I could see men pissing, talking, kneeling, crowding stalls, humping over urinals, cupping brown glass vials beneath their faces. I could see David in a crowd by the sinks. He stood with his back to me, in front of a long mirror framed with small round lightbulbs. His head was bowed. He was scooping water from the faucet and drinking it, so that his beard glittered red and silver. As I watched, he slowly lifted his face, until he was staring into the mirror. His reflected image stared back at me. I could see his pupils expand like drops of black ink in a glass of water, and his mouth fall open in pure panic.

"David," I murmured.

Beside him a lanky boy with dirty-blond hair turned. He too was staring at me, but not with fear. His mouth split into a grin. He raised his hand and pointed at me, laughing.

"Poseur!"

"Shit—shit . . ." I looked up and David stood there in the hall. He fumbled for a cigarette, his hand shaking, then sank onto the floor beside me. "Shit, you, you saw—you—"

I started to laugh. In a moment David did too. We fell into each other's arms, shrieking, our faces slick with tears and dirt. I didn't even notice that his cigarette scorched a hole in my favorite shirt till later, or feel where it burned into my right palm, a penny-sized wound that got infected and took weeks to heal. I bear the scar even now, the shape of an eye, shiny white tissue with a crimson pupil that seems to wink when I crease my hand.

It was about a month after this happened that we moved to Queenstown. Me, David, Marcy, a sweet spacy girl named Bunny Flitchins, all signed the lease. Two hundred bucks a month gave us a small living room, a bathroom, two small bedrooms, a kitchen squeezed into a corner overlooking a parking lot filled with busted Buicks and shock-shot Impalas. The place smelled of new paint and dry-cleaning fluid. The first time we opened the freezer, we found several plastic Zip-loc bags filled with sheets of white paper. When we removed the paper and held it up to the light, we saw where rows of droplets had dried to faint gray smudges.

"Blotter acid," I said.

We discussed taking a hit. Marcy demurred. Bunny giggled, shaking her head. She didn't do drugs, and I would never have allowed her to: It would be like giving acid to your puppy.

"Give it to me," said David. He sat on the windowsill, smoking and dropping his ashes to the dirt three floors below. "I'll try it. Then we can cut them into tabs and sell them."

"That would be a lot of money," said Bunny delightedly. A tab of blotter went for a dollar back then, but you could sell them for a lot more at concerts, up to ten bucks a hit. She fanned out the sheets from one of the plastic bags. "We could make thousands and thousands of dollars!"

"Millions," said Marcy.

I shook my head. "It could be poison. Strychnine. I wouldn't do it."

"Why not?" David scowled. "You do all kinds of shit."

"I wouldn't do it cause it's from here."

"Good point," said Bunny.

I grabbed the rest of the sheets from her, lit one of the gas jets on the stove, and held the paper above it. David cursed and yanked the bandana from his head.

"What are you doing?"

But he quickly moved aside as I lunged to the window and tossed out the flaming pages. We watched them fall, delicate spirals of red and orange like tiger lilies corroding into black ash then gray then smoke.

"All gone," cried Bunny, and clapped.

We had hardly any furniture. Marcy had a bed and a desk in her room, nice Danish modern stuff. I had a mattress on the other bedroom floor that I shared with David. Bunny slept in the living room. Every few days she'd drag a broken box spring up from the curb. After the fifth one appeared, the living room began to look like the interior of one of those pawnshops down on F Street that sold you an entire roomful of aluminum-tube furniture for fifty bucks, and we yelled at her to stop. Bunny slept on the box springs, a different one every night, but after a while she didn't stay over much. Her family lived in Northwest, but her father, a professor at the Divine, also had an apartment in Turkey Thicket, and Bunny started staying with him.

Marcy's family lived nearby as well, in Alexandria. She was a slender Slavic beauty with a waterfall of ice-blond hair and eyes like aqua headlamps, and the only one of us with a glamorous job—she worked as a model and receptionist at the most expensive beauty salon in Georgetown. But by early spring, she had pretty much moved back in with her parents too.

This left me and David. He was still taking classes at the Divine, getting a ride with one of the other students who lived in Queenstown, or else catching a bus in front of Giant Food on Queens Chapel Road. Early in the semester he had switched his coursework: Instead of theater, he now immersed himself in French language and literature.

I gave up all pretense of studying or attending classes. I worked a few shifts behind the counter at the Queenstown Restaurant, making pizzas and ringing up beer. I got most of my meals there, and when my friends came in to buy cases of Heineken I never charged them. I made about sixty dollars a week, barely enough to pay the rent and keep me in cigarettes, but I got by. Bus fare was eighty cents to cross the District line; the newly opened subway was another fifty cents. I didn't eat much. I lived on popcorn and Reuben sandwiches from the restaurant, and there was a sympathetic waiter at the American Café in Georgetown who fed me ice cream sundaes when I was bumming around in the city. I saved enough for my cover at the discos and for the Atlantis, a club in the basement of a fleabag hotel at 930 F Street that had just started booking punk bands. The rest I spent on booze and Marlboros. Even if I was broke, someone would always spring me a drink and a smoke; if I had a full pack of cigarettes, I was ahead of the game. I stayed out all night, eventually staggering into some of the District's worst neighborhoods with a couple of bucks in my sneaker, if I was lucky. Usually I was broke.

Yet I really was lucky. Somehow I always managed to find my way home. At 2 or 3 or 4 a.m. I'd crash into my apartment, alone except for the cockroaches—David would have gone home with a pickup from the bars, and Marcy and Bunny had decamped to the suburbs. I'd be so drunk I stuck to the mattress like a fly mashed against a window. Sometimes I'd sit cross-legged with the typewriter in front of me and write, naked because of the appalling heat, my damp skin gray with cigarette ash. I read *Tropic of Cancer*, reread *Dhalgren* and *A Fan's Notes* and a copy of *Illuminations* held together by a rubber band. I played Pere Ubu and Wire at the wrong speed, because I was too wasted to notice, and would finally pass out, only to be ripped awake by the apocalyptic scream of the firehouse siren next door—I'd be standing in the middle of the room, screaming at the top of my lungs, before I realized I was no longer asleep. I saw people in my room, a lanky boy with dark-blond hair and clogs who pointed his finger at me and shouted, "Poseur!" I heard voices. My dreams were of flames, of the walls around me exploding outward so that I could see the ruined city like a freshly tilled garden extending for miles and miles, burning cranes and skeletal buildings rising from the smoke to bloom, black and gold and red, against a topaz sky. I wanted to burn too, tear through the wall that separated me from that other world, the real world, the one I glimpsed in books and music, the world I wanted to claim for myself.

But I didn't burn. I was just a fucked-up college student, and pretty soon I wasn't even that. The following spring I flunked out of the Divine. All of my other friends were still in school, getting boyfriends and girlfriends, getting cast in university productions of *An Inspector Calls* and *Arturo Roi*. Even David Baldanders managed to get good grades for his paper on Verlaine. Meanwhile, I leaned out my third-floor window and smoked and watched the speed freaks stagger across the parking lot below. If I jumped I could be with them: That was all it would take.

It was too beautiful for words, too terrifying to think this was what my life had shrunk to. In the mornings I made instant coffee and tried to read what I'd written the night before. Nice words but they made absolutely no sense. I cranked up Marcy's expensive stereo and played my records, compulsively transcribing song lyrics as though they might somehow bleed into something else, breed with my words and create a coherent story line. I scrawled more words on the bedroom wall:

I HAVE BEEN DAMNED BY THE RAINBOW
I AM AN AMERICAN ARTIST, AND I HAVE NO CHAIRS

It had all started as an experiment. I held the blunt, unarticulated belief that meaning and transcendence could be shaken from the world, like unripe fruit from a tree; then consumed.

So I'd thrown my brain into the Waring blender along with vials of cheap acid and hashish, tobacco and speed and whatever alcohol was at hand. Now I wondered: Did I have the stomach to toss down the end result?

Whenever David showed up it was a huge relief.

"Come on," he said one afternoon. "Let's go to the movies."

We saw a double bill at the Biograph, *The Story of Adele H.* and *Jules et Jim.* Torturously uncomfortable chairs, but only four bucks for four hours of air-conditioned bliss. David had seen *Adele H.* six times already; he sat beside me, rapt, whispering the words to himself. I struggled with the French and mostly read the subtitles. Afterwards we stumbled blinking into the long ultraviolet D.C. twilight, the smell of honeysuckle and diesel, coke and lactic acid, our clothes crackling with heat like lightning and our skin electrified as the sugared air seeped into it like poison. We ran arm-in-arm up to the

Café de Paris, sharing one of David's Gitanes. We had enough money for a bottle of red wine and a baguette. After a few hours the waiter kicked us out, but we gave him a dollar anyway. That left us just enough for the Metro and the bus home.

It took us hours to get back. By the time we ran up the steps to our apartment we'd sobered up again. It was not quite 9 o'clock on a Friday night.

"Fuck!" said David. "What are we going to do now?"

No one was around. We got on the phone but there were no parties, no one with a car to take us somewhere else. We rifled through the apartment for a forgotten stash of beer or dope or money, turned our pockets inside-out looking for stray seeds, Black Beauties, fragments of green dust.

Nada.

In Marcy's room we found about three dollars in change in one of her jean pockets. Not enough to get drunk, not enough to get us back into the city.

"Damn," I said. "Not enough for shit."

From the parking lot came the low thunder of motorcycles, a baby crying, someone shouting.

"You fucking motherfucking fucker."

"That's a lot of fuckers," said David.

Then we heard a gunshot.

"Jesus!" yelled David, and yanked me to the floor. From the neighboring apartment echoed the crack of glass shattering. "They shot out a window!"

"I said, not enough money for anything." I pushed him away and sat up. "I'm not staying here all night."

"Okay, okay, wait . . ."

He crawled to the kitchen window, pulled himself onto the sill to peer out. "They did shoot out a window," he said admiringly. "Wow."

"Did they leave us any beer?"

David looked over his shoulder at me. "No. But I have an idea." He crept back into the living room and emptied out his pockets beside me. "I think we have enough," he said after he counted his change for the third time. "Yeah. But we have to get there now—they close at 9."

"Who does?"

I followed him back downstairs and outside.

"Peoples Drug," he said. "Come on."

We crossed Queens Chapel Road, dodging Mustangs and blasted pickups. I watched wistfully as the 80 bus passed, heading back into the city. It was almost 9 o'clock. Overhead the sky had that dusty gold-violet bloom it got in late spring. Cars raced by, music blaring; I could smell charcoal burning somewhere, hamburgers on a grill and the sweet far-off scent of apple blossom.

"Wait," I said.

I stopped in the middle of the road, arms spread, staring straight up into the sky and feeling what I imagined David must have felt when he leaned against the walls of Mr. P's and Grand Central Station: I was waiting, waiting, waiting for the world to fall on me like a hunting hawk.

"What the fuck are you doing?" shouted David as a car bore down and he dragged me to the far curb. "Come on."

"What are we getting?" I yelled as he dragged me into the drugstore.

"Triaminic."

I had thought there might be a law against selling four bottles of cough syrup to two messed-up looking kids. Apparently there wasn't, though I was embarrassed enough to stand back as David shamelessly counted pennies and nickels and quarters out onto the counter.

We went back to Queenstown. I had never done cough syrup before; not unless I had a cough. I thought we would dole it out a spoonful at a time, over the course of the evening. Instead David unscrewed the first bottle and knocked it back in one long swallow. I watched in amazed disgust, then shrugged and did the same.

"Aw, fuck."

I gagged and almost threw up, somehow kept it down. When I looked up David was finishing off a second bottle, and I could see him eyeing the remaining one in front of me. I grabbed it and drank it as well, then sprawled against the box spring. Someone lit a candle. David? Me? Someone put on a record, one of those Eno albums, *Another Green World*. Someone stared at me, a boy with long black hair unbound and eyes that blinked from blue to black then shut down for the night.

"Wait," I said, trying to remember the words. "I. Want. You. To—"

Too late: David was out. My hand scrabbled across the floor, searching for the book I'd left there, a used New Directions paperback of Rimbaud's work. Even pages were in French; odd pages held their English translations.

I wanted David to read me *La lettre du voyant*, Rimbaud's letter to his friend Paul Demeny; the letter of the seer. I knew it by heart in English and on the page but spoken French eluded me and always would. I opened the book, struggling to see through the scrim of cheap narcotic and nausea until at last I found it.

Je dis qu'il faut être voyant, se faire voyant.

Le Poète se fait voyant par un long, immense et raisonné

dérèglement de tous les sens. Toutes les formes d'amour, de souffrance, de folie; il cherche lui-même . . .

I say one must be a visionary, one must become a seer.

The poet becomes a seer through a long, boundless and systematic derangement of all the senses. All forms of love, of suffering, of madness; he seeks them within himself . . .

As I read I began to laugh, then suddenly doubled over. My mouth tasted sick, a second sweet skin sheathing my tongue. I retched, and a bright-red clot exploded onto the floor in front of me; I dipped my finger into it then wrote across the warped parquet:

DEAR DAV

I looked up. There was no light save the wavering flame of a candle in a jar. Many candles, I saw now; many flames. I blinked and ran my hand across my forehead. It felt damp. When I brought my finger to my lips I tasted sugar and blood. On the floor David sprawled, snoring softly, his bandana clenched in one hand. Behind him the walls reflected candles, endless candles; though as I stared I saw they were not reflected light after all but a line of flames, upright, swaying like figures dancing. I rubbed my eyes, a wave cresting inside my head, then breaking even as I felt something splinter in my eye. I started to cry out but could not: I was frozen, freezing. Someone had left the door open.

"Who's there?" I said thickly, and crawled across the room. My foot nudged the candle; the jar toppled and the flame went out.

But it wasn't dark. In the corridor outside our apartment door a hundred-watt bulb dangled from a wire. Beneath it, on the top step, sat the boy I'd seen in the urinal beside David. His hair was the color of dirty straw, his face sullen. He had muddy green-blue eyes, bad teeth, fingernails bitten down to the skin; skeins of dried blood covered his fingertips like webbing. A filthy bandana was knotted tightly around his throat.

"Hey," I said. I couldn't stand very well so I slumped against the wall, slid until I was sitting almost beside him. I fumbled in my pocket and found one of David's crumpled Gitanes, fumbled some more until I found a book of matches. I tried to light one but it was damp; tried a second time and failed again.

Beside me the blond boy swore. He grabbed the matches from me and lit one, turned to hold it cupped before my face. I brought the cigarette close and breathed in, watched the fingertip flare of crimson then blue as the match went out.

But the cigarette was lit. I took a drag, passed it to the boy. He smoked in silence, after a minute handed it back to me. The acrid smoke couldn't mask his oily smell, sweat and shit and urine; but also a faint odor of green hay and sunlight. When he turned his face to me I saw that he was older than I had first thought, his skin dark-seamed by sun and exposure.

"Here," he said. His voice was harsh and difficult to understand. He held his hand out. I opened mine expectantly, but as he spread his fingers only a stream of sand fell onto my palm, gritty and stinking of piss. I drew back, cursing. As I did he leaned forward and spat in my face.

"Poseur."

"You fuck!" I yelled. I tried to get up but he was already on his feet. His hand was tearing at his neck; an instant later something lashed across my face, slicing upwards from cheek to brow. I shouted in pain and fell back, clutching my cheek. There was a red veil between me and the world; I blinked and for an instant saw through it. I glimpsed the young man running down the steps, his hoarse laughter echoing through the stairwell; heard the clang of the fire door swinging open and crashing shut; then silence.

"Shit," I groaned, and sank back to the floor I tried to staunch the blood with my hand. My other hand rested on the floor. Something warm brushed against my fingers. I grabbed it and held it before me—a filthy bandana, twisted tight as a noose, one whip-end black and wet with blood.

I saw him one more time. It was high summer by then, the school year over. Marcy and Bunny were gone till the fall, Marcy to Europe with her parents, Bunny to a private hospital in Kentucky. David would be leaving soon, to return to his family in Philadelphia. I had found another job in the city, a real job, a GS-1 position with the Smithsonian; the lowest-level job one could have in the government, but it was a paycheck. I worked three twelve-hour shifts in a row, three days a week, and wore a mustard-yellow polyester uniform with a photo ID that opened doors to all the museums on the Mall. Nights I sweated away with David at the bars or the Atlantis; days I spent at the newly opened East Wing of the National Gallery of Art, its vast open white-marble space an air-conditioned vivarium where I wandered stoned, struck senseless by huge moving shapes like sharks spun of metal and canvas: Calder's great mobile, Miró's tapestry, a line of somber Rothkos, darkly shimmering waterfalls in an upstairs gallery. Breakfast was a Black Beauty and a Snickers bar, dinner whatever I could find to drink.

We were at the Lost and Found, late night early August.

David as usual had gone off on his own. I was, for once, relatively sober: I was in the middle of my three-day work week; normally I wouldn't have gone out but David was leaving the next morning. I was on the club's upper level, an area like the deck of an ocean liner where you could lean on the rails and look down onto the dance floor below. The club was crowded, the music deafening. I was watching the men dance with each other, hundreds of them, maybe thousands, strobe-lit beneath mirror balls and shifting layers of blue and gray smoke that would ignite suddenly with white blades of laser-light, strafing the writhing forms below so they let out a sudden single-voiced shriek, punching the air with their fists and blasting at whistles. I rested my arms on the rounded metal rail and smoked, thinking how beautiful it all was, how strange, how alive. It was like watching the sea.

And as I gazed, slowly it changed; slowly something changed. One song bled into another, arms waved like tendrils; a shadow moved through the air above them. I looked up, startled, glanced aside and saw the young blond man standing there a few feet from me. His fingers grasped the railing; he stared at the dance floor with an expression at once hungry and disdainful and disbelieving. After a moment he slowly lifted his head, turned and stared at me.

I said nothing. I touched my hand to my throat, where his bandana was knotted there, loosely. It was stiff as rope beneath my fingers: I hadn't washed it. I stared back at him, his green-blue eyes hard and somehow dull; not stupid, but with the obdurate matte gleam of unpolished agate. I wanted to say something but I was afraid of him; and before I could speak he turned his head to stare back down at the floor below us.

"*Cela s'est passé,*" he said, and shook his head.

I looked to where he was gazing. I saw that the dance

floor was endless, eternal: the cinder-block warehouse walls had disappeared. Instead the moving waves of bodies extended for miles and miles until they melted into the horizon. They were no longer bodies but flames, countless flickering lights like the candles I had seen in my apartment, flames like men dancing; and then they were not even flames but bodies consumed by flame—flesh and cloth burned away until only the bones remained, and then not even bone but only the memory of motion, a shimmer of wind on the water, then the water gone and only a vast and empty room, littered with refuse: glass vials, broken plastic whistles, plastic cups, dog collars, ash.

I blinked. A siren wailed. I began to scream, standing in the middle of my room, alone, clutching at a bandana tied loosely around my neck. On the mattress on the floor David turned, groaning, and stared up at me with one bright blue eye.

"It's just the firehouse," he said, and reached to pull me back beside him. It was 5 a.m. He was still wearing the clothes he'd worn to the Lost and Found. So was I: I touched the bandana at my throat and thought of the young man at the railing beside me. "C'mon, you've hardly slept yet," urged David. "You have to get a little sleep."

He left the next day.

A few weeks later my mother came, ostensibly to visit her cousin in Chevy Chase but really to check on me. She found me spread-eagled on my bare mattress, screenless windows open to let the summer's furnace heat pour like molten iron into the room. Around me were the posters I'd shredded and torn from the walls; on the walls were meaningless phrases, crushed remains of cockroaches and waterbugs, countless rust-colored handprints, bullet-shaped gouges where I'd dug my fingernails into the drywall.

"I think you should come home," my mother said gently. She stared at my hands, fingertips netted with dried blood, my knuckles raw and seeping red. "I don't think you really want to stay here. Do you? I think you should come home."

I was too exhausted to argue. I threw what remained of my belongings into a few cardboard boxes, gave notice at the Smithsonian, and went home.

It's thought that Rimbaud completed his entire body of work before his nineteenth birthday; the last collection of prose poems, *Illuminations*, indicates that he may have been profoundly affected by the time he spent in London in 1874. After that came journey and exile, years spent as an arms trader in Abyssinia until he came home to France to die, slowly and painfully, losing his right leg to syphilis, electrodes fastened to his nerveless arm in an attempt to regenerate life and motion. He died on the morning of November 10, 1891, at 10 o'clock. In his delirium he believed that he was back in Abyssinia, readying himself to depart upon a ship called *Aphinar.* He was thirty-seven years old.

I didn't live at home for long—about ten months. I got a job at a bookstore; my mother drove me there each day on her way to work and picked me up on her way home. Evenings I ate dinner with her and my two younger sisters. Weekends I went out with friends I'd gone to high school with. I picked up the threads of a few relationships begun and abandoned years earlier. I drank too much but not as much as before. I quit smoking.

I was nineteen. When Rimbaud was my age, he had already finished his life work. I hadn't even started yet. He had changed the world; I could barely change my socks. He had walked through the wall, but I had only smashed my head against it, fruitlessly, in anguish and despair. It had defeated me, and I hadn't even left a mark.

Eventually I returned to D.C. I got my old job back at the Smithsonian, squatted for a while with friends in Northeast, got an apartment, a boyfriend, a promotion. By the time I returned to the city David had graduated from the Divine. We spoke on the phone a few times: He had a steady boyfriend now, an older man, a businessman from France. David was going to Paris with him to live. Marcy married well and moved to Aspen. Bunny got out of the hospital and was doing much better; over the next few decades, she would be my only real contact with that other life, the only one of us who kept in touch with everyone.

Slowly, slowly, I began to see things differently. Slowly I began to see that there were other ways to bring down a wall: that you could dismantle it, brick by brick, stone by stone, over years and years and years. The wall would always be there—at least for me it is—but sometimes I can see where I've made a mark in it, a chink where I can put my eye and look through to the other side. Only for a moment; but I know better now than to expect more than that.

I talked to David only a few more times over the years, and finally not at all. When we last spoke, maybe fifteen years ago, he told me that he was HIV positive. A few years after that Bunny told me that the virus had gone into full-blown AIDS, and that he had moved home to live with his father in Pennsylvania. Then a few years after that she told me no, he was living in France again, she had heard from him and he seemed to be better.

Cela s'est passé, the young man had told me as we watched the men dancing in the L&F twenty-six years ago. *That is over.*

Yesterday I was at Waterloo Station in London, hurrying to catch the train to Basingstoke. I walked past the Eurostar terminal, the sleek Paris-bound bullet trains like marine animals waiting to churn their way back through the Chunnel. Curved glass walls separated me from them; armed security patrols and British soldiers strode along the platform, checking passenger IDs and waving people to the trains.

I was just turning toward the old station when I saw them. They were standing in front of a glass wall like an aquarium's: a middle-aged man in an expensive-looking dark blue overcoat, his black hair still thick though graying at the temples, his hand resting on the shoulder of his companion. A slightly younger man, very thin, his face gaunt and ravaged, burned the color of new brick by the sun, his fair hair gone to gray. He was leaning on a cane; when the older man gestured, he turned and began to walk slowly, painstakingly down the platform. I stopped and watched: I wanted to call out, to see if they would turn and answer, but the blue-washed glass barrier would have muted any sound I made.

I turned, blinking in the light of midday, touched the bandana at my throat and the notebook in my pocket; and hurried on. They would not have seen me anyway. They were already boarding the train. They were on their way to Paris.

CHRISTMAS IN DODGE CITY

BY BENJAMIN M. SCHUTZ

6th & O Streets, N.W.

(Originally published in 2005)

Sharnella Watkins had never walked into a police station in her life. She'd been tossed in delirious or drunk, carried in kicking and screaming, and marched in on a manacled chorus line. But walk in on her own, never. That would have been like sex. Another thing that if it was up to her, she'd never do.

She checked both ways before she crossed the street, searching for witnesses, not traffic, and clattered over on her nosebleed heels.

She knocked on the bulletproof plastic at the information center.

The desk sergeant looked up from his racing form. "Help you, ma'am?"

"I'd like to talk to that detective, the big one. He's bald and he gots a beard down in front, ah, you know, ah Van Dyke they calls it, oh yeah, he wears glasses, too."

"That's detective Bitterman, ma'am, and why would you like to talk to him?"

"It's personal."

"Well, he's working now. Why don't you come back when his shift ends?"

"When's that?"

"Six o'clock."

"I can't wait that long. Can you give me his phone number? I'll call him."

"Sorry, ma'am, I can't do that. Unless you're family. You aren't family, are you?" The desk man sniggered. Big Bad Bitterman and this itty-bitty black junkie whore.

"No, I guess you're not. Sorry 'bout that." The desk man looked down, trying to root out a winner in all those optimistic names.

Sharnella knew the truth would be pointless, but along with a nonexistent gag reflex, the other gift that had kept her alive on the streets all these years was the unerring ability to pick the right lie when she had to.

She leaned forward so that her bright red lips were only inches from the divider and sneered. Then, shaking her head, she said, "You think you're so smart. Well, lets me tell you something. It ain't me what needs him. He's been looking for me. He wants to talk to me. And now, I'm telling you both, to go fuck yo'selves. I ain't coming back, and I ain't gonna talk to him and . . ." She got close enough for the desk man to count her missing molars: "I'm gonna tell him it was your sorry bullshit what pissed me off and he should see you 'bout why he can't solve no cases no more."

The desk man had been following her little breadcrumbs of innuendo and found himself ending up face to face with Mount Bitterman. The explosion wouldn't be that bad. Bitterman had made enough enemies that if he declared you one, you'd as likely be toasted as shunned. Bitterman never forgot and never forgave.

The desk man had endured too much inexplicable disappointment and loss to risk an angry Bitterman.

As Sharnella turned to walk away, the desk man said: "Hold your horses, bitch. This is his number at headquarters."

He wouldn't write it down for her, hoping her memory would fail. She'd be fucked and Bitterman would have no cause. As she backed away, mouthing the numbers to fix them in her disloyal mind, the desk man said, "You know Bitterman only listens to the dead. I hope you find him soon."

Across town, Detective Avery Bitterman reached down and pulled on his dick. One of the advantages of a closed front desk. He'd notice himself doing this more since his divorce. A dispassionate review told him that it wasn't for pleasure but rather to reassure himself that he was still all there, a feeling he had less and less often these days.

The receptionist at headquarters told him that he had a call from a Sharnella Watkins and that she said it was an emergency. "Put it through," he said.

"Is this Detective Bitterman?"

"Yes, it is. How may I help you?"

"You probably don't remember me, but I remembers you. You arrested my boy Rondell. You was the only one who didn't beat up on him. You wouldn't let nobody hurt him."

Bitterman shook his head, remembering. That's right, ma'am. I wouldn't let them lynch him. I thought it would be more fitting if your son got sent to Lorton, where he could meet the two sons of the woman he raped, sodomized, and tortured to death. Those mother's sons and some friends tied him down, inserted a hedge shears up Rondell's ass, opened him up and strung his intestines around him like he was a Christmas tree. When, to their delight, this didn't kill him, they poured gasoline over him like he was a sundae and set him on fire.

"No, I do remember you, Sharmella."

"SharNella." She knew she was right to call this man. He remembered her. He would help her.

"It's my baby, Dantreya. He's gone, Mr. Bitterman. I know he's in some kind of trouble . . ."

What a fuckin' surprise. "Ma'am, I'm a homicide detective. You want to go to your local district house and file a missing persons report. I can't help you with this."

"Please, Mr. Bitterman. They won't do anything. They'll just say, 'That's what kids do,' and with me as a mother why not stay out all night. But he's not like that. He's different than my others. He's a good boy. He goes to school. He's fifteen and he never been in no trouble. Never, not even little things. He likes to draw. He wants to be an artist. You should come and see what he draws. Please, Mr. Bitterman, he's all I got left. It's Christmas tomorrow. I just want my baby home." Wails gave way to staccato sobbing.

Sharnella's tears annoyed Bitterman. I'm a homicide detective, that's what I do, he said to no one. I can't deal with this shit. It ain't my job. Come back when he's dead. Then I'll listen.

"Ma'am, I'm sorry. I understand how you feel. But the beat cops can keep an eye out for him. You tell them where he's likely to go. That's your best bet, not me. I'm sorry. I gotta go now."

Bitterman hung up over her wailing "No's." Where was he going to go? He was head of the cold case squad. These days, everything was a cold case. Arrest and conviction rates were lower for homicide than for jaywalking. The killers were younger, bolder and completely without restraint. The law of the jungle, "an eye for an eye," would have been a welcome relief. The law of the streets was "an eye for a hangnail." Everything was a killing offense. Motive was nothing, opportunity and means were ubiquitous. Children packed lunchbox, thermos, and sidearm in their knapsacks for school. The police were the biggest provider of handguns. Three thousand had disappeared from the city's property rooms to create more dead bodies that the medical examiner's office couldn't autopsy, release or bury. That for Bitterman was the guiding symbol of his work these days. Handguns on a conveyor belt back to the streets, and the frozen dead serving longer and longer sentences in eternity's drunk tank.

The phone jerked Bitterman back from his reverie.

"Mr. Bitterman, this is Sharnella Watkins. Don't hang up on me. I can help you. My boy's gone, 'cause they want to kill him."

"Who's they, Sharnella?"

"The 6th and O Crew."

"Sharnella, you said your son had never been in trouble. The 6th and O Crew is nothing but. Why am I listening to this?"

"He didn't do nothing. He was coming home from school with a trophy he got at a art show, and Lufer tried to take it from him, but my baby wouldn't give it to him and when Lufer tried again he hit him with it and knocked him down and my baby ran off. He said Lufer went to get his gun and was yellin' that he'd kill him for sure. And he would, that boy's purely mean. He kill you for no reason."

"Sharnella, this still doesn't help me. Get to the help-me part or I'm hangin' up."

Sharnella had never given a policeman a straight answer in her life. But her baby was in danger. Sharnella never stopped to think why she felt so differently about this child, her fourth, than any of the others, only that she did and that his death, after all the others, would kill her too.

"This boy, Lufer Timmons. He's killed a bunch of people. That's what everybody says. Everybody afraid of him. They say he's the Crew's main shooter. But he does it when it ain't business, just 'cause he likes it. And he said he'll kill my boy. Doesn't that help you, Mr. Bitterman?"

The Crew favored death as a solution to all its problems. Giving the delivery man a name was a help. "Tell you what, Sharnella. You go over to the station house like I said and give 'em all the information about your son. Bring a picture, a list of all of his friends and where they live, and where he's been known to hang out. Tell them to fax me a copy of all that. I'll look into it."

Her story was probably 90 percent bullshit and 10 percent horseshit for flavor, but Bitterman knew he'd check it out. You turned over every rock and picked up every squiggling thing. That was his motto: No Corner Too Deep, No Corner Too Dark.

Bitterman tried to remember Sharnella from her second son's trial. She'd started dropping babies at fourteen and was done before twenty. That'd make her around thirty-five now. She looked fifty. Flatbacking and mainlining aged women with interest. Beginning as a second-generation whore, Sharnella's childhood had been null and void; her prime had passed unnoticed, one sweaty afternoon in a New York Avenue motel.

Bitterman was more aware of time than ever before. He'd lifted and run and dragged his ugly white man's game to basketball courts all over the city. Elbow and ass, he rebounded with the best even though he couldn't jump over a dime. No one ever forgot a pick he set or an outlet pass that went end to end, but he remembered not to shoot too often or try to dribble and run at the same time. His twenties and thirties didn't seem all that different, but now at forty-five he knew he wasn't the same man. Bald by choice, rather than balding. Thicker but not yet fat, slower both in reflexes and foot speed. Maybe mellowing was nothing more than realizing that he couldn't tear the doors off the world anymore. The long afternoon of invincibility had passed.

Sharnella's second son, Jabari, had killed a rival drug dealer in a rip-off attempt that also killed a nursing student driving by. Her only daughter, Female, with a short "a" and a long "e," so named by the hospital and then taken by Sharnella, who liked the sound of it, had died of an overdose of extremely good cocaine at the age of sixteen. Everything she delivered died or killed someone else.

Bitterman called down to Identification and Records.

"Get me the file on Lufer Timmons. If there's a picture make a copy for me and send it up with the file. And see if there's a file on Dantreya Watkins."

Bitterman sat at his desk awaiting the files, massaging his eyes.

Bitterman had tried to catch a case of racism for years, a really virulent one, but to no avail. He had mumps when he needed anthrax. It would have made his job so much easier. No sadness for the wasted lives, no respect for the courage of the many, no grief for the victims, no compassion for the survivors.

He'd been a homicide cop in a black city for almost his entire adult life. He'd seen every form of violence one person could do to another. He'd seen black women who'd drowned their own babies, and ones who'd ripped their own flesh at the chalk outlines of a fallen son. Men who'd shot and stabbed an entire family, then eaten the dinner off their plates and men who'd worked three jobs for a lifetime, so their children wouldn't have to. Bitterman just didn't get it, how anyone could conclude that they were all of a kind, that they were different and less. He wished he could, it saved on the wear and tear.

When he opened his eyes again, he saw the Lufer Timmons file on the desk and a note saying no file on that Watkins. Maybe he was his mother's pride and joy.

Lufer Timmons had been raised by strangers, starting with his parents and moving on to a series of foster homes, residential treatment centers, detention centers and jails. Now at seventeen, he was well on his way to evening the score with a number of crimes to his credit starting with the attempted rape of his therapist at the age of eleven.

Bitterman studied the picture of Timmons. Six-one and a hundred sixty-eight pounds. He had a long face with deep crevices in his cheeks, thin lips, a thin nose, prominent cheekbones, and bulging froggy eyes. Bitterman pocketed one photo, Xeroxed the page of known associates and family and put the file in his desk drawer. A call to operations yielded the very pleasant news that one of his known associates was currently in custody at the downtown detention center.

Bitterman drove slowly along "The Stroll" looking for Sunshine, as in "put a little Sunshine in your day," her marketing pitch to the curbside crawlers. Sunshine was a six-foot redhead, natural, with alabaster skin, emerald green eyes and surgically perfected tits. Bitterman had decided that Sunshine was going to be his Christmas present to himself. He wasn't even sure he wanted to have sex with her. He just wanted to look at her, all of her, without having to hurry, like when she was on display, so he could memorize her beauty. Lately he'd been thinking about what he had to show for forty-five years, and all the fucks of a lifetime hadn't stayed with him as sharply as his memory of her on a warm summer's eve, leaning against a lamppost, trying to stay one lick ahead of a fast-melting vanilla cone. Her tongue moving rapidly up the sides of the cone until anticipating defeat, she engulfed the whole mound and sucked it out of the cone. Beauty baffled Bitterman. It seemed fundamental and indivisible. He could not break down his response into pieces or explain it away by recourse to another force or power. Sunshine was perfect and her beauty touched him in a way he couldn't avoid. He hoped that she wouldn't be easy to find. He knew that she would turn out to have bad teeth and bray like a donkey.

Lafonzo Nellis was waiting for Bitterman in interrogation room six. Bitterman sat down and the guard left.

"So, Lafonzo. Tell me about Lufer Timmons."

"Fuck you."

"Glad we got that cleared up. Let me give you some context, here, Lafonzo, before you get into more trouble than you can get out of. Because it's Christmas, God gave me three wishes. The first is a known acquaintance of Lufer Timmons in custody, that's you. The second is to have you locked up but not papered. The third is up to you. See, if you don't talk to me, that's okay. I hear that Lufer is a reasonable man, fair with his friends, not likely to do anything rash. I'm gonna leave here, head over to 6th and O and start asking about Lufer, and talking loud about how much help you were to me. The street bull who brought you in hasn't papered you yet. He can let you go and he doesn't have to explain a thing. You're just DWOP: Dropped Without Prosecution. Now, I hear that a lot of your buddies saw you get busted and righteously, too. How you gonna explain being out of here right after we talk? Huh?"

"You ain't got the juice to make that happen."

"Oh, yeah. You been around, Lafonzo. Let's get a reality check here. You know that a street bull's got two jobs. His shift and court time. Court time is time and a half. You sit on

your butt, you drink coffee, you tell lies, you hit on the chip-
pies, nobody's shooting at you, and it's time and a half. Now, I
just promised that guy I'd list him as a witness on my next two
homicide trials. They're usually three or four days each. Easy
time, easy money. What do you got to offer him?"

Lafonzo had a friend who was a cop and he'd pocketed
$100,000 in court time and he'd only made three arrests all
year. Lafonzo had a vision of trying to 'splain everything to
Lufer. Lafonzo made his mind up immediately and forever.
"Okay, okay. What do you want to know?"

"We'll start with the easy stuff. I got a picture of Lufer
from his last arrest. Look at it, tell me if he's changed
any."

He slid the picture across the table. Lafonzo didn't pick it
up. "Yeah, that's him. He ain't changed none."

"Okay, so tell me about him. What's he like?"

"He's a crazy man. I mean, what you want to know? He's
in the Crew, 6th and O. You know what that means. I don't
got to tell you. Let's just leave it at this, if there's trouble,
Lufer fixes it. Period. Understand?"

"We're getting there. If I was to go lookin' for him, where
would I find him?"

"Dude moves around a lot. See, there's plenty of other
people, like to find him, too, you see what I'm saying. If he has
a pad, it's a secret to me."

"What kind of car does he drive?"

"A 'Vette, a black one."

"You know the year, the tags?"

"No, man. Why should I care?"

Bitterman knew he'd find no such car legally registered to
Timmons.

"Okay, where does he hang out? I'm gonna put a man at

6th and O with his picture every day from now on. So where else will he show up?"

Lafonzo was running out of room for evasions; a full-blown lie was called for here. But present danger prevailed over the future.

"They's a few bars he fancies. Nairobi Jones, Langtry's, the Southeaster."

"What else can you tell me? Any trademarks, things that he favors?"

"I don't know. He always wears that long coat. You know, the ones that go down to your boots."

"A duster?" Bitterman was finally interested.

"Yeah."

"What color?"

"Dark. Dark red."

"Like burgundy?"

"Yeah."

"What's it made of?"

"Leather. Musta cost plenty."

"What about a bandana?"

"Yeah, that too. He wears it around his neck, not on his head."

Glory to God. The red leather duster and the bandana could make him "Johnny-Jump-Out," wanted in six daylight shootings. Bitterman put what he knew from the files together with Nellis's information and began to understand his quarry a little better.

"He fancies himself quite a shootist, doesn't he?" Bitterman began. "No back of the ear, hands tied, in a dark room for him. I admire that. Straight up in your face, shoot and shoot back. He must have quite a reputation in the 'hood. You don't fuck with Lufer Timmons, do you?"

"What do you need me for? You seem to know everything."

"That I do, Lafonzo. I know that Lufer steals a car when he's gonna whack someone. He's got a driver he trusts. He cruises the streets till he finds his target, then he jumps out, which is why we call him 'Johnny-Jump-Out.' No pussy bullshit drive-bys for our Johnny, no, he jumps out, calls the target by name, pulls his piece and does it right there, trading gunfire on the street, broad daylight, then back in the car and he's gone. Cool customer, our Lufer, drawing down on a man telling him you're gonna kill him and then doing it. Nice gun he uses, too, .44 Magnum. Holds on to it. Does he wear a holster, Lafonzo?"

"Yeah."

"Tell me about it."

"What for?"

"Because I want to know, Lafonzo."

"It's on his left hip, facing the other way."

"A cross-draw, how elegant. And so cocky. Most guys just shoot and throw down. He doesn't think he's gonna get caught. I know he wears armor because one guy hit him right in the chest before Lufer put one between his eyes."

"So how come you know so much, you ain't got him yet?"

"All we had was an M.O. No pattern to his killings. Now, I know that there isn't one. Lufer gets hot, you get shot. Now I've got a name, a description, and some places to look for him. He got a name for himself? All the great ones had nicknames. What about Lufer?"

"Fuck, man, he don't need no nickname. You hear Lufer Timmons looking for you, that's like hearing the Terminator wants you."

Bitterman pocketed his photograph and smiled at Lafonzo. "I guess you'll be wanting to spend some time indoors, right?"

Lafonzo sat up straight. "Don't you be putting me out there, now. That motherfucker'll kill me."

"Relax. I'm not gonna screw around with you. I'll make sure you're papered and held, maybe get you a nice high bond you can't post. How's that sound?"

"Great. Fuckin' great. Thanks."

No other city in the world had as much of its population behind bars. Even the bad guys prefer to be in jail rather than on the streets. Bitterman was optimistic about nailing Timmons. A guy so caught up in building a reputation wouldn't be able to wait for it to be bestowed upon him. He'd help it along with plenty of boasting. All they had to do was find the right pair of ears. Secondly, he liked his gun too much. Holding on to that was a mistake. If they found that, they'd match it to bullets in his six victims. Once he was off the streets, they'd go back and talk to the deaf, dumb, and blind who'd seen and heard everything and convince just one of them to talk. Once gone he would not be coming back.

Bitterman left the detention center to get an arrest warrant from a judge. If he got it soon, it'd make the 3 p.m. roll call for the next shift. By tomorrow morning, every active duty officer on the streets would be looking for Lufer Timmons. A Christmas present to the city.

Dantreya Watkins had been going about this all wrong. He'd approached the "gangstas" on the street looking for a piece and received the short course on urban economics: Desperation drives the price up, not down. Once his ignorance of makes and models was established, his "brothers" tried to sell him .25-caliber purse guns for four hundred bucks. Poverty only served to delay his fleecing. After three unsuccessful tries, he knew enough to ask for a .380 Walther. That seemed to be a respectable gun. He found a kindly gentleman who sold him such a gun and a full clip of ammo for three hundred bucks, which was all the money he could steal from his mother.

It wasn't until later, in an abandoned warehouse when Dantreya squeezed off a practice round and saw the cartridge roll out of the end of the barrel, that he learned that the clip was full of .32-caliber ammo and completely useless. Dantreya was now armed with a three-hundred-dollar hammer.

Dantreya's descent into the all-too-real world, far from the comics he read, rewrote, and illustrated in his room, was now complete. He was waiting nervously at the side of his friend TerrAnce's house for TerrAnce to get his father's gun for him. In exchange, Dantreya had offered TerrAnce his entire collection of X-Men comics, which they would go get as soon as TerrAnce lifted the gun from his father's holster in the closet.

TerrAnce pushed open the ripped screen door with his shoulder and, holding the gun carefully in both hands, took the steps, one at a time. He walked around the side of the house and approached Dantreya, both hands grasping the trigger and pointing the gun at him. Dantreya stepped aside as gracefully as any matador and took the gun out of his friend's hands.

"Thanks man," he said, as he spun the chambers of the revolver. The bullets looked like the right size. Now, all he had to do was find Lufer Timmons. His older friends could help with that.

TerrAnce looked at him expectantly. Dantreya slipped the gun into his jacket and shrugged, "Hey man, I gotta go. I'll get your stuff and bring it right back."

That said, he took off across the street and ran up the

alley away from his friend TerrAnce, now crying with all the disappointment an eight-year-old has.

Bitterman pulled up to the corner of 6th and O. He got out and put the cherry on the roof to simplify things for the locals. Up here, a white man with an attitude had to be crazy or a cop. Bitterman wanted to make sure they made the right choices.

Fats Taylor was poured over a folding chair.

"The fuck you doin' up here, Bitterman?" Fats asked, his chest heaving with the effort of speech.

"Just came up to hear myself talk, Fats. You bein' such a good listener and all."

"I hear everything, sees everything, and knows everything." Fats chuckled and smiled.

And eats everything, Bitterman thought.

"I'm looking for a faggoty little nigger, name of Lufer Timmons, you know him?"

Fats's face sealed over, as smooth and black as asphalt in August.

"Well, you listen, Fats, and I'll talk myself. This little queer thinks he's a real pistolero, a gunslinger. Well, I think he's a coward. I know who he's shot, where, when, and why. Pretty tough with kids, and cripples, spaced-out druggies, welshing gamblers that don't carry. You tell him I'm looking for him, Fats. And you know who I've put in the ground."

Bitterman closed his show, went back to his car and drove away. Fats could be counted on to spread the word, emphasizing every insult. A punk like Timmons, to whom respect was fear and fear was all, wouldn't let this pass. Bitterman was already wearing armor and would until Lufer was taken in. Although facing a .44 Magnum he might just as well be wearing sun block.

Bitterman repeated his performance in Nairobi Jones and the Southeaster.

For fun, in Nairobi Jones, he told them he was Charlie Siringo, the Pinkerton who single-handedly tracked the Wild Bunch until they fled to South America. In the Southeaster he was Heck Thomas, one of the legendary "Oklahoma Guardsmen."

Bitterman wanted Lufer to stay put, and challenging him would do that. He wanted him angry and impulsive, so he insulted him. He wanted him confused, so he multiplied his pursuers.

Bitterman drove over to Langtry's via all the "cupcake corners" in the first district. His latest ex-partner had suggested that the politically correct term for these young ladies was "vertically challenged," and they should be so described in all police reports. Bitterman got himself a new partner. He'd seen only a few working girls out on the sidewalks. Cold weather and the new law that allowed the city to confiscate the cars of the johns caught soliciting had forced one more evolution in the pursuit of reckless abandon. Now the girls drove endlessly around the block until they pulled up alongside a likely customer. The negotiations had more feeling than the foreplay to follow. Then a quick sprint to lose a police pursuit and the happy couple was free to lay down together, take aim and miss each other at point-blank range.

Sunshine's Mercedes was off line. Bitterman figured she was probably curled up with some rich young defense attorney in one of the city's better hotels. Next to a Sugar Daddy John, a Galahad Defense Attorney was a girl's best chance to get off the streets and get some instant respectability. Just another reason to hate those scumbags. Bitterman gave up after talking to Betty Boop. She'd shown up around the same time as

Sunshine, and Bitterman had fancied her, too. Now her looks had gone like last week's snow.

Bitterman pulled up across the street from Langtry's and started over when he saw Sunshine's Mercedes. He turned back and got into his car to consider his options. If she was in Langtry's alone, he'd pick her up and put her somewhere until he was done looking for Lufer and then celebrate Christmas Eve with her. If she was somewhere else nearby and he went in looking for Lufer, he'd miss her when she came out. He didn't like that plan much. Of course, she could be with someone else already. As long as it wasn't some fuckin' defense attorney he'd flash some badge, heft a little gun, and requisition her on police business. Bitterman decided that this year the city could wait to get his gift.

He hadn't been this excited since he was four years old and came down in the middle of the night to see if Santa had brought the baseball glove that would make him Willie Mays. Just give me this one thing, Lord, just because it's something I can ask for. Everything else I lack is so huge, so vague, so damned close that I don't even know what I'm looking for.

Dantreya Watkins hurried halfway down the alley, then slowed and moved cautiously along the wall to the intersection with the street. He was trying to think of what his heroes would do. Batman would swoop from the dark and knock Lufer down, then disarm him, tie him up, and leave him for the police. The Punisher would kick down a door and come in guns blazing. Dantreya tried to conjure courage but all he got was a tremor in his legs and a wave of nausea. He turned back to the alley and threw up all over his shoes. Courage had not delivered him to this place. He had nowhere near enough money to pay for Lufer's death, and he could not imagine running away to live elsewhere. He could leave his world as a superhero, but not as himself. Like his mother, he had an allergy to the police and would not take a step toward one. He knew Lufer was a guarantee of death, only the date on the death certificate was missing. His fears and beliefs, what was impossible and what was certain, had brought him to this alley. His mind had painted him into a corner and it didn't bother with a small brush.

The tremor in his legs increased and Dantreya gripped the pistol in his pocket even tighter, hoping that would slow down the shaking that surged through him. He thanked God for the gun. Without it he knew he was a dead man looking to lie down.

Forty minutes later Lufer Timmons in his long red duster pushed open the door to Langtry's and stepped out onto the sidewalk. Avery Bitterman sat up, cursing his luck that Timmons would be the one to show first. Timmons held the door and his companion stepped out into the night. She really was lovely, a thick mane of brick-red hair, pale skin and deep dimples when she smiled. Sunshine, in her knee-high boots, towered over Lufer, who traveled up her length slowly, appreciating every inch of her. He was gonna love climbing up this one. Lufer wasn't particularly fond of white meat, but that crazy honky who'd been jivin' with him put him in the mood to fuck this bitch cross-eyed, then maybe mess her up some. Called him a faggot, a punk. He'd show him who the real man was. First he'd teach this white bitch about black lovin'. That'd ruin her for white dick. Then he'd go find that motherfucka, kneecap him, make him beg for the bullet, then shove his gun all the way up his ass before he did him. Lufer smiled, goddamn that felt good. Life was good to Lufer, offering him so many avenues to pleasure.

Sunshine slipped her arm through his and they walked down the street, Lufer showin' off his prize and she whispering in his ear about what she had in mind for him. Bitterman let them pass his car, then got out and walked up the opposite sidewalk. Oh my, he said to himself as he felt something leak out of him. Sunshine was still as beautiful as ever, but her smile as she lay her head on Lufer's shoulder was not one he wanted anymore. He couldn't kid himself about what they would mean to each other, not any longer anyway.

Lufer pushed open the door to a three-story walk-up between a Brazilian restaurant and an erotic lingerie store. Bitterman pulled out his radio, gave his location, who he was watching, and called for backup. If he'd been able to see down the alley across the way, he'd have seen a slim figure back away, turn and run to the fire escape and quickly begin to climb.

Bitterman crossed the street and stood by the door to Timmons's crib. He opened his jacket and thumbed back the strap on his holster. A level-three vest was supposed to be able to stop a .44 provided it wasn't too close, but they said the shock would flatten you and you got broken up inside even if there wasn't penetration. Where the hell was backup, Bitterman thought.

He scanned the street in both directions and saw nothing. Right now he was the thin blue line.

A shot rang out, then another, then a scream and a third one.

Bitterman yelled into his radio, "Shots fired, I'm going up!" He pulled the door open and heard things falling, scuffling and screaming from above. Both hands on his pistol, he followed it up the stairs. He hit the second floor and pointed his gun at all the doors and then up the stairs.

The noise was coming from the door at the far end. Bitterman closed in rapidly and pressed himself against the wall. He reached out with his right hand and touched the doorknob. It was unlocked.

"Wonderful, I get an open door but no backup," he said to himself.

Bitterman slowly turned the knob. The noises had stopped.

No banging, no screams. When it was fully turned, he flung it open and stepped through into what he hoped was not the line of fire.

Lufer was on the floor. His pants were down around his knees. Sunshine was under him, twitching. Lufer's cannon was in his hand and there was a bullet hole in the sofa. There was also one in his neck, and the blood was pooling under his chin.

Bitterman saw a young boy to his left, holding on to a snub-nosed .38. The gun was jumping around like it was electrified. His left leg tried to keep time but it couldn't. There was a large stain on the front of the boy's pants.

"Put down the gun," Bitterman barked, but the boy didn't respond.

Bitterman searched his face. His eyes were wide open and unfocused.

"Put down the gun," Bitterman asked, more gently but to no avail.

The boy was clearly freaked out by what he'd done. Maybe he could get close enough to disarm him.

"Son, please put down the gun. You're making me nervous the way it's shaking there. I don't know what happened here, but I know he's a bad man. Why don't you tell me what happened here."

Bitterman edged closer to the boy, who was facing away from him. Maybe he could get his hand on the gun, then hit him in the temple with his pistol. At this range he couldn't afford to let the boy turn. Even shooting to wound him wouldn't work. An accidental off-line discharge could be fatal this close. Should he tell him he was going to reach for his gun, or just do it? And where the fuck was backup anyway?

Bitterman moved slowly toward the boy until he was about two feet away. If he turned on him he'd have to shoot him. He had no choice. Why wouldn't he just put the gun down and make this easier on both of them?

Bitterman slowly reached out for the gun. The boy's eyes snapped into focus and he tried to pull away. Bitterman grabbed for the gun. It swung up toward his face, he pulled it down toward his chest and slammed the kid in the head with his pistol. The .38 went off and Bitterman fell back gasping. Dantreya Watkins hit the floor and lay still.

Bitterman, on his back, reached up and touched his chest. He could feel the .38 embedded in the Kevlar. God, did he hurt and was he glad he could say it.

He lay there on his back, like a Kevlar turtle, his hands clenching with the pain of each breath. He saw Sunshine push Lufer Timmons up off of her, until she was clear of his now and forever limp penis, roll out from under it, stand up and stagger to the door without a backward glance. Bitterman tried to call out to her for help but could only groan instead, as she banged her way down the stairs. The front door slammed and Bitterman lay there in the enveloping silence waiting for the sounds of backup: screeching tires, sirens, pounding footsteps. Above all else he wanted there to be someone in a hurry to find him. Bitterman closed his eyes and whispered, "Merry fucking Christmas."

AFTER (EXCERPT)

BY MARITA GOLDEN
Woodmore, MD
(Originally published in 2006)

The bullets discharge from the muzzle of Officer Carson Blake's sixteen-round Beretta with the tinny, explosive popping sound of a toy gun. He will not remember exactly how many shots he fires so wildly. Fires with pure intent. Fires, he is sure, to save his life. In the first seconds after the shattering sound of the bullets subsides, he would say, if asked right then, that he had fired every bullet in his gun. Never before has his gun been so large. Never before has it weighed so much. He's dizzy and breathless. His heart beats so fast, he can't believe he is still standing.

When he shoots the man, everything, all of it, unfolds as if in slow motion. He wants to look away. He dares not turn his gaze. The first bullet boring through the man's thick neck riddled with razor bumps, the force twisting his head to the side, as though he is looking with those astonished, horribly open, not yet dead eyes to see where the bullet comes from. The second bullet piercing the skin of the black leather jacket, lodging in the flesh of his shoulder. The third bullet, fired at his groin, bringing him to his knees and then onto his face, sprawled flat out on the parking lot forty feet from the entrance to the Chinese restaurant The House of Chang.

Carson stands staring at the man on the pavement, his body a bloody heap illuminated by the fluorescence of the mall parking lot lights, and sees the cell phone a few feet from the man's hand, and he prays for the ground beneath his feet to shift in a cataclysmic rumble and swallow him whole. *A cell phone*, he thinks, unbelieving. *A cell phone.* Not a gun. He hurls a howl, deep and guttural, into the night. Sinking to his knees, he touches the man, turns him over onto his back, sees the bulbous, bloody wound in his neck, smells the sharp odor of his sodden groin, desperate now to find, to feel, a pulse. There is none. There is only the cell phone. Looking up in desperation, Carson sees a sky unfamiliar and frightening, in which he can fathom not a single star, a vastness that makes him wish for wings.

Carson tries to stand but cannot, and he crawls a few feet away and vomits. When there is no more sickness to spill from his gut, he wipes his mouth and shouts at the dead man, through trembling lips stained with a blistering splash of tears, "What the fuck were you doing? Why didn't you just do what I said?"

There is nothing on this night that hints at disaster. After twelve years on the force, Carson can tell when a shift will be hell on wheels. On those shifts, the dispatcher begins reciting an address and an "incident" (car crash, domestic disturbance, robbery, brawl, accident, murder) even before Carson is belted behind the wheel. Then there are the calm, quiet shifts when hour after hour he's numb with boredom, cruising the nine square miles of his police service area, and after a couple of hours he begins looking for a safe place to park and take a nap.

But he can't get bored. Because bored he won't see the obvious—the missing tags on a beat-up hoopty driven by a carload of young punks looking for trouble and determined to find it. But this night he is bored by 9:45, when he walks into a 7-Eleven near the litter-filled streets of a housing project known as "The Jungle" to buy coffee and a doughnut: Carson ignores the group of high school–age boys hanging out in front of the store at almost ten o'clock on a school night, rapping, jonin', joking, lying. Matches waiting to be struck. *Don't they have homes?* Carson wonders for the thousandth time, then recalls what he has seen in some of the homes these boys live in—rats, roaches, three kids sleeping on the living room floor, toddlers playing near stacks of cellophane-wrapped crack cocaine, no heat in the winter, stifling ovenlike apartments in the summer, overworked mamas, long-gone daddies. Those homes make the parking lot of 7-Eleven seem a step up in the world.

Still, why the hell were they standing outside to talk? *Just hangin'.* He'd read somewhere that this was street corner culture, an integral part of the Black experience. Some urban ritual. But this is Prince George's County. No inner-city street corners here, like in nearby D.C. *But niggahs,* he thinks sullenly, *can turn anyplace into a ghetto.*

Nearly all the arrests he's made, all his stops, involve boys like the ones he barely looks at as he passes by, feeling them grit on him with a steely stare because he's a police officer. To them he's a cop and he is, in their eyes, the enemy. He's fed up with arresting young Black males—aimless, directionless, often involved in nonviolent crimes that set the stage for all the shit that hits the fan in their young lives. Just last week he was called to the scene of a shooting and saw a kid no more than seventeen, dressed in spanking new jeans, two-hundred-dollar Air Jordans, and a Phat Farm sweatshirt, loaded into the Emergency Services vehicle, *dead.* Shot in the back while standing outside a Popeyes, from the passenger side of a Crown

Vic that careened past the spot where he stood munching on a spicy chicken breast and a biscuit while talking to his baby's mama. The car didn't even slow down to make the hit. As Carson watched the EMS vehicle drive away, he wondered how many hits the kid had made. Revenge, payback, and a brutal, bloody synchronicity ruled the lives of too many of the young men he arrested. He saw precious few truly innocent victims. Predators, that's what he calls them, kids like that fourteen-year-old who walked into a convenience store in Oxon Hill and tried to rob it at 5 a.m. and ended up stabbing the Korean owner to death. *What the fuck?* Carson sometimes wonders. *God damn, my people, my people,* envisioning the future of the race in every act and every choice these young men make. He's tried to talk to them, standing in groups like these or in handcuffs in the backseat of his cruiser, but he might as well be speaking Mandarin.

So yeah, he is tough, and he is hard on their Black asses. There but for the grace of God . . . He has a son who in his worst nightmares turns into a wannabe thug giving these young bloods a run for their money. None of it makes sense. On more than one shift he's arrested suburban Black boys from *Leave It to Beaver* homes, hungering to be criminals, proving their street smarts by being stupid enough to land in jail. He's arrested boys with a plasma TV in their basement and their father's BMW SUV and mom's Lexus and their Honda parked in the garage. He'd been a young punk once too, angry, feasting on his own sense of deserved and superfluous rage at a world he couldn't control and that he was sure would never give him room. But bored, this night, Carson doesn't even say a word, just figures his presence, the patrol car, the weapon the boys know is in his holster, will do all the talking for him.

He swaggers past the cluster of boys, all of them dressed in baggy jeans and oversize shirts, blue bandanas tied around their cornrowed heads. Carson strides a bit more forcefully than usual, preening to let them know that the convenience store is his turf, not theirs.

Everybody thinks it's postal workers who are the major victims of workplace crime. It's really the immigrants and teenagers and retired giving-my-own-business-a-try sales-clerks behind the counters of convenience stores who are the most vulnerable workers in America. It's always open season on them. Every damn day of the week is a "good day to die" for one of them somewhere in the land of the free. By just standing at the magazine rack, thumbing through copies of *Hustler* or *Newsweek*, or shooting the breeze for a half hour with whoever is working, Carson can stop a crime.

Because Carson doesn't tell the boys to move on, to go home, they continue to stand outside, as loud and boisterous as if they were playing video games and sipping forties in their liv-ing room instead of standing in a public place. He could get them for congregating beneath the *No Loitering* sign, but he doesn't.

He and Eric used to debate all the time which was worse, more dangerous: the boredom that makes you lazy, careless, stupid, or the nights of pure adrenaline, responding to pri-ority calls back to back. And don't let it be another officer down. But that's why Carson is out here. Why he's a cop. He loves the rush. The risk. Everything on the line. The pressure. The chance to change somebody's fate, save a life, because he got there in time to catch the burglar, prevent some jerk from giving his wife an ass-whooping and turning her into a corpse. Or maybe he stops a killer on the side of Route 450, pulls him over because the knucklehead is driving a car with broken taillights, expired plates, and when he runs his license through the computer he discovers this is a live one, the kind of scum they build prisons for, and when he searches the car he finds a weapon. And not just any weapon, but one that's loaded and has been used in a murder.

Still, 95 percent boredom. That's Carson's average week. Sometimes his average month. This isn't nearby Washington, where there are weeks when somebody gets killed every night. This is the 'burbs. But still.

On this March night, a night when it is not quite spring, when it's a chilly forty degrees, there's this flat-out wide-faced moon in the sky. A moon so big and awesome it's like a gigantic neon eye or face. A full moon, bursting the seams of the heavens. Milky and liquid and trembling. It's not white but some strange kind of orangey yellow, like no moon Carson can ever recall seeing in the sky. *The full moon.* That's the only odd thing. The only unexpected thing on this night, when Carson has given a couple of speeding tickets and the radio has been mostly silent.

Carson isn't superstitious. Not like Steve, who keeps a rabbit's foot in his wallet, or Eric, who recited the Twenty-third Psalm, closed his eyes and said it silently in the squad car before he pulled out of the station lot. *"The Lord is my shepherd, I shall not want."* No, Carson figures all that just attracts catastrophe. Why depend on luck instead of yourself? Why close your eyes to pray when what you fear could be closing in? So that moon, which he will tell Bunny about if she's awake when he gets home, that's the only strange thing so far this night. His patrol service area includes everything—the area around Martin Luther King Boulevard, the weathered houses and streets of the working-class neighborhood near the FedEx Field football stadium, and the moneyed community called Heaven's Gate. It's mostly the area around King Boulevard that keeps him busy with burglaries, robberies, drug traffic. But this night, one hour before his shift ends at midnight, Carson congratulates himself. It's been quiet. Maybe too quiet, even for a weeknight. But there is nothing in the quiet that makes him think that the worst will be saved for the last moments of his shift.

Half an hour after leaving the 7-Eleven, he's making one last swing around Enterprise and Lottsford roads, past million-dollar houses and the estates behind the barriers of gated communities. He isn't doing *that* well, but with his salary and the $25-an-hour part-time security work he performs, and Bunny's recent raise, they are a $150,000 household and he lives fifteen minutes away. He doesn't live in Heaven's Gate, the community he's just passed that has been written up in magazines and even the *New York Times* as symbolic of Black suburban progress. He lives in Paradise Glen, and Carson is just as happy in paradise as he figures he'd be in heaven. He knows police officers who drive Jaguars and Benzes, have high-six-figure salaries, and are in debt up to their ears, cops addicted to doing nothing but working and making money the way some are in the grip of booze and women.

Carson spots another squad car parked in the lot of Kingsford Elementary School. When he pulls up beside the cruiser, he immediately sees that it's Wyatt Jordan. The fluorescence of the parking lot lights glows on his massive shaved head. Carson parks beside Wyatt and gets out. He stretches his arms and shoulders as he walks around to the other side of his cruiser. Jordan's thick, rumbling laughter is the only sound besides the occasional car cruising past on Enterprise Road. The conversation, which Carson hears through Jordan's half-open window, has the sound of an easy, illicit dialogue, and he figures Jordan is having phone sex. There are all kinds of rumors about Jordan, that he's hooked on Internet porn sites, and Carson knows he's a player, has seen him in action. He's been busted more than once for stopping by his girlfriend's house for a quickie while on duty, and his wife waited for him to get off his shift one evening and jumped out of her Volkswagen and charged after him with a baseball bat.

"Drama Queen" is Carson's nickname for Jordan. He's got no respect for cops who let their lives become a public mess. He knows Jordan from a distance, and he's fine with that. But hell, he can shoot the breeze for a minute. Jordan ends the call and snaps the cell phone shut.

"Am I interrupting something?" Carson asks, leaning on the side of the cruiser, letting a wide, wily grin spread over his face.

Jordan extends his beefy arm out the car window, a raucous laugh rumbling up from his chest. The two men slap palms and shake hands. "Come on, Blake, ease up—I know what you heard, and it's all true."

"All the hardheads must be working a new shift or stayed home instead of risking running into you," Carson says.

"That's what it looks like. Only real action I had tonight was a domestic disturbance call over near Bowie High School. By the time I got there, the dude didn't wanna press charges."

"Say what?" Carson laughs at the thought of where this story is headed.

"No joke." Jordan opens the door of his cruiser and lifts his bulk out, leaning on the side of the car. He's six-seven, two-seventy-five, and solid as a rock.

"You heard me. Dude was getting a Mike Tyson work-over by his girlfriend. He had a black eye. I did the counseling routine. When I got there and saw what was happening, I figured she kicked his ass over another woman. But she claimed he stole some of her money. In my man's defense, though, she had about three inches on him. He was drunk and kept telling me he called 911 'cause he didn't wanna hit no woman."

"So this was love and money?"

"Yeah, you know, half the calls are rooted in one or the other."

"You going to the cabaret at the Chateau Saturday night?" Carson asks.

"I'ma get my ticket at the door," Jordan says.

"I ain't gonna tell you what I had to do to get Saturday night off—I owe Benson big-time," Carson says sheepishly.

"Out with it, tell me . . ."

The two men stand gossiping, trading an easy banter that makes Carson ponder that this is the first time in a long while that he's really talked to Wyatt Jordan. Jordan finally looks at his watch and says, "I better start heading back in. And I hope like hell I don't run into anything on my way."

Jordan pulls out of the lot and Carson sits in his squad car, savoring the silence, the night, and once again looks at that damned full moon. He has decided to follow Jordan in when a car with no lights speeds past on Enterprise Road. He should just let it go, let it slide. He'd been thinking about his warm bed in the moments before the car sped by. But he isn't that kind of cop. He doesn't let much slide. He didn't become a police officer to let shit slide. There have been several carjackings in the area in the past month, and Carson wonders if the idiot speeding by with no lights is some teenage car thief who could cause a fatal accident or some psycho like the predator who waited outside the home of a doctor a mile away and shot him outside his house, stole his wallet, and used his credit cards an hour later, or maybe some kid from D.C., out joyriding in the county.

Carson pulls out of the parking lot and puts his lights on, radioing in to the dispatcher, "I'm behind this guy who's speeding, no lights, and he's not stopping."

"Do you have backup?"

"No."

Carson hears Jordan's voice break into the call: "I'll head back over there."

Carson's all up in the ass of the car, glued to the vehicle, but the driver won't stop. The black Nissan crosses the intersection and finally the driver abruptly pulls into the near-empty parking lot of a strip mall. By the time the car has stopped and he's parked behind him, Carson's skin is tingling and he's tense, buoyed by the involuntary adrenaline rush that's an invisible body armor, priming him for action.

"Get out of the car, sir!" Carson yells, approaching the vehicle, his Beretta pointed at the man behind the steering wheel with his hands in the air.

"Open the door slowly."

The door opens and the driver steps out as Carson moves back. He's twenty-five or twenty-six, Carson guesses, clean-cut, sober-looking, with a serious, proud, unflinching face. He's wearing expensive jeans, a bulky sweater, a leather jacket, and Timberland boots. His hair is braided and he's got a chiseled, tough/soft handsomeness that reminds Carson of the Black male models he's seen on the pages of *GQ*, advertising Hugo Boss suits, or the actors on Bunny's favorite soap opera, *The Young and the Restless*. He's that smooth. And for all his disarming good looks, the man standing before him could be a robber, a murderer, or just an unlucky SOB caught speeding when he thought no cops were around.

"Turn around, face the trunk of the car," Carson orders. "On your knees. Put your hands behind your head." The man drops to the ground and faces the trunk of the car.

"What did I do? Why was I stopped?" he asks, his voice injured, surprised.

"What'd you do? You crazy, man? Fleeing an officer. Driving with no lights."

"What? I wasn't eluding you. I didn't realize my lights weren't on. I mean, I had an argument with my girlfriend and I've been f'd up all evening," he says, turning to look at Carson to make his point.

"Where's your license? Your registration?"

"In my wallet in my back pocket."

Carson begins to approach the kneeling man when he sees him drop his left hand and reach inside his waistband.

The quick, small movement chills the night and freezes Carson's blood.

"Put your hands up!" he shouts, a surging infusion of fear flooding his insides, as liquid and warm as blood.

He's no longer a pretty boy but a looming threat. The man is holding an object in his left hand, smooth, hard, shiny as the moon in the sky.

"Put your hands up!" Uncertainty balloons inside Carson. The words bruise his throat as he issues them with a force he hopes the man will immediately respect.

"I'm not . . . It's not . . ." the man pleads, again turning his head to face Carson and in one swift move rising from the ground.

Where is Jordan? Carson wonders, another surge of fear sliding down his spine. Pointing the object at Carson, the man steps forward.

"What's in your hand?"

"Look, I said it's . . ." the man insists, taking another step toward Carson, pointing at him with the hand holding the object. The night, the sky, the stars overhead: they all swirl around him, a dreamy encroachment. Carson is alone. In a darkened parking lot. And terribly afraid.

"Drop what you're holding and put your hands behind your head," Carson orders as his finger trembles, a whisper away from the trigger.

"Officer, I said . . ."

It's his fingers and his hands, both of them clutching the Beretta, it's even his body, that pulls the trigger. All he sees is the man's hand and the object pointed at him in the moment he fires his weapon for the first time ever.

Wyatt Jordan pulls into the strip mall parking lot and parks a few feet away from Carson and the body on the ground. Two minutes ago he heard Carson radio in to the dispatcher that there had been a shooting: "Shots fired." Through the radio system that connected Carson to the dispatcher and Wyatt to them both, Wyatt heard Carson's voice, shell-shocked and unraveling. *Damn,* Jordan thought, accelerating toward his destination as he heard Carson's call, wondering who was down and what he would find.

Walking from his squad car to Carson's cruiser, Wyatt Jordan realizes that Carson Blake is no longer a fellow officer he just barely knows. As the first to arrive at the scene, he will be bound to Carson from now on by the kind of knowledge both men can only submit to but never fully understand.

Jordan examines the man on the ground, scans the area around the body for a weapon, sees the cell phone, and then walks over to Carson, slumped in the front seat of his cruiser.

The driver-side door of the car is open. Jordan crouches down beside Carson and pries the gun from his moist, steely grip. "What happened, Blake? Are you okay?"

"I thought it was a gun, I swear, I thought it was a gun." The words are breathy and heavy, whispered like a confession. Jordan sees before him a mere remnant of the man he had joked with half an hour ago.

Wyatt Jordan looks away, seeking relief from the face, from the husky sound of Carson's sobs as he weeps into his hands. Jordan lets his eyes scan the circumference of the parking lot and the darkened houses across the street where people are sleeping. Then he turns back to Carson, his large beefy arm enfolding Carson's shoulders, cradling him in a stiff embrace. He doesn't know what else on earth to do.

Emergency Medical Services is the first to rumble into the parking lot of the strip mall and begin examining the body. Soon the lot is ablaze with high-beam-intensity lights from fire trucks, a fluorescent halo hovering over the length and breadth of the search for shell casings and other evidence around the body cordoned off with yellow tape. More than two dozen men and women are swarming around the scene, from Internal Affairs, Homicide, Evidence, the Criminal Investigation Unit; the president of the Fraternal Order of Police and the district commander are there as well. Other officers, hearing what happened on their radios, mill about, curious and concerned, all of them thanking their private gods that on this night they are not Carson Blake.

Carson's sergeant, Melvin Griffin, arrives, and after talking to the crime scene investigators he sees Carson and Wyatt Jordan sitting in the backseat of Jordan's cruiser. He approaches them. At the sight of Griffin, Carson rises slowly from the backseat, and Griffin, a trim, gentle-eyed man of medium brown complexion, whose handlebar mustache and large, mournful eyes make him appear more solemn than he is, reaches for Carson, puts his arm around his shoulder, and says, "Come on, walk with me."

"You okay?" Griffin asks as they walk slowly away from Jordan's cruiser. Because this question seems the most puzzling inquiry he has ever heard in his life, Carson says nothing, although his gratitude for the question is immeasurable. Carson and Melvin Griffin walk away from the hive of activity immediately surrounding the crime scene, to a secluded space in front of the post office, Griffin's arms fatherly, sheltering, on Carson's shoulders.

"Obviously you were in fear for your life?" Griffin asks, standing at Carson's side, not looking at him, but waiting, Carson knows, for the only answer he can give. The answer he will have to give.

"Yes," he mumbles.

"You thought he had a gun." Carson hears not a question but a statement.

"Yes."

"Well, then this looks like a clean shooting to me," Griffin concludes, casting his gaze back to the site they have just walked away from. "Take care of yourself and make sure you take your ten days. You call your wife?"

"Not yet."

"Call her, son—it's gonna be a long night."

Griffin begins walking back toward the fire trucks and squad cars, the investigators, the officers from Internal Affairs who Carson knows want to talk to him, gently leading Carson back toward that assembly with him.

"No, no, can I just have a few minutes?" Carson asks.

"Take all the time you need," Griffin tells him, and walks

away, leaving Carson in the shadowy darkness outside the post office.

He feared for his life. He thought the man had a gun. If he had done the right thing, if he had done the only thing he could do, why did he now wish that he'd been rendered mute so that he could not speak, or blind so that he could not see what that fear and those thoughts had wrought?

No, he had not called Bunny. He wouldn't. He couldn't. He'd have to tell her this face-to-face.

"Be sure to take your ten days," his sergeant had told him. Ten days before he had to make an official statement to anybody about what had happened, about what he had done. Ten days that would turn into weeks. Ten days to get his story straight? Ten days to keep silent, when all he really wants, even now, forty-five minutes after he has killed a young man holding a cell phone and not a gun, is to talk, to explain. But this is Maryland, and the state has legislated ten days of silence for a police officer after a shooting. Ten days to live alone in his own head, the last place he wants to be.

He can't stay in the shadows forever, he knows, so Carson heads back to the others, still feeling the shadows engulfing him no matter how fast he tries to walk. He is still a police officer, and he has to bear witness to what has happened. To what he has done. He tells the story of the stop and the shooting to Margery Pierce, an investigator from the Criminal Investigation Division. She's a red-haired, blue-eyed, frumpy matron Carson has seen at other major crime scenes like this one, and her hand rests on Carson's shoulder as he leans against her van and talks to her, hearing his own voice as though from a great distance, as though it belongs to someone else. When Margery walks away, Lester Stovall from Internal Affairs steps toward Carson, asking first, like Margery, like everyone, if he is okay, and then before Carson can answer says, "Can you tell me what happened?"

Just as Carson is going to answer the question, Matthew Frey, the Fraternal Order of Police lawyer, walks out of the crowd surrounding the scene and puts his hand on Carson's chest like a barrier between Lester and Carson and says to Lester, whom he knows and respects, "You know I get to talk to him first."

Matthew Frey wears a wrinkled trench coat over a white shirt and khakis. He had hurriedly dressed in the bathroom of his Clinton, Maryland rambler after hanging up from the call from the president of the Fraternal Order of Police. Gently shaking his wife awake, he told her where he was going. He has defended police officers for eighteen years. In his office desk in Largo, he keeps a twenty-inch billy club that his grandfather used when he was on the force in Baltimore. Matthew Frey stands before Carson, trying to gather quickly how much he can handle, if he is an officer who will fall apart because of this night or one who will turn to stone. No matter how long he looks at Carson, he cannot tell for sure.

Carson sees Matthew Frey's longish gray-white hair and his pencil-thin lips and reads in the man's blue eyes that he is perhaps the only person present whose job is to protect him.

Frey walks with Carson to his Volvo, and they sit in the front seats.

"You smoke?" he asks Carson, offering him a cigarette.

"Naw."

"Then I won't. You called your family?"

"I can't bring myself to do that just yet."

"I understand. You okay?"

"Not really." This is the first time Carson has answered

the question. The first time he has spoken what he knows unalterably to be the truth.

"When you're ready, I want you to tell me what happened. Take your time. Tell me everything just as it happened, as much as you can recall."

Carson recounts the incident, filling the narrative with all the questions and the doubts that plague him, working through the silences that strangle him and hurtle him back into the moment with the retelling. "I know now that I should've waited for Jordan. He radioed he was on the way. It all happened so fast. So goddamned fast. I lost control. I mean, before I knew it he was reaching into his waistband and had turned around and was on his feet. On his feet, facing me. It couldn't have been more than a few seconds before I lost control of the stop. That's not supposed to happen, I know. But once he was on his feet, facing me, he was holding this object—he wouldn't drop it like I kept telling him to. He kept trying to tell me something, but I wouldn't listen, I couldn't take the chance. He looked like a good kid. He gave me some lip, but he wasn't at all what I was expecting. I was afraid for my life. I thought he had a gun."

Frey listened, knowing that memory is fractured and heightened, made suspect by the lingering effects of trauma. Every time an officer tells him details of a shooting he's been involved in, Frey recalls the conclusion of his favorite writer, Gabriel García Márquez, that life is not what one lives but what one remembers. Carson tells him much more than he needs to know. The days and weeks and months looming ahead of Carson will be even more crucial than this moment, as he helps him to remember the incident in ways that would render what happened inevitable rather than criminal. "You don't have to make a statement when you go back to CID. Get one of the other officers to take you and I'll meet you there. I'll help you fill out the Discharge of Firearms report. You'll be asked what happened. You're not to say anything. Do you understand?"

"Yeah."

"Have you ever fired your weapon before?"

"No." Then Carson asks, "What's gonna happen to me?"

"I don't want you to worry about that tonight. I'll protect your rights. Just know that."

Carson has been in CID many times but never like this, with the eyes of the few officers in the building offering him so much compassion, never with those same officers stopping in the hall to pat him on the back, tell him he'll be okay, to ask how he is.

In an office next to the area where roll call is held, Carson is asked by a Colin Barnes if he wants to make a statement. Barnes at two-thirty in the morning wears a cashmere jacket over a cream-colored shirt with a silk navy-blue tie and large silver cuff links, stylish as always amid the grimy gray funk, the stale, listless air, the battered furniture and indifferent decor that Carson knows too well and that weigh on him with an awful heaviness at this moment.

Then Barnes reads Carson the Advise of Rights form: *You have the right to remain silent. Anything you say can and will be used against you.* Carson is now a cop who has been Mirandized. He signs the form.

"Don't people know when you say 'Drop what you're holding,' we mean drop what you're holding?" Colin murmurs irritably as he places the form before Carson to sign.

The Discharge of Firearms report asks everything from the type of weapon used in the incident to how much sleep Carson had in the last twenty-four hours. The single eight-line paragraph that Frey tutors him on will be used for a press release that the Office of Communications will send to the media.

Carson agonizes over the brief paragraph, which contains the sketchiest rendering of the event even as it answers the primary who, what, when, where. The only question left un-answered is why. Carson hands Barnes the form studded with erasures, damp with sweat, the cursive script small and tortured.

"You been given a replacement weapon?" Barnes asks.

"No, not yet."

The gun used in the shooting is now evidence. He can't leave CID without a gun. On administrative leave, he is still a police officer. Still expected to protect and serve if he sees a "situation," while gassing up his car or shopping for a new pair of shoes. He's got to have a gun. He could be on some thug's kill list. Maybe he's got enemies he doesn't even know about among all the people he's arrested and helped send to jail. He's responsible for *his* life. The lives of others. And his Beretta gives him all the authority he needs. The one or two times he's left home without his weapon he's felt naked, like a moving target. His Beretta is a strap-on body part. He wants a gun but can't imagine holding it without remembering how he held it moments before the shooting, with focused, unfamiliar horror and dread. If he had to fire his weapon again he is not sure that he could.

Matthew Frey waits with Carson for Derek Stinson, the armorer who provides officers with new weapons. Stinson, a small, monklike man who like Matthew Frey was awakened from sleep, arrives carrying the metal case that is with him at all times. He's an ex-cop who keeps a collection of guns in his St. Mary's County home.

Stinson places the metal case on the same desk that Carson used to sign the Miranda forms and to write the report of the shooting. The four guns lie in the case embedded in foam, with magazines for each gun. Stinson gently lifts the Beretta and a magazine from the hold of the foam and offers them to Carson. Carson holds them in his dry, ashen palms with a reverence that stills the moment. Derek Stinson tells him, "In situations like the one you were in tonight, this is your only friend."

After Carson has put the new Beretta in his holster he tells Stinson, "I'd never fired my weapon at a suspect before. I never wanted to have to do it, but still I wondered what it would be like. Now I'd give anything not to know."

At 5:30 a.m., Carson unlocks the door to his house, weak with the desire to see the faces of his children. It is a desire that fills him like hunger. Like thirst. He walks quietly in the dark to his twin daughters' room, which he painted pink for their birthday. The night-light plugged into the wall socket casts an eerie frosting of muted half-light over the room's darkness. Barbie posters claim nearly all the space on the walls. Stuffed teddy bears, dolls, and Beanie Babies are scattered all over the carpeted floor. Standing in the doorway, Carson is stunned by the cheeriness of the room and it nearly buckles his knees, nearly sends him crashing onto the floor, but he steadies himself and walks to the bed of Roseanne, lying on her side, sucking her thumb reflexively in her sleep, her body curled, snail-like, beneath the sheet. Carson wipes the tiny beads of sweat from her forehead with his fingertips. Leaning closer, he listens to the heavy grunt of her breathing. He closes his eyes and allows that sound, the slightly asthmatic, ragged breathing of his daughter, to drench him like rain.

After a few moments Carson pads softly over to Roslyn's

bed. She is sprawled on her back, arms and legs akimbo. A gentle fluttering of her eyes behind her closed lids makes it seem as though she's merely feigning sleep. Roslyn's left leg twitches several times and she turns on her side.

In Juwan's room, the boy sleeps too, a copy of *Treasure Island* tucked beneath his pillow. Carson stares at the face slack with sleep. He looks deeply into the face of a son that he is sure, even before this night, he has already lost.

Carson stands outside Juwan's door and considers the steps he will have to take to enter the room where his wife, Bunny, sleeps. The thought of those steps fills his mind like a forced march. Bunny wakes up at 7:00 a.m. Maybe, just maybe, he will have a reprieve until then. He knows he won't be that lucky but walks back downstairs anyway, slumping into a chair at the breakfast nook in the kitchen. He is more than tired, feels an ache that is primordial and awful in his bones and in his skin. He'd like to make a cup of coffee but doesn't want to make any movements that would signal that he is home. There have been other times in his twelve years on the force when he was hours late because of a fatal accident. Sometimes he had a chance to call. Sometimes he didn't. Bunny knew this was part of The Job. Shit happened. So she would have guessed, Carson convinces himself, that shit happened last night. To someone else.

If he can just be alone for a while. So that he doesn't have to face Bunny, to tell her what he did. Even if alone means having nothing and no one to distract him from the images and the memories of the shooting playing over and over in his head. A videotape that on the ride home he promised that he would only allow to play for fifteen minutes of every hour, a promise he has absolutely no power to keep.

The clock on the kitchen wall ticks in all this silence, too loudly, and when he finally switches on the kitchen light to see that he has been sitting in the breakfast nook for half an hour, Carson hears Bunny coming down the stairs. She stands in the kitchen doorway, bundled in a terry-cloth robe, her hair in rollers.

"I couldn't sleep. I haven't been able to sleep all night," she complains, yawning and walking over to the table. "What's wrong? Why are you so late?" she asks sleepily. "Why are you sitting down here? Why didn't you come to bed?"

"I know I should've called," he begins.

"I was worried . . . I started to call the station," Bunny whines.

"I'm sorry."

"Carson, sorry just doesn't cut it. You don't seem like yourself. You look strange, Carson, what's wrong?" she asks, sitting down heavily beside him.

He thinks he will tell her calmly, slowly. Instead, the words speak themselves, stumble out. "I'd given him the ticket. The stop was over. I was on my way home."

"Carson?" Bunny asks, saying his name like a question, and to Carson his name sounds as odd as the inquiry he has heard, it seems, a thousand times this night, *Are you okay?*

"It was dark. Hell, I didn't know. How could I? All he had to do was drop what he was holding. Like I told him. Then I would've known."

"Carson, you're scaring me."

"It happened so fast." And that is the truest thing Carson has thought or said this night. "It happened so fast. I killed a man. I stopped him because he was speeding and driving with no headlights."

"And you killed him?" Bunny whispers, rising so quickly she nearly falls, clutching the collar of her robe tight at her throat and covering her mouth with her hand. Carson stands and walks to Bunny as if he could protect her, save her, from the wrath of what he has done. They cling to each other. Never before have they held each other with love so total and so blind.

ABOUT THE CONTRIBUTORS

RHOZIER "ROACH" BROWN, while serving a life sentence for murder, founded the Inner Voices, a drama troupe that was allowed out of prison more than eight hundred times to perform their brand of social drama. Largely as a result of the group's success, President Gerald Ford commuted Brown's sentence to immediate parole. The play *Group Work* was nominated for three television Emmy Awards and won Best Social Film at the New York Film Festival. A television documentary titled *Roach* was created about his life story. Later, he worked as a special assistant to Mayor Marion Barry for offender affairs and has been active in endeavors dealing with prisoners and former prisoners, both as the director of community-based programs and as a political activist. Brown played a key role in getting legislation passed that gave ex-offenders the right to vote in D.C. elections. He has also worked as a television and film producer.

PAUL LAURENCE DUNBAR (1872–1906) was among the first African American poets to garner national eminence in the U.S., gaining popular recognition for his collection *Lyrics of a Lowly Life* (1896). Although born in Ohio, Dunbar attended Howard University in Washington, D.C., where he lived in LeDroit Park. Shortly after his marriage to fellow poet Alice Ruth Moore, Dunbar took a job at the Library of Congress. His time there was short-lived, however, as he blamed the library's dust for his worsening tuberculosis. Dunbar's other poetry collections include *Oak and Ivy* (1893) and *Majors and Minors* (1895), and his poems and short stories were published in *Harper's Weekly*, the *Sunday Evening Post*, the *Denver Post*, and *Current Literature*. What was originally established as the first high school for African American children in Washington, D.C. was renamed in honor of Paul Laurence Dunbar and continues to carry his name after a recent relocation to the Northwest quadrant of the city.

MARITA GOLDEN is the author of twelve books of fiction and nonfiction. Her most recent novel, *After*, was named a 2007 Outstanding Work of Fiction by the Black Caucus of the American Library Association. She is president emeritus of the Hurston/Wright Foundation.

JAMES GRADY is a former investigative reporter and author of the best-selling novel *Six Days of the Condor*. He has spent his career writing from Washington, D.C., publishing more than a dozen novels and numerous short stories—including a selection in the original *D.C. Noir*. Also active in movie and TV writing, Grady's literary work has won two Regardies Short Fiction awards, garnered an Edgar nomination, and received Italy's Raymond Chandler Medal, Japan's Baka-Misu Award, and France's Grand Prix du Roman Noir.

ELIZABETH HAND is the multiple award–winning author of nine novels and three collections of short fiction. Since 1988, she has been a regular contributor to the *Washington Post Book World,* the *Village Voice,* and *DownEast Magazine,* among other publications. She lives on the coast of Maine.

LANGSTON HUGHES (1902–1967), most notably recognized as a founder of the cultural movement known as the Harlem Renaissance, was a poet, short story writer, and playwright. After traveling throughout Africa and Europe as a young man, Hughes moved to Washington, D.C. for a period of time in the 1920s, where he lived at the 12th Street YMCA. There he was part of the blossoming literary scene, publishing poetry in the Howard University–associated journals *The Crisis* and *The New Negro.* Influential in his rhythmic, jazzlike writing style, his other works include *The Weary Blues* (1926), *Not Without Laughter* (1930), *I Wonder As I Wander* (195), *Tambourines to Glory* (1958), and a series of books involving the character Simple.

EDWARD P. JONES is the winner of the Pulitzer Prize for Fiction, the National Book Critics Circle Award, and the International IMPAC Dublin Literary Award. Born in 1951, Jones was raised in Washington, D.C., where he lived until attending Holy Cross and later the University of Virginia, earning his MFA. He won the PEN/Hemingway Award and a Lannan Foundation grant for his first book, *Lost in the City* (1992), a collection of short stories about working-class African Americans living in D.C. His other works include *The Known World* (2003) and *All Aunt Hagar's Children* (2006). Jones once again resides in D.C., where he continues to write.

WARD JUST was a war correspondent in Cyprus for *Newsweek* and a key reporter for the *Washington Post* during the Vietnam War. Among his impressive catalog of fifteen novels, four short story collections, and one play, Just's novel *An Unfinished Season* (2004) was a finalist for the Pulitzer Prize for Fiction in 2005, and *Jack Gance* (1989) won the *Chicago Tribune* Heartland Award for Fiction. Just's work often revolves around Washington, D.C., highlighting the influence and repercussions of national politics and policymaking on American citizens.

JULIAN MAYFIELD (1928–1984) was a novelist, essayist, playwright, actor, and political activist. In 1962, he lived in Ghana and was a speechwriter for President Kwame Nkrumah and editor of the *African Review*. He was the acknowledged leader of the African American community that settled in Ghana to assist Nkrumah in his dream to unite Africa. In the early 1970s, Mayfield lived in Guyana, South America, assisting President Forbes Burnham in the establishment of a national service to help feed, clothe, and house its citizens. Documentation of his colorful career in the arts and politics can be found at New York Public Library's Schomburg Center for Research in Black Culture.

JULIAN MAZOR was born in Baltimore in 1929 and grew up in Washington, D.C. He has also lived in New York, London, and Ireland. He is a graduate of Indiana University and Yale Law School and served in the air force. His two short fiction collections, *Washington and Baltimore* and *Friend of Mankind and Other Stories,* include stories that originally appeared in the *New Yorker*.

LARRY NEAL'S (1937–1981) early work, including "The Negro in the Theatre" (1964), "Cultural Front" (1965), and "The Black Arts Movement" (1968), helped define the Black Power era. Working together with Amiri Baraka to open the Black Arts Repertory Theatre/School, Neal continued to publish his essays and poems in publications such as *Drama Critique, Black Theatre, Negro Digest, Performance,* and *Liberator*. He taught for a time at Howard University in D.C.; Neal's story in this collection describes—from a female point of view—the four-day student protest and campus takeover of 1968. Howard was the first university to be successfully closed down by student activism and would serve as the model for the Columbia University shutdown later that year.

GEORGE PELECANOS is an independent film producer, the recipient of numerous international writing awards, a producer and an Emmy-nominated writer on the HBO series *The Wire*, and the author of fifteen novels set in and around Washington, D.C. He is the editor of the best-selling first volume of *D.C. Noir*.

BENJAMIN M. SCHUTZ (1949–2008) was the author of the acclaimed psychological thriller *The Mongol Reply*, as well as previous novels and short stories featuring private eye Leo Haggerty. His fiction has won both Shamus and Edgar awards. He was a forensic psychologist who lived in the Northern Virginia suburbs of Washington, D.C.

ROSS THOMAS (1926–1995) worked for over twenty years as a reporter, foreign correspondent, and political strategist. He turned to writing at the age of forty and produced his first novel, *The Cold War Swap* (1967), which won an Edgar Award, in just six weeks. Writing twenty-five novels over the course of his twenty-nine year career, often under the pseudonym Oliver Bleeck, Thomas's works include *Chinaman's Chance* (1978), *Out on the Rim* (1987), and *Voodoo Ltd.* (1992). In 2002, he received the first Gumshoe Award for Lifetime Achievement.

JEAN TOOMER (1894–1967) was born Nathan Pinchback Toomer in Washington, D.C. An African American whose maternal grandparents both had Caucasian fathers, he resisted racial classification even from childhood, switching between an all-black school in D.C. to an all-white school in New Rochelle, New York, then back again. Although he studied at the University of Wisconsin, the Massachusetts College of Agriculture, the American College of Physical Training in Chicago, City College in New York, and New York University, he never received a degree. Among his most prominent works, *Cane* (1923) is considered to be a crucial text of the Harlem Renaissance and the Lost Generation; the novel explores the societal position of African Americans in the South during the early 1900s.

RICHARD WRIGHT (1908–1960) was born to a sharecropper and a school teacher in Mississippi. He was the author of several novels, short stories, and nonfiction works that are among the most powerful and controversial pieces of American writing. A major participant in the Harlem Renaissance, Wright helped redefine race relations in the twentieth century. His first story, "The Voodoo of Hell's Half Acre," was published in 1924 in the *Southern Register*. Wright's other works include *Uncle Tom's Children* (1938), *Native Son* (1940), *Black Boy* (1945), *The Outsider* (1953), *Eight Men* (1961), and *Haiku: This Other World* (1998). In 1940, *Native Son* became the first national best seller by a black writer in American history.

Also available from the Akashic Books Noir Series

D.C. NOIR
edited by George Pelecanos
384 pages, trade paperback original, $14.95

Brand new stories by: George Pelecanos, Laura Lippman, James Grady, Kenji Jasper, Jim Beane, Ruben Castaneda, Robert Wisdom, Jim Patton, Norman Kelley, Jennifer Howard, Jim Fusilli, and others.

"[T]he tome offers a startling glimpse into the cityscape's darkest corners . . . fans of the genre will find solid writing, palpable tension, and surprise endings."
—*Washington Post*

BROOKLYN NOIR
edited by Tim McLoughlin
350 pages, trade paperback original, $15.95
*Winner of Shamus Award, Anthony Award, Robert L. Fish Memorial Award; finalist for Edgar Award, Pushcart Prize.

Brand new stories by: Pete Hamill, Arthur Nersesian, Ellen Miller, Nelson George, Nicole Blackman, Sidney Offit, Ken Bruen, and others.

"*Brooklyn Noir* is such a stunningly perfect combination that you can't believe you haven't read an anthology like this before. But trust me— you haven't. Story after story is a revelation, filled with the requisite sense of place, but also the perfect twists that crime stories demand. The writing is flat-out superb, filled with lines that will sing in your head for a long time to come."
—Laura Lippman, winner of the Edgar, Agatha, and Shamus awards

BROOKLYN NOIR 2: THE CLASSICS
edited by Tim McLoughlin
312 pages, trade paperback, $15.95

Classic reprints from: H.P. Lovecraft, Donald E. Westlake, Pete Hamill, Jonathan Lethem, Colson Whitehead, Carolyn Wheat, Maggie Estep, Thomas Wolfe, Hubert Selby Jr., Stanley Ellin, and more.

"This collection of reprints is packed full of literary treats."
—*Mystery Scene*

"[T]he perfect companion to McLoughlin's successful all-original anthology, *Brooklyn Noir*." —*Publishers Weekly*